A
LOVE
MOST
FATAL

A MAFIA ROM-COM

MORELLI FAMILY BOOK ONE

KATH RICHARDS

To my three siblings. I love you.
Don't try to guess who is who here—I promise it doesn't work like that.

AUTHOR'S NOTE

Thank you for picking up *A Love Most Fatal*. I hope it's as fun to read as it was to write.

Before you get started, please know that this is an adult, mafia rom-com—so while it is both romantic and comedic, beware that there are also mature themes you may expect in a mafia romance. In this book you will find blood, murder, violence, death, gun use, organized crime, and on-page sex.

VANESSA

THE GRANDFATHER CLOCK TICKS AWAY IN THE FRONT ROOM; THE sound is the only thing grounding me through another infuriating meeting in which a man tries to pawn his nephew/widower-brother/cousin from the mainland off on me as a reasonable marriage candidate.

Apparently, marriage shouldn't be anything more than a business deal.

Because that worked *so well* for me the last time.

I hear the men out because it's rude not to when we've been in business together for so many years—generations, for some. But sitting through these asinine meetings is not good for my health. I'm not entirely sure what it feels like to have high blood pressure, but if anything were going to bring it on, it would be this. I always leave with a headache, which should be coming on any second now, along with—

"I'm sure you both can find an arrangement that is suitable to your... more physical needs."

And bingo. Cue the headache.

I take a sip of tea, now lukewarm after Ronaldo prattled on for twenty minutes all about the great ways this relationship would benefit us both, and set the mug back down. A marriage with his family would be practically useless to me. Still, I listen because it would be more annoying to hear him moan about my disregard for tradition and clan loyalty.

Ronaldo's cup has, once again, made its way to the wooden tabletop instead of the coaster provided.

"Your cup," I say. Because he has some sense of self-preservation, he moves it onto the coaster.

His face displays a calm surety, but he's picking at a loose thread on his Gucci pants. He's off balance while talking to me and doesn't exactly know where he stands. He knows that I hold more power than him in this city, a lot more, and he probably knows that I have multiple men in his employ keeping tabs on his dealings, though he doesn't know who. He was afraid of my father, and that fear remains for my father's heir, but he doesn't know precisely how to account for the fact that his heir is a woman.

"Are you saying that your nephew is going to cheat on me, Ronaldo?"

After a beat of shock, his eyes nearly bulge out of his crusty skull, and a vein in his forehead twitches. If I were a man, he would extend this same curtesy.

"Well, no, Vanessa, that's not what I—"

It was.

"Enlighten me, then. What sort of arrangement do you mean?" I ask, my tone almost generous.

His lips are thin, floundering open and closed while he puts coherent words together in his pebble of a brain. "Of course, James will have needs, and I presume anyone in your position would as well."

"Ah." *Needs.* "And if you wanted him to marry my younger sister, would she be extended such liberties as well?"

I think this question might be what breaks him: a concept so incomprehensible I can't *really* mean it. As a rule in our world, women cannot take lovers. They ought to be pure, loyal creatures who belong to their father, then husband, or their son if their husband dies. But of course, men are welcome to their pick of lovers, so long as they're not a part of the clan, lest they embarrass their wives. Foreign women are fine, but God forbid they be from the homeland.

Ronaldo clasps his hands and leans forward with a patronizing smile.

"Your sister would be a different situation. You understand," he says. *She's not in charge*, is what he means. My power doesn't extend to her.

"Sure. A wife could never undermine her husband's status in that way," I agree with a shrug.

Ronaldo looks relieved, relaxing back into his chair, like finally I'm showing some reason.

"Right." He takes a sip from his coffee, the ends of his gray mustache coming back wet.

"And James would never do anything to embarrass me," I say.

Ronaldo's head keeps bobble-heading on. James would never take an Italian lover, only Polish or Russian, he thinks I mean. As another man said last week, his nephew wouldn't ever piss in his own pool. *Great. Cool.*

"Wonderful. So, infidelity of any kind from James will not be tolerated. You understand," I echo.

He chokes, and then places the mug directly on the table next to his coaster, a bit of coffee splashing over and landing on the wood. Before I can correct him for a third time, though, he hurries to pull a handkerchief from his pocket and sops up the spill, replacing the cup again to its coaster.

Before this house was mine, it was my father's, and he was very particular about his things. He liked them kept nice; credenzas dusted, wood floors polished, settees and ornate rugs free of bloodstains. Capos knew if they were invited in his home they were not to disrespect it. Perhaps it was his attention to detail that made him such a good don. Even with him gone, I'm glad that fear still lives in Ronaldo.

"If you think fidelity is beyond his capabilities—"

"No," Ronaldo is quick to jump in. Cute that he thinks this can be salvaged. He bobs his head, though his eyes show that he doesn't quite understand. He can barely fathom how a man can or should be faithful to his wife, but I carry on anyway.

"And James is prepared to move to my estate, of course."

Another brief hesitation, and then, "Of course."

I know his nephew James has a sizable home of his own, one with a garage large enough to hold all of his trophy cars. He would throw a fit about moving. But really, just what do they expect? That I'd move my entire base of operations? And for what, to preserve his ego? It's laughable.

I'm not actually considering this, and I haven't since Ronaldo entered my home with cologne assaulting my nostrils, but I put on a show that I'm thinking it over. I let my gaze coast over the rug, the custom wallpaper, the tall windows, and the many pieces of art and pottery collected over the years. This room alone is probably worth more than the man sitting in front of me.

"Just a few more questions," I begin.

Leo, my head of security and favorite cousin, is standing by in the room, large and intimidating as ever, and I can tell he's trying to hold back a smirk. He's seen this song and dance as often as I have and knows what's next. He calls it *The Finisher* because if the bit about monogamy doesn't send the old men into a rage, this usually will.

"Has he given much consideration to the name?" I ask.

Ronaldo stills his fidgeting.

"The name?"

"His surname," I clarify. "I won't be taking his, but I wondered if he'd given any thought to taking mine."

I say it with as straight of a face as I can muster while Leo tries not to laugh. Ronaldo stutters his response, trying to temper himself before doing what he likely wants to do: throw his cup across the room for the blatant disrespect of me even humoring such an idea. Doing this would end badly for him, so he must choose his words wisely while also telling me to kindly *fuck the fuck off if I think his nephew would ever consider changing his last name to Morelli.*

"Certainly you don't mean this."

"And why not? If James was marrying Mary, you would expect nothing less of her, no? Because he holds more power than her, right? He doesn't hold more power than me."

"I didn't realize Mary was on the table for discussion."

"She isn't."

"But they might make an excellent pair, no, *cara?*"

"No." I stand and smooth out my pants, conversation over. "And don't call me dear."

It was a crafty attempt, pivoting to my sister when he realized I was too obstinate to be a viable option for his nephew. Mary, though, would be infinitely worse.

"We're done here. Go before you start offending me."

"Vanessa, this would benefit more than just us," Ronaldo says, standing to match me. His face is reddening by the second and that vein protrudes further on his forehead. I nod at Leo, who comes over and puts a hand on his shoulder.

"My answer is no, Ronaldo. It's time for you to leave. *Ciao.*"

He does leave, lacking the smug smile he arrived with. Once the door is closed behind him, I pinch the bridge of my nose and roll my shoulders.

This was the third meeting of its kind this month, and I'm not positive how many more I can sit through before I start murdering innocent men. Well, as innocent as a criminal can be.

I waste no time trading my slacks for spandex and my heels for sneakers before making my way to the basement for evening training. I suspect Leo is off in the guest house—well, *his* house— doing the same.

5

Mary is already in our gym stretching when I get downstairs, still fuming from the meeting.

"So, are you engaged, then?" Mary asks.

"Please murder me if I'm ever desperate enough to agree to marry James Sinclair. And make it a slow death. Painful."

Mary laughs and lunges further into her stretch, then moves through the rest of her flow, practically folding herself in half before standing up.

"I thought he would at least offer the younger one," Mary says. "What's his name again?"

"Ryan," I groan. James is annoying, but his brother is insufferable, a lecherous prick that I had to suffer through all of high school with. "Ronaldo thought you might be a better match. Fewer demands."

"I would eat him alive."

"You should've seen his face," my cousin calls from the base of the stairs, his suit traded for workout clothes. "Completely nuclear."

Mary holds her water bottle up in a mock cheers. "Do you think he'll retaliate?" she asks.

"No. Ronaldo's a moron, but he's certainly not that brainless," I say.

"At this rate, you're going to run out of men to say no to." Leo says this like it's funny, but the truth of it strikes a little too close.

There are a few powerful families in this city; The Morellis and the Donovanns secure the top of the list, so it's reasonable that all other families in our employ want to marry up.

I start on my warmup: a quick mile, some stretching, and drills on the bag, while the other two start sparring on the mat.

I am not opposed to marriage, and in fact, I would like to have somebody by my side who would also share my bed, my stresses, and my pains. This is all very appealing to me. I have my mother and my sisters, Leo, too, and I know I can lean on them, but these relationships are not the same as having *a person*.

Ultimately, it *is* lonely at the top. But Mafia men are often cruel; it comes with the territory for us all. Our emotions must be hardened to some extent if we are to follow tradition so stalwartly. *Alphaholes*, some call them.

There are no shortage of men looking for a bride, but very few that are looking for a partner. I know it's expected that I marry, and soon, but I can't risk marrying someone who will undermine my position at every turn when I need him to help me.

I know no men whose egos are strong enough to demure to me in this way.

But there's no avoiding the topic, because of the slight problem of an heir. Or lack thereof.

One of my sisters would take over if I was to die prematurely, nobody is more prepared than they are, but that is not something I want for them. Mary would do it; she's got an extreme sense of duty that I adore, but she wouldn't be happy in charge.

Willa's kids are an option, but my niece and nephew are two of the most perfect children in the world. The thought of them having to kill or be killed makes me ill.

Adoption is an option, but this then begs the question of how will this baby be raised? Who will be doing the raising? I believe I am the least equipped person to raise a baby, maybe on the planet. Perhaps second only to Mary. Willa has her own children, and my mom is still young, not even sixty yet, but I can't just expect her to constantly babysit the child I bring into this world.

And a man hiring a full-time nanny is fine, but me trying such a thing might cause mass upheaval.

I increase the pace of my drills, my heart rate climbing as I think about the double standard of it all. Men in this world have very few worries, as far as I'm concerned. There's the running of things, but that's just business. A job. They have wives to worry about the running of everything else—their homes, children, social calendars, house staff, gifts, and relationships. I don't have that luxury.

I pound my fists harder into the hanging punching bag, trying to beat the frustration out of me, like if I hit this bag of sand enough, I will suddenly be calm about the whole life, marriage, and baby situation. I go at this pace until my lungs burn, and a towel hits my face to get my attention. I use it to wipe the sweat from my neck and look at where Mary and Leo have been sparring.

"Your turn," Mary says.

I spar with Leo for a while, then with Mary, and then we run some drills, two versus one kind of stuff, jiu-jitsu, etc. It's the routine. Leo's been training with us since we were kids. His dad was my dad's only brother, and chief of security, so he was always around.

Our training was intense and vigorous. My father knew we would never be stronger or larger than the men in our circles, and thus, we needed to be better prepared. We needed to be smarter, more agile, and better with weapons—his three little fighting machines—because we wouldn't always have a security detail with guns to watch out for us.

We keep up with our exercises like our lives depend on them because they in fact do.

Just as I get Leo into a leg lock, my phone starts to ring. I wait for him to tap out before crawling over to my bag to answer it.

"Hi," I answer, out of breath.

"Oh, thank God," my sister says, as if she's been calling me for hours.

"What's the matter?" I ask, immediately on edge. Leo and Mary both still as I click the call to speaker.

"I need you to go to Artie's parent-teacher conference tomorrow," Willa says. I can't help the eye roll that mirrors Mary's before she goes back to work on the speed bag.

"No," I say.

"Yes," Willa says. "Please, Ness, it'll be like twenty minutes tops. It's at 2 PM at the school."

"If it's so short, why can't you go? Or better yet, your husband?"

"We're both busy," she says, like this explains it perfectly. "Getting together the paperwork for the Monson bid is taking longer than I expected, and Sean's got fires to put out at three sites tomorrow. But we missed the last conference and really can't miss this one."

I sigh for so long that she asks if I'm still there. Working in a family business means we all have a job; if it doesn't get done, the rest of us are affected.

"Can he do it on the phone?"

"No, this guy is a real tight ass. He also has a tight ass, if that at all sways you towards saying yes."

I take the phone off speaker as Leo laughs from where he's still sprawled out on the mat.

"Artie won't be able to play if we don't get this sorted," Willa explains. "Please, can you just go talk to him? His godmother and beloved aunt is just as good as his own mother if you think about it."

I can't help but laugh at the absurdity of it. This sort of request is not infrequent from my older sister. If she wasn't so damn good at carrying the weight of our company's legal department on her shoulders, I would begrudge her more. I roll my head until my chin is resting on my chest.

"Fine." I mutter, and can practically see Willa grinning through the phone.

"Thank you forever."

"You're welcome," I say, then add "forever," before hanging up.

2

NATE

I'M RUNNING LATE. AGAIN.

Punctuality is important to me, it really is. I'm just not always very good at it.

I have very good intentions, and I tend to leave myself more than enough time to get where I'm going, but in the ever-moving current that is a day, something always comes up. There's a longer line at the post office when I need to return an Amazon package, or the man I play pickleball with on the weekends wants to play "just one more quick game" and I agree, even though I know it's never quick. Inevitably, I'm rushing, and today is no different.

Freeway traffic isn't normally so excruciating, but city planners love to make everyone miserable by closing entire lanes in the middle of the day. Lovely, really.

It's a term week, which translates to a week off for the kids to do whatever it is middle schoolers do now that they have phones and a week for teachers to prep for the last term of the year. Also the allotted time for the final parent-teacher conferences. I schedule all of mine on Monday and Tuesday, making for two mammoth days of meetings with parents. If they miss, they miss, and they can go ahead and send me an email. But Artie Donovann's mom begged (literally) that I reschedule for today, *any time, really*, and she promised she wouldn't miss it, swore on her mother's life she'd be there, etc., etc.

I was home for the day when she called, and I'd just realized that I'd forgotten my laptop in the classroom, so I told her I would make the allowance just this once. I'd be going to campus the next day anyway, and Artie is a good kid, although he is on my shit list this semester.

The guys I usually play pickleball with at the Y were meeting at noon, so I thought I would have just enough time to get in some games before booking it over to the school. However, I did not account for the spirit of Satan being in the entirety of the city's driving population today, so now I'm going to be late.

My phone keeps ringing, my mom most likely checking in to see if I've found a date for my cousin's wedding yet, but my phone is in my gym bag in the back seat. After it starts ringing a third time, I give in and answer on my watch.

"Ma?"

"Hi, sweetie. How are you?" she asks before launching into vivid detail about the ham she's making for her book club tonight and just how awful the lines were at the grocery store this morning. "It sounds like you're in the car. What are you doing? I thought you had the day off," she says after a couple minutes.

"I have a bit of work to tie up," I say.

With no preamble, she starts in on my cousin's wedding and how it's important that I don't show up alone because of how it will look to the rest of the family (whatever that means) and I can barely hear her, so I'm fiddling with the volume control on my stupid watch, all while pulling into the school's parking lot right behind a black Land Rover, which abruptly slams on their brakes. This, in turn, gives me no time to brake, resulting in me crashing the front of my Prius into the back of this car probably twelve times the cost of mine.

And a parent, no doubt.

"Shit, fuck," I say, and my mother gasps through the watch's little speaker. "Mom, I gotta go, I'll talk to you later." I press the screen of the watch until the call ends and pull into a spot next to the car. She gets out first, an absolute force of a woman storming to my door with her arms up.

I climb out of my car and try not to think about the fact that I'm still in my gym clothes while this woman looks like she is about to step into a meeting with high-level executives. She looks pissed, too, like I've ruined her day along with every other shitty driver in this godforsaken city.

"What the hell happened?" She asks when I haven't said anything for half a minute, just staring at her. I close my mouth, which was hanging open slightly, and look at the back of her car. There's a dent, but it's a small one.

"I'm sorry," I say, "but you're the one who stopped short after a turn."

"Because there was a *kid*," she yells, and god, why is she so pretty while she's yelling at me?

I look in the direction she's pointing, and sure enough a student and his father are getting into an equally nice vehicle just down the row.

"You weren't paying attention," she accuses, one manicured finger pointed right at me. I think it's black nail polish, but on closer inspection, it's blood red, which feels foreboding to her scratching through my skin for hitting her two-hundred-thou-sand-dollar car.

This still feels like not entirely my fault, and much more the fault of the kid and his dad for not using the crosswalk, but there is a fire in this woman's eyes that I do not want to stay on the other side of for long. Not when I still need to change for my meeting which is *oh*, I glance at the cursed watch, seven minutes away.

"Look, I'm really sorry. Let me give you my insurance and we can get this squared away."

She stares at me for a long moment, like she's trying to see if I'm actually sorry, and I try to look as penitent as I can while wearing gym shorts and the "I <3 BJ" T-shirt my cousin Rex got for me in Beijing last year.

She lets out a breath before nodding, releasing me from the staring contest spell so I can retrieve my insurance information from my cluttered glove box. She takes photos of her bumper and mine—which is in much worse shape than hers, to be clear—then of my ID and insurance card. I learn from her ID that her name is Vanessa Morelli, and the whole thing is done in less than four minutes. She's already on the phone with someone and waves me away once she has everything she needs.

"Sorry again," I mouth, and she gives an absolutely lethal eye roll that I will be thinking about for the next three weeks while I shower and every time I close my eyes to sleep.

My mom has sent me a dozen texts since hanging up on her, and I quickly tell her that I'm fine while I tug my loafers on in the staff bathroom by my office. When all is said and done (I do have to re-button my shirt because I missed one in my haste), I walk into my classroom with one minute to spare and am stowing my gym bag beneath my desk just as Mrs. Donovann knocks on my door.

"Come on in," I say and look up to find, not Mrs. Donovann, but the woman whose car I just hit in the lot, Vanessa. I know it's not Mrs. Donovann, because I've met her before, and Mrs. Donovann's hair is honey blonde and she has gentle eyes; this woman's hair is a shiny dark brown with matching eyes that cut through me like knives.

She stops at the door, both of us staring at each other trying to sort out what the other is doing in this classroom. She stares at my body, and I glance down at my clothes, worried. The button is fixed, everything is tucked in, and my zipper is up, I look great.

It's the best button-up shirt that I own, it's got tiny little stripes on it.

"You changed," she says.

"I did," I reply.

"That was absurdly fast." She looks almost impressed, and I have to wipe a surprised smile from my face.

"Yeah, I've, uh, got a meeting." I peer behind her to what I can see of the hall, which is otherwise empty. Not a Donovann in sight.

Her eyebrows shoot up on her forehead. "Willa didn't tell you," she says.

It's time for my eyebrows to move because I know the name Willa, Willa being. . . Willa Donovann. Donovann-*Morelli*, I now recall. Willa, who has obviously sent this woman, Vanessa, in her stead. Because of course I would need to have a meeting with her after just making an ass of myself in the parking lot.

"She didn't tell me. But please, come in." I gesture to the desk set up in the front of the room, two chairs on one side, one on the other. I suddenly wish I had a better set up for her to sit in, something classier than a table that I had to use three Clorox wipes on to get all the pencil-drawn penises off its surface.

She takes a seat and crosses her legs, and I catch sight of the red bottoms of her shoes as I sit across from her. Her phone buzzes in her bag and she glances at it before closing her eyes briefly, as if recentering herself after whatever bullshit she just read. I am desperately nosy and wish I knew what it was, but I am in no position to ask.

"I'm Artie's aunt, Vanessa Morelli. Willa is sorry she couldn't make it, but something came up."

"Sure, no worries," I say, though Mrs. Donovann's ardent assurances that she'd be here today ring through my mind.

I open Artie's file and flip to the page of his list of approved adults who have access to his school information. Sure enough, Vanessa Morelli is on the list.

We sit quietly for a moment that is thick with the fact that I just hit her car. The ridiculousness of it dawns on me so thoroughly that I have to close my eyes and laugh just a little or I'll combust.

To my surprise, Vanessa gives a laugh, too.

"Look, I am very embarrassed and would love to go hide in that closet there," I choke out as I point at the little door in the back of my classroom, which makes her smile wider. "Can we start over? Like pretend some jackass in the parking lot didn't just hit your very shiny, very nice car with his very old, environmentally conscious, baby blue Toyota?"

Her smile is everything to me, like it might make my brain melt the way her cheeks push up her eyelids and she tries to keep her lips closed.

"Okay," she agrees, and holds a hand across the desk for me to shake. I do. "I'm Vanessa."

"Nathaniel," I say. Then, "Nate Gilbert. Good to meet you, Vanessa."

"You too."

3

VANESSA

"Now, Artie is just an awesome kid," Nate starts, his voice in teacher-talking-to-parent mode. "He's a joy to be in class, and exceptionally smart. I am very impressed by him, and that isn't something I say about all of my students."

I think about Willa's text, the one that said Artie was failing this class and that I needed to "do anything you need" to fix it. Whatever Willa thinks *that* means.

"If he's so excellent, then why is he failing?"

Nate nods, as if he was expecting this question, and pulls a paper out of the file folder in front of him. He slides it across the little desk to me, and I scan it briefly. Artie's grades. Tests and in-class participation all A's, but the mile long list of other assignments all zeros.

"No matter what I do, I can't get Artie to turn in any of his homework. He seems to believe that homework is an 'antiquated practice used to make young people miserable,'" he says, obviously quoting the little shithead, who I recognize as quoting Mary.

He's twelve.

I try not to sigh.

"This argument is ringing a bell," I say.

Artie is all of the things his teacher described; smart and joyful and wonderful, but he's stubborn, too. No doubt he'd been digging his heels in about this all semester since Mary planted the seed in his head. Sometimes I believe some of the adults in my family would fit right into middle school.

"His grade has suffered, but further, he's nearly started a revolution in the class, a quarter of his classmates also opting to not submit the quarter's worth of assignments."

If I didn't think my godson was meant to play basketball, video games, and be the otherwise untouchable prince of the family, I would say that he was meant to lead. Perfect heir potential if he wasn't too good for this world.

"I see."

"And the thing is, I think he is doing the homework. He comes to class prepared to participate every day, but when it comes time to turn things in, he says he doesn't have it."

Now, I do sigh, because it sounds just like him. He does do homework, I've seen him do it as recently as last night, and he even helps his twin sister with hers when she doesn't get it.

My phone buzzes in my bag again, no doubt Willa telling me to get on my knees for Artie's cute, weird teacher to get him to give her son a better grade before the end of term.

"What grade does he need to finish the basketball season?" I ask.

"It's his GPA, he needs at least a 2.5."

"Seems high." Higher than when I was in high school at least. Most of the athletes I knew were barely scraping by in their classes. But Artie's in the seventh grade, what does he need a GPA for?

"Low Bs across the board. A couple of C-pluses would be fine. Totally doable," Nate explains.

"And because of your class, he's. . ."

"Sitting at a 2.2."

Nate hands me a few more papers from the folder; his grades from his other classes, all much the same story. Except for his extracurriculars. He's got an A in P.E. and painting. Good for him.

"As you said, he's a great kid. If you suspect that he's doing the work, is there a way you can give him partial credit?"

"I can't give him credit for work that I have no proof that he's done."

"But you said he's always prepared in class. He participates?"

"Yes, Artie is extremely bright, but his little cohort of anti-homework followers aren't faring so well," Nate explains.

He wants me to just agree and say that I'll talk to Artie, I know he does, and trust me that's what I want, too. I really, *really* do.

But if I don't at least attempt to sway him, Willa will ride my ass to hell about not trying harder.

In this spirit, I narrow my eyes at the man. "I don't see how their grade is his fault."

"No, of course not," he amends. "Each student is responsible for their own grade, and it's not Artie's fault that people listen to him, but his disruption in class is leading to negative pressure from his peers."

"How?"

"It's not uncommon that they'll loudly boo the students who do turn in their assignments. Do you see how this creates a hostile environment for the other kids? The ones who've done their work but feel like they'll be ostracized unless they don't turn it in?"

I take this new information in, blinking at the discovery that my twelve-year-old nephew has started a literal anti-homework union in his math class. I would be impressed if it wasn't so aggravating.

"I'll talk to him, I will," I promise. "That is unacceptable, you're right. In the meantime, though, can you put his grade up, just enough so that he can play in next week's games? It would mean the world to him."

It's Nate's turn to narrow his eyes.

"And it would mean the world to *me* if he stopped his tirade on my class. So, it seems we are at an impasse."

"Even just once?"

He doesn't dignify this with a response, and I am once again cursing Willa for making me handle this.

"Look, is it money that you want?" I reach for my bag on the seat next to me, fully prepared to give him a hundred dollars. "You want me to tell the insurance company it was my fault? What."

Nate looks truly gobsmacked now, like he's trying to sort out what I am joking about and what's serious. I pull out a hundred-dollar bill and set it on the table, and his expression contorts to disdain.

Unsure of what he's looking for here, I set another bill on the table. Teachers don't make that much, so surely this is enough to change a couple of grades. He doesn't budge, his eyebrows only ducking further over his eyes.

"Not enough?" I ask.

Nate closes the folder in front of him and pushes his chair back from the table. It makes a hideous scraping noise on the linoleum.

"That is more than enough," he says. For a second, I think it's all good to go, that he's not the hardass Willa said he is, but then he continues, "This is entirely inappropriate Mrs. Morelli—"

"Ms." I correct, and he doesn't miss a beat.

"—Ms. Morelli, I don't know what kind of school you think this is, but I cannot be *bought*."

I huff a laugh.

Everyone can be bought.

I put another hundred on the table, which only seems to anger him further. He throws Artie's file on his desk and starts packing other things into the backpack he came with.

"It's time for you to go," he says.

"We're not done talking."

"We are. I'd be happy to meet with Mrs. Donovann-Morelli next week, but please let her know that this level of entitled bribery will not be accepted coming from her either."

For once, I've been rendered speechless.

I talk to a lot of men every day, scary men, sensitive baby men who throw tantrums when they don't get their way, ones with at least one gun on their person at all times, but rarely do they shut me down so concisely and sternly as this middle school math teacher just has. They know what I'll do to them if they do. This man doesn't know anything about me though, so he goes on:

"And just what kind of school do you think this is? Like, have you had success with this tactic before? Do you just carry around hundreds of dollars to bribe people with all the time?"

I don't usually need to resort to bribing, as demands and threats are my first preferred options, but I don't tell him this. I slide the money back into my purse and settle into my chair for the rest of his rant which he shows no sign of stopping now.

"I like Artie, I really do, and now I like him even more knowing that he's ended up so normal coming from a family of spoiled socialites who pay off their problems instead of, oh I don't know, having a normal conversation about them? Truly, what the hell were you thinking?"

I'm silent at the question, and he looks as if he's just now realizing that while I was out of line, what he's just said is more so. He squeezes his eyes shut and drags a hand down his face, a gesture I'm all too familiar with in myself.

"I think you should leave," he repeats, now sounding more tired than furious.

I stay sitting a moment longer before I nod and push up from the desk. I'm not used to men calling me entitled or spoiled, no matter how true either of these things may or may not be. It's almost refreshing, being talked to as if I'm a normal, albeit unhinged, aunt and not someone that's killed a number of people I will not disclose with my bare hands. I should feel embarrassed, put in my place.

Instead, I'm fucking *thrilled*.

"I'll talk to Artie," I say once I reach the door. His head snaps in my direction. "He'll have his missing assignments in by Monday. Can't do anything about the other kids, though. Maybe try that stern talking to, though. See how they fare."

After another silent moment of his eyes studying my face, he gives the briefest nod.

"Thank you," he says.

With one last glance at his face, his body, his hands now relaxed on his backpack strap, I leave, sliding my sunglasses on my nose before getting outside.

* * *

EVERYONE'S already eating by the time I finally get home, gathered around in the kitchen, Willa and my mom standing, Willa's kids sitting at the island stools. Mom's already put together a plate for Leo who kisses her on the cheek and goes to join Mary and my brother-in-law, Sean Donovann, watching football in the living room. The meatballs smell delicious, and my stomach garbles at the spices in the air.

My meetings went way too long after I left the school, dragging on until I almost made Leo knock someone out just because he spoke too slow. Damn southerners are not meant for Boston, and I stand by that.

"Here, Princess." Mom offers me a plate after I get through my own round of cheek kisses and hugs.

My niece, Angel, is wearing a shirt and pants with a skeleton printed over her own bones; her Halloween costume that she's worn at least twice per week since October. She says she's paying homage to this singer and that I wouldn't get it because I'm too old and know nothing about music. I tell her, singer or not, she looks badass.

Before I've even taken a bite, Angel's pulled out her sketchbook and is bustling to where I stand to show me her latest work. She, like her twin, is too good for the world she's been born into. I'm never entirely sure how they got to be so sweet with their dad the way he is (Irish, mafioso, second in line to the Donovann estate, etc.) but maybe that's exactly how: Sean acts tough, and can be as scary and hideous as he needs to be—and with his lot, he does. Often. But he's got a soft spot for Willa. An even softer spot for his kids.

"I'm going to shoot hoops," Artie says through a mouth full of food as he brings his plate to the sink.

"Nope," I say and point back to the stool he just vacated.

He looks warily back at me, his mom told him I met with Mr. Gilbert no doubt, and he's afraid of what I'll do to him. He should be, it means he knows he's messed up.

"Sit," I say and take my time looking at some of Angel's new drawings. A still life of some fruits and vases, a pencil drawing of a tennis shoe, a cartoonish portrait of their cat. I delight in the fact that, at almost thirteen, she still wants to show me her artwork.

"Beautiful," I say. "You're getting really good at shading, look here, Willa." I point at the tennis shoe and nudge my older sister. Willa hums in agreement.

"Very good, baby," Willa says, and Angel beams.

I give Angel one more kiss on the forehead before starting on my own food. Angel tells us about her day while Mom starts packing up leftovers. Artie squirms in his seat, waiting to hear his fate after the parent-teacher conference.

"So, what happened with the teacher?" Willa finally asks. "Can he play?"

"Oh, he can play," I say, and Artie lets out a breath. "If he turns in all his homework by Monday."

"What?" he whines.

"What happened?" Willa asks.

I shoot Willa a look. "What happened is that your son has started a small revolution in his math class that's led to bullying."

"I don't do any of that," Artie says. "I'm not a bully."

"No, but the bullying has come at a result of you disrespecting your teacher."

"Mr. G and I are cool. I don't disrespect him!"

"By being obstinate and not doing what you're told—what your teacher assigns to help you learn—you're disrespecting him and his time. You also disregard your parents' time by making them deal with it, and furthermore, since I had to talk to him about it, you're disrespecting *my* time."

"What—"

"Artie," Sean barks from the living room. "Don't fight with your godmother."

He looks to his own mother like she might defend him, but after one look at me, she doesn't push it, just shrugs and gives her agreement.

Artie groans.

"You're doing it, Arthur Donovann-Morelli, and tell your posse to knock it off," I say with finality. I'm using my stern voice, which is different from what Leo calls my scary voice. That one is saved for the people who've wronged me. "Make it right."

He sighs, but eventually nods. I give him a hug and mess up his mousy brown hair which he tries to put back in place.

"I love you," I tell him, and he says it back. "Now go get to work."

He scatters to the front room to do homework, and his sister follows him with her sketch book. They're far past the age of it being deemed "cool" to do everything together, but they still do. I adore them.

Willa and I are on dish duty since Mom cooked. I wash, and she dries.

"Did you try to pay him off?" Willa asks quietly.

"Yeah," I admit. "He was so pissed, he yelled at me." I can't help but laugh about it and she follows suit while I tell her exactly what he said, special emphasis on the spoiled, entitled socialite of it all. I can barely remember the last time someone talked to me like that.

"He's got balls," she says. "You scare *me*."

I splash her with some of the sudsy water. "Just what the hell did you mean when you said to *do anything*? Did you want me to give him a blow job so your son can play basketball next week?"

Willa splashes me back and cackles. "Don't pretend you didn't want to!" She lowers her voice. "All the moms are into him. He's not, like, traditionally hot, but he's got something about him, no? I'm in a walking group with a few of them, and I swear he's all they talk about sometimes."

"How do you have time to be in a walking group?"

"I don't, but those moms gossip nearly as much as the rest of the legal department and I like to be in the loop." She twirls her finger next to her head. "For the kids."

Willa, a nosy person first, mother second.

"But be honest, it was hot when he was yelling at you, right?"

"Willa!"

"Like, just a little? Come on, you can tell me," she teases.

"We're done here." I pull the plug on the sink and try not to smile too wide. Willa is my older sister, but she's always been my closest friend. She can get me into the biggest of headaches, but I suppose it's the job of family to give you headaches and help when you have your own.

I am about to retire to my room for a much-needed hot shower when Leo's phone starts ringing. He takes it in the other room, and I am almost certain that it won't ruin my night, but the look on his face when he returns says that was wishful thinking.

"What?" I ask when he's hung up.

"Shipment is missing at the boat yard," he reports. I try not to sigh too loudly as I change course and head toward my office with Leo, Mary, and Sean trailing behind me. It's going to be a long night.

4

NATE

As much as I tried to ignore the problem of needing a date for my cousin's upcoming nuptials, my parents will not let me forget. Dad just had a procedure on his knee this month, so they will not be able to make it for the wedding, which means it's extra important that I go and show all my extended family that I am doing well, or better yet, *great*.

I answered a call from my mom on a whim at the start of my prep period and now have been listening for ten minutes about things I should and shouldn't say about my current life. My cousin Rex is rich, he works some job in stocks, and his sister is a travel influencer, so there's a bit of insecurity on my parents' part that their only son is, you know, just shaping the minds of the next generation and teaching the valuable skills of mathematics that they will take into their lives.

"Tell them about how you are working at a private school now," my dad says in the background of my mom's phone.

"Good idea, Grant. And who are you bringing again?"

"Ma, I have to go," I say. "More on this later, I love you."

I disconnect the call before she can say more and beeline for Jenna's classroom. She's my closest friend, both at this school and in general. She teaches seventh to ninth grade English and when I get to her classroom, she's in the midst of taping paper chains to her wall. Her countdown to the end of the school year.

"One of the kids started shit-talking *Macbeth* today, and I should get faculty of the year for not failing him," she says as soon as I'm settled in at one of the desks.

"Bravo," I say and then cut right to the chase. "Will you go with me to Rex's wedding?"

I can't see Jenna's face, but I already know what she's doing.

"Don't roll your eyes, say yes."

She turns back to face me after taping the last of her students' chains, this one neon pink and green, and with a sigh, comes down from the step stool to sit across from me.

"You're my best friend," Jenna says.

"Thank you."

"But I will not go with you to that tool's wedding."

"He's not so bad." I throw my hands up and lean back in my chair. "And you can't punish me for the crimes of my family. Attending weddings together is our thing."

Calling it 'our thing' is maybe a stretch, since we've only been to three weddings together in our five years as friends, and we have many other things we do with a much more frequent cadence: begrudgingly training for a 5k she signs us up for every October, not-so-silently judging parents when our students reveal secrets about their home lives, taste testing ice cream flavors at every shop in the city. But weddings are one of our things, and if they aren't, then I am officially trying to make them one.

"One, I love you, but I do not want to go. Two, I think I'm seeing someone," she says.

"Who?"

Jenna doesn't answer right away, but a bit of a smile tugs at the sides of her mouth and she schools it to be neutral.

"Jenna. . . "

She leans on the table like she's sharing a secret. "Do you remember the woman from the gym who we thought was checking you out because she kept staring at you when we were on the stair stepper?"

"Leopard leggings? And a kid?"

"Yes. She came up to me last week—"

"When?" I ask.

"Thursday, you were lesson planning—anyway, hand to God, she asked if you and I were seeing each other."

"And you said. . ."

"I said no, you're actually my strange little brother, and then I told her that I like girls, to which she said that she'd love to take me out for drinks."

"No fucking *way*," I slap both palms on the desk.

"Way. So we went to drinks on Friday."

"How did you not tell me this? *Days* have passed. Did you make out?"

"Yes," Jenna ignores the first question.

She and I have slightly different understandings of the term "best friend." Namely, I believe we should talk on the phone once per day, even when we already have plans to see each other, and that she should send me texts when the slightest inconvenience happens. She, on the other hand, prefers to not touch her phone for sometimes tens of hours at a time.

"Hot?" I ask.

Jenna nods solemnly. "So hot."

"This is the biggest thing that's happened to us all year, why are you just telling me?"

"Because I knew you would react poorly when I also told you that I really can't go to that wedding because I'm seeing her again this Friday."

I squint at Jenna, dutifully trying to decide which emotion will win: indignation that she is skipping out on a wedding that I also am dreading, or elation that she's going out with the hot mom that wears matching workout sets and bench presses twice as much as I do.

"Don't be mad." Jenna reaches a hand across the table and pats my arm. "You'll find someone."

The list of women I know who I could ask on dates is quickly dwindling as they either keep moving out of the city or getting married, which Jenna knows because she is the one I always bring to said weddings.

"How?"

"Ever heard of a dating app?" The bell rings before she can start her familiar rant, and I quickly remove myself from her classroom.

* * *

THE MONDAY after term break is usually a wash for everyone. Even with the best intentions to start the final term strong, the kids are too buzzed on the week they had off and the fact that in two short months it will officially be summer vacation. I didn't get to sleep until stupid late despite going to bed early. My upstairs neighbor has been on a reggae kick and loves nothing more than playing it well into the night while he does his gaming streams. I've watched a few, they're fine.

So, after a long day of giving all my students what I call a planning day—AKA they set goals for how the rest of the school year will go and then we watch part of *October Sky*—I stand at pick-up duty fueled only by the third cup of burnt coffee I had after lunch and the promise that after all of these kids clear out I'll be able to drive home and fall directly into my bed until tomorrow.

Pick-up isn't an arduous task, all we have to do is make sure there are no fights and the kids aren't getting kidnapped, which is easy enough. It's a drag, but we all do our time.

One of the kids has left a softball in the small patch of grass, and I pick it up.

I toss the forgotten softball in the air a few times as I stroll down the sidewalk past the cars that surpass my salary. A horn immediately startles me from my important focus on the ball, and when I turn to look, I am met with a black Land Rover with the darkest tinted windows I've ever seen in my life (they *cannot* be legal). I should recognize the car immediately, but I must be really out of it, because it takes the passenger side window gliding down for me to realize who's inside.

Vanessa Morelli. Artie's aunt, or godmother, or whatever, perched in the driver's seat of the black Land Rover that I drove my car into last week. I've been waiting on a call from my insurance after filing the claim, but it hasn't come.

She's got these tiny sunglasses slid low on her nose that she's peering over with a smirk hinting at a shadow of a dimple into her cheek. As if her face isn't already perfect, she needed to have a dimple. Sure.

"Hey," she calls.

"Hello," I say, and make to walk on, but she inches along the sidewalk keeping up with me in the slow-moving line of cars.

"Did Artie get all of his work in today?" she asks, and she has to stop driving or else she'll hit the one in front of her, so I stop too. I'm very reluctant about it all, though.

"He did," I say. "Did you write his speech?"

"Speech?"

"Speech," I repeat, but really, speech isn't right; it was a performance. A whole monologue. The boy should be in theater. "He gave a rousing, pro-homework manifesto. Stood on his chair and everything."

Vanessa laughs, her eyes lit up at the image, and really just what does she need with a dimple like that anyway? I stare a beat too long before I nod at the space in front of her and she moves her car forward to close the gap, me walking beside her. I resume tossing the ball because that is something I can focus on without forgetting how insufferable she was last week.

"I'm sorry, by the way," she says.

I'm not sure I heard her correctly.

I look back into the car and she's pushed the sunglasses onto her head, which has pushed her hair from her face, because seeing more of her face is exactly what I need when trying to hold a grudge right now.

"It wasn't cool," she says. "I recognize that."

"How big of you," I say, and then after a moment, "Thank you."

We're making eye contact like we know each other, not like I just hit her car and told her to fuck off last week, and the light honk of the car behind her startles us both to move forward.

"I'm sorry too," I say. "I don't have a habit of yelling at my parent-teacher conferences."

"Well maybe you should. You're good at it."

She's smirking, like a cheeky, devious little angel, and I wish I had something clever to say back, but the smirk has sent me into a mute state. Artie shows up with his twin sister in tow, and they both offer me their fists to bump, which I do, because I am not a monster. They climb into the back seat of their aunt's car and each lean forward to plant a kiss on her cheek.

"Bye, Mr. G.," Artie says out the window and gives a salute. I mimic the gesture, earning a grin from the boy.

Vanessa leans her head back into my view. "Bye, Mr. G.," she mimics, before pulling out of the pick-up line and away from the school.

I notice that her bumper is already fixed.

5

VANESSA

IN THE BRIEF SOLITUDE OF MY OFFICE, I RUB MY TEMPLES IN soothing little circles. When work is especially bloody, I see that purple-red color of blood each time I close my eyes for hours. At the heart of it, I do not want to kill people. None of us do, we aren't murderers. You don't want someone like that on your team, someone who *likes* killing.

It's not fun, it's not sport, it's horrific usually, but unfortunately, it's business.

We do what we have to when we have to, because if we don't, someone else will get us first.

Every crime family comes with its dangers, and ours is just the same. Some deal in drugs, people, gambling, fake money—whatever they're good at. Before I was born, my father's uncle was a relatively small fish in a massive pond. He was a runner, then a lackey, then, after getting his hands dirty enough, an advisor. By the time he became the boss, my father was seventeen. They expanded into weapons, buying and moving product into the country so it could be sold to the highest bidder.

I will not pretend that this is ethical.

But, again, it is business.

Now, we've only expanded our horizons; our importation of technology and weapons means that we can move very expensive products into the country and sell them to well-paying clients who want to feel safe, protected, bigger than everyone else. It also means that when something goes missing, it's not an inexpensive problem that can be easily ignored. We're not pushing pot here.

Willa's husband Sean and his brother, Cillian Donovann, breeze into my office, ending my moment alone, and sit heavily in the chairs across from the desk.

"Nothing?" I ask, though their faces tell me everything.

"The other families are clean," Sean says.

Cillian tilts his head left to right as if weighing the statement. "Well, clean is relative."

"They didn't steal our shit," Sean clarifies. "No reason to believe the Garzas did it."

"What about the Orlovs?" I ask, though I have no reason to suspect them. This boss, Maxim, hasn't caused us any trouble since taking over, but that doesn't mean he *won't.*

"Wouldn't risk the relationship," Sean says. "And apparently he's got his own problems."

The Garzas, the Orlovs, the Morellis, and the Donovanns run this city, each of us staying in our own lanes for the most part. Of course there are sub families, ones that report up, and every decade or so they get a hankering to play king of the hill and topple whosoever is on top. Those are some of the messiest problems to deal with because it's not about taking out faceless strangers. That's *personal.*

"We'll find them," Sean assures.

A shipment of highly technical weapons was stolen last week and still have yet to be located. There were hundreds of small explosives, tiny little things that are easy to hide, almost unnoticeable, but pack a huge punch. We had buyers across the country ready to shell out ungodly sums of money, but then the shipment went missing. More are already on their way, but that's money we eat if they aren't found. It's not like there's insurance on illegal materials.

The cameras were tampered with and none of our guys had a damn detail to share. It's not that nobody knows who stole the shipment—someone knows—it's that they aren't talking.

I think about what the last five days have entailed, which is a whole lot of *not* finding whoever's been messing with my shit. Cillian and Sean brought in a suspect on Thursday during dinner, which normally wouldn't be a huge issue, but it was an obligatory dinner with one of the Old Heads who still not-so-secretly wishes my father was still alive and in charge. The kind of dinner where I must listen to slightly veiled misogyny and pretend that I respect him more than I do because clan politics are delicate.

The dude the Donovanns brought in was bleeding all over the front walk and the entryway while Mary was in the middle of dishing up lasagna for everyone. She'd quickly handed the serving tools over to my mom, who entertained the Old Head and the kids with Willa, while the rest of us took the joker to the basement.

I would prefer to not do business in house like this, but desperate times call for unsavory measures.

Cillian said the guy was the closest they'd found to the missing shipment; the owner of the last car the security cameras picked up before going down. He wasn't in the clan, just a wannabe gangster known for selling firearms to kids.

Prick.

He was tight-lipped, only opening his mouth to shout profan-ities at us, and he lost consciousness after Mary worked on convincing him for the better part of an hour. Her white sweater was completely soiled, stained deep red down the front and on the sleeves, and she would have joined the family for dessert looking just like that if I hadn't told her to go change.

The guy was dead by the time we went down again a few hours later, though Mary swore she'd been easy on him. Said no way could he have died from that beating, even if he was on blood thinners, but sure enough, there was not a heartbeat to be found. She and Leo took care of his body, but god, it's exhausting work running about like that while there are guests upstairs.

"It's only a matter of time before we smoke them out," Cillian says now. He's all confidence—in fact, he's *always* all confidence about things like this. Someone steals his shit? He cuts off their fingers. Someone betrays him? He kills them. It's like this life doesn't faze him. As the head of the Donovann family, he's got to be tough. I'm just glad he's on my side because he'd be a son of a bitch to kill.

"You're right," I sigh.

It's not the stuff going missing that's really upsetting me, it's the disrespect of it. A container of bombs disappearing is inconvenient, but ultimately pennies in the grand scheme of the year. We aren't going out of business because of a few missing boxes.

But a bad egg in the operation? That could cost a fortune if left to rot.

Sean looks down at his watch and stands from his chair. "I've got to be on one of the sites," he explains. "OSHA violations abound, apparently."

I close my eyes to the news, trying to hide the uncontrollable roll of my eyes. Running the workings of the mafia clan is a business in itself; there's the logistics of employees, shipments, transportation, orders, and every other detail. Then, of course, there's the deals to be made, individuals to be bought out, and relationships to be fostered. The construction business, though, is what lets us do the things we really want to do and gives us more capital to do it. So, nothing gets to be ignored.

On the side of Morelli Construction, Sean manages the

construction sites, Willa handles the legal, I'm the acting CEO. All these roles would be a lot if we weren't *also* managing some of the largest crime operations in the city.

"You look stressed," Cillian says once his brother leaves. I let myself slouch in my chair until my head is resting on the back of it. If he was anyone else outside of my family I wouldn't show such fatigue, but Cillian has been on our side since I was eighteen. He's earned our trust with his partnership, and I've seen him low, exhausted, or with bloody fists in defense of someone from my family. He's not blood, but he is one of us.

"I can't stand this stuff. Like there's a rock perpetually in my shoe, and until we find who did it, I'll never walk comfortably," I say.

"Anyone in your clan you think might have it out for you?"

I think about this, scrolling through names and faces in my mind. "I pissed Ronaldo Sinclair off last week, but he's too much of an idiot to retaliate."

"Why him?"

"Because I wouldn't marry his nephew. You know James?" Cillian nods. "And I wouldn't give him Mary for either him or his brother Ryan."

Cillian whistles.

"She'd kill him in his sleep."

"I know." I stand and look out the window to the back yard. Mom is hard at work in the garden, weeding and planting and otherwise making sure it's going to be the most beautiful garden in the neighborhood.

It's nice to see her outside again. For over a year after my father died, she didn't touch the garden. It was something they did together, him following her around telling her what troubled him, her listening, adding her input where she could.

Cillian meanders over until he's by my side and leans against the wall on the other side of the window frame.

"How many this month?"

"Hm?"

"Marriage proposals."

"Oh." I sigh. "Just three. A notable one from the Barga family, though."

"They'll send their son here from California?"

"Well, I'm a hot piece of ass," I say. My father made quite a name for us in his tenure, drawing eyes of crime families across the country. I think his cooperation with them is what made him such a strong leader. It's a fine line for me to walk in his stead, interfacing with crime lords a world away. "Obviously they didn't offer their favorite son. Probably not even the spare. They'd send the third in line. He's probably nineteen."

"Did you kill them for even offering?"

"No. Figured that would make traveling to California very difficult," I say. Every inquiry has come from a place I understand, a place that craves security. My family could offer that. "The funny thing is that they always ask if I'd arrange for a match with Mary if not for myself. They have no idea what a handful she'd be."

"They'd be lucky to have her," Cillian says, which makes me smile. He and Mary haven't always gotten along—something about Cillian gets under her skin, always has—but Mary at least hasn't threatened to strangle him in a few years, which is progress. She tolerates him. He recognizes that she's an asset.

"She'd take over from within. It would take three weeks. If that."

"All the more power for you, then."

"I suppose."

Cillian is older than Willa and Sean, mid-thirties I think, but he is like me in that both of us became the heads of our families much younger than we intended. He's a peer, and practically family. The Donovann's used to be enemies to us, but when Willa and Sean fell in love, our fathers eventually agreed that the match would be an advantageous one.

It's been a fruitful partnership, our combined families.

"Why don't *we* get married?" Cillian muses.

I smile at my friend, but his lack of laughter tells me that he isn't joking. I mirror his pose, leaning against the wall facing him.

"That desperate for an heir?" I ask.

"Aren't you?"

I look out the window instead of answering. Outside, Mom stands and dusts dirt off her hands and knees.

"I'd like to train my nephew, but his godmother wants better things for him," Cillian teases.

"Well, I heard that your nephew's godfather is a rotten mobster, so maybe she's onto something there."

Cillian rolls his eyes.

"She sounds smart," I add. "Probably beautiful, too."

He huffs through his nose, which is about as much of a laugh you'll generally get from him, and we lapse into a silence. The air conditioner kicks on and blows cold air through a vent on the floor between us.

I remember Artie and Angel's baptism. Cillian and I both held Artie, Mary and Leo held Angel. Four godparents for the two tiny creatures. Artie was so tiny, his head fit in the palm of my hand, and his little fingers were wrapped around Cillian's pinky. The truce was so new still, not even a year since Willa and Sean's wedding. I was just seventeen.

Willa decided she didn't want to be the head of the Morelli family—she wanted to take care of the law side of the business, and give her kids all the attention she was able. Father had just announced that I would inherit his position instead. I was terrified, though strong enough not to show it. I'm still terrified. Afraid I didn't learn enough before he died, or that I won't be able to hold onto the power I have. Worse, I worry that I won't be able to protect them in the end.

I suppose he must've feared the same, though if he did, he

never said so. There's so much he never said—or maybe didn't feel like he needed to say, at least not yet.

I thought I'd have another twenty-five years to prepare.

"What about your niece?" I ask. He glares at the concept.

"I've watched *her* godmother gut several men. I do not wish to be one of them."

"That's fair." Mary is lethal, a sharp blade, but her goddaughter is as sweet as they come, and Mary will do every single thing to keep her that way.

"*Yeah*," he echoes, mocking, and I let out a small laugh.

After another quiet moment, I release a heavy breath. "I would be a bad wife," I admit. This is a truth I've never spoken aloud, one that I've been harboring for the better part of a decade. "I don't know that I'm made for relationships like that."

"You *would* be a bad wife. You work too much," Cillian says, then smirks. "I'd be a shit husband, though, so it evens out."

We watch each other, both surveying how serious the other is, gauging if the other is actually considering the offer. I have considered this. More than once, in fact. He and I are the same; too young to have so much power and responsibility, unmarried, in need of heirs. We would make sense as a pair.

Cillian's hot, too, in his brutal way. He's a mobster and he looks the part; tattoos on his hands and neck, buzzed hair, sharp clothes. He's a friend, which is more than could be said for most of the men in this community. I trust him, which means something. It's a tempting thought, but if I'm going to have an arranged marriage it should be with someone who can offer something I don't already have. Our families are already so tied with Willa and Sean, there would be no power gained for either of us.

I break first, turning to look at the portrait of my parents over the fireplace. My dad's large hand on my mom's shoulder, protective even in the painting, his gaze daring anyone to touch her. Their love was epic, something my sisters and I used to daydream about, a love that started as duty but blossomed into something much larger.

Our father was dear to us, and loyal to her. After having Willa and me, Mother almost died giving birth to Mary, and he never made her try for another. And though Leo was the obvious choice for heir—his nephew and godson is nearly as good as a son, and much of the clan expected him to—he didn't doubt his daughters could handle it. He cared for and believed in us in a way that most men in this world are incapable of.

I feel the familiar burn in my throat when I think too long about my father. As to not cry, I say, "Your dad would roll right over in his grave if he knew you married an Italian. Another Morelli in the family, no less. Is that the kind of generational karma you want?"

Cillian huffs again, and the tension floating with the dust between us ebbs.

"Sean did it," he reminds me.

"Sean's the spare."

"I know," he says, and walks back around the desk. He shrugs his suit coat over his wide shoulders. "It would give my Ma a heart attack."

"Couldn't have that," I say, though my disdain for his mother is no secret, nor her disdain of me. The truce between our families has never been enough to make her a pleasant woman in the slightest, and generally I try to like women, especially off-putting ones.

I push off the wall and step back to my desk, opening a folder then closing it.

"I talked again with Mr. McGowan," Cillian says. "He wants to accept your bid for the building."

I don't let myself celebrate this. "But?"

Mr. McGowan always has stipulations and has made every part of this process a unique hell. First, the back and forth on the proposal was egregious, and he's somehow even worse now that we are discussing a contract. He wants us to build it, because we are the best, but he will act like he's doing us a favor at every fucking turn.

"But he still doesn't want to work with you directly on the contract," Cillian says gently, like he knows it will make my stomach boil, which it does. "He's old, he's Irish, he's. . . rooted in tradition."

"So, what? He can see the quality of work we do, but he refuses to acknowledge that I'm the one in charge? Jackass."

"He is," Cillian agrees. He presses his fingertips on my desk and waits until I meet his eyes. "But this is four hundred million dollars we're talking about."

I heave a long sigh. Cillian is generally removed from the workings of Morelli Construction—he has his own dealings for the Donovann clan that keep him plenty busy—but he has been instrumental in getting deals for new builds from the old Irish of the city. They want what we can offer in terms of unofficial add-ons (see: rooms and basement levels not listed on any blueprint for the less above-board dealings), but they only want it so long as they can go through Cillian. It's been over a decade since Willa and Sean got married, tying our families together, but some prejudices run deep.

It doesn't help that I'm a woman—a disgrace in their eyes, even if they don't say in so many words.

"I'll pull the deal right now," he says. "It's up to you."

He means it. There's no judgment behind those pale eyes.

"Keep moving forward," I say.

After a moment, Cillian knocks on the desk. "Okay."

"Nice watch, by the way," I say, and he looks at the gleaming thing on his wrist like it's just fine. *Pretty nice* instead of thirty-five thousand dollars of vintage gold and leather Rolex. Cillian loves his watches.

"This old thing?" He heads for the door but pauses before he can step through to the hallway. "Teasing aside, Ness, I would marry you. If you needed, of course."

Cillian smiles and I give my best estimation of a genuine one in return. It feels a bit stale on my lips.

"Thank you, Cillian."

He leaves without another word, his gait so sure in every step. I recognize the confidence, so much of what we need to be is the same, but I need to be tougher, smarter. He isn't underestimated by default.

6

VANESSA

MORELLI FAMILY TRADITION RULES THAT WE TRY TO MAKE IT TO ALL of Artie's basketball games. Angel doesn't play any sports, but for a time she did ballet, and we went to every performance, holed up together in the studio which smelled like hairspray. Tonight is not the last game of the season, but it is the last home game and Artie is starting. His math grade somehow made its way to a very respectable B- after submitting a massive stack of assignments.

The gym is relatively quiet, mostly just parents and coaches since the bulk of the student section won't show up until the high school games later on. Artie is on the C team, which is all of the middle schoolers if I'm to judge by just the size of the players. Artie is not the best by any means, but he is improving. I would know, seeing that Willa throws a fit if any of us are so much as late for a home game.

We've mostly moved on from the crisis with the bombs, but I still feel restless. Like I can't let my guard down for even a second. I still don't know exactly who sabotaged us, and that's not a comfortable feeling. We ruled out most of the other families in the city, but I can't shake the feeling that it's someone who knows how we work. The motive, too, concerns me. If it's someone that just wanted some money that is one thing—a problem, but ultimately not a huge one—but if someone wants to use the weapons against us. . . Well, then that's a bigger issue.

The sharp trill of the ref's whistle reminds me that now is not the time to dwell. Now is the time for me to cheer for Artie like the good godmother I am, tell him to get back up and not worry about it when he misses a free throw, scream when he manages to sink a three. We *were* the loudest people here, but a few of the student council students have shown up by now, and not to be outdone, are chanting for the boys. The cheerleaders, too, with their pleated skirts and high ponytails are cheering on the sidelines.

Artie gets subbed for another kid who's faster than him, but not as good at making baskets, and we all send him thumbs up when he looks at us from the folding chairs that make up the bench.

"I'm going to get a so-da," I say, exaggerating the O because it makes Angel giggle. "Anyone want anything?"

They all wave me off, Mary and Angel are huddled over a Nintendo Switch, and Sean and Willa are leaning close, whispering something or other back and forth. The two of them have always been like this, excruciatingly in love. Their mushiness never fades, and I will not pretend that part of me doesn't envy this level of love and devotion.

Leo is sitting a few rows behind, his back against the cinderblock wall as his eyes scan for potential danger, and I don't have to say anything to know he'll follow me.

It feels good to stretch my legs, I swear I'm experiencing hypertension from all this shit happening, but I don't let on.

Before I reach the lobby, I spot Artie's math teacher leaning against a wall typing on his phone, a school lanyard hanging around his neck. I see what Willa meant about him being weirdly hot. His light brown hair sits in messy waves and his shoulders are slightly pulled forward, but he's got a sharp jaw with a shadow of a beard and, bad posture or not, he seems somewhat built. Not exceptionally tall, but at least six foot. He is handsome, I think. Not mafioso handsome, but most definitely math teacher handsome.

He sees me looking at him as I'm about to pass and his face lights up in recognition. I nod and look away, but he slides his phone in his pocket as he heads my way.

When he sidles right up next to me, I send Leo a look that translates roughly to *this is fine* before he thinks to interfere.

Of all the people here, I would guess that Artie's math teacher is the least dangerous.

Today he wears an outfit much like the one he had on the last two times I saw him: a button-up with the top button undone, rolled at the sleeves, a tie pulled from his neck, black JCPenney dress shoes. The shirt isn't fitted, unless he's aiming for a sort of rectangular fit.

"Ms. Morelli," he greets. "What a surprise."

"Mr. G.," I say. "Nice to see you again."

He gives a sort of mock bow, his hands remaining in his pockets. "Come around here often?"

"Required attendance," I explain. "Family mandate."

"How supportive of you," he says. His eyes are a striking green, and they flit to my face and then away, scanning around the gymnasium instead of meeting my eye directly even though *he* is the one who approached me.

"And you?" I ask.

"Oh, I don't have to come to the games, but middle school basketball is better than any professional sport. More inspiring, more exciting."

"I couldn't agree more." We round the corner into the lobby. "Were you also in need of a mid-game soda?" I ask.

"Always," he says. "But these booths live in the dark ages. Cash only."

"Oh?"

He bobs his head in an exaggerated nod. "Luckily for me, I ran into someone who I have under good authority carries a number of large bills on her person at any given time."

I would balk at the audacity of this man if he wasn't also somewhat amusing.

"Very lucky for you." We join the brief line outside of the concession booth.

"I just hope she knows that I would love a bag of sour Skittles," he says and I can't help it, this time, I laugh aloud. Leo's head darts in our direction at the sound. "And a water."

I'm next in line and repeat his order, adding on three cans of soda for me, Leo, and Sean. I get a sleeve of Starburst for Mary and Angel to share, and then I slip the goods into my bag.

I'm not entirely sure why I did what he said, maybe because I'm seldom ordered around and wonder how far he'll take it. It's not like I'm scared of him. I could kill this man in no less than a dozen ways, many of which with just my hands, but he seems harmless enough. It's disarming. I don't think he could hold his own in a fight, and that fact endears him more.

Nate pops a few sour Skittles into his mouth and his lips pucker at the taste. He wipes the powder from his fingers on the side of his slacks.

"I've got another favor to ask," he says.

"Do tell," I say as we walk down the track towards the other side of the court where everyone sits. Little squeaks of sneakers on the floor sound from the court below us.

He stops and leans on the rail looking over the court and I watch his eyes scan the students running back and forth. He's nervous, I'm sure of it now. I can see it in the tension in his shoulders, the way he gnaws on the inside of his cheek.

"Hear me out," he starts after draining a quarter of his water bottle. "There's a wedding."

I pride myself on my ability to school my face into an unfazed expression in all critical conversations. A vital skill. But I can't control my eyebrows now, and they've shot halfway up my fore-head, which is as alarming to Nate as it is to me because he rushes to continue:

"It's my cousin Rex, and he's the fourth cousin in my family to get married, and my parents are getting antsy that not only am I working with children instead of with investments, but I am also unmarried."

"Oh, wow," I say before I can hold back. It's startling how much there is to process there, and I can barely begin to before he barrels on.

"So, you see, it's a big deal that I go and tell my aunts and uncles that I work at a fancy private school now and an even *bigger* deal that I bring a date."

"Reasonable." I'm lying, but I nod. We are both leaning against the railing and facing each other, and the scoreboard above our heads beeps.

"I don't have one, though. A date. I need one." After a pause, he adds, "I want you to be my date."

My jaw falls open before I snap it closed again. I have once again been left without words by this strange man.

"Why?"

"Because I don't know very many women."

"Flattering," I say, wry.

"And even if I did know many women, *you* might be the most beautiful one."

I blink at the relative ease in which this man just delivered a flirty compliment. Him calling me beautiful also makes my neck flush, but I will not be investigating why that is at this time.

I look down at the court instead. In the stands, Willa and Mary are staring at us, Willa waggling her eyebrows and Mary squinting at Nate. I would flip them off if there weren't so many children here.

"And while teaching children about fractions and finding the hypotenuse of a triangle is apparently not 'grandson of the year' material, having you there to escort me would most definitely put me in the running."

I throw my hands up. "You're kidding! The hypotenuse might be the most important thing they learn all year."

"Finally," Nate breathes, "someone who gets me."

He pops another palmful of Skittles in his mouth, and once again, winces. It doesn't look like a wholly pleasant experience, eating sour candy, but he carries on.

"The wedding is Friday and if I don't have a date, my mother may never forgive me, and then I won't be invited home for Thanksgiving or Christmas. All of the major holidays will be spent alone with my dog eating grocery store sushi. Is this what you want for me, Ms. Morelli?"

I consider, a smile pressing into my cheeks.

I'm not sure why I'm humoring this—boredom maybe?

No, he's charming in his way. He's totally unlike nearly every other man I spend my time around. Those men are macho with shallow egos, cruel, and they struggle in our every conversation to balance the respect they know my position deserves with how much respect they feel they ought to show me as a 28-year-old unmarried woman.

Nate is nothing like that. He talks to me like I'm an equal, like he can just request I buy him sour Skittles and tell me I'm spoiled and entitled with no recourse. It's rare.

"You don't do dating apps?" I ask.

"Please don't relegate me to a dating app, Vanessa, it's unsafe! I could be in very real danger. I'm sure non-murdering women are on there, but which of them is going to say yes to a date with a stranger in two days?"

I blink at his use of my first name after so much Ms. Morelli, and further, at his assumption that I've never murdered anyone. It's not lost on me how much danger he's in just by speaking to me in public, where anyone can see and think he's working with me.

I should say no. Obviously, I should say no, if only because I have no reason to say yes. But I *want* to say yes.

The realization surprises me and I'm halfway to convincing myself that I only feel this way because of all the drama recently, but before I can make it all the way to that conclusion, I am speaking again.

"What time?" I ask as the buzzer sounds off behind me again, longer this time, the end of the third quarter.

Nate looks astounded, like in a million years he wouldn't have thought I'd actually say yes.

"I can pick you up at six."

"I'll come to you," I say. Leo would rather drive me and keep watch through the evening, which reminds me that I will have to try to explain this to Leo and, *shit*, my sisters. Willa is going to have an absolute heyday about this.

"Alright, wow. Shall we, I don't know—exchange numbers?" he asks.

"I have yours," I remind him. "From when you. . . hit my car?"

"Right. Yes. Well, I am looking forward to it." Nate starts backing away. "And I'm leaving now before you tell me you were joking."

"Okay."

"O-kay," he repeats and with one last nod walks away. I watch him go for just a moment, not entirely sure how I ended up here.

7

NATE

I TRY TO KEEP MY AFTER-HOURS TIME AS CAREFREE AS POSSIBLE, particularly Friday nights when the most adventurous thing I'll plan is the rare occasion I can convince Jenna to go to trivia night with me. Now though, I am as unchill as I've ever been and am most definitely freaking the hell out. I can't stop checking my hair, even though it looks the same as it did the last time I looked, and we're going on ten minutes that I've paced around my apartment waiting for Vanessa.

Vanessa is hot, like stupid hot. She is hotter than me, I am aware. I would probably have to be an Avenger, or a fucking vampire to be as hot as she is. And despite trying to bribe me like some sort of criminal or nefarious millionaire, she apologized and has been friendly ever since. Charming, even.

Hot, and charming. Deadly combination.

We've texted three times in the last couple days, and I feel like I'm seventeen again. The first time my phone pinged with a message from her I called Jenna back-to-back as many times as it took until she grumpily picked up. She had no constructive advice for me, all her message ideas either too flirty or too stiff.

The text exchanges were brief. I gave her my address, told her she could wear whatever she wanted, but I for one would be in my best. I over-thought this one to death before clarifying that I was joking and would not be wearing my very best, just my almost-best, and whatever she wanted to wear would be perfect. But probably not white.

She'd sent back a "Haha" and I overanalyzed it for an hour.

Ranger lets out a huff on the couch, tired of my anxious steps, and I walk over to pat him on the head. He's an old dog but a good dog, maybe the best dog. A terrier mix, the runt of his litter that I have to bathe way too frequently now, but he is a good dog.

He hates the pacing, which is fair. I suppose I would too if he was the one pacing.

I check my hair one more time and crunch down on three orange tic-tacs.

I'm in the process of smelling my armpits one last time when my buzzer goes off indicating that she's downstairs. Or at least I hope it's her because I can only look in the mirror and fuss so long before I start making things worse.

"Who is it?" I ask into the intercom.

"Ness," she says, then corrects herself, "Vanessa."

"I'll come right down."

"Actually, can I come up and use your bathroom?"

I freeze and try to recall the last time I cleaned the bathroom and catalog every embarrassing thing that could exist there.

"Sure," I say and buzz her in.

The elevator never works, so she's got four flights of stairs to climb, which gives me at least ninety seconds to speed clean my entire house. I start on the bathroom, shoving everything on my counter into the drawer. This makes it look too clean, suspiciously clean, so I grab the hand lotion and deodorant and place them back. It can only be a good thing that she know I am moisturized and smell good.

I'm thankful that I'm not a very messy person, but she will

have to walk through my bedroom to get to the bathroom, so I pull straight my comforter and kick my slippers under the bed.

I am also debating whether or not the slip of her nickname means that *I* can call her that but decide that best practice would be not. It's then that I hear the knock at my door.

I give Ranger one more look before opening the door and good lord, she looks gorgeous. *Hot* hot, Vanessa is wearing a short, black dress. Her lips are painted deep red, and her long hair is pulled back into a low ponytail, no flyaways.

"Vanessa," I say finally, and she stands a bit taller.

"Hello," she says, and steps past me into my apartment. We look at each other for a moment too long and Ranger barks at her feet, startling the both of us.

"Christ," she whispers, looking down at the dog. I kneel down to scratch behind his ears before I pick him up. "What is that?"

"This is Ranger," I say. "He's really sweet, just wanted to introduce himself."

Vanessa looks unsure about the said sweetness of the dog, which I cannot blame her for. Ranger has not aged all that gracefully. I can admit, even, that he is a bit ugly, but I think he's ugly in the way that makes him all the more endearing and precious. After another moment of the two assessing each other, she nods.

"Good to meet you, Ranger," she says. I deposit him back on the ground and Ranger's tail thumps before he meanders over to his bed, circling three times before settling.

I show the way to the bathroom and do some breathing exercises while I wait for her to come out. I lean on my kitchen counter aiming for casual when I hear the toilet flush, but that feels wrong, so I stand and prop one hand on my hip, which is somehow much worse. I end up crossing my arms over my chest as she comes out of the room and can only pray that I look normal.

"Shall we?" I ask.

"Definitely."

* * *

WE WALK to the wedding because the venue is just a few blocks away, and even though I live in a just-okay part of town, the place is *nice*. It's an old mechanic's shop turned into a hip, industrial party space that rich people pay way too much to rent.

I did offer up and down to drive since Vanessa's wearing such high heels, but she said no to each one of my offers because she likes walking and that I would be amazed at the things she can do in her heels. (This made my neck hot because I just kept thinking about things she potentially does in those high heels and my mind isn't better than that of my fourteen-year-old students, it's just better trained.)

I lied about not wearing my best because the suit I am wearing is, pitifully, my best. I feel entirely underdressed next to her, but if she feels the same, she doesn't let on.

When we get to the venue, I am impressed with how nice it really is. But then again, my uncle Dave is never one to hold back costs on a party, and a wedding is about the biggest party you can have. My cousin Sasha's wedding still shows up in bridal magazines, and that was three years ago; she posts about it every time, so I am very up to date on how often she's been written about.

"Greeting line first?" Vanessa asks, eyeing the line of people waiting to hug and congratulate my cousin and his blushing bride.

"They already had the ceremony," I explain. "Don't take a shot every time you hear the words 'intimate' and 'special' because you might get alcohol poisoning."

"Duly noted."

It would have made my mom's whole year if Rex asked me to be a groomsman in his wedding, but I didn't make the cut. He didn't even invite me to the *ceremony*, though he and I are close, in my estimation. The ceremony was just for a handful of their closest family to make it really *special*, a little note in the invitation told in fancy script.

Come celebrate with us afterward. Food, sweets, dancing, an open bar, and love in the air.

Gag.

"So, fill me in. What do I need to know? Who are the main players?" Vanessa says as we join the greeting line.

I point to the bride. "Phoebe. Very nice, makes delicious fruit salads, can't remember what she does for work, though she told me it has something to do with content creation."

"Pretty dress," Vanessa notes.

"The groom is my cousin, Rex, full name Reginald. He works in stocks and more recently, crypto. He's the oldest, and favorite, grandson. Every few months we get together for basketball or he invites me for drinks with the *bros*."

"Do you like him?"

"I do, actually," I admit. "He was the closest thing I had to a brother growing up, so he bugs the shit out of me sometimes, but he's good. He's. . ."

"Family?" she finishes.

"Family." We are about three couples away from the front, and I now can see my uncle and aunt are receiving as well. Phoebe's parents too, I presume, though I have never met them. "Next is Aunt Barb next to Uncle Dave. He's my mom's brother, and they are competitive in a very weird, adult way. Their other daughter Sasha is the one in the pink dress over there. Beware, she will be recording many videos on her phone, and if you're too friendly, she'll try to teach you a dance."

"Speaking from experience?"

I give a grim nod and it lights up her face. Before she can ask more though, we're up and Rex is pulling me into a hug, exclaiming how glad he is I could make it. My uncle tunes in, resulting in another round of hugging, my aunt even brings Vanessa in for one.

"You look familiar, have we met?" Rex asks Vanessa before we can say all our congratulations. Phoebe's eyes go wide.

"Oh my god!" Phoebe's hand darts to Vanessa's forearm. "You're Vanessa Morelli."

Vanessa takes all these strangers touching her in stride, looking as pleasant as ever.

"I am," Vanessa agrees. "Though, I'm sorry I'm not sure I know where we've met."

"No," Phoebe says. "I was the one in charge of getting quotes for last year's 30 under 30 at *The Post*. We talked on the phone."

I recall now that she isn't a content creator, but a content curator. She has a journalism degree. Honest mistake.

"*Right*. Phoebe?" Vanessa says.

"Yes!" I hope Phoebe never realizes that Vanessa maybe only knows her name because it was displayed on four different signs at the entrance. "Babe, she was like the biggest picture on the spread."

"That's right." Rex nods. "Cool that you could come to our wedding with Nate-Man."

"Yes. Nate-Man," Vanessa holds my arm like we really are here on a date, and I feel like she's touching me with a live wire. "Well, congratulations, you look very beautiful, Phoebe. And beautiful together."

Phoebe beams, I mean she just glows under this small praise from Vanessa.

"We'll leave you to the masses, but we'll see you on that dance floor," I say, and it has the intended effect of making Rex laugh and give one of his signature huge claps on the shoulder.

My aunt and uncle do look impressed as we walk away arm in arm. *You're welcome, Mom.*

"You didn't tell me you're famous."

"Hardly. Just a local thing. Shall we buffet?"

If she means to divert my attention, it works, because as with the rest of the wedding, no expense was spared on the food, and being so nervous has worked up an appetite.

After piling my plate with three kinds of salads (pasta, potato, green) and a literal steak, we find our way to an empty table. We take turns observing guests, guessing their jobs and hobbies until some of my other family members make their way to the table and we have to make small conversation about my job, where in the world I met such a catch as Vanessa, how my dad's surgery went, onward and onward.

Exhausting work.

It's a relief when it's time for cake cutting, speeches, and then of course the actual eating of said cake which is a peach, rhubarb, fluffy masterpiece. Sitting next to Vanessa through it all reminds me of what it felt like to date as a teenager. My palms sweat and I keep wiping them on my slacks wondering what it would be like to hold her hand and praying that they stop sweating in the case of such a thing.

Hand holding would be far too forward, I decide, but decide that an arm around the back of her chair when the music starts playing is reasonable. I need to lean closer for her to hear me, after all. It's casual. Very cool.

"So, what sort of stuff do you like to do? When you're not at basketball games or strangers' weddings."

Vanessa's face turns towards mine and I swear she looks down at my lips which makes my heart stutter in a way that almost concerns me.

"I like to run," she says. "My sister and I do a lot of fitness classes together."

"Artie's mom?"

"Her, but my other sister, too. Willa is the oldest, I'm in the middle, and then there's my little sister Mary who I live with. We all get together and work out every week." She takes another bite of cake.

"Any brothers?"

"None," she says. "You? Siblings?"

"Only child."

"Sounds boring," she says, then looks sorry she did. "I didn't mean—"

"No, it was in a way. Cousins were good growing up, at least, and my parents are awesome. They live in Connecticut."

"Do you see them often?"

"Every month or so, and I spend most of the summer there, but they want me to move back. I think they want me back home just so they can set me up with unsuspecting local women."

"They must miss you."

"Maybe."

I think about my parents, the cruises they go on, the way I introduced pickleball to them but they have far, far eclipsed me. My dad's baked goods, my mom's books all over the house, anything used as a bookmark. They want me to have kids so bad, I know. They were in their thirties when they had me and now that I've just entered *my* thirties they are antsy to see me start a family.

"What about you?" I ask. "What's your family like?"

"Well, you've met Willa. She's always been sort of the princess of us. Married Sean when she was like barely nineteen. Then there's me and Mary. She and I live with our mom, and us kids took over my dad's business when he died."

"I'm so sorry. When did he die?"

"Just about four years ago."

"How old were you? Young to take over a company, right?"

"Yeah." She breathes a laugh. "I was 24. Fresh out of grad school and yes, I was definitely overwhelmed. But we made it work."

"What is the company?"

"We do construction," she says, and something clicks in my mind. The 30 under 30 list in *The Post*, Phoebe freaking out. "Wait, like Morelli Construction?"

She nods. "That's the one."

"You took over Morelli Construction when you were only 24 years old?"

"I did. Some of the key shareholders weren't thrilled, but I think I've proven my worth by now. Mostly, hopefully."

Morelli Construction's name is practically everywhere. You can't go a block without seeing their signs on the fences of huge projects around town.

"And it's a family affair? All of you?"

"Willa went to law school to step in as chief legal officer, her husband does operations, and Mary. . . she's in charge of the more special projects." Vanessa lifts a shoulder, and in doing so, her ponytail falls to her back. I look for a moment too long at her collarbone and clear my throat.

"And you like that? Working together."

Vanessa looks to the dance floor while she thinks. Rex and Phoebe twirl around together, her head on his chest, a serene look on Rex's face.

"Sometimes it's hard, but family is important," Vanessa finally says. "It means something to have people you would do anything for and know that they'd do anything in return."

I like this idea, the loyalty involved with loving someone so much that any ask isn't too big.

In the slow swell of the music, I'm looking at Vanessa and she's looking at me, and I think we might kiss or something, but then the song ends. One of Rex's college friends comes over the speakers to get everyone to the floor for a conga line and limbo, and I'll be the first person to admit that group dancing is a delight.

"You don't have to dance with me, but I will be tearing up that dance floor for at least thirty minutes before we can leave."

Vanessa grins, a wild light on her face. "Lead the way."

8

NATE

I take Vanessa to get ice cream on the way home, because even though we've been together for three hours, I can't let her go yet. I have this sneaking suspicion that if I let her out of my sight, I'll never see her again, and I would very much like to see her for as long as I possibly can.

I keep asking her questions, looking for whatever it is that should signal to me as a red flag, but I think she may be perfect. She's hard-working, devoted to her family, funny, and beautiful. Her face lights up when she's excited, and when she laughs, it always looks like it surprises her. I like listening to her speak, holding my breath as she thinks before she answers a question. I could learn from her in this regard, the way she listens to the question in its entirety. I bumble and barrel through speaking, often saying stupid shit before really thinking it through.

I'm better at talking to kids; they're little twerps sometimes, but they are so good. I love that they're always learning, their little minds working over new concepts and growing as they do. It's easier to be myself around them because they all think I'm an old loser anyway. Plus, I don't need kids to think I'm cool, I need them to trust me and know that I'm trying to help them learn and that I'm a safe person they can talk to if they need to. They don't need to be embarrassed around me because I do my best to be as embarrassing as possible around them.

I've never really felt confident around adults in the same way, and especially not Vanessa with her perfect body and sharp mind and assessing gaze that is drawing conclusions about me that I cannot predict.

"Where did you go just now?" She spoons another bite of ice cream into her mouth.

"Was trying to figure out how to get you to like me," I admit, and *that*, that is what I mean by not thinking before I open my damn mouth.

Vanessa's dimple makes itself known, and it's so cute I want to do something absurd like kiss it. She shivers, just barely, but I see it. I stop walking and she follows suit with a questioning look. I shrug off my suit coat and drop it over her shoulders, silently hoping she won't think it's weird.

She smiles wider, switching her ice cream cup between her hands so she can slide her arms through the sleeves, which are too long on her. I take a step closer and roll them up so they're not past her palms. When I'm done, I realize how close we're standing.

"Hi," she says.

"Hi." My grin is making my cheeks ache, and I incline my head to keep walking. We do, but our shoulders are closer than they were before.

"If you want me to like you, I guess that means I'm officially forgiven for trying to bribe you into academic dishonesty?" Vanessa asks.

"I guess it does," I say.

She scrapes the last bite of her ice cream, which is the most sugary atrocity I've ever seen: gummy bears, nerds, and sour gummy worms mixed into a strawberry ice cream. The choice surprised me. For as clean cut and severe as she is, I thought she might go with a dark chocolate fudge, maybe, or a plain vanilla.

I wonder what the sweetness tastes like on her tongue, but quickly dismiss the thought and the accompanying images it procures.

"So, what does a normal day look like in the life of Vanessa Morelli?"

"My sister drags me on a run before the sun comes up, usually. Then breakfast which is my favorite meal of the day—my mom likes to cook." Vanessa sighs and shrugs. "Then most of the day is taken up by meetings and visiting sites and potential sites. I meet with a lot of investors and check-in on various projects, which is as boring as it sounds."

"And after the riveting nine to five?" I nudge.

"After that excitement, I go home, see my sisters, the kids make an appearance a few days a week. I know I'm making my life sound really exciting, but of course there's the basketball games and the random parent-teacher conference to fill in on occasion."

She shoots me a look at this, and I'm done trying not to smile like an idiot around her.

"What do you do for fun?" I ask, the one thing glaringly absent from her schedule.

This stumps her, and we're quiet as she thinks about it for the length of half a block.

"It's fun to go to Artie's games, or to watch TV shows with my mom at night. I like movies, too, but I don't go out to see them like I used to in college," she says. She squints at nothing. "I guess I don't prioritize fun."

"And do you date?" I ask. I can't understand the world we live in if Vanessa Morelli is a single, non-dating individual.

I think I see her cheeks redden under the streetlights.

"No," she says. "I don't really."

I have no sensical words in response, and she must see this because she takes pity on me and fills the silence.

"I'm not anti-dating, I'm just. . . busy. I was engaged once. Before grad school, an old family friend, and my first boyfriend."

"What happened?"

"He wasn't what I thought. Didn't like that I wanted to go to grad school and work for my dad. Wanted me barefoot and pregnant. He was intimidated by. . ." She waves her hand in an encompassing gesture in front of her. "He didn't want me to be in charge."

My mind paints a very clear fantasy, unbidden, in which Vanessa and I live in domestic bliss. I've quit my job, just for a few years, just until the youngest is in pre-school, and Vanessa runs the world all day before she comes home to be with me and our two babies. After the children are asleep, after a delicious dinner I made, unless we ordered in, we make love and in fact make another baby, a third, a girl who we name Vanessa Jr. She has my nose.

I think there is something wrong with me.

"He sounds like a jackass," I say, and I hope she doesn't hear how my voice has dropped an octave into the gravelly, horny territory. "I'm sorry you had to go through that."

"Me too," she says. "Better to have found out before the wedding, though. Sometimes I imagine what if I'd gone through with marrying him. My dad would have still died, and I would have still wanted to take over the business, but I wouldn't have the support of my husband which would make what I do a whole lot more difficult."

"I'm glad you have your family as support. I can't imagine taking on something like that alone."

Our walking has slowed past a leisurely stroll, and I'm starting to think that she doesn't want this night to end either. That sort of thinking breeds too much hope, though, and it is much too soon to let myself be hopeful.

She's looking up at me, her big brown eyes focused on my face, assessing my reaction in light of her latest confession. After a moment, she turns back to the sidewalk, and fuck it, I grab her hand and she lets me lace my fingers through hers.

"What about you, then? Do you have hobbies?" she asks.

"My friend Jenna and I go to the community center a few times a week. Pickleball or kickboxing, stuff like that. Otherwise, I like reading." I don't mention that sci-fi is my favorite genre, but I will if she asks.

"What is pickleball? A card game?"

"Like table tennis but human-sized."

"Isn't that just tennis?"

"No, no, Vanessa. Tennis is tennis. Pickleball is kind of like tennis, but smaller. More like ping pong."

"I've never heard of it," she says.

"You must not spend much time with middle-aged people."

This earns me a laugh, and I revel in the sound like it's a heated blanket.

We are just about to my building, and I slow my steps further until we've stopped walking. I'm still holding her hand as we stand under the lamp post bathing us in yellow light.

"I've had a really nice time tonight," Vanessa says. "I don't get to do this very often."

"Me too."

I'm bad at stuff like this, holding hands in quiet moments on the precipice to another moment. I never know how to gracefully tip from one into the next.

She makes it easy.

"Nate?"

"Hm?"

"You can kiss me," she says, and I don't waste any time.

I let one hand slip around the back of her neck as my mouth descends on hers, her lips warm and pliant against mine. I deepen the kiss when one of her hands snakes around my waist and sigh into her open mouth.

Her tongue tastes like sugar and strawberries, and it dances with mine. I'm backing her up into the alley between my building and the next one for some semblance of privacy, and she moves willingly, her tongue still enthusiastically traveling around my mouth, pressing against my teeth, making me let out these involuntary moans. I press her against the brick wall while bringing our bodies flush together, one of my thighs pressing between her legs.

She sucks my tongue into her mouth which makes me lose my mind.

I'm barely thinking, just feeling her hands so eager traveling over my torso and into my hair as I draw her closer and pour myself into her mouth. I want to consume her and be consumed; I am lightheaded from this kiss and her soft hands.

I recognize that we could be inside my apartment within two minutes, less if we hustled up the stairs, but I can't even consider the idea of stopping this, not when she's grinding against my thigh and pressing her tits into my chest, not when she's biting my lip and huffing little breaths in my ear as I trail a mess of kisses up her throat.

My hand is traveling up her side and skating across her bare back beneath my jacket when she goes still. I follow suit and look at her questioning.

Did I go too far? Was I too much?

"Are—"

"*Sh,*" she puts her finger to my lips and is looking just behind me like she's listening for something.

The only thing I hear is my heart still beating in my ears and my neighbor's reggae playing through his window upstairs. A car rolls past, and I'm pretty sure they can't see us shrouded in the dark, but I still shift to cover her body more.

Vanessa lets out a breath and relaxes her shoulders, and I

think whatever gave her pause has passed, but then I hear it too. The footsteps from the street behind us are so quick, I don't even have time to untangle myself from Vanessa before palms are landing on my shoulders and yanking me away from her.

I am on the ground, the breath knocked from my lungs in the space of a breath. Another man has sprung for Vanessa, but she jumps from his reach. I want to move, to help defend her, but a boot lands on my chest and presses down before I can.

"I'll shoot him," the man above me says, and Vanessa halts. The other man still approaches her.

There's a gun pointed toward my face, and I cough, trying to sputter some sort of surrender. I have two credit cards with decent, but not great, credit limits, but I'll give them whatever they want.

I put my hands up by either side of my head; Vanessa does too. The other man stalks towards her, and I see that he's got a gun pointed at her.

"Come on, we can work something out," I rush to say, and his foot presses harder on me. I am about to yell watching the other man reach to grab Vanessa when she moves faster than lightning.

Many things happen at once.

First, I see Vanessa twist her attacker's arm, dislodging his gun, which she quietly fires twice before I can even hear the man grunt. I only know it fired because of the light and the way the other man standing over me hiccups back and falls to the ground, releasing the weight from my chest as he does.

Did she just—

I scoot away and push myself to standing, my breath still ragged. I want to help Vanessa somehow, but she's handling herself just fine. She expertly fights the man that's at least double her size. In a flurry of moves I barely see, she's brought him to the ground beneath her and shot another two rounds into his head. My stomach lurches, but I keep the bile down.

Red is spattered on her neck and face and my suit coat.

"Are you okay?" I ask even though, despite a split lip and splatter, she's looking mostly calm, just a quiet rage simmering.

Vanessa spits blood onto the back of the man's head and nods.

"Did he hurt you?" she asks.

I shake my head.

She steps past me to survey the other man, the one who was holding me, and lands a hard kick to his side. Mind you, she's done all this wearing her very tall heels. When he doesn't move, she spits on him too and retreats to where her purse had fallen off in the fray.

"I'll call the police," I say, already digging in my pocket for my phone.

"Not yet," she says.

I pause, my finger hovering over the call button, and my hand is shaking. She comes close and looks me over, her fingers trailing over my face for a moment before she takes my phone and locks it.

"It's okay," she says. "We're okay."

I watch as Vanessa pulls out her own phone and taps the screen before pulling it to her ear.

"Get Tony over here," she says after a moment. "Two of them. . . We're good. Yeah, he's good. See you soon."

After hanging up the phone, she slips it back into her purse. My whole body is shaking now, and I haven't made myself look at the dead men because I've never really looked at a dead person before, and the thought of seeing *two* now up close horrifies me.

"Are you in pain?" she asks, and her voice is so gentle.

"No," I say, and my voice is so loud I try again, quieter, "No."

"I'm sorry you had to see that."

"What is happening?"

Her lips press together into a thin line. The red of her lipstick has smudged a bit around her mouth from our kissing, and I imagine it's smeared across my lips as well.

"Business," she says. "I can't explain here, but I'm going to

handle it. I need your help moving them further into the alley."
She nods at the dead men, and I still don't let myself look at
them. Just the fact that their bodies are next to me, dead and
unmoving, feels like a weight on my chest, like a monster beneath
my bed I'm afraid to look at.

"We'll start with this one. You can get his feet. Okay?"

"Vanessa, we need to call the police, we can't move
them, we—"

"Nate, you need to trust me right now. I need you to say
'okay.'"

I take a shaky breath and squeeze my eyes shut. I am pretty
sure when I open them this will all still be happening, but I let
myself hope that it won't.

When I open my eyes, she's still in front of me wearing my
suit coat, a small trail of blood on her chin. I swipe it lightly with
my thumb and she barely winces.

"Okay," I say, and do what she tells me.

9

VANESSA

NATE DOESN'T SPEAK WHEN LEO ARRIVES WITH TWO BODY BAGS. HE remains silent as we deposit the dead men in said body bags, and still doesn't speak when Leo and I haul them into the back of the car. He just stands, blood on his hands, which are limp at his sides, and has a haunted look to his eyes. By the time Tony and the other boys have arrived to clean up the rest of the scene, he still hasn't spoken.

I told him he could go upstairs after Leo got there, only because he looked like he was about to vomit everywhere, but he stayed. He didn't help, mostly just stared into the middle distance, but he didn't try to run or call the police either, which is good. I think he's in shock.

When it's clear that the team doesn't need any help with the rest of the cleanup, I lead Nate into his building and up the stairs to his apartment. Leo trails a flight behind us, quiet steps so Nate won't hear.

Nate's hands are shaking too much to get the key in the lock, so I take them and open the door before following him in. The dog appears and circles at our feet and on second look it really is perhaps the most hideous little dog I've ever seen. Nate drops his suit jacket on the back of a chair, picks the ugly dog up and holds him to his chest before he begins a bit of quiet pacing.

His living room is small but cozy. There's an old gray couch with the left cushion mostly sunk in, a multi-colored quilt that looks well-used, and a stack of DVDs on one side of the television. I also see a few candles, which is maybe why it smells so nice in here. Citrusy. There are some framed pictures on the wall, but not many. A Star Wars art print.

There's also a baseball bat leaning against his coffee table, a small wooden one, and I would guess that's Nate's only form of a weapon in this apartment.

Nate stops his pacing and looks at me.

"That wasn't a random attack," he says, not a question.

"It wasn't," I agree.

"Are you an FBI agent?"

I purse my lips and shake my head.

"CIA?"

"No."

"FDA?"

"Not that," I say. Nate puts the dog back on the ground, and it sniffs at my heels for a moment, licks the top of my foot lightly, and settles next to me.

"Is it a secret?" Nate asks. "Like, are you undercover? Can you not tell me? Do I need to go into witness protection now?"

The smallest laugh escapes me at the absurdity of the idea. "No, you don't have to go into witness protection. You'll be fine."

"So you are a spy? I won't tell anyone. Promise."

I open my mouth to lie to him, but close it before I can. Telling him I'm part of law enforcement might make him feel better, but it won't keep him safe.

"Not exactly, no."

"Did you know those guys were going to be here?"

"No," I say, and it's the truth. "I had no idea that would happen tonight." I'd never seen those men before. Criminals, not from any of our circles, but Boston is a big city.

"Who were they?"

"I'm not sure." I have a feeling I'll be up through the night trying to answer that. I let a big breath fill my lungs and hold it for five seconds. "My job leads me to have some. . . enemies."

"Enemies that want to kill you? What the hell kind of business are you running?"

I say nothing, though I do cross my arms and wait as he circles around the drain that is the truth about me. His brown hair is mussed from the scuffle, a patch hanging over his forehead. His eyes, previously so filled with light and humor, are wide and wary.

I remind myself that as uncomfortable as this evening must be for him, at least he's still alive.

"Those men you called downstairs," he nods towards the window. "They didn't even question it. Does this shit happen often?"

I still say nothing, and it looks like he's almost got it. It looks like the truth is at the front of his brain but he won't let himself guess it.

His mouth falls open and he turns to me.

"Are you caught up in a gang or something?"

I don't give any affirmation of this, but I don't deny it either.

"Holy shit, Vanessa." Nate comes closer to me, his voice dropping lower. "Do they have something on you? Are you trying to get out?"

I bury my face in my hands because he really wants to think the best of me. I think optimistic must be his default; he probably smiles at strangers in the grocery store.

"No, I—" I'm interrupted by a light knock on Nate's front door, which makes Nate jump and reach for the bat. I hold a hand out to stop him from attacking and retreat to open it.

Tony pokes his head in. "All clean out there, boss. We'll come back when the sun is out to make sure."

"Thanks, Tony."

He nods then looks at Nate, who is watching the exchange with trepidation and wide eyes, white showing around the whole iris. Still white-knuckling that fucking bat.

Tony sticks a hand through the door to hold a fist out to Nate.

"Good to meet you, bro," Tony says. Nate stares at it for seconds before mechanically raising his arm to bump Tony's fist with his. "Ah, lemme take your shirt. I'll get the blood out of it and bring it back tomorrow."

"Oh, that's—" Nate looks at the shirt, just realizing the stains of blood on the fabric. He looks again like he's going to throw up. "Don't worry about it."

"Nah, that's a nice shirt. My ma has good stain stuff, you'll never know." Tony holds out his hand, this time his palm up and open. Nate leans his bat against the wall before he tugs on his tie and unbuttons his shirt, stripping it off to reveal a tight white tee beneath and a hint of some of the muscles I knew I felt when we were making out. He's lean and fit in a very practical way. Not like he works out for hours every day, but like he might be able to run a half marathon if he trained for a couple months.

Nate balls up the button-up and hands it over. I also give Tony the suit coat, which was another casualty to the blood.

"Thank you, Tony," I say again, and this time he does leave, the door clicking shut behind him. I am about to say something to Nate, anything, when Tony opens the door again.

"Oh, Leo says he's going to wait in the hall to take you home."

"Great," I say, and this time we listen for Tony's steps to retreat before trying to speak again.

"Vanessa, are you—"

"It's not how it looks."

"You don't work with those guys? Those criminals?"

"They're not criminals," I defend, though they are. We all are. He just made it sound so dirty.

"Right, because normal, non-criminal people know how to clean up bodies and get blood stains out of clothes." He's whisper-yelling, and I step closer to him.

"Would you rather we left them there?"

"No, I would have rather we call the *police*, Vanessa. What the fuck?"

I try not to roll my eyes, but it's fruitless. "I told you I'd handle it, and I did. I am."

"Yes, but why wouldn't you let the police handle it if you're not a criminal?"

I don't have a reasonable response to this and he knows it. Nate takes a step closer, crowding me towards the wall not unlike he had been an hour ago under very different circumstances. An hour ago, he looked at me like I was a revelation, like I could have been a goddess or some apparition.

Now, he looks horrified, and desperate to believe I'm not what he thinks I am.

I bite my lip only to remember that it was split in the fight. The sharp pain and the metallic taste make me flinch and Nate takes a breath.

"Tell me I have this wrong. Tell me I can't call the police right now and tell them what just happened because you're a spy, and that it'll mess with your operation—just, don't tell me what I think you're saying. Don't tell me you're a fucking criminal. Please."

My stomach turns knowing that I'm even worse than what he thinks. I'm not just a criminal, I'm *in charge*.

"It's. . . sensitive," I say, and after a shocked silent moment, he pushes away from the wall, from me, like I'm a curse or a plague. "Nate, listen to me."

He can hardly look at me, his lip curled up in a sneer as he recalibrates the night, the woman I was with the truth he knows now.

"You can't call the police," I start in a rush, my voice belying how out of control I feel. "There's hardly an officer in this city that's not in somebody's pocket and if you call this in, you *will* be in danger."

I don't mention what I'm afraid of, that he's already in danger. That there's already a hit on him because he was seen with me by whoever it was that was out for my head tonight.

"You need to stay safe," I say. "I can keep you safe, but only if you keep your head low. Don't go poking into things you don't want to be a part of."

He wants nothing to do with me, I can see that clearly on his face, a cocktail of disgust and regret. But I need to know that he won't do anything stupid.

"Nate," I grab his wrist, and he pulls back from me.

"What, because you'll kill me if I don't?"

His words sit heavy in the space between us until I pull back my outstretched hand and set my shoulders.

"You're safe," I say. I put on my best face, the one that shows nothing, the mask that's all too familiar for me, the one I haven't had to show him before. He watches the change, his eyes narrowing as I compose myself. "So long as you aren't an idiot."

I've opened his front door and am halfway through when he calls my name. I don't turn because he'll see the hope on my face if I do, but I stop.

"Whatever shit you're involved in, keep it the hell away from me."

Leo stands just outside the door, and his eyes are soft and sympathetic when I meet his. No doubt he heard everything.

I turn over my shoulder and peer into the apartment for the last time. I allow myself one look at Nate, his eyes full of hate and confusion.

Was trying to figure out how to get you to like me, he'd said, not even an hour ago.

I swallow the lump in my throat and nod.

"Goodbye, Nate."

I pull his front door shut behind me and walk past Leo without acknowledging his sympathy. He knows me too well, always seen right through me, like my sisters. It's why he's such a good bodyguard.

"Station someone here," I say as we descend the old staircase. "No one touches him."

* * *

WHEN I GOT HOME from the date with my hair still a mess and my dress ruined, my family could tell enough that I didn't want them asking any questions. I might guess that Leo called ahead to let them know not to pry.

The next day the search began in earnest. The two men that attacked us weren't affiliated to any clan, just non-denominational hitmen for hire. We questioned their small organization first, then let Mary take to her more unsavory methods. If threats and a good beating don't work, then Mary with a knife usually will, and this time was no different. Twenty minutes with Mary in charge and we learned that the two men were hired by an anonymous buyer who only communicated through burner phones, and paid in cash.

Another dead end.

We let the hitmen live, and they all looked at my little sister with a terrified sort of respect. She's small, but fierce, I don't blame them. They won't be trying that again, no matter how much cash someone offers them to try to off me. For letting them live, they said they'll even do some work for free, whenever we need.

Nate is safe, so my sources say. He leaves his house for school, then returns right after, only leaving to take that dog out, and even then, only small distances around the building.

I try not to think about him and the havoc I wreaked on his life.

Four days after the attack and with no discernable movement, I gather my sisters, Leo, and my mom in the living room for a family meeting. I look at the photo of my parents on the wall, looking for answers in my dad's eyes, which are just like mine. They yield nothing.

Sean and Cillian show up ten minutes late, fresh off some bullshit of their own they had to deal with, and I don't wait to dive right in.

"We need to go on lockdown," I say.

They all blink at me while this settles in.

"A bit extreme, no?" Leo asks.

"Let her talk," Cillian chides and leans forward so his elbows sit on his knees.

It is extreme. We were kids the last time there was a lockdown. Dad didn't tell us much about it, but a few months later, we all dressed up in our matching black dresses and attended the rat's funeral. Perfunctory, really, since Dad was the cause of death. It was someone Dad trusted, and if he hadn't killed him, that trust would have cost him his life.

"We need to tighten the circle, at least until we figure this out. If it's a lower family messing with us, then we can't give them the power of knowing our every move."

"But if we tighten too much, they'll suspect we're onto them," Mary points out.

"As far as they know, we go on business as usual. But when shit goes wrong, we need to know about it first-hand. That means showing up where we usually send someone else. Someone who could be paid off to mess with evidence."

"That's grunt work," Willa says. "We're running a business here."

Mary is right there with her. "You want us to go to warehouses and look for clues? We're in charge, Ness, we're not on *Scooby Doo*."

"Be nice to your sister," Mom says, but she looks wary too.

"Do you really trust that every lower family would die for us?" I demand. "That their loyalty can't be bought if they're desperate enough?" Mary crosses her arms and thuds back against the couch. "I've narrowed our circle of trust to the people in this room, everyone else is on probation."

"Tell us what to do, boss," Leo says, and I'm grateful for his easy acceptance.

"Mary and Leo, you're on visits. Clubs, fronts… Check in and tighten up loose ends. If they miss so much as a dollar on their dues, I want to know about it. Willa, I need you to make sure we're square with our city connections. Police, DEA, Governor's office, FBI, our guy over imports—send them gift baskets if you want, schedule lunches for me with them, offer a donation, you know them best."

"Consider it done," Willa says. She's already making a list behind her eyes.

"Sean, do what you need to make sure the lackeys and construction employees are happy. Buddy up, give bonuses, whatever."

"Right." Sean nods, his arm still wrapped around Willa's shoulders.

"Mom, I need you extra gossipy with the other moms. Anything you can find from them, find it."

She pulls her shoulders back and nods.

"Cillian, run your clan as you see fit, but if you suspect someone on your side is the cause of this, make them talk," I say.

Though we work together on many things, the Donovann family is still separate from the Morelli family, with Cillian's own dealings just like I have mine. It's business. But if the rot is on his side, we need to find it and cut it out before it festers.

"And when people get suspicious about us butting our noses where we usually couldn't be bothered?" Mary asks.

"Then you say you're doing quality assurance," I tell her. Her attitude is getting on my nerves, and I level a stare at her. "You wanted to be in charge of enforcement, Mary, I need you to fucking *enforce*."

I don't break eye contact with Mary, her eyes shooting flames at mine. I might be terrified of a look like that if I didn't grow up with her. We fought like cats as kids—worse as teenagers—but always came back together. We all trust each other enough to push each other, but right now I need her to trust me.

"I hear you," I say, my voice softer. "We need to do this."

After another tense moment, she releases a breath and looks away. She swallows her pride with a silent exhale and nods.

"You're right," she says. "We'll find them."

I give her a small smile and then let my shoulder relax from the rigid posture I've been maintaining.

"It's a good idea," Cillian says. I don't need his assurance, but it feels good to have it.

"It's not forever," I say. "Just for now."

Just until I can figure out who the hell is threatening my family.

* * *

It's been a full week since my date gone awry with Nate, and Willa's finally reached her threshold of minding her business about it. Honestly, I'm surprised she's been able to hold out this long.

"Did you kiss?" she asks once she's about three miles into her treadmill run.

"I almost got him killed."

"But did you *kiss*, Vanessa?"

I keep doing my stationary exercises on the ground in front of her just waiting for her to lose her patience. After another half-mile, she throws a hand towel at me.

Mary and Sean spar on the large mat, and Leo beats on a punching bag, but I am certain they're all listening. Everyone is so damn nosy in this family.

"Yes," I say, hoping she'll leave it at that.

"I fucking *knew* it," Mary says.

"Called it," Willa adds.

Leo is smart to stay silent after I level a glare at him.

"It was nothing," I say. *Best kiss of my life,* I do not add. "Nate made it perfectly clear that he does not want to see me again after that."

"Bullshit," Willa says. "You're a dime, what did he say?"

I finish my set of crunches and lie back on the mat for a few seconds before looking back at my older sister. She looks perfect, even while running. Her perfectly highlighted hair is pulled into a braid thumping against her back and her cheeks are barely red. She doesn't even look that sweaty.

"He may have told me in no unclear terms to keep myself and my crime the hell away from him."

Willa hums, speeds the treadmill up a bit.

"Prick," Sean scoffs.

"No, that's not so bad. People can adjust!" Willa says.

I watch one of the propeller fans on the high ceiling slightly shaking as it makes its rounds. I've already come to terms with the fact that I will not be seeing Nate Gilbert again, not even a parent teacher conference. Tony and a couple of other guys are set up outside his place on a rotation, though, and they send me texts directly every day with updates, usually letting me know that he's staying inside aside from teaching or walking that dog.

"Do your lunges," Willa says. I get up. "I think you should call him, you need to get laid. How long has it been?"

"*You* need to get laid," I say back, though I know for a fact that she does not need to get laid. Her and Sean are open with their love to an uncomfortable level. Like, still borderline making out during family movie nights kind of stuff.

It has been at least a year since I last had sex, and that is a generous estimate. I might guess closer to two.

"I'm not saying you need to marry the guy, Ness, just send a text. He already knows your secrets."

"It's not worth it," I say. "He could never be a part of this."

Nate is better than us—too good for organized crime.

We work out independently for a while, my family finally taking the hint that I don't want to talk about it. Willa makes her way onto the mat and drops down next to me after she's hit seven miles.

"Do you think the attack could be *because* you went on a date?" Willa asks.

"Hm?"

"Like, you keep saying no to proposals and then these old heads hear you're hooking up with some math teacher from Connecticut and something breaks in them? First, you tell them their 22-year-old son isn't a good fit and then," Willa snaps, "you start dating some guy who's never so much as gotten a speeding ticket?"

I don't want to say yes, don't want to admit that it's very likely that these stupid fucking old men are deciding to question my authority in a way they never would my father. Doesn't matter that my work has made us all wealthier, has brought us into this century. They would trust me more if I was married, and more so if I was married to one of their sons.

If I had a husband, they could believe that he was secretly making moves for me with me as his little novelty puppet.

"Maybe," I say.

I shouldn't have killed both of the men that attacked me. I'll admit that I got a bit too heated, it's just that I hate being caught off guard. Especially on the singular night I decided to take off for myself.

Willa stands from where she was just folding herself in half and reaches a hand down. "Fight with me?" she asks, and I let her pull me up to fight until I'm not thinking about marriage or math teachers anymore.

10

NATE

NINE DAYS HAVE PASSED SINCE WHAT I HAVE BEEN NOT-SO FONDLY referring to as The Incident. I don't know who to talk to about this, so I have been writing in my journal.

Journaling is a practice I usually only turn to about once per quarter, and even then just a few paragraphs here and there, waxing poetic until I get bored. This week alone I've filled more than two dozen pages in my free time after school and during my prep periods.

I've been journaling about whatever comes to mind, but what has come to mind most recently, is in depth explorations of the lives those men *might* have lived if they hadn't attacked us. If Vanessa hadn't murdered them right in front of me before spitting on and kicking their still-warm corpses.

This usually turns into me thinking about how my life would've been different too, if I didn't see any of that.

Other times, I just write song lyrics or practice my cursive. Keeps the mind active.

I've been keeping the book with me because not only am I stressed, I'm also paranoid. I am certain that my apartment isn't safe, my dog isn't safe, and while we are at it, I am in fact not safe.

I have no security.

I'm thinking about moving, but I moved in nine years ago and my contract says the landlord can only raise the rent up to fifty dollars a year, and the first couple years they didn't even think about it. Thus, my rent is ludicrously cheap and I would be remiss to let that go.

I'd have to sell half of my belongings to move, and my belongings really aren't worth much to begin with.

Jenna has been hounding me about the date, saying that I wasn't texting her very much which either meant I was too distracted having hot sex with my wedding date, or I was spiraling into a deep depression. I told her it was a secret third thing that I could not talk about and she shouldn't ask, and because Jenna respects boundaries more than I think a best friend ought, she *didn't* ask.

Well, she didn't until I missed the kickboxing-dance fusion class we go to and now she knows something is really wrong and she's come directly to the source. She doesn't even knock after I buzz her up, just uses the spare key she keeps and walks right in.

She drops her gym bag on my kitchen table and stares wide-eyed around my room: the cave-like atmosphere with my blinds and curtains shut tight, the jigsaw puzzle to which I have been giving a half-hearted attempt. Then she spots the journal and snatches it before I can grab it.

"Oh, my god, you're journaling." Jenna holds the book in one hand while strong-arming me away from her with the other. "If you don't tell me what happened, I will call your mother."

And I know that she will, so I stop fighting her and let my shoulders droop.

"You cannot laugh," I warn. "This is very serious."

Jenna mimes an oath.

I'm not positive that Jenna will not be in danger by learning this, and in fact, I am pretty sure that she *will* be, but the journal is a soulless receptacle for my anxieties, and Jenna is my closest friend and greatest confidant.

"I think Vanessa is in the mafia," I say, because this is the conclusion I've come to after days of googling and rewatching *The Godfather* (1 and 2) and *The Sopranos*.

Jenna, bless her, doesn't laugh.

"Tell me more about this," she says.

So I do. I tell her about walking home and about the things Vanessa said about family and taking over her father's company, things that I didn't think were weird at the time, but now think were suspicious. I tell her about the make-out (she screams, high-fives me, asks for details which I do not give because there are more important things about this story), and then I tell her about the men, the one who knocked me on my ass who I watched die, how I watched him die, and the way Vanessa quickly handled the other man as if he wasn't four times her size.

Other than saying, "No fucking way" every sixteen seconds, she doesn't stop me.

"And then she. . . spit on him?" Jenna says.

"Stop looking impressed, that is not impressive, Jenna. She's probably a sociopath."

"Yeah, no, sure, you're right, go on."

I tell her about the efficient clean-up like they'd done it a million times before, the team of tattooed and scary men that reported to her and were there minutes after she called, and the conversation afterward.

"What did they do with the bodies?" Jenna asks, not nearly alarmed enough about the fact that there were any dead bodies to begin with.

I shrug because really it is anybody's guess, but if I did have to guess (which I have, many times, in my journal), there was a boat or a meat grinder involved. I can hardly think about it without getting pukey.

"Could she be a spy?"

"She all but admitted to being a criminal," I say. "All the guys called her 'boss' and she runs that big company, and she told me not to call the police and, Jenna, I think I'm going to be a target of the mafia for the rest of my short life."

"Okay, now hold on," Jenna says. "You're being dramatic again."

"Jenna, I watched two men be murdered. I think you could afford to be more dramatic right now." I'm whisper-shouting again, though it would be difficult for any of my neighbors to hear me with the music so loud upstairs.

"Did you see the guy in the red Corolla outside?" I ask, whispering like he also might hear us from the curb.

Jenna's eyebrows furrow and she gets up to peek out of my window, the metal blinds clinking as she moves a slat. I swear Ranger's tail thumps at the slash of sunlight on the floor; the blinds have been drawn round the clock, all of my plants are in crisis.

"Who is he?"

"Tony," I say. "He was the one who got the blood out of my shirt. He sits out there and makes sure nobody comes back."

"Is he nice?"

I loath to admit that Tony is exceptionally nice. He nods at me when I leave my house, has knocked on my door and offered to walk Ranger multiple times, and even brought me a burrito once. Tony has the kind of face that could either be thirty-five or nineteen depending on the light, and he acts like I'm part of his family. Really, he called me 'Cousin' yesterday.

"You think she's his boss? Or like, *the* boss?"

"I guess, maybe," I say, though yes, I do think that. "Both."

"Holy shit," Jenna breathes, absently scratching behind Ranger's ears. "Did you throw up? When you saw the dead guys."

"After she left." I am known to have somewhat of a light stomach.

"But crime is like. . . a man's world, no? *Godfather* shit?"

"I will not pretend to know the intricacies and workings of the mafia, Jenna. Maybe they've entered the 21st century."

She takes a moment to process all of this, bending one of the metal blinds again to get another look at Tony and chewing on her bottom lip. She's still in her gym clothes and the baby hairs on her forehead have dried against her skin. Ranger licks at her leg until she picks him up and gives him a kiss on the head.

"Well, if she's got a guy posted out of your house, you're under her protection, right?"

"Sure, but for how long? When Tony goes away, then what?"

"You know how to fight, what about the self-defense classes?"

"Did you not hear the part where I floundered on the ground while Vanessa literally killed them?"

"You could get a gun?" she says and scrunches her nose up at the thought. "Could become a real gun nut."

I had thought about that too, but the thought made my skin itchy.

Jenna quickly pulls away from the window, but then returns and waves stiffly, presumably to Tony.

Jenna deposits Ranger back on the ground before punching my shoulder, not lightly. "Why didn't you tell me sooner?" she demands.

I hold my now injured arm and stare blankly, letting myself blink three times before responding.

"Did you not hear the mafia part of all of this?"

She throws the foam football from my shelf at me, and I dodge it before it can hit my face. Next is a pillow, which I don't dodge in time. "You have to tell me things!"

"I tell you everything!" I defend. "I didn't want you to be in danger too."

When there's nothing else soft for her to throw at me, she seems to realize that now is not the time for her indignation. She makes the face I recognize as an apology, and I make one back.

We sit on the couch and stare at my covered windows while Ranger settles on the floor between our feet.

"I think you should call her," Jenna says after a sigh.

"What?"

"Tell her you're freaking out and you need to know you'll be safe."

I've considered this and promptly dismissed the idea over a dozen times now. I'm pissed, obviously, but what really gets me is how much I enjoyed myself with her before the night turned sour. Vanessa was charming and funny and hot in a way that distracts me when I think about it for too long. If I call her, she might unintentionally remind me of these things, and what I need is to remember that she is dangerous and any affiliation with her is likely to get me killed or thrown into prison, or both.

But then I think about that kiss and how it was, without any doubt, the most affecting kiss of my existence, the one I will be comparing all kisses to going forward. What I need to do is forget all about Vanessa and that stupid kiss that I have angrily jacked off thinking about every day this week. She's a criminal for Christ's sake. I do not need to be thinking about her in any way, especially not in a horny way.

"Do you want to stay at my place for a few days?"

"Laura would love that," I say. Her roommate, Laura, has long since tried to convince Jenna that I was not worthy of her friend-ship, and by being friends with me, she was perpetuating a series of things that I am not nearly online enough to understand, according to Jenna.

Laura tolerates me, and that is a trial for her. I can't imagine how she would react if I was there for longer than twenty-four hours.

"She'd get over it."

"It's okay," I say, and then stalk over to the window to look at Tony. She follows and peers over my shoulder as Tony eats a huge sub and bops his head to music we can't hear. "I've got him."

11

NATE

Tuesdays are, by far, the most cursed day of the week. It's probably not the day's fault, but we live in a society, and because we do, Tuesdays are cursed. It's like a Monday without any of the notions that this can be a fresh new week, the steep incline to the crest of the hill that is Wednesday afternoon. Smooth sailing from there, but Tuesday? No.

Today, barely past 7 AM, things are already bad because I spilled Jenna's and my Tuesday Iced Coffees down the front of my shirt before school. I thought I had an extra one in my car, or at least a sweater or something, but last month I cleaned out my trunk which was really a great thing for past-me to do at the time, but has left current-me almost late for work in the last week of school, rushing home to change. It's fine. It's Tuesday.

I cruise up my apartment building stairs and my neighbor must have taken his Adderall early this morning because the reggae is already blasting. (I asked, he said he can't code without it, and really, who was I to keep him from his livelihood?) My shirt is still sopping wet, sticking to my chest, and my pants are soaked too. I am about to unlock my door when I see that my handle has been busted and is hanging loose from its socket.

Light from the big windows I've started leaving open for Ranger comes through a small crack between the door and shines onto my dirty ass shirt.

I weigh my options because I honestly do not have time for this, but I've been gone for just over an hour with the gym and the coffee run, so if someone broke into my damn apartment they might still be here. I could call the police, but I can't stop thinking about what Vanessa said about the cops eating out of the overflowing fists of the city's criminals. She didn't say this in so many words, but I got the picture.

I didn't see Tony outside the building, probably because he doesn't need to watch my place if I'm not here.

I could call—

No.

I'm not going to call the very person who is most likely the reason someone has broken into my apartment in the first place.

But then again, if it is her fault she should pay for my busted doorknob and whatever possessions have been stolen in there. Reparations for emotional damages, too. I can type up an invoice.

My right eye is twitching but I shake out my arms a few times to psych myself up. I need to be ready for anything.

Slowly, I push the door open with my pointer finger, opting not to call anyone until I know how bad the damage is. The door squeaks on its hinges and I stop, cursing the old building with its old fucking doors, and then resume my progress. I toe off my dress shoes and creep down the entrance hall to the living room which looks just as I left it. Nothing is too far out of order, as far as I can tell, but Ranger isn't sprawled out snoozing in his usual sunny spot.

I whistle for him, and he barks in response. My head snaps to the sound and he's sitting in front of my bedroom, tail thumping against the wood floor.

"C'mere," I whisper and, after whining and walking himself in a circle three times, he does. I scoop him up and kiss his head a dozen times before venturing onward, him still cradled in my arms like a newborn. My bedroom door is shut, which I swear is not how it was when I left this morning, but if a burglar wanted something from my apartment, it probably wouldn't be my old clothes.

It takes four deep breaths to get my feet to move forward, and I don't put Ranger down because I'm too afraid that he'll get snatched by the boogey man in the rest of my unexplored apartment. I slowly step across the floor to my bedroom and the wood only creaks in the one spot it always does, the one I should have avoided, but still nothing sounds from beyond my bedroom. No sudden movement, nothing jumping out at me from my bathroom or cupboards.

A car honks from the street below in its normal fanfare, and it nearly makes me scream or throw up or, I'm not sure, my adrenaline is so high.

I decide I will call Vanessa, because something is very wrong, though I don't know what, and it is absolutely her fault.

This is exactly what I tell her when she picks up the phone, I whisper it, and she doesn't understand, so I have to repeat myself, louder this time, and I still haven't opened my bedroom door, because I just know there's something in there.

"Nate?"

"Yes, this is Nate," I snap. "Someone was in my house, might still be in my house."

"Where are you? Are you okay?"

"Home, and no—"

There's a creak behind my bedroom door and a yelp escapes from me.

"Nate?"

"I just heard something," I whisper.

"Do you have a gun?" Vanessa says.

89

"No, I do not have a fucking gun," I snap, though I am cursing myself for not listening to Jenna when she told me I should buy one of her dad's pistols off him.

"Get a knife then, a kitchen knife will be fine," Vanessa says through the phone. I want to talk back again but I hear a loud thud, like something just dropped off of my bookshelf. Taking as few steps as I possibly can, I grab my biggest kitchen knife from the block and hold the phone between my shoulder and my ear, still cradling Ranger in the other arm. He has no clue the danger we are in.

"Do you have it?" Behind her voice, I hear honking through the phone. She's driving, maybe driving here, or maybe just on her morning commute to do crime around all of Boston. "Nate."

"I have it."

"Good, now don't move."

This is not the advice I thought she would be giving me right now, I thought she might say to leave and potentially be ambushed on the street again, or to barrel in there and go all slasher-flick on whoever has broken into my apartment.

She's right, staying put sounds like the best option.

Vanessa spouts some commands to someone on the other side of the line before her voice is back in my ear. "We're on our way."

It sounds like she's about to disconnect the call and my stomach lurches. "Wait—"

Vanessa is quiet, waiting. I hear the car through my phone's little speaker, imagine her racing through the city, hitting morning traffic. I squeeze my eyes shut.

"Please don't hang up."

A beat passes, but I know she's still there. "Okay," she says, and her voice is so soft. I almost let myself take comfort in it.

Almost.

Ranger sneezes in my arms and I start sniffing too. It smells almost like. . . smoke.

I turn my gaze to my bedroom door and sure enough, I see smoke seeping out beneath the crack of the white door, crawling across the scratched and stained floor towards me.

"Shit," I murmur.

"What is it?" Vanessa asks.

The fire alarm starts beeping; I spring into action, dropping the knife on my kitchen table and setting Ranger on the ground before retrieving the tiny fire extinguisher under the kitchen sink. I don't even have to psych myself up to open the door, I'm too worried about all my shit getting burned to a crisp, the whole building catching fire with it.

There's a good amount of smoke in the room, but I find quickly that the source is a small fire in my metal trash can, the one from the bathroom. Ranger barks at it with all his might, like doing so will scare it into submission.

My phone slides to the ground with a thunk while I pull the pin and squeeze the lever on the extinguisher, covering the fire in white foam. The smell burns the inside of my nose and my eyes, ammonia and ash.

The fire alarm keeps up its beeping, but my bedroom window is wide open, most of the smoke left in the air flowing out of it. I never leave my window open without the screen because this is how bugs get inside. It's the window with the fire escape which is horrifying to me.

I hate that someone could be out there right now watching me, waiting to shoot me and Ranger through each of our heads.

My closet is empty, and my room is otherwise unoccupied. My shelf looks untouched, the frames on my wall not even off kilter. I don't see anything immediately off as my eyes scan the room, just the window, the foam in the trash can still making its crunching noise as it falls to liquid.

Vanessa is shouting something through my phone's speaker on the ground and I pick it up and press it to my ear.

"I'm fine, it's fine," I say. "Someone started a fire in my trash can."

I climb onto my bed and hold down the button on my fire alarm until it stops beeping. Ranger is still barking, though; howling and growling at my bathroom door like the old piece of painted wood is the one that started the fire.

Vanessa is speaking something in my ear, but the gut churning foreboding feeling in my stomach is back as I step down and approach my closed bathroom door.

I shouldn't open it.

I very much should *not* open it.

"What's happening?" Vanessa demands, then yells to someone on her side of the line, "*Go faster!*"

Now that I've joined Ranger on the ground, his barking has quieted to a growl, and despite the ongoing internal conflict regarding whether I should open the door, I twist the handle, cold in my slick hand, and push into the bathroom.

The lights are off, but I smell it first: a thick scent, sweet and coppery, and accompanied by a steady dripping sound into my tub. I cannot hear Vanessa through my phone, just the dripping in the tub. I cannot feel anything except for dread in my spine, it holds me hostage and I don't want to move, but I can't not, I have to turn my head, I have to make sure someone isn't there waiting to shoot me. It feels like I am moving slowly, my arm lifting to flick on the light before my sight is filled with red.

Red *everywhere*.

It's so, violently red. That's what surprises me most at first, the fact that it looks like corn syrup and food dye splattered against my mirror and the walls and all over the floor.

My eyes find the source, a man hung up in my shower, his arms suspending him in the air, one tied to my shower head, the other strung up to the curtain bar.

His neck, his torso are both—

I fall back onto my ass and Ranger starts barking again, loud howls at the man whose stomach was sliced open, his insides on my tile. *Tony.*

"Nate," I hear through the phone, loud and insistent. *"Nate—"*

"Get here," I say, before promptly losing the entirety of my breakfast.

12

VANESSA

Nate remains silent for the whole ride to my house, and I'm not sure if that's because he's angry and traumatized or because he's trying not to heave all over my leather back seat. When I peer at him through the rearview, he's just petting the ugly little dog's head as we drive, a numb look in the near distance.

Leo got him to change from his work outfit that was stained with what looked like coffee and throw up into a mismatched hoodie and sweatpants—but his face is ghostly. I'd think he was sick with the flu if I didn't know better.

He's a mess.

I'm a mess. Shaken. Leo knows it too, though he's wise enough not to mention it. He didn't question me when I rushed into the car, or when I sped across the city weaving through many a bus lane to get to Nate. I've always loved this about Leo; when it counts, he listens. So, when I told him to help Nate pack a bag and get him to the car, he didn't question that either. Lockdown or not, the math teacher was coming with us.

I surveyed the grisly scene in the bathroom while they packed. I allowed myself to cry a total of four tears before I squared my shoulders and took a closer look at the work done to

Tony. Sweet, loyal Tony, who was exceptional at chess and who loved his family deeply.

It was a butcher job, fast and hideous, someone had slashed through Tony's artery first before the work on his torso. There was no obvious calling card as to who did this, no "X" on his neck, no slashes to the face, no note, just the nightmare of one of our best guys cut to ribbons in defense of someone who isn't even part of the family.

This is how his parents will see it, at least.

I have an intense urge to flee the country at the fact that I'll have to pay his parents a visit this afternoon to break the news. I don't have time to think about what I'll say yet, not when I still don't know what the hell to do with the shivering man and sleeping dog in my back seat.

My eyes gravitate toward him through the mirror again, and when his gaze clashes with mine, I nearly jump.

"My classes," he says. "It's the last week of school, I need to get a sub."

Leo clears his throat and turns to look at the distraught, greenish man. "Willa called the school." His voice is gentle. Leo is a scary dude, but he's always had the better bedside manner of us.

Nate and I make eye contact again before I look back to the road.

"Where are we going?" Nate asks.

"My house," I say. "You'll be safe."

"For how long?"

"Until we figure out who came after you," I say. For my sake, I pray that it will be brief.

His expression curdles into a glare. "It was a message for you, wasn't it?" Leo and I are quiet, which I suppose is answer enough because Nate goes on. "Just what the hell kind of work do you do?"

"It's sensitive," Leo says, which earns a scoff from Nate.

We will tell him. At this point, we have to. He's in too deep, and for as much danger as I've already put him in, it would be worse if he was kept in the dark. I'm not looking forward to his blatant judgment, though. He already looks at me like I'm vermin and he is leagues above me.

Traffic is stop-and-go as we make our way across town and it's just past nine in the morning by the time we pull through the gate. There's a sharp ache just behind my eyes in my skull, but I can't take the day off. I have seven meetings I'll need to rearrange.

"I'll tell you everything you want to know later," I say as I pull into the garage beneath the house. I wonder what it looks like to him, the manicured lawn, the heavy trees surrounding the property, the garage, the fleet of vehicles. Growing up here, the home has always been a comfort to me, a sanctuary where we could be ourselves, but I wonder if it feels cold and intimidating to him.

"What about my place? What about—"

That haunted look returns to wash over his face and his lips press into a hard line.

"Someone will be by to clean your apartment today. If you want to move, we will help you relocate to another apartment when this is all over and will maintain your expenses in the meantime."

"Jesus," Nate mutters and swings his legs out of the car, still holding the dog. He doesn't put it down as Leo retrieves the two duffels from the trunk.

I lead them into the house, aware of every picture on the walls, the marble floor tiles, the way there's no pile of sneakers by the door—I compare every immediate detail to his lived-in apartment, a place that will probably never be comfortable for him again after seeing what he did.

We move in a line down the hallway, past the kitchen where Mary and Mom are still eating breakfast, and to the base of the stairs.

"Welcome to our home," I say because Mom has poked her head around the corner and will flay me herself if I forget my manners so thoroughly. "Leo will help you get settled in upstairs and we'll talk when I get back later."

"When?"

I look at my watch. "Later," I say again. "Tonight. Someone will be up with lunch in a few hours unless you're hungry now?"

"And you'll be doing what?"

"Working," I say because he probably doesn't want all the details and even if he does, I don't have the patience nor composure to give them to him.

"Ah let me guess, murder? Money laundering, maybe? Selling drugs to children? What's on your docket?"

"Meetings," I correct.

"*Great,*" Nate says, but it's dripping with derision. He leans closer to me, not close enough that I can smell him, but close enough that I'm reminded how green his eyes are, dark wells full of ire. "Well, you just let me know when you're able to pencil me into your busy schedule. I'll be here."

Leo's face is impassive, but I know if I peer down the hall at my mom, a smirk will be scribbled across her face. It's her way; she thinks people don't talk to me like this enough, which is admittedly the reason we're in this mess to begin with. I wanted to feel normal for one singular evening. I wanted to go to a wedding and lose myself in a room of strangers and pretend I was a woman who someone could talk back to without fearing for their life.

And now, this.

As if he has any idea where he's going, Nate starts trailing up the stairs, effectively dismissing himself.

I roll my eyes before inclining my head for Leo to follow him before Nate can start opening doors or letting the dog piss on my mom's carpet.

When they're out of sight, I look down the hall at where Mary and my mom stand looking amused.

"Don't even start," I warn, and then head for my office.

13

NATE

I tried to stay awake to huff and puff around the room until someone got annoyed with my stomping and told Vanessa to come back, but the shock and adrenaline wore off in an hour leaving me exhausted. I told myself I'd only lie down for a little while, but woke hours later with a not-small amount of drool on the pillowcase beneath me and a new light coming through the thin curtains covering the balcony doors.

This really isn't a room so much as it is a suite, one with its own bathroom, walk-in-closet, hardwood desk, ornate chair, and a settee.

When I've managed to rub the sleep out of my eyes, I peer out onto the balcony and see that it is a great wide one that extends on either side of the door, presumably connected to the other bedrooms on the floor. I am about to step out to investigate more when a gentle knock sounds. Ranger doesn't bark, but does jump down from the bed to the settee to the floor and thumps his tail against the plush carpet.

I clear my throat before calling whoever it is to come in, and it takes a single glance to know that the woman who comes in must be Vanessa's mother. She's young, younger than my mom, and has the same black hair as Vanessa, only cut in a bob and peppered with gray streaks. There is nothing homely about her, like there's nothing homely about her daughters. But her mother has a softness about her where Vanessa is hard lines and sharp glances.

"I brought you some lunch," she says and holds up a tray like an offering. "I hope you like sandwiches."

"Thank you," I say, and take the tray from her before setting it on the desk. The metal tray holds way more than just a sandwich; I spy what looks like a plate of fruits and veggies, a bottle of apple juice, and maybe even a slice of carrot cake?

"I didn't realize how hungry I was until right now."

She searches my face, I'm not sure what she's looking for, but she seems satisfied with what she finds and nods.

"Sorry about what happened to you," she says. "Two boys in two months is a shame."

I don't correct her that it was in fact three, two the first time, one today, and it doesn't really feel okay, so I don't say it is. Ranger, ever polite, hasn't barked but is positively shaking waiting for this woman's attention. She notices him and a smile flits over her eyes.

"That's Ranger," I say, and she squats down to scratch his head, looking perfectly poised as she does.

"Well, you and Ranger come downstairs when you feel ready. This room is no cell."

It's another two hours before I take her up on that offer and venture downstairs with Ranger at my feet to find a backyard for him. I bring the tray full of empty plates down with me; it was maybe the best meal I've eaten in weeks, everything fresh and full of flavor. The sandwich had pesto and some melty cheese that makes my mouth water when I think about it now, and the cake. . . that carrot cake was on a different level of cakes, and if nobody is around, I may have to execute a heist of sorts to take the rest of it.

I walk slowly through the house, like someone might jump out at me and ask me what I'm doing down here, but there's not a person to be seen sitting beneath the chandelier in the dining room, nobody cooking in the kitchen outfitted for a small team of chefs, no signs of life in a cozy living room other than an unfolded blanket on the gray couch. It doesn't take long to find a door to the massive backyard. Ranger and I snoop around the perimeter, him giving everything a thorough sniffing inspection.

There are two additional buildings here, a guest house and a small greenhouse. I peer into the latter but don't investigate. I stroll by some garden beds, and trellises of vines with little green grapes growing on the stems. Also, there's a covered pool, and nearly as much outdoor furniture as I have indoor furniture in my entire apartment.

This kind of yard would've felt like magic to me when I was a kid. Even now, I'm not positive that there isn't fantastical life hiding between the trees at the perimeter of the yard, but the events of the last ten hours sully the grandeur of the place.

I suppose this is what blood money can get you: a gorgeous house with a spectacular yard and comfortable beds. That's why crime rates are so high. Somehow, the thought only serves to make me angrier, an indignant rage scorching between my bones.

I leave Ranger lying in a patch of sunshine and march back into the house. I'm looking for Vanessa, or the big bodyguard guy, or anyone who can explain to me what the fuck is going on, but again I find no one.

I do stumble upon an office, one with a thick rug, high ceilings, and a tidy fireplace. I decide immediately that it must be Vanessa's. It's sleek but well-used. Put together and tidy, but the photos on the wall and around the room give the personal touch of someone who loves their family.

Plus, it smells like her, which frustrates me further. Whatever perfume she wears is rich and floral and tingles in my nose.

It's warm in here, the yellow afternoon light casting through the window onto plush carpet. It bounces beneath my feet, and I belatedly slip off my shoes and hold them by the backs in one hand. I can imagine her at the desk, shoulders just bent forward, lower lip between her teeth while she concentrates. The idea is almost too human for what I've worked her up to be in my head.

Larger than life. A villain.

Now would be a good time to poke around her desk, but I've never been so good at snooping. The thought alone of sneaking around and getting caught knocks up my heart rate and makes my palms sweat.

On her desk sits a little gold frame holding a family picture. Vanessa has a bright youth in her eyes, she was a teenager, maybe, and she is crowded next to who I recognize as Artie's mom, Willa in a bright white gown. There's another smaller sister, too—I guess Mary—and on either side of them are their parents. It's a beautiful photo, not posed by a photographer as much as pulled together in a moment. Her dad has a glass of wine in his hand and is looking at his girls like he couldn't be happier with them.

They look so alive, so full of love and joy. Her dad doesn't look like an evil criminal—just like a man. A dad with graying hair and a mustache. He looks fancier than *my* father, but my dad shops almost exclusively at Costco, so that isn't difficult.

I stare at the photo for multiple minutes before I decidedly place it back on the desk, retrieve Ranger from outside, and retreat into the room to wait. I don't need to be snooping around this place, finding things that make her look less like a monster; that's in fact the opposite of what I need.

Ranger settles in a spot by the door, almost wistfully, huffing.

I wait.

When I venture downstairs again a few hours later, there is someone in the kitchen moving about, cooking something that is making my stomach garble. I creep past them hoping to evade their notice as I seek out Vanessa. I don't find her immediately, but I do open doors at random to two bathrooms and a laundry room before I reach one that is partially open already, music streaming from inside.

I don't knock, I just use my pointer finger on the handle to slowly pull open the door and it swings outward to reveal a staircase down to what I can only assume is a murder dungeon. I steel myself before descending and when I get there, *murder dungeon* doesn't seem that far off.

The floor and walls are concrete, there's this big home gym set up and a couple of closed doors that I imagine lead to plexiglass psycho cells. Like on that Netflix show about the stalker, but more than one of them for double the murdering.

I do find Vanessa, and she's wearing a tight little workout set and beating the absolute shit out of a punching bag in the corner. She doesn't hear me when I come in, but how could she over the 2000s divorced dad rock playing over the speakers?

It appears that working out is higher on her list of priorities than, oh I don't know, explaining to me why my life has been sent through a garbage disposal. She owes me an explanation, or at least an apology, but here she is, throwing her whole body into punching that bag, her ass looking ridiculously good while doing so.

I watch for a moment too long before remembering my mission and how much of a menace she is, and I force my eyes decidedly away.

There's a complicated sound system and I fiddle with it, accidentally turning it up louder before cutting the song completely.

Vanessa lobs a few more combos on the bag before finally turning around to look at me. She doesn't look surprised, which pisses me off more. It's not like she'd forgotten; would she have even come to find me if I hadn't sought her out?

I prop my hands on my hips, and look only at her face, not her tan skin shining with sweat. "Where have you been?"

Vanessa uses her teeth to undo the velcro on one of her gloves and then pulls off the other before tossing them onto a bench. I can't help but notice that she looks exceptionally tired, a weight about her face that would almost make me feel a sting of compassion for her if she wasn't the reason there may still be a dead man strung up in my bathroom, dripping his guts onto my new bottle of shampoo.

"Working," she says.

I scoff, I can't help it. I'm still not entirely sure what her job is, but I doubt an afternoon workout constitutes work payable. Vanessa unwraps a long wrap from her hands as I approach, and she hardly glances up as I do.

"What's on your agenda for the rest of the day? Think you can squeeze me in, or should I just keep watching TV in your guest room?"

"Nate," she bites, and it sounds like a warning.

I decide to dive straight into it: "Am I ever going to be able to go back to my apartment again? Did you do the same thing with Tony that you did the last two guys?"

She looks pained at the reminder, her eyes shutting on a wince. Invoking his name reminds me of the way he was left, and my stomach lurches, all that red coming to mind.

"We took care of it," she says, and there's that mask of indifference I saw earlier, that icy wall she puts up to hide what she's feeling. I want to smash it. What little is left of my composure snaps.

"How? Chopping him up and throwing away the little meat pieces? You were vague the last time this happened and now look where that landed us."

"It's better if you know less—"

"Who does that protect, me or you?"

Vanessa's hands fist at her sides as she glares at me, but I don't stop there.

"And do tell, is this how all your first dates end up? Or do they usually not live long enough to meet the family? I should consider myself *lucky*."

"Jesus, Nate—"

"And please enlighten me, do you often pretend to be a normal human to unassuming men you meet? Or do they end up in the meat grinder, too?"

Vanessa twists away from me and slams one of her palms on the punching bag before putting her hands on the back of her head and walking across the gym. Her back is rigid, and I can't see her face.

I go on, because I can't let shit rest and I'm desperate for her to admit that she's feeling anything as horrible as I've been since walking into my apartment this morning. "I deserve to know what the fuck is going on if I am just as likely to die any day."

Vanessa stalks back to me until she's just in front of me. Without her heels she has to look farther up to meet my eyes.

"Do you want to know where I just was?" she asks, and her voice is steady. The punching bag sways on its chain. I want to say something else about her blazing around the city shooting people, but something about her tone gives me pause.

"No guesses?" She turns her head so I can see the side of her face. When I still say nothing, she turns back to me and there's no hiding the sting in her eyes, the glassiness on the surface. "I sat with a couple as they wept to learn that their youngest son would need a funeral. Closed casket," her voice waivers on the last bit, but she keeps it together, looking just past me.

"He died because he was protecting *you*," she says. "Because I asked him to. Because I couldn't help myself. Because I just *had* to go to that wedding with you."

Vanessa's voice is so quiet, but in the stillness of this concrete room, it feels enormous.

"So, I'm sorry, Nate, if I didn't think to run home to fill you in on all of my comings and goings."

I have the wherewithal to be chagrined.

Vanessa takes a big breath and I watch her chest rise and fall with the motion.

She pulls her shoulders back and meets my eyes again. That mask is back, but there's a crack in the foundation now.

My comeback, whatever it might have been, gets caught in my throat. I still want to say something to fill the silence, something mean or hurtful, but she feels bad enough, it's written all over her face.

"Dinner's ready," someone says from behind us. My gaze snaps to the base of the stairs where a young woman who looks mostly like Vanessa leans against the wall shooting fire at me with her eyes. Like if I was a village, I might be pillaged and burnt to the ground after one glare.

"Thanks," Vanessa says. She goes to brush past me but stops at my side. "We'll talk after we eat."

"Right," I whisper and follow the two of them up the stairs to dinner.

14

VANESSA

Despite how much I've had to do today, it's somehow still Tuesday. As soon as we sat down for what I anticipated would be a quiet, awkward dinner, I watched out of the window over the sink as Leo rushed out of the guest house with his phone pressed against his ear.

I took a long breath to steady myself for whatever fire he was about to bring, and sure enough, as soon as he came through the back door, he was waving me over. I grabbed a full plate for me, and one for Leo, and led him into my office where we'd work through dinner and for another three hours afterwards.

By the time the problem was sorted out, it was almost 10 PM, and I swear I could feel the weary tiredness between my bones making me move slower. I took as searing of a shower as I could manage and tried very hard not to shed any tears, not until I was done for the day and in bed where I could cry as much as I needed.

I'm not one of the hardened people who never lets themself cry; that would be emotionally inefficient. Instead, I allow myself a small amount of stress crying at least twice per month, and that helps keep me level-headed.

Now, I stand at the door of my guest room and listen to Nate moving on the other side. I imagine him pacing, or rifling through his duffle for something soft to sleep in. I imagine the dog already asleep somewhere, getting its hair everywhere.

I knock.

He answers it immediately, poking his head through the crack. I spot a bare shoulder too, and it's more defined than his shirts let on. When he sees it's me, he does a double take, maybe because I'm wearing no makeup, my hair dripping water onto the shoulders of my nightshirt.

Or maybe I really do just look as bad as I thought when I was applying my third layer of eye cream.

"You came," he says, thankfully lacking that note of derision that's been there all day.

"I said we'd talk. So, let's talk."

A long moment passes before Nate jerks his head and steps back from the doorway letting me in. I follow behind him and look at his pale back as he pulls a T-shirt on. He's got freckles on his shoulders.

The room doesn't look very settled into, his clothes are still in their bags, but the bed looks like it was slept on, and his hair is damp too, so he's at least showered and rested some. The dog is passed out on the little dog bed Nate brought, his tongue lolling out of his mouth.

"Please sit," Nate gestures to the chair, my chair, in my house, but I do as he says, and he settles on the bench at the end of the bed.

"The stuff you want to know about," I start, then pause attempting to communicate this in a way that won't immediately earn more of his scorn. "You can't un-know it."

"You said I was safe," he reminds me.

"You are safe," I agree, "But you aren't totally tangled up yet. You still have some plausible deniability."

His lips twist up into what is almost a smirk, which is the last thing I thought I'd see from him after today.

He waves his hand around, gesturing at the room. "Seems I'm already pretty tangled up."

I let out the big breath I was holding. "What would you like to know?"

"Are you a drug dealer?" he asks first.

"No," I answer, which is true for the very most part. True enough that I don't feel bad.

I, personally, am not dealing drugs. That is for the lower families to facilitate.

"So, the cartel?"

"No involvement there." *If I can help it.* I can't always, though. They want smart weapons as much as anyone else.

"Your dad—was he like The Godfather?"

"Something like that, yes," I admit. "He was a powerful man."

"And you, what? Inherited his job? "

"Yes. Family business."

He mulls on this. "You're a boss, then?"

"I am," I agree.

"In the," Nate lowers his voice like someone might overhear, "mafia?"

I don't tell him that I'm moreover *the* boss, depending on who you ask (baby steps here), but I tilt my head in assent.

Even though he was the one who supplied the guess, he still looks shaken by my answer.

"We sell weapons, mostly," I explain. "All sorts of technologies. We build a lot of security systems, too. That's the primary thing."

"And your construction business?"

"That's real. Just another thing. We do a lot of totally aboveboard projects, but we also do. . . specialty builds," I say.

"For illegal stuff?"

"Yes, for illegal stuff." There can be no subtlety here, apparently.

"Have you ever been to jail?"

"Never."

"Are you worried about getting caught?"

"Not presently."

My dad made sure the police in this town were with us, and the ones that weren't knew not to mess with us. He laid a lot of that groundwork, and now my sisters and I just maintain the relationship. I give out a lot of presents and bonuses come the holidays. The list includes our few contacts in the larger agencies —the departments who *theoretically* want nothing more than to stop organized crime entirely, but in *practice* much prefer the benefits of looking the other way.

I make sure it stays that way.

"Who attacked us the night of the wedding?"

"Two privately hired hitmen from a non-affiliated organization."

"And who hired them?"

I press my lips together in a tight line. "That's what I've been trying to figure out."

"And until you do?"

"Until I do, I think you should stay here. You'll be safe in this house. It's not forever, just for a while. Not even the whole summer. You'll be able to sleep easy and leave the mafia far behind you by the time you have to go back to work in the fall."

I watch Nate's Adam's apple bob as he swallows.

It's a crazy offer, I know that, but I'm desperate. I won't have anyone else killed because of my one-night lapse in judgment. As soon as we figure out who is targeting us, hopefully Nate will be persuadable about moving back to Connecticut where I can be sure that he is free to live his happy little life of pickleball and kickboxing classes.

He'll marry a nice local girl, a baker or someone who owns a bookstore, and they can have as many tall, bookish kids as they want and we will keep tabs on him, but he will be safe, and this will all be a wild memory that I will pay him handsomely not to share.

"Okay," he finally says.

I know he'll have more questions tomorrow, but I think that this was more than enough after the day we had. I stand and offer my hand for him to shake.

He stares at it warily, before standing himself. He sort of towers over me when I'm not in my heels, and I lift my gaze to meet his. Slowly, he raises his palm to meet mine, and when I take it, it's so warm wrapped around my hand. My index finger falls at the base of his wrist and beneath his skin I can feel his thrumming heart.

"Alright, then. The summer." I give his hand one definitive shake and then step back, ready to make my hasty exit and bury myself in my bed.

I'm almost out of the door when he says my name.

"Hm?"

"What about my class for the rest of the week? Can I leave?"

I chew on my bottom lip thinking about this.

"You're not a prisoner here," I say. "If you want to go, I'll send you with Leo, but I wouldn't advise it. I can't guarantee that someone won't come for you again. They obviously think you're a way to get to me, making you valuable."

He bobs his head. "And vulnerable."

"Yes," I agree. "That too."

With as much of a smile as I can muster, I bid him goodnight and stride down the hall until I finally sink into bed behind the safety of my closed door.

* * *

WHEN I COME DOWNSTAIRS in the morning, my mom is in the kitchen (expected) in total stitches laughing at something Nate's just said (unexpected, unsettling, and frankly unfair that he's won her over so immediately). She's cradling the ugly little dog in her arms and scratching its neck while obviously enamored by a story Nate just told.

He notices me first, standing in the doorway like a specter, and stands up straighter before holding his mug up in greeting— it's my favorite green mug, surely poured by my traitorous mother.

"Morning," he says.

"Vanessa, baby," Mom says. "You didn't mention that he has a dog."

I look at the creature, who looks back, apathetic to me, secure in its knowledge that he's aligned himself with the most powerful woman in the house.

I try not to sneer at the dog, which is more gremlin than canine.

"Yes, well." I pour my coffee into a just-fine mug and pretend it makes no difference to the quality of my morning.

"You've got a beautiful garden, Mrs. Morelli," Nate says.

Mom practically purrs. That garden is her pride and joy in the summer months, sometimes I think she likes it more than her daughters.

Not more than her grandchildren, though.

"My dad has a garden. It's smaller than yours, but I helped with it growing up. You can't find better tomatoes than from a garden."

I'd swear someone was feeding him lines, Mom basically says this every night we eat food that comes from the garden or greenhouse.

"My girls used to help, but now they're too busy to be bothered."

"Oh, Ma." I let her kiss my cheek as she slides by me towards the oven. She's making a frittata, *nearly done, just ten more minutes,* the smell of which is making my mouth water.

"I would love to help you with it today if you have any work to do on it. And maybe a tour of the greenhouse?" Nate says, and that answers the question of whether he decided to go to work or not.

Mom, ever delighted, tells him how she would love that, calls him such a nice boy, and then repeats the sentiment to me five times. Seriously he should put Mom Charming on his résumé because what the hell?

The dog starts wiggling, and upon being placed on the floor, runs in quick circles and huffs out of his nose until Nate takes the myriad of hints and excuses himself to let him outside.

Mary shuffles into the kitchen looking somehow more tired than I feel and I hand her my mug which she is quick to drain. Mary is ever the definition of the corny "don't talk to me 'til I've had my coffee" shirts, though she'll bite your head off if you say as much.

She sets my now-empty mug down on the counter and I pour us both another.

"Mom, you can't fall in love with the math teacher," Mary says, obviously having heard some of Mom's awestruck fussing. "He's had his tongue in your daughter's mouth."

"Mary!" I say at the same time as Mom says, "He has?"

"Why didn't you tell me you kissed? He is very handsome." She raises her eyebrows a bunch of times.

I groan.

"He also called Vanessa mean things," Mary points out.

"Yes, but he had quite the shock. Who can blame him?" Mom says.

"Enough, *please*," I refrain from dragging my hands down my face, but it's a Herculean effort. "Can we talk about anything else?"

"Patrice called," Mom says, and I can't help my sigh this time. It's too early to be sighing like that. It's an omen for the rest of my day, I think.

Patrice, or Patty as we call her, is one of the mob wives from my mom's generation. She, much like Willa, can't keep from butting into other people's business.

"Okay, maybe not *anything* else."

Mom ignores me and keeps on. "Her cousin's boy is thinking about moving to town. Wants to be closer to family."

"Closer to someone's family," Mary mutters.

"He wants a job?" I ask, too hopeful that this is all he's looking for.

"He wants a wife."

Because of course he does.

"I thought Patty was on my side about this. She told me last month she's a feminist."

"She was," Mom agrees. "She is. But then her cousin heard you were still single and going on dates."

"One date. One." I'm whining now, I can't help it.

Even if the men are seen as the ones "in charge" of their households, we all know that their wives hold more power than they'd ever admit. If they think I need to get married too, their husbands will be trying to throw anyone they know my way.

"Who else?" I ask. Patty works in a very tight-knit clique of other mothers, my ma included, and if she's got it in her head that I should be married, the rest of them do too.

Mom stands straighter, but she can't hide the truth written all over her face.

"Please, not all of them," I groan. When she doesn't deny it, I do plant my face in my palms, makeup be damned. "I cannot deal with this right now. Not when I've got," I motion in the general direction of the backyard, "all of this going on."

"Then you might need to show them you're serious about finding a husband," Mom says. Her lips are downturned.

She doesn't like this either but knows even more than me that we are nearly powerless to stop it. These women are determined, which I love about them until their determination is aimed at changing something about *me*.

"She's right," Mary says. "It would take very little prodding for their crusty-ass husbands to try to revolt against you. Until now, they haven't wanted to cross you out of respect for Dad. Your position too, sure, but their fear of you has only rivaled the fear of their wives."

"This is so twisted." They are two of the few people who I'd let see me like this, griping about the inherent unfairness of everything slouched over the counter with my head in my hands. Mom rubs a circle on my back.

"It's not that they don't want you in charge, they do, but they want you to uphold tradition too. Family is very important to them."

"Family is important to me. The most important thing," I say. Both my immediate family and the larger family as a whole. It's why I do everything that I do, I'm not just building a fortune for myself, there's a whole network of people I am looking after.

"Ultimately, no husband means no baby," Mary says. I hate when she's practical. "And no baby means no heir."

"I don't have time to try to find a husband."

"I know, baby." Mom pushes my overgrown bangs behind my ear. It makes me feel like a kid again. "There's never enough time for matters of the heart."

I set my shoulders and take one last big breath, holding it for four seconds before letting it out.

"Will you make me a list?" I ask my mother. "If you can get the names of everyone interested, I can start looking through it this week."

"I think that would do it," Mom says. "You show them you're seriously considering their options, they'll back off. At least for a while."

The egg timer that's lived in the kitchen for as many years as I've been alive dings, though I barely have an appetite for the frittata at this point.

When I look out the kitchen window to the backyard, Nate is

standing on the grass with his eyes closed and head tilted back, like he's getting in his morning photosynthesis. The dog rolls on the lawn like it's the most spectacular grass he's seen in his life. It's surreal to see him there. Neither of them belongs.

"So he'll stay?" Mary asks at my side, also peering out the window.

"He's staying," I agree.

Mom wraps an arm around my shoulders and pulls me towards her. "This is going to be fun."

15

NATE

I USED TO DAYDREAM ABOUT VACATIONS LIKE THIS. WHEN I WAS IN my second year of teaching and doing grad school in the evenings, I would get home from work and my classes, and then I had to work on my lesson plans, or my grading, or my *own* assignments. Then, as I collapsed into my mattress that was just on the floor (no headboard, no box spring), I would close my eyes and fall asleep imagining days where I had no responsibilities and no obligations.

In my fantasies, my perfect day looked like this: I had no alarm set on my phone—it was charging in the kitchen, not even on my nightstand—and I would wake slowly, after fourteen hours of sleep. I would make something simple but delicious for breakfast. I could try a new recipe; I had all the time in the world after all. I would eat and maybe shower and get into fresh sweatpants, and then I would plant myself on the couch for approximately eight hours to read or watch movies or catch up on the seasons of TV I'd missed with my busy schedule. Then maybe I would go on a walk if I felt so inclined. Pick up a chocolate croissant down the street, and maybe a pizza for dinner. (At this point of the fantasy, I would usually meet a beautiful woman at the pizza shop, our orders getting mixed up, and we would laugh about the coincidence of both of us asking for extra banana peppers and olives and that woman would eventually become my wife and Ranger would love her as much as me and our three children.) I could stay up as late as I wanted and could do it all again the next day because it was my vacation and I had nowhere to be.

This sounded like true bliss.

Now, I've been on a nothing-to-do staycation for nine days and I am beginning to feel like I was a fool to think I would love doing nothing for this long. Day one was nice. Vanessa's mother Claire showed me around the garden and greenhouse and together we toiled at it for a few hours, a companionable work that reminded me of my dad. Delightful.

I met the house staff; a private chef who comes a few days a week as well as the weekly housekeepers. They came before lunch and stayed until dinner, which was as delicious as you'd expect a homemade meal by a private chef to taste. Then, I wrote in my journal, took a long shower, and climbed into the pillow-top bed with the 400 thread count sheets—it felt a bit like a night in a hotel.

Really, I've been relatively relaxed, despite the fact that I'm sheltering for my life in a mafia household with a family of well-dressed criminals.

But now a week has passed, and increasingly, I feel like my brain might explode out of my eyes from quietly relaxing in this massive house. The gardening has been great, but it's my one activity. Vanessa is mostly gone, though she shows up for dinner, not a hair out of place, and we politely ignore each other. Claire and Leo talk to me, while Mary either pretends I do not exist or stares at me like she's casting some sort of incineration spell on me from her mind. Leo is actually very cool, not at all as terrifying as his build and demeanor would give off.

The only time I've left the Morelli estate was on Monday

when I was escorted by both Leo and Vanessa's freaky sister Mary to clean out my classroom—it turned into a whole thing. Jenna was there and she ribbed me with questions about the house, Vanessa's family, etc. She asked if I saw them doing crimes, like if they were dragging bodies into the living room every other night, and she seemed a little let down when the answer was no. She also couldn't resist trying to flirt with Mary, who *actually* cracked a small smile at Jenna's attempts. I didn't know Mary's mouth moved that way, it was a shock.

In true Jenna fashion, she'd only been answering about a third of my calls and texts, and now, she's about to pack up for a two-month trip journeying alone around Spain and then Italy and Croatia, staying in hostels and working random jobs along the way. She's been planning this for a year, and I am certain this means she'll be even less accessible. And I will be here, in Vanessa Morelli's house, cooped up and going absolutely out of my mind.

Ranger is having the time of his life, though. He gets to run outside as much as he wants and is completely tuckered out by day's end. The cook loves dogs and has been meal prepping and feeding him these raw dinners that are absolutely ruining him for dry food for the rest of his life, so that's great for me.

I'm especially angsty about it all tonight, tossing and turning in the most comfortable bed I've ever slept in on freshly laundered sheets. After a few hours of this, I push out of bed to investigate the leftovers situation in the fridge, which is when I find Vanessa lounging on the couch watching what I immediately recognize as the second *Fast and Furious* movie.

I love this movie, and I won't pretend that I don't, so I scrounge in the fridge for a leftover piece of homemade pizza and settle on the far end of the couch, as far away from her as I can be. She closes a folder full of papers she was looking at before turning to assess me with her face neutral. She's not wearing any makeup and she has a light smattering of freckles on the tops of her cheeks and across her nose. Also, these freaking glasses I've never seen. Clear rounded frames that she takes off and sets on top of the file folder she was looking at.

Reading glasses? Vanessa Morelli doesn't have perfect vision?

She wears a hoodie I see her in sometimes, oversized and faded with BOSTON across the chest, and the tiniest pair of shorts that I avoid looking at. Vanessa pulls a blanket across her bare legs.

"Do you like this movie?" She nods at the TV.

"Of course." The second movie is not the best of the franchise by any means, but it might be in my top four. "It's pure fun. We meet Roman and Tej who are basically unrecognizable from their characters by number seven."

She looks me over like it's a surprise to hear that a 30 year old man would be interested in the most iconic racing and action franchise of the last two decades. I was seven when the first one came out, it was like my bible.

"It is," she says, and looks back at the TV.

We watch for a while, me chewing bites of my cold pizza and her resting her head on her propped-up fist. It's something to do, and it makes me feel less lonely even if it's Vanessa I'm sitting with.

"Have you been comfortable here?" Vanessa asks after another twenty minutes of the movie quietly playing from the screen. Her voice startles me from the warm quiet that enveloped us.

"I've been comfortable," I say, then shrug.

"What is it?"

"No, I mean, I am comfortable. You have a wonderful home." The nicest house I've ever seen in person, with collectibles displayed on shelves like I might display little Lego sets, and a *staff*. It's not a house so much as it is an Architectural Digest home tour. The video would be called something like "Inside Vanessa Morelli's Stunning Boston Estate" and Vanessa would lead the tour with aplomb and humble charisma.

"The bed is great," I add.

Vanessa rolls her eyes. "But what?"

"But what, what? I said I like it."

"No, you said you were comfortable. That's not—"

"I'm bored," I say before she can pick apart my response more. Her pretty little mouth rounds into an O. "Out of my fucking *mind* bored. I haven't chilled this much since middle school and even then, my mom had me in summer basketball leagues."

"You want to play basketball?"

"Well, maybe," I say. "I've just been sitting around. All day. I haunt your house, eat your food, and bother your mom—"

"You've been helping her in the garden," she corrects. "She loves it."

"There's only so much gardening to be done. It's not a farm, Vanessa."

Vanessa crosses her arms over her chest, a gesture that's becoming a familiar sign of her thinking. "What then? Do you want an XBOX? What's a hobby you've been dying to get into but felt like you never had time for or couldn't afford? Just say—"

"No, like I'm thinking about applying for a job." Though the offer of getting into a hobby free of charge is tempting.

"Isn't it your summer break? Why do you want to work during your break?"

"It is, but I usually travel a little and go down to Connecticut and help my dad with his bookkeeping for two months."

"You want to do my books?"

This is very much not what I meant—for one, I don't want to be culpable of any of her money laundering schemes or whatever it is she does. "No, that was just an example; I *can* do books."

"I have a team of accountants on my payroll, salaried with benefits. Plus, lest you forget that one week ago you were calling me a rotten criminal so, no, I'm not letting you near my books."

In a cartoonish display of frustration, I throw my hands up and let them fall back to my lap. "I didn't say I want to get near your books. It was just an example," I say again. "I can do many jobs. I am exceptionally capable."

Vanessa has the gall to look wary of this.

"I'm thinking about applying for a remote customer service gig. Or maybe getting some new certifications."

Vanessa rubs a spot on the middle of her forehead. "Are you trying to make me feel bad for providing a place that is too relaxing while you are hiding from potential scores of hitmen?"

"No! No, you—" I pause and let out a big huff. "You asked how I was liking your house. I was trying to be honest with you."

"Well, when you decide you want to take up embroidery or something, let Leo know. He'll order whatever you need."

She sounds annoyed with me. Or maybe just annoyed at large. Frustrated?

"What's got you all," I gesture vaguely at her body, indicating the overall tense, tired, beleaguered essence of her.

She grabs the manilla folder that's been resting precariously on the arm of the couch and drops it in my lap. I haven't even opened it and I know it's going to either be incriminating information about the Morellis or the most exciting thing I have seen all week. Well, probably the latter either way, I don't know that three seasons of *The Vampire Diaries* counts as exceptionally exciting.

"I need a husband," she says before I can look at the contents.

My brain short circuits at this. For a moment, I believe she's proposing a reluctant marriage with *me*.

Marrying Vanessa would do the opposite of expediting my transition from her house and back into my own, and in fact would probably only serve to entangle us more—this time financially and legally.

Plus, if I'm going to have any sort of wedding, I'll have to invite my parents and they'll probably fall right in love with Vanessa themselves, which will incur the impossible task of telling them that she doesn't love me, she only loves crime and money and legacy and maybe the members of her immediate family.

"Nate?"

"Hm?"

She nods at the folder, and I look down at it. Slowly, I pry the cover open and am met with a long list of names, some with little check marks next to them, some little exes, others violently crossed through. "I've been trying to find a husband."

"Oh." *Oh.* A husband who is, very reasonably, not me. Sure, sure. "Why?"

"There's a delicate balance in my culture. . . certain traditions that need to be upheld," Vanessa explains, and I wonder if she means as an Italian American or as a mob boss, but I figure now isn't the right time to ask.

"You're still young though, right? This isn't like some old maid situation."

"I'm twenty-eight," Vanessa agrees. "I've practically aged out of eligibility in these circles, but it's not my age that's the issue. It's my position."

Ah, a mob boss issue then. Right.

"I need to marry someone who will benefit the family, and they need to be secure in the fact that I will always outrank them. But if I'm searching, everyone has a relative they want to be considered."

I look back at the list, and flip through a few more pages. There are three pages alone of names. I count four Lorenzos as I skim.

"So, what, you have to consider all of them? Like *The Bachelorette*, or something?"

"Or something," Vanessa says. "I need a system to go through all of these men, most of them just to say I considered the offer."

"But you hope one of them will be good enough." The marks next to the names take on new meaning, the checkmarks are few, but they look hopeful. The ones crossed through, now appear angry. "You want to marry one of these guys?"

"No," Vanessa says, "but I think we've learned that I don't get to make decisions based on what I like."

I will not investigate the meaning of that remark, I will not let it endear her to me. She chooses to do the things she does, she's not a criminal by accident.

"Sorry, I don't know why I'm telling you this. I need to sleep." Vanessa uncrosses her legs from beneath her and moves to stand up, but I'm back to looking at the list.

"Why don't you put them in categories? Looks like you've already started doing that." I scan over the ones that are only a little crossed out versus the ones that are violently slashed through. "Have the ones you really can't stand fill out an online form or something."

"Like an application?"

"Sure," I say. I flip a page, then close the envelope. "Tell them it's a screening, nothing personal. Thirty questions or so. You're a busy woman. What do they expect, an in-depth interview for each of them?"

I offer her the Folder of Men, but she is looking at me like she's just realized something. If humans had bulbs over their heads, hers might be lit up.

"What?" I ask, afraid of the thought that's making her look like she's on the brink of a scientific discovery.

Vanessa takes a deep inhale through her nose. "I will hire you to interview them."

Oh.

She's *lost her mind*.

"Vet them for me," she says, rushed. "You were just saying you want a job and you're right; I can't take this massive project on alone. Too busy."

"That is a *ridiculous* idea."

"No, think about it, you'd be great! It would keep you busy. Leo will be your bodyguard."

"What would I even ask them?"

"Up to you," she shrugs. "That's part of the job. I'll pay you. Bunches."

As compelling as being paid *bunches* sounds, Vanessa is most definitely not thinking clearly. If she was, she would just tell me to fuck off and stop complaining, or something. Not this.

"I'm not working for the mafia, Vanessa," I insist.

"You wouldn't be working for the mafia, you'd be working for me."

"What's the difference?"

Vanessa levels a wry glance my way. "I exist outside of my job."

"How very humanist of you," I snipe, but she waves me off.

"Whatever." Vanessa stands up and stretches her arms over her head making her sweatshirt reveal a sliver of her stomach. "Do it, or don't. I don't care."

The credits roll on the TV, the last of the movie having passed by without me realizing.

I'm inclined to believe that she's joking, but really, how often does Vanessa Morelli joke?

I let myself imagine what this would look like, me vetting her list of criminals to find her perfect mafioso spouse so that she can make little mafia babies.

"It's not safe," I say, my voice quieter than I would like.

"You'd have Leo," she points out. "He's a good fighter. One of the best."

"Yeah, I'm sure he is." The man is absurdly massive, he would probably have a successful fighting career if he wasn't into organized crime. "But the night of the wedding and then again in my apartment," I trail off for a moment, remembering the blood, the three bodies drained of life in front of me. "I was useless."

Vanessa presses her lips together into a tight line, but there's something sympathetic in her dark brown eyes. I swallow the lump that's found its way to my throat.

She's hearing what I haven't said. That I'm scared all the damn time, even in her fortress mansion, because someone could come for me at any time and no amount of beginner kickboxing classes at the Y would save me.

"Did you bring gym clothes?" Vanessa asks.

I blink at the question. "I brought some." Or I think I did, at least.

"We'll train you," she says, like it's simple. Decision made. Vanessa shuts off the TV and stands.

I stand, too. It's still a shock looking down at her without her heels. "What?"

"You want to be safe? We'll teach you." Vanessa nods. "Meet in the basement at 5 PM tomorrow."

"Oh, I—" My tongue is uselessly searching for syllables. "Okay."

"Okay." She pats my arm like she's my coach and this was a good talk. "If you get bored, come up with a list of questions and have them on my desk by Friday. My family might have some ideas."

Vanessa sidesteps me and begins walking out of the living room, clicking off lamps as she goes.

"I'll think about it," I say, still gaping at her like an idiot.

"Give me an answer sooner than later." She smiles again. I hate how much I love to see it. "But at least take me up on the training. You can't be bored if you're physically exhausted."

16

VANESSA

This morning I wrote a dollar amount on a scrap of paper and dropped it on the island in front of Nate while he ate a heaping serving of Mom's oatmeal bake. I could've just said the number out loud, but the extra drama was worth it when his eyes nearly fell out of his skull at the price I was willing to pay for his help.

We went back and forth for ten minutes, him saying it's not nice to lie about money to teachers who, famously, make too little money, especially in this great state of Massachusetts, even at private schools—to which I assured him that I wasn't lying at all and Willa would even tell him what to do so that he didn't have to pay taxes on it.

This went over as well as you might expect it to with him; he was indignant that I thought he wouldn't want to pay taxes, but Mary pointed out that nobody wants to pay taxes and he shouldn't be such an ungrateful prick.

He shut up then, looked down at the number again, and agreed.

I set him loose on the project and joined Mary and Leo on some rounds; first to a few construction sites, and then on the late payment visits. They've been doing more of these since I called for the lockdown, but I've attended some. Mary is more than frightening enough to get people to pay up, but some people just need to be reminded that they wouldn't have the lives they do, the luxuries they so appreciate, without me. It usually scares them straight. Nobody wants a cold visit from the boss.

We are headed to the third such visit when my phone starts buzzing with a call from Cillian. I answer it on speaker so Leo and Mary can also hear.

"Morelli," I say, just like my dad used to.

"I think I can get McGowan to agree to $410 million," Cillian says without preamble.

That's great, more than I expected he'd be able to get, but still not quite enough for all the modifications McGowan wants. Leo's eyes cut from the road to me with a brief shake of his head.

"Push higher," I say. "The best we can do with his absurd security specifications is 450."

Cillian clicks his tongue through the phone. "He feels entitled to a discount. For all the goodwill he's shown our families in the last decade."

Mary mutters a slew of curses under her breath at this. McGowan is practically geriatric, Irish, and has been nothing but a dissenting thorn in our family's side since Willa and Sean got married. He thought it was unreasonable to expect that the good Irish folk of the city would just accept the Morellis with open arms and has made that abundantly clear over the years.

He's rich as sin, and has old city connections that we don't want to lose.

"That is the discount. Make him think he's getting a good deal over my head."

Mary huffs again, louder this time. "You want him to think you're an idiot?" she whispers.

"McGowan is the idiot, Mary. It doesn't matter what he thinks, he'll be dead in ten years."

"I'll try," Cillian says. I think that's the end of the call, but he keeps going. "And what's this I hear about a middle school teacher?"

"What did you hear?" I pinch the bridge of my nose.

"First, that you went on a date with him and nearly got shot?" His disbelief agitates me. God forbid a woman have a social life. And I did *not* almost get shot. "And then Artie said that he hasn't come to your house in a week because his teacher is your new boyfriend, and he needs to settle in."

Leo laughs, Mary grumbles that he's not good enough to be my boyfriend, and I try not to think about all the ways I want to kill Willa.

"He's under our protection," I say.

"Christ, he's actually staying with you?"

"Just for the summer." Not that it's any of Cillian's business. "He's harmless."

"He's an outsider," Cillian is using the stern voice he takes with Artie and Angel when they're being rowdy. "He should move states if he feels unsafe. Not *stay in your house*."

"He's defenseless. Couldn't hurt a fly, much less betray Boston's most powerful families. Why don't you come meet him sometime?"

"Ness—"

"Goodbye, Cillian." I hang up before he can bother me anymore. I'm not much one for friends, but if I was, Cillian might be my closest one. Though he acts like my fucking father sometimes which pisses me off.

The rest of the afternoon is as expected, if not bloodier. I don't know how Mary stomachs the unsavory sides of enforcement, but she's the one who asked for this job. If I had it my way, I'd put her in charge of something else. Maybe we'd expand more into casinos or something. But no, she wants to punch people. One way to get her wiggles out, I guess.

One of our club owners decided to stop paying back our

generous and gracious loan and thought we wouldn't notice. He proceeded to make a poor-taste comment about Mary's outfit, which ended about as well as anyone would expect: multiple broken bones in his face and hands.

He did pay up, though, and his blood on Mary's bare legs was enough to make the next guy comply without argument or preamble.

By the time we get home, it's half past 5 PM and Nate is pacing around the kitchen wearing sneakers, a massive T-shirt, and blue basketball shorts. The man loves to pace almost as much as he loves wearing clothes two sizes too big for his body.

"Nervous?" Mary asks. When he catches a glimpse of the dried blood on her legs and face, he really does look nervous.

"No, you guys are just late." He shifts on his feet. Leo pats Nate's shoulder as he walks past him to get changed and Mary and I go up the stairs to do the same.

"Go downstairs and start stretching," I call from the second story. He looks warily at the basement door like whatever is down there might bite him.

"Should we go easy on him?" Mary asks, but her smirk belies her intention. She couldn't go easy on him even if she wanted to, which she most definitely does not.

* * *

"START ON THE TREADMILL," I point to the machine next to the one Leo is already running on. "Three miles. No more than ten minutes each."

"I can't do that," he says immediately. "How about one mile?"

"How about five?" Mary bites back.

"Do what you can for thirty minutes," I reason. "Just don't stop running."

Mary and I do our stretches before going through our weight training circuit together on the rack in the corner. At some point,

Mary turns up the music loud enough to drown out Nate's panting. After about fifteen minutes, Leo leans over and hits some buttons on Nate's treadmill while giving him advice that I'm unable to hear. He slows down substantially, though, and looks moderately less miserable for the second half of the run. He's still quite sweaty by the end of it.

The drills go about as well as I expect. Nate is generally fit; I am certain he could lift a good amount of weight and can stay energized enough for a sports game, but he's not a fighter.

Leo demonstrates the drills and critiques Nate's form in a way that is nicer and more patient than Mary could ever be. Nate doesn't have much power behind his punches yet, but he will after enough practice. No concerns. It's the sparring that does him in.

He starts with Leo, who is instructive and gentle on him. Then it's my turn.

"Keep your hands up," Mary yells again from the side of the mat. He overcompensates and isn't fast enough to block when I land a hit to his stomach. It's a light hit, but he still grunts.

"Why aren't you hitting her? Hit her!" Leo repeats the direction again and I think Nate might be sick.

I slow my feet and lower my gloves.

"He's right," I say. "You have to hit me."

"But what if I hurt you?" He drops his arms to his sides, and I press my lips together to not smile. I pop a quick hit to his face, not too hard, but enough to startle him.

"What the fuck?"

"Did that hurt?" I ask, and hit him again, then one more time, until he puts his hands back up. "See, you're fine. Puffy gloves. I'll be fine."

Nate glares at me but leaves his hands up.

"Here." I drop all fighting stance and come up beside him. He tenses like I'm going to get him again, which is a good impulse. I lightly tap my glove to his stomach, then his sides. "Tighten here, and here."

I use one of my feet to nudge his stance open. "Wider. Like this." I demonstrate, bent knees, arms loose, core tight. "Good. Now hit me."

I make my way in front of him again and lower my gloves enough that he has a clear shot. He's miserable about it, but his stance looks better, and after a few seconds, he hits me.

It doesn't hurt at all, more of a light tap with the bouncy glove and he looks panicked like he might want to shower me in apologies, but Leo hoots and calls that he's doing great.

"Again," I say, and he does, a little harder this time. "Another."

After three more hits, each stronger than the previous, I grin and put my gloves back up. Leo starts the timer, and we take turns sparring for the next half hour. At some point after going against Leo, Nate loses the shirt confirming that, while lean, he is in fact more cut than his baggy button-ups give him credit for. I blink a few times at the sight of his chest, which has more freckles and hair than I expected, then clear my throat and call for him to switch and fight with Mary next.

He's the most afraid to fight her; she pulls her punches the least and is relentless on the offense, but it makes him less reserved; he hits harder and quicker which is exactly what I hoped would happen.

I'm sure that they would both hate to admit it, but he'll learn the most from her.

When we call it for the day, Nate's face is sunburn red and his hair wet with sweat as he sits on the mat nursing a bottle of water.

"Good work today," I say. "Tomorrow, we do 6 AM."

"You're kidding," he groans and looks to Leo for sympathy. "She's kidding, right? Do you hate yourselves?"

"We have to stay sharp," I say. "You too if you're going to be interviewing mafiosos."

This makes the men sound more dangerous than they are—the men Nate will be interviewing are mostly kind of losers, but losers with guns. If he can fight better than them, he'll be fine, and with us teaching him, he will.

"Get cleaned up for dinner. Artie and Angel are coming and they're going to have a lot of questions for you."

NATE

AFTER THREE DAYS OF TRAINING WITH THE MORELLIS IN THEIR murder basement, movement of any kind is a torture. I want to say that I can tell I'm already getting stronger, but I just feel like I've been through a few turns in a taffy stretcher.

I am ready to collapse into my bed after dinner, but Vanessa has other plans: a crash course on the Morelli Family. Artie and Angel are sent to what I refer to as the fancy living room (it has no television) with bowls of ice cream and their video games while the rest of the family spreads out in the comfortable living room (the one *with* a television).

Willa, previously only known to me as Mrs. Donovann-Morelli is here with her husband Sean who I'd never met formally. His hair is practically white it's so blonde and he watches his wife like she's the center of the universe. Seems nice.

Willa hooks up a laptop to the television for her presentation titled "Finding Mr. Morelli."

"Let's begin," Willa says. She stands next to the television, a little remote in her hand like the one I use in class for my Power-Points. "Nate, if you have questions, don't hesitate."

"Great," I say and sit up a little taller. I am in the middle of the long sofa between Claire—the matriarch Morelli—and Leo, trying not to spill my coffee on either of them or the couch which must run for more than half of my salary. Sean leans back in the lounge to our left, Vanessa on the love seat to our right, and Mary on the ground in front of her. A real family movie night.

Willa moves to progress to the next slide but stops. "Where's your notebook?"

I jolt and reach for the journal on the ground in front of me, spilling a bit of coffee on my leg in the process. I look for a table to rest the mug, but can't quite reach it, and really everyone is staring at me now, so I offer the mug to Leo who grunts before taking it.

I open the notebook and click my pen. "Right. Ready."

Willa clicks to the first slide, a family picture that I recognize as the one framed on Vanessa's desk from Willa's wedding.

"You've met all of us except for Dad," everyone bows their head briefly in remembrance and it seems like the right thing for me to follow suit. Willa clicks the remote. "Here is a larger family tree."

She clicks to the next slide which has a diagram detailing all extended family; uncles, cousins (an incredible number of cousins), and some grandparents.

"For obvious reasons, no one on this tree will be considered as potential marriage candidates for Ness. This said, many of these—" Willa's remote doubles as a laser pointer, which she now uses to circle the further parts of the tree. "—people have cousins not related to us by blood that they will want to be considered."

"Right," I sit up straighter and lean forward. I'm not sure what to write in my notebook, so I just scrawl and underline 'cousins' and return my attention to the screen. Willa progresses to the next slide.

"Here is the preliminary list of men my mother has put together based on conversations with the other Ma's." The slide shows about fifteen photos of various Italian or Irish men and their names beneath. I count four named "Nicky".

Mary stands and, from a black leather tote, pulls out a stack of manila envelopes much like the one Vanessa gave me and drops them on my lap.

"Review details about them before your interviews. It's important that they believe you know exactly who they are."

"What happens if they think I don't?"

"You lose their respect," Vanessa says from her seat. She's staring at the screen with her lips curled in an approximation of disgust at the men listed.

"Sure, makes sense," I mutter.

The next slide has no pictures, but at least 40 more names. I recognize some from the list Vanessa showed me earlier this week.

"Tier two, these are the men that are less appealing, but we still must consider as to not upset the family."

"Dear God," Vanessa rubs her temples. "Mom, you really want me to consider marrying Ricardo Guerra? Be serious."

"His uncle is in charge of the shipyard, stupid, you're going to consider him," Mary says, and Vanessa sighs. I write that down in my journal.

"Go on," Vanessa nods at Willa.

"There's some shorthand you're going to need to know," Willa says. "But before I go on, we must be clear that this is all incredibly sensitive information and if you tell anyone outside of this room what you've learned, go to the police, or otherwise disseminate this information, we are not liable for what may or may not happen to you. Not to mention the NDA."

I clear my throat, trying not to choke at this, and then nod. I signed the document before dinner after spending too many hours trying to parse through the legal jargon.

"Okay," I say.

"I need confirmation, yes or no," Willa says.

"Yes," I say, "I mean—no, I won't tell anyone. Yes, you can, uh, trust me."

Willa and Vanessa share a look before Willa goes on.

On the screen now are several letter codes.

Without going too deep into the specifics of the business, Willa briefly explains each code: Rx is pharmaceuticals, which relies on SH (shipping and handling), transit, and distribution. Then there are codes for tech, construction, weapons, gambling, and explosives. I try to jot down the codes and their meanings, but there are so many, and they all seem to rely on at least three others.

Willa explains that everyone has a job, sometimes two, and they need to feel heard to keep doing those jobs. Quite a few men on the marriage list do not expressly have a job in one of these sectors but are the nephews of people who do. For instance, bottom of tier one is Romeo, whose father is a coroner—*best in the city, only one they trust.*

"Everyone is connected," Willa says, "and each folder has a list of connections for you to familiarize yourself with. The tech guys are smarter than the shipping and handling guys and you're going to need to tailor your questions accordingly."

I have no idea how I will do that, but I nod and scribble a note of it.

"Everybody is important, and they need to feel valued. That's how the ship moves, how people carry on. How *we* make money so *they* can make money to provide for their families."

"Right, makes sense," I say.

"Ultimately, we're all family," Vanessa says. "And family takes care of family."

This is very *Fast & Furious* of her, but I don't mention it.

"Next we need to talk about you," Willa says, and the next slide has a photo of me on it. It's from last year's faculty and staff Christmas party, Jenna and me with matching hideous sweaters and margaritas. *Did she pull this from my Facebook?*

I'm trying not to feel like my privacy has been violated, but when Leo and Mary both snicker it's hard not to get defensive.

"As a teacher, you have an endearing style," Willa explains. "You're very easy to trust, like you've never been to a dry cleaner, and you've had the same loafers since college. Kids love that."

She sounds so genuine, but I am pretty sure that cannot, in any world, be a real compliment.

"For these meetings, you'll need to adopt a new look." The next slide is a collage of men pulled from various fashion advertisements—a vision board for a classier, sleeker me.

Amidst the smoldering faces, I see shiny black shoes, black fitted suits, button ups showing far too much chest, veiny arms with thick watches, and intimidating hands with rings adorning more than one finger. Also, the hair is always sleek, kempt, gelled back, not a curl in sight.

I peer down at my own hands, wide palms and long slender fingers, which are kind of knobby at the knuckles, if I'm being honest. You put a big watch on me, and it will look absurd.

"First, your clothes." Willa rifles in her big leather bag and pulls out a sheet of paper that she hands to me. This is not a digital family, apparently. "A list of all of the items you'll need."

Everything is categorized, three different pairs of shoes, button ups in three different colors (or non-colors: gray, white, black, two of each), pants, accessories, hair products—

"I don't know how to find all this stuff, and even if I did, I don't think I could afford it," I say. Even with the unhinged amount of money Vanessa is going to pay me, buying nice items in each category would quickly eat up two months' pay.

"You don't have to worry about that, sweetie," Claire pats my knee like my own mother would. "We have a shopper."

A shopper. Of course. Reasonable.

"We'll pay," Vanessa says. "Consider it your uniform."

"Great." Because it's a brilliant idea to take even more money from the mafia. "Anything else?"

"Your hair," Willa says.

I thought the slide show was done, but no, the next slide has numbered photos of four different men with different, though similar, haircuts. All smooth, which my hair has never really been.

"You can choose between one of these hairstyles and our stylist will show you how to use the products." Willa clicks off the TV and goes to sit on her husband's lap, presentation concluded. "Any questions?"

"Who will I say I am, then? What credentials does a middle school teacher from Connecticut have to find Vanessa a husband?"

"Great fucking question," Mary mutters, loud enough for everyone to hear. Vanessa tugs one of Mary's braids and Mary pastes on a saccharine smile. Looks unnatural.

"If they ask, we imply you're a consigliere. Leo and Willa have already started the rumors," Vanessa says. I don't know what that word means or even how I will spell it to Google it later, but I think in *Godfather* terms, we're pretending that I'm equivalent to Tom Hagen, which is hilarious. Math teachers are known to make rock-solid consultants. I can understand why Mary can't keep from rolling her eyes every twenty seconds.

"It's an honor," Leo says with a heavy pat on my back. "Don't fuck it up, brother."

"Right." I should have more questions, everyone is looking at me like they're just waiting for me to ask something, but they've made themselves very clear: do my research, act the part, get new clothes, and fix my gross, stupid hair.

"I should be good." I open one of the folders without really looking at the pages, and skim over my spare notes. "Yep. No questions."

This was not the summer I intended, but at least I have something to do.

18

VANESSA

My eyes are burning as I stare at the spreadsheet that accounting sent over, the numbers blurring together. I don't usually look at reports like this, but three sites have come in over budget this month, and not by a small margin by any means. My site managers have written lengthy explanations to state exactly why this is the case, all referring to their spreadsheets and noting where cuts can be made. Whatever the problem is, trying to get to the bottom of any of it is mind-melting and not in my purview.

"You've looked better," a low voice says from my doorway. Cillian leans against the frame, a crooked smirk on his face.

I lean back in my chair with a huff and rub my eyes.

"Thank you kindly, asshole."

Cillian holds his wide, tattooed hands up in surrender. "I thought honesty was our top rule in this relationship. That and, of course, never go to bed angry."

"Sure, sure." I stand from my desk chair and stretch my hands over my head then roll my neck back and forth. Cillian slides my glass of water across the desk to me and I take a sip.

"What do you need?" I ask. "I didn't think you were coming here today."

"Was in the area." Cillian picks up a piece of paper off my desk and holds it up to squint at it. "Picked your darling mother up one of those butter cakes. Just who are you interviewing with questions like these?"

I try to pull the sheets from his hand, but he holds it up out of my reach and my pride is much too large to try to jump for it.

"I told you I've been looking for a husband," I say.

"And what does *this* have to do with finding a good husband?"

"You wouldn't know what it's like having to vet men to make sure they won't murder you in your sleep or get half of the town pregnant."

"Well, have you had any luck so far?"

I stalk back to my chair and drop into it. "No."

"How many have you interviewed?"

"Recently, none. The math teacher is going to do it," I say.

Cillian barks a laugh at the idea of Nate sitting across from various men in the mafia and asking them questions about how tenderly they might treat a woman, namely me.

"I know," I say with a sigh and swivel my chair in a full circle. When I'm back to facing him, he's not laughing anymore, but still grinning. "But not all of us can just go on unmarried until their soulmate comes along."

"You think I'm looking for my soulmate?" Cillian asks.

Cillian has never been one for serious relationships. I don't think I've known him to have even one long-term girlfriend, everyone in that area of his life is temporary. But that doesn't mean he wouldn't, probably, if he met someone.

"Isn't everyone? Looking for someone who matches them?"

"Ah you see, those are different things. You can meet any number of people who match you, who would make good partners, but I don't think soulmates exist, not like that."

Willa mentioned once that Sean and Cillian's parents had a

loveless marriage. We were never so unlucky as to have a home with no examples of love.

"Whether they exist or not, I'll be lucky to find someone generally compatible on that list." I point to the folder of men. "I can only do my best to find someone half-decent who knows his place."

"You want a weak man?"

I don't say no, but to hear it put like that, that's certainly not what I want. What do I really want? Someone who pushes me, who makes me think about every side of a problem, someone helpful, and loyal, someone who won't make me and our children miserable.

"I want someone that I can trust."

"Am I on your list?"

I laugh but cut off when he doesn't join me.

He quirks an eyebrow. "You don't trust me?"

"I trust Leo, but he's not on the list."

"Yes, Ness, because Leo is your cousin," he says.

"And you're family."

Cillian glances again at the paper and then hands it out to me. "Let me sit for an interview."

I scoff but after a quiet moment, I meet his eyes. "Don't ridicule me for doing my duty."

Cillian only nods and points again at the paper. "Ask."

After another unyielding moment, I sigh and lean forward to look over the typed list of questions Nate dropped on my desk this morning. I haven't been able to review them yet, so they're as new to me as they will be to Cillian. I motion for him to take a seat and then I get up, only to sit on the other seat next to him. He scoots his to face mine and when we're all settled in, I take a deep breath and nod.

I start with a simple one: "How many children do you want?"

"A whole brood of them, if I'm lucky," Cillian says. "I like the sound of *five*."

"You're lying," I say.

"I'm not. I always wanted more siblings." Cillian pockets his shirt's cufflinks and rolls the sleeves up his forearms as he speaks. It's possible the man may have more rings and watches in his rotation than my sisters and I combined.

"And how will you treat this basketball team of children?" I ask.

"Fairly."

"How do you mean?"

"I won't shield them from this life like you have our niece and nephew. I will teach them and treat them with respect. We all have obligations, and they must understand that. Petulance can only be tolerated for so long."

"Before what? You hit them?"

"That depends."

"On what?"

Cillian shrugs. "Is the child a little boy or a 30-year-old menace? The man-child may need to be knocked around if he's fallen too far from grace."

"Hm." I hadn't considered my children as adults living and making decisions as old as I am now. They exist in my mind more as a concept than breathing things that will actually take my place. It's not something I like to imagine too concretely.

Next question.

"And how do you feel about moving?"

He doesn't laugh like I expect him to, and doesn't scoff at the mere thought of relocating from his family home.

"Would I get my own office like this one?" He waves his finger in a circle.

"Maybe a bit smaller," I say.

"Good, yours is too large. Who needs a fireplace in their office? Citizen Kane?"

I skip the three questions about sex because I do not want

Cillian to think of me as a sexual creature on this decent Friday afternoon.

"What do you do if a beautiful woman propositions you?" I ask.

"I remind her of the beautiful woman I have at home." His eyes snake for the barest moment down to my chest before returning to my face, which, *so much for not thinking about me as a sexual being.*

"What if your wife wants to do business you have no part in? What if you aren't included in everything?"

"Will she extend me the same courtesy?" Cillian leans forward, his forearms on his knees.

I consider this. Too much outside business could lead to a loss of power, but Cillian has his own dealings to maintain, ones I'm glad not to have to manage, ones that are already pivotal to my own dealings.

"Some," I say.

"Then, some."

"Would you ever consider marriage counseling?" This is obviously a question added by my mother, who swears up and down it was the one thing that saved her and Dad's marriage in the beginning after they had Willa.

"I don't like it—someone having access to my most personal matters—but I would consider it." This is more than can be said for the other men I've spoken to thus far who would divorce before they considered a counselor.

I look at the rest of the questions, many of them I already feel like I know the answers to. He has that going for him, I suppose; the years between us.

I make up my own question, "And what if she can never love you?"

Cillian doesn't answer at first, but moves his hand over my knee, his fingertips barely brushing the bare skin there. I meet his eyes, so piercing blue with the afternoon sun lighting up his face through the windows.

"Consider this my hat in the ring," he says, his voice low.

"Why?" I whisper.

"I can't stand the thought of you marrying some idiot," he says, and leans closer still, his breath warming my cheek. "It'd be bad for business."

This makes me crack a smile, and he follows suit. He moves to stand, but first presses a loud kiss on my cheek, just like Willa does.

"Are you staying for dinner?" I ask.

"Can't. But I will be here for the pool party. Gotta see what the fuss is about with this teacher."

"Ah." My mom's doing each year when it's finally warm enough outside to swim. I'd forgotten about the pool party, much like I'd been forgetting any social engagement for the last three weeks.

I flick my hand in a wave and he offers a mock salute before leaving me be in my office, the quiet and dust settling around me in his wake.

19

NATE

Despite what I've seen over the last weeks here, the Morelli family does in fact take breaks, usually in the form of a family gathering. This morning started with an "easy" training (easy being three miles on the treadmill and a full body lifting workout) and then we all dispersed to get ready for the first pool party of the year. It's tradition, a whole event celebrating their crystalline pool with bright blue tiles being warm, clean, treated sufficiently, and ready to jump into.

I am on the invite list, I think by merit of my being in the right place at the right time—namely a protected prisoner in their home.

Willa, Sean, and the twins show up for the fun along with a man I've never seen before who doesn't spare a glance in my direction, much less introduce himself. I slather sunscreen on myself while everyone greets one another.

"This is Cillian," Willa says to me. "My brother-in-law."

She pats said brother-in-law on his shoulder, and Cillian doesn't force a smile, he only looks me over like I'd been below his notice and he is now forcing himself to pretend he cares for propriety's sake. I'm not a short man, but I am still a few inches below his sight line.

I would hold out my hand for him to shake, but it's still greasy from the sunscreen, so I offer my fist instead. Like in another life we might be two bros playing basketball at the rec center.

"Nate. Nice to meet you."

He looks at my fist and commits the cardinal sin of leaving me hanging until I drop my arm back to my side. *Monster.*

"The teacher," he says with a generous amount of derision.

I know with a bone-deep certainty that Cillian is not fun at parties, not the guy you ask to help you move, not the person you want as your neighbor if you need a package brought in. He looks more ready for a yacht club than a backyard pool party. My swim trunks are almost a decade old, probably purchased at the same time I got my slides that squeak against the cement. Cillian wears a cream, silken button-up, unbuttoned enough to show the top of his tattooed chest and neck, and shorts that look nicer than my best slacks.

Just how can he make me feel woefully underdressed for a pool party? I didn't think you could mess that up, the only dress requirement is a swimming suit.

Basically, I hate him.

Artie, at least, is casual, though maybe I shouldn't take comfort in matching with a 12-year-old.

"Yep, I am a math teacher," I say, rubbing more sunscreen on my face. "Though you'll have to forgive me, your reputation doesn't precede you."

"Uncle Cillian, are you going to swim?" Angel yells while Artie uses all his lung capacity to blow up a floatie.

"No, Angel. Maybe next time," he says. I'm not convinced.

Cillian squints at me before shaking his head and walking away, not another word wasted on the likes of me.

Seriously, who needs a *gold watch* at a pool party?

Vanessa and Mary come outside then, Vanessa in a tight little wrap dress, Mary wearing all black, as is her way. Both have sunglasses perched on their noses and Vanessa pushes hers onto her forehead to give her niece and nephew kisses on their cheeks.

Cillian, I notice, offers his own cheek for her to kiss which she does without fare. Seeing them next to each other, Cillian looking down a great many inches to her perfect face, it dawns on me that *he* is the kind of man Vanessa is looking for. Huge forearms, tattoos swirling over his limbs and up onto his neck, a strong alpha male type. And if he's part of the family, he's already got the criminal thing going for him.

He is the kind of man that ends up with Vanessa Morelli, the kind who can protect and defend her, or at least fight alongside her.

He has the look.

But if he's so perfect, why isn't he on the list?

Next to me, Artie throws the mostly inflated floatie into the pool and dips his toe in the water, using my forearm for support. He hoots.

"Mr. G., it's so warm. ANGEL! Come feel the water!"

His little sister deposits her sketchpad and pencil bag and scurries over to do the same, using my other arm to steady herself while she splashes her foot in the pool. After being deemed sufficiently warm enough, she and her brother squeal. Being with his family, away from the assessing eyes of other 12-year-olds, has made Artie seem younger. It's heartwarming, I don't usually get to see students in their natural habitat with the people they like the most.

"Can we get in, Grandma?" Artie asks. Claire is already laid out on a chair, basking in the late morning sun.

"Yes, babies," she calls. Artie plunges into the pool without a second thought, soaking me and his sister immediately, to her delight. She's a little more timid, but I give her a thumbs up and she pencil dives in after him.

"Mr. G., Mr. G., you have to get in!" Artie hollers and who am I to deny this?

I toss the bottle of sunscreen onto my towel and jump in after them. I have been practicing my cannonball for many years, so the kids are amazed by the splash and their joy is more important than the milk-curdling glare Cillian sends my way for getting a teaspoon of pool water on him.

God forbid any water gets on his chino shorts.

Leo follows suit, then Sean, and eventually Willa, Vanessa, and Mary wade in, opting to chat in the shallow end of the pool. Cillian finds a chair and talks with Claire, never joining the fun, even when Claire leaves him to paddle some laps back and forth.

My arms are still completely wrecked from the week of grueling training with the Masochistic Morellis, but I launch Angel as many times as she asks and let Artie ride on my shoulders for a game he made up called Viking. I'm the horse; we charge his dad and Leo with pool noodles until they pretend to die, throwing themselves backward into the water and inevitably splashing their mother and aunts in the process.

It's the most fun I've had since getting here, and after a couple of hours, everyone is starving and sun kissed, despite Willa's liberal sunscreen application with her spray bottle on the whole family.

"Come eat!" Willa calls to her kids, who float on their backs, arms spread, eyes closed.

"Five more minutes," their dad says, and Willa allows it. And because she's nicer than either of her sisters, she chats with me while we make our plates.

"I think you're already getting stronger," she says. "You look strong."

I can't say that I look any different after four days of them kicking my ass, but I thank her anyway and take a seat next to her under the patio.

"You're good with kids. Is that why you're a teacher?" she asks.

"I like kids," I agree. "I wanted to get a PhD and teach college accounting, but I did a student teaching internship in my undergrad and loved it. Middle schoolers are hilarious and much smarter than I thought."

"They are funny," she agrees. We both look out at her twins, their ankles hooked together while they float on the surface of the water.

"Yours are sweet with each other," I say. Willa beams and absentmindedly puts a hand on her stomach.

"They are."

She calls to Sean to get the kids out of the pool for lunch, five minutes up, and they make their burgers with puddles of water pooling beneath their feet.

Vanessa hasn't put the wrap back on, instead sporting just her green bikini, and the sight of her skin is making my brain short-circuit.

I recognize that she is no longer a romantic possibility and will live a long life with a loving criminal, but she's still the hottest woman I think I have ever seen, in real life or on TV.

"You're staring," Mary says, plopping into the seat next to mine.

I clear my throat and take another bite of burger, but my eyes flick back to Vanessa, who now looks at me curiously. I nod in her direction, the first acknowledgment I've given her in hours, and she does the same before continuing her conversation with her mother.

* * *

SOMEWHERE AFTER MY thirtieth (a frugal estimate) piece of watermelon, the kids have dried off and changed, now asleep with messy damp hair on the couch as a Godzilla movie plays on the TV. I stand in the kitchen snacking on the fruit, everyone spread out either inside or out as the party winds down. It's strange to see them all not worrying about work, just a Saturday with nothing to do other than talk and swim and eat and relax. It's so very summer, and I find myself wanting to take a nap on the couch as well.

Jenna sent a bunch of photos of her travels thus far, many of which with the random strangers that she's made into friends on her way. I reply to each of them with more questions than I know she'll answer and ask her to please, pretty please, FaceTime me the next time she has a decent Wi-Fi connection. She says she will, but only if I promise to give her a virtual tour of the mansion and let her talk to Mary who she thinks sounds fun.

Not the word I would use.

"What is it you have on her?" A voice startles me from my texting. Cillian.

"Who?"

"Ness," he says, and I can't help but think the use of the nickname is calculated. A subtle brag. Very *I-have-an-intimacy-with-her-that-you-do-not.*

"It might be easier if I did have something on her." I snap the lid onto the fruit bowl and slip past him to put it in the fridge. "Just the wrong place, wrong time. One ill-advised date that ended in a shooting. I'm sure you get it."

"What I don't get is why she has a soft spot for you. Maybe it's her maternal instinct urging her to take care of something helpless and pathetic." Cillian doesn't pretend to say this flippantly, he is all eye contact and broad shoulders pulled back into perfect posture.

What the hell is this guy's deal?

"Are you this charming with everyone, or just with me?" I ask, but he ignores the question and leans closer to me.

"I don't trust you."

"Hm," I agree. "And just what do you think I can accomplish? As you pointed out earlier, I'm only a math teacher."

"A math teacher interviewing mobsters." He laughs. "Rich that anyone would believe you're a *consigliere*."

I grab a cup and pour some of the orange mango juice from the counter while I try to come up with a response to the bullshit this dude is going on about. I've never been one for macho posturing, but I'm starting to think I should practice comebacks for moments like this one.

Cillian puts a punishing hand on my shoulder. There must be a pressure point directly beneath his thumb because my shoulder involuntarily drops in response.

"Don't search too hard," Cillian says, and offers the most disgustingly handsome smile I've ever seen. His row of bottom teeth are perfect, and commercial-white. What a dick. "She'll come to her senses soon."

Speaking of the she-devil, Vanessa walks in through the back door, her sandals slapping against the tile floor.

Cillian takes the glass of juice from my hand and brings it to Vanessa.

"Thanks," she says, and takes a long sip. "Just what I wanted."

Cillian smiles and winks at me over her head.

I hate that fucking guy.

20

NATE

BECAUSE FIGHTING ISN'T ENOUGH, THEY WANT ME TO BE GOOD with guns. Vanessa swung by my room after morning training to tell me to get dressed to go out. Leo then drove us to a private, indoor shooting range where they unloaded five boxes of different guns on a table and handed me a pair of ear plugs and glasses.

"You don't get these in the real world," Vanessa says. "But hopefully in the real world you won't be shooting inside a concrete building."

Leo laughs in a way that tells me this scenario is more common than I would like to believe.

"Do you have a gun?" Leo asks and I don't mean to wince, but I do. I think my face has been in an uncomfortable grimace since we walked in the door.

Mary takes a bite out of an apple from where she perches on the counter. "Have you ever held a gun?"

"Yes." That's a lie. I've held many laser guns, but I don't think that's what they mean.

"You're a teacher, shouldn't you have one?" Leo asks.

"Now *that's* a hot button topic," Vanessa mutters, and before anyone can follow that thread, she holds a pistol out to me. It's black and smaller than I thought it would be. As to not look entirely horrified, I take the gun from her, my fingers ghosting across the back of her hand as I do.

It's heavier than I thought it would be. I don't even hover a finger over the trigger.

Vanessa holds up what I recognize from video games as a magazine and a box of bullets.

She jerks her head towards one of the bays and I follow her there holding the gun at my side. Is it illegal to walk with a gun out in front of you? Or is it more just common safety, like how you hand scissors to your neighbor in class? Wait, are there laws about gun safety that I need to know before shooting a gun?

"Here." Vanessa presses a few bullets into the magazine's sleeve and hands it to me to do the same. It looked easy when she did it, but it hurts my fingers as I try to push metal bullets into their metal case. She loads a second magazine while I finish mine.

"These are .22s." She holds up one of the little bullets. "They're not the best, but they're good to learn with. Could kill someone under the right circumstances."

I gulp and pluck the bullet from her hand to add it to my now-full case.

"Great. Now put in a magazine and load the gun."

She makes it sound so easy, and after a moment of messing with it, I guess it is. I have the clip in place and am working on pulling back the hammer when shots fire in the bay next to us making me jump. It's just Mary shooting a much larger handgun than the one I'm holding, with what looks like a very casual amount of focus on the target in her lane. Her shots slice the center of her paper to bits, nonetheless. Makes it look rather easy.

"This is the safety." Vanessa points to a little switch where my pointer finger can reach. I slide it down and then back up into place.

Vanessa turns away from me and messes with a couple of buttons on the stall's wall and suddenly a tall sheet of paper drops down ahead of us. It's a target with one big striped circle in the middle and four smaller ones at each corner.

"Shoot it," she says and steps back.

"But I don't—"

"Just try," she says.

I don't know anything about holding a gun aside from what I've seen in video games and movies, but I raise the gun shakily in front of me and take a big breath. There's nothing inherently scary about this thing. Other than the possibility of blowing up, or misfiring, or any number of possibilities my mind is readily supplying me with right now.

I don't know where to hold it, but I lift my arms and try to look down the top of the barrel to the target. My eyes have a hard time focusing and I might be going cross eyed, but before I can overthink it more, I pull the trigger.

Nothing happens.

"The safety," Vanessa says.

Right.

I flick the safety down again, return my arms to their position and pull the trigger before I can work myself up about it.

It's startling the way my wrist jerks backwards with the recoil on this little gun, and I gasp when a hot piece of metal hits my arm. I almost think I've been shot, but when I look down, my skin is unmarred, and I see a little metal case drop to the ground beside me.

"Very natural," Vanessa says. I hit the paper at least, but just barely. There's a hole in the white space surrounding the targets, not actually within one. "Now, what did you learn?"

Vanessa is no teacher, but I recognize the pedagogy of the exercise. *She's* the natural.

I swallow and look down at the thing. "I have to tighten my wrist more."

"Try that."

I do, locking my wrist so that upon pulling the trigger, it doesn't get jerked back as much. It works, marginally, and the bullet pierces the paper in the farthest ring of the big target. Not my intention, but at least it's in a target.

I look back at Vanessa for more instruction and she nods. A couple of bays down, Mary and Leo are firing round after round of shots at their targets. I understand why we need the ear plugs; it sounds like the thunder.

"Hold it up again."

I do as she says, holding the gun like I had the last two times and look out at the paper. I try not to jump when Vanessa comes up beside me, so close that her mouth is near my ear. Her hands come on my shoulders. "Relax these."

I inch them away from my ears and can't help but tighten my abs when her hand ghosts over the front of my shirt.

"Tighten here," she says. "And stand up straight."

I follow her directions, adjusting my stance and posture with every firm touch of her fingers on my body. She's so close that I can feel a hot breath on the bare skin of my neck.

I clear my throat.

"Good," she says. I've got goosebumps up my arms that I pray she cannot see.

"Now aim and shoot."

I take a deep breath, steadying myself, and then pull the trigger. It goes almost where I want it, much closer to the middle than my last attempts at least.

"Good. Empty both magazines, and then we'll move to the bigger guns."

Vanessa stalks off in her clopping heeled boots to Mary's bay, leaving me with my homework and the feeling of her hands lingering on my torso.

I blink away my lewd thoughts and raise the gun again.

* * *

I FEEL beyond strange in my new clothes, but I will not deny that I look. . . hot in them. A man measured my whole body a few days ago, and when we came back from the shooting range today, I had a whole new wardrobe filling half of the walk-in closet. Dress clothes, semi-formal, business casual, and even exercise options are hung up or laid out in the drawers. There are five pairs of new shoes, too, all which fit great and probably cost more than any shoes I have ever once owned.

In preparation for our first interviews, I put on a fitted gray button-up and pants that were hanging next to it. I thought maybe they were too small at first, but when I looked in the mirror, I realized that, no, this is just what clothes look like when they fit me.

I look like a new person.

There's a light knock on the door followed by Claire poking her head inside.

"That looks handsome," she says and comes in fully. She's much sweeter than her daughters. Mary, especially, bears little resemblance personality-wise.

Ranger circles at her feet until she picks him up and scratches his neck. Spoiled dog.

"Thanks," I say. "For all of it, I mean. The clothes, and the compliment."

"Thank the girls," Claire says. "They're the ones with the style."

I look in the mirror again and nod.

"The hairdresser is here," she says. "Come on down when you're ready. I'll have her cut Leo's first."

"Great, um, thank you."

It still feels wrong accepting all this treatment from them. First living in their huge house, now wearing hundreds of dollars' worth of clothes picked out just for me and getting in-house haircuts? I need to remind myself that I didn't choose this. It's not like I'm asking to be here and mooch off them, more like living in a house of criminals was somehow the safest of my choices.

Claire takes Ranger with her on her way out, leaving me alone in the room to assess myself in the mirror.

The hairdresser is a young woman named Anette who smacks gum and chatters with Claire and Mary about people I've never met. She pulled a stylist's chair from a closet I'd never peeked in and she leans it all the way back so she can wash my hair in the sink, talking all the while.

She then uses the pedal on the back of the chair to raise me up and down while she snips pieces of my hair seemingly by vibes only. Leo's hair looked good when I came downstairs, which is the only reason I'm not more concerned by her practices and lack of focus.

"You have good curls," she says. "You Jewish?"

"No. But thank you."

"Girlfriend?"

"No," I say.

"The dog is his, though," Mary says. Anette looks long at Ranger who's sleeping in the dog bed Claire bought him for downstairs. He's lightly snoring—it's not his fault, he's old.

"Cute dog. I'll cut his hair, too, if you want."

After twenty minutes of spritzing my head with a spray bottle, cutting the sides with an electric trimmer, snipping at the top, and snapping her gum, she gives me one last long look and nods. Various creams are applied, which all smell fantastic.

"Here." She hands me a handheld mirror and, maybe it's because I've only been to Great Clips for the last decade, but I didn't know that my hair could look like this. Smooth on the sides, not cut too short, and softer than it has ever, ever been. No frizz. I think this must be how Vanessa feels every morning when she wakes up perfect.

Leo walks back into the kitchen, where Anette, Mary, and I are still quiet, assessing my Steve Rogers level transformation. "Oh shit."

"I think I see it now," Mary says, squinting.

Anette spits her gum into the trash. "The dog next?"

* * *

THE STRANGEST OF all of the strange developments of late is that, somehow, Vanessa and I have fallen into a routine of watching movies together after everyone's gone to sleep. This came about the night of the pool party when, both of us not being able to sleep, gravitated to the leftovers in the fridge. She was already on the couch eating a piece of cake and, after a quiet moment, invited me to sit. Another action movie played on the TV.

We watched in relative silence, but when she said, "Same time tomorrow?" as casually as she might ask for my coffee order, I gave a dumbfounded yes.

We've had five of these movie nights now, and tonight I sit on the couch beneath a massive soft blanket, eating chopped watermelon from the same big bowl as Vanessa, each of us with our own fork. Her hair smells like coconut conditioner and we both have these lime green eye masks beneath our eyes.

I let the watermelon dissolve on my tongue as the action movie plays out on the screen.

"I like this one more than five," she says. "But eight is the best."

"I support your opinions, even though you've never been more wrong."

Vanessa laughs through her nose and drops her fork into the now empty bowl of red juice. I offer some of the popcorn, but she shakes her head.

Her cheeks and forehead are lightly pink from time spent in the sun on sites today, and with no makeup on, I can see that smattering of freckles I imagine will only get darker as the summer goes on.

I have an absurd urge to rub my thumb across them. I keep my hands to myself.

Vanessa pulls the extra blanket from beside me and drapes it over her lap, getting comfy. Action movies must be the great unifier because this time two weeks ago she could barely look at me and now we're sharing a blanket.

I've been here a month and I'm already getting complacent. Too comfortable.

"Have you figured out who's trying to kill you?" I ask, though I know the answer.

"Lots of people want to kill me," she says. "But no, if you're asking if it's safe to leave yet, it's not."

There's no use complaining about it, so I slouch down on the couch and lean back. "At least your sister has cool kids for me to hang out with."

"They are cool," she agrees. Her eyes are slightly closed but she cracks them to say the next part. "I think my godson is obsessed with you."

"That's because I taught him the joy of fractions and PEMDAS this year."

"Ah, PEMDAS."

"By the way, your brother-in-law is a total dick bag," I say, then rush to clarify: "Cillian, not Sean."

Vanessa snorts. "A dick bag, you say."

I throw a piece of popcorn at her, and she laughs louder.

"He *is*. Told me he thinks I have bad intentions."

"And do you?" Her head is tipped back on the throw pillow as she speaks, her dark brown hair tucked into a braid on her shoulder.

"Yes, I'm thinking about taking what I've learned and starting my own mafia. I would invite you, but I think it should just be teachers."

"Bummer," she says with a click of her tongue. "Well, that's just Cillian. He's protective, is all."

She looks beyond sleepy, so I don't try to press my point that the guy has weird vibes and, further, is probably into her.

Her eyes slip shut again and after a couple of minutes, I feel her toes wedge beneath my leg.

"Do you want to lay out?" I ask, ready to move, but she's already asleep.

NATE

I WAS UNDER THE IMPRESSION, FOR SOME REASON, THAT THE MAFIA was run by very few people.

As it turns out, everyone has a godson, brother, cousin, nephew, or a guy-who-goes-way-back. Everyone in Vanessa's circle has three men (minimum) for her to consider, and it's my job to do that considering.

I've been at it for two weeks.

They know me now—consigliere for the Morelli family is apparently no title to be trifled with because after an assessing stare, the men usually lean back and talk to me like I'm an equal. The real consigliere is Willa, and if not Willa, then Leo, and if not Leo, then Mary. I am many, many degrees separated from the actual position, but these men don't need to know this.

I'm starting to get my footing as I get to know the types of men on this list. Vanessa and I sort them into three categories: goon, obedient soldier, or *capo* material. Goons are most common, they're stupid or they're violent or they are stupidly violent. Capos are harder to come by, because they must both recognize power and know how to use it. Middle managers, basically.

Vanessa says she wouldn't entirely mind a stupid guy so long as I think he could be useful and loyal to her in the long run. He can be stupid but not corruptible, violent but only when he needs to be, a good fighter but not someone that will want to *fight her*. Arguing is okay, but ultimately his pride cannot be so large that he would undermine her decisions. An underlying tenderness would be appreciated.

"How the fuck am I supposed to know if a man is secretly a sweetheart?" I asked after my first days of interviews.

She shrugged. "Use your judgment."

So, along with my list of questions, I started giving the men increasingly detailed scenarios and thought experiments to get their minds working. I've also considered DNA tests, because now she wants to know if they have good genetics—if their kid would be a fighter.

Leo joins me for every interview, either sitting at the table or standing somewhere nearby. Sometimes, when he knows the man, he shakes his head when they lie about one of the questions. I underestimated how helpful having him with me would be.

"How many men have you killed?" I asked one man (the first Tony of the week) hoping to give him pause, but he just squinted off, puffed on his cigar. He was no less than twenty years older than Vanessa, a small forest of gray nose hairs visible over his mustache.

"How many I've killed or how many I've *had* killed?" he asked.

I put a mark in the Capo category and moved on to the next question.

The next day, I *started* my interviews with the scenarios: "You and Vanessa go to the opera…"

"What is at the opera?" the new, much younger man asked. He was fresh from the motherland which was a mark in his favor. "I would never do that."

"Yes, well Vanessa asks you to go—"

"I tell her no," he said. "We stay home and make love instead."

"No," I said, "you've got a daughter."

"Oh, you're mistaken. I don't."

"No, I mean imagine," I said. "You've got a daughter, and she wants to go to the opera. It's her birthday."

He considered this more carefully and nodded. "We'll go for her birthday."

"But when you leave the opera, a homeless man approaches you—"

"Is he strong?"

"What?" I asked. Leo turned to me with a tilted head like this was a reasonable inquiry.

"Is the man strong?" the candidate repeated.

I blinked. "Yes, he's double your size, and he's got a gun—"

"I offer him job," he said before I could get to the part where the homeless man in the situation threatens them with said gun. I took note of this, marking "interrupting" in the cons list, but "enterprising" and "virile" in the pros column.

Later that day, we met a man in his office (a morgue—he is a mortician, to be clear). "Say you're approached by another woman, not Vanessa," I began, "and she propositions you."

He thought before answering, a trait which most of the men do not have.

"Is she Italian?" he asked.

"No?" I looked to Leo for help.

"She's Polish," Leo supplied.

The mortician was quiet in his white lab coat, hands held in his lab waiting for me to go on, but that was it, that was the whole scenario.

"Do you sleep with her?" I asked.

His lips drew back over his teeth in some semblance of displeasure, and I was about to pen "loyal" in the pros column when he spoke:

"Of course I have sex with her," he said and smiled. Oh, because he and I? We were in on a little boy's club truth, apparently. Most of them act like this, like because I am a man, I must speak their misogynistic crime language.

His face fell serious. "I do wear a condom, of course."

"Of course," I agreed, and drew a line directly through his name.

Some of the interviews are short. I get what I need very quickly, no blood work required. The last one of today, for instance; we sat down, and after a few pleasantries I dove right in.

"Imagine that you have a young daughter—"

"Only sons," he said, and I crossed his name right off the list.

Overall, the men fail.

"These guys suck," I say now, and throw the files on Vanessa's desk. She thumbs through looking over the notes I'd written for each. "Are they all like this?"

"Yes," Mary says before taking a huge bite out of an apple. "All of them."

"If they're not rude, they've got this fragile masculinity, and if not both of those things, they seem like bloodthirsty creatures, barely human!" I drop into one of the chairs across from Vanessa's desk with a huff.

"Oh, don't be dramatic." Willa files her nails as she leans against the windowsill. "Ness is much more bloodthirsty than them."

"Not a single redeeming quality for any of them today? Think hard," Vanessa asks, and I shake my head, grim.

"Maybe if you were interviewing for an aggressive flag football team, but otherwise no," I say. "Although multiple wanted you to know that they carry a Colt .45."

"They're researching," Willa says. "How sweet."

"Our dad's gun of choice," Vanessa explains. "How many have you met this week?"

"Thirteen," I say. I lean further into the chair, my head now lulled onto the seat back. "I'd fire them if I was you, honestly. Don't get within ten feet of any of them."

"This isn't helpful." Vanessa holds the back of her neck for a moment before shutting the file folder and pushing it away from her. "The moms are antsy. They want me to date these men like I'm the fucking bachelor."

"Bachelorette," Willa corrects.

"Does that make Nate your Jesse Palmer?" Leo asks.

Mary and Vanessa speak at the same time: "Who?"

"Maybe Nate's standards are too high," Willa says, then points her nail file at me. "You can't rule them out just because they've killed a few men."

"Vanessa's the one who told me that a likelihood of hidden tenderness was a requirement! And at what point does the number of men they've killed become too many?!"

Everyone in the room gives my question serious thought—though the obvious answer is not much higher than one, right?

"Number doesn't matter if they have a good reason," Mary says.

I can only blink in response. She's just like them. If I was interviewing Mary, I would cross her name off the list right now.

Vanessa pushes up from her desk and takes a moment to straighten her skirt and smooth her already perfect ponytail; the picture of composure. "I don't have time to think about this today. We have visits to make."

I don't know what takes place on their weekly visits, but I hear through the wall that Mary always takes a shower immediately afterwards, probably to wash cold blood off her hands. I might guess visits equals murder, poisonings, torture, etc. but I am open to the idea that it's something much more civilized.

"Pick two of them and invite them to dinner on Monday. Call it a follow-up," Vanessa says. "I don't care who. Rumors will spread that I'm considering and that will appease them."

I wouldn't let any two of these men into my home, but I nod anyway and give her a thumbs up. "You got it, captain."

22

VANESSA

THE KIDS COME OVER MOST SATURDAY NIGHTS FOR A SLEEPOVER because it doesn't matter how many years they've been married; Sean and Willa still go on weekly dates and then probably have sex loud enough to wake their neighbors. They are as in love as they've been since high school.

Usually the kids come over for movies, ice cream, crafts with their grandma, video games with Mary—there's never a shortage of family members to entertain them, but tonight in a strange sequence of events, the kids are left with just Nate and myself.

Mary is God knows where doing whatever it is she does when she sneaks out on the weekends, Mom is out with a few of The Mothers, and Leo is making his appearances at our gambling establishments.

And Nate, well, Nate doesn't leave.

I didn't want him to assume he had to entertain two 12-year-olds on his Saturday night (not that he is one to have plans), but Artie beelined upstairs and knocked on Nate's bedroom door before I could tell him otherwise.

Angel doesn't even have her shoes all the way off before Nate and Artie are ambling down the stairs, talking about the Switch game Artie brought for them to play tonight.

"Auntie." Angel grabs onto my forearm and lowers her voice. "My stomach is feeling weird."

"I'm sorry, baby." I pull her under my arm for a hug. Nate and Artie walk past towards the living room. "Have you eaten? Let's get you something."

I poke around the fridge and find a Tupperware of Mom's bean soup that she made yesterday while Angel fills me in on the slumber party she went to the night before.

"Will you ask Mom again if I can get a phone?" Angel asks, her head resting on her arms on the counter.

"Yeah! Will you?" Artie yells from the living room.

"You have a phone," I remind them, and they both sigh with different levels of dramatics. The two share a flip phone that can call and send texts.

"But we can't have apps," she says.

I ladle enough soup for the four of us into a pot.

"You have an iPad, though," I point out. The twins also share that, and there are screen time limitations. Willa is better about all that childhood development and parenting stuff than I imagine I would be.

Personally, I love screen time. I get it. This is why I am meant to be an aunt and not a mother.

I nod toward the living room. "And then there's the Switch. You're swimming in technology, miss."

"I do love my Switch," she says, and looks off in her dreamer stare.

She looks so much like Willa with her plump pink cheeks and light soft hair that her mom braids into various complicated styles. Today, it's in a simple braid that's tucked under her over-sized tie-dye fleece hoodie. Willa has always loved dress up and that extends to her kids, but she lets them wear the bright-colored, tacky pieces that are rite of passage for little kids. I love that about my sister.

Nate comes into the kitchen with his dog jingling in behind him as I'm serving soup into four bowls; he leans a hand on the counter next to me. I'm getting used to having to look up to meet his eyes at night. The dog circles a few times before dropping into the bed that now lives in the kitchen despite my protests.

Nobody listens to me in this house.

"Do you have any Tums?" he asks in a quiet voice. "Artie's not feeling great."

"What's wrong with him?"

Nate shrugs. "Maybe he's constipated, I don't know. Kids have stomach issues all the time."

He's so good with the kids, always confident when he talks with them, like they aren't the most delicate of creatures.

"Angel, too. There's a medicine cabinet in the bathroom down the hall. Check there."

"Got it," he says and strides out of the kitchen.

Angel is still sitting at the counter with her head resting on her forearms and when I rub circles on her back, she turns to look up at me. She's pale, the pink of her cheeks turned to red splotches and a slight sheen on her skin.

"Oh, sweetie, you really aren't feeling good, are you?"

Her lower lip wobbles and I know she's going to start crying.

"No," she says, and her voice cracks. I pull her in for a hug and her little body shaking goes tense and still. There may be something behind what people say about a woman's intuition, because I know in an indescribable way that she is about to vomit and move into action, grabbing the nearest receptacle (in our case, the now-empty glass Tupperware the soup was in) and sliding it in front of her. The dog, maybe sensing danger, vacates his bed and the kitchen.

She does vomit, retching into the bowl.

"Nate?" I call loud enough that he'll hear from down the hall.

He rushes back into the kitchen, plastic bottle of Tums rattling in his hand.

He sees my niece groaning over her bowl at the counter and doesn't even pause before retrieving two mixing bowls from the cabinet to the left of the fridge. He hands one to me and practically sprints into the living room with the other to help Artie with what feels inevitable. Even in my distress, I'm a little surprised that he knew not only exactly what was needed, but right where to find it. Has he been here for a month already? Is that all it takes? Only 25 days to learn someone's kitchen and how to help them in crisis?

"I'm sorry, Auntie," Angel says after breathing heavily over the bowl for a few moments, the heaving temporarily abated.

"Don't be sorry, sweetie." I take out two bobby pins from my hair and secure her bangs behind her ears before I hand her the fresh bowl. "Hold this right beneath your face, I'm going to take you to the bathroom so you can throw up there, okay?"

"Okay," she says, the most defeated, miserable agreement in history, and her tears have welled and flowed over her eyelids. We are walking delicately to the bathroom down the hall when I hear Artie retch from inside.

Angel, hearing this, starts crying harder and almost throws up again. There are two bathrooms downstairs, so I steer her towards the other one on the other side of the house, walking faster until we are kneeling in front of the toilet where she heaves again.

This goes on, Angel throwing up until her stomach is empty, and then throwing up more bile until she's thoroughly exhausted and cannot throw anything more up because there is nothing more to expel. At this point, we sit with our backs against the floral wallpapered wall, Angel leaning against my chest with the bowl cradled in her arms.

Nate pads down the hall in his socks, and for reasons unknown, no shirt.

Reading my expression, he explains, "The shirt was a casualty to the stomach bug. I rinsed most of it off, though."

I wince. "Sorry to hear that."

"Artie's taking a shower upstairs, and I think I've cleaned up the bulk of the. . . material in the kitchen."

"You didn't have to clean that," I say. If it smelled anything like the rest of it, it was probably heinous.

"How are you feeling, Miss Angel?" he asks, ignoring what I just said. Angel gives a weak thumbs up, not opening her heavy eyes. "How can I help?" he mouths.

I look down at Angel, so sweet and exhausted. She needs a shower and clean pajamas and then to sleep this off. Her brother, too, it sounds like.

"I'll get her upstairs and cleaned up, you get fresh bowls and put the big throw blanket in the dryer."

"The one on the couch?" he asks, and I nod. "On it."

Nate pads away without another question, off to move through the house like he's lived here forever.

"Nate's nice," Angel murmurs. "I like his dog."

I kiss her head. "Let's get you upstairs, little."

* * *

AFTER SHOWERING, brushing their teeth, and making them drink as much Gatorade as they could without throwing up more, it takes nothing for the kids to fall asleep on half of my bed. They lie close together, Artie's head pressed against his sister's shoulder, her ankle on top of one of his. It reminds me of when they were babies. They always napped together, cuddled up like nothing could be more natural or comforting.

I run my fingers through Artie's damp hair and my heart constricts like a fist is reaching into my chest cavity and squeezing at how much I love them.

My door pushes open slowly and Nate pokes his head

through the crack of the door. Seeing the kids asleep, he steps inside quietly with the soft throw blanket overflowing in his arms. He lays it over them and it's big enough to stretch over me as well. The heat of the blanket fresh from the dryer warms my pajamas and seeps into my skin.

He leaves the room without saying anything, and I find myself disappointed that he didn't want to stay. On a normal night, we'd be watching a movie together downstairs or laughing about the things he heard in his interviews that day.

Maybe it's all too cozy for him, he doesn't want to be friendly with a monster.

I hear his steps up the stairs with the jingling of Ranger's collar following behind. The noises of the dog used to grate my nerves, but there's something familiar about them now. A constant reminder of the heartbeat of the house, so many of us living inside.

I'm about to sink further into bed and try to rest when Nate is back in my doorway, this time holding a tray with two mugs.

"I brought tea," he says.

He's never been in my bedroom before today, but he makes himself right at home, moving stuff on my nightstand so that he can set down the tray and waiving his hand so that I scooch over towards the kids making room for him to sit. He pulls the blanket over his legs as he sits beside me with his back against the soft headboard.

His hair is wet, little drops of water on his neck and the collar of his sweatshirt, and I watch the damp skin on his neck as he situates himself.

"Here," he says. My eyes move first to his face, then down to the mug he's holding out to me. I take it and decide that the best thing to look at is the steam that floats off the top. I'm not thirsty, but I love the hot cup in my palms.

"Thank you."

"You know, every day it gets less glamorous to be you than I thought," Nate says.

"Maybe being an aunt isn't glamorous," I say. "But otherwise, being me is pretty deluxe."

He gives me a wry look like he sees right through that and then burns his tongue on his tea. We both laugh, but quietly, to not wake the little ones.

"They adore you," Nate says, looking at the drooling kids. They both wear old college shirts of mine, and beneath them, their chests rise and fall as they sleep. Artie makes tiny snoring sounds.

"I was so young when Willa had them, and she was so young, I had no clue what they would be like. But Willa wasn't afraid. She was so confident, so in love."

"And you?"

"I was seventeen. I didn't know anything about babies, and Willa was so sure it would work out. She was going to have the kids and raise them and be the best mom and go to law school, and to her credit, she's done all those things."

Angel shifts, and her head burrows against my side, the same way she did when she was a baby. There were two months where she'd only sleep if she was in someone's arms or pressed right against her brother. I remember being so petrified of breaking them when they were that small.

"Do you want kids?"

"In the abstract, yes," I say. "This legacy won't die with me."

This legacy being the family, the responsibility, the business. If we weren't in the position we are, none of them would be safe.

Ours isn't just a life you can get out of, it's a generational curse, or blessing, I'm not sure, but as my father always used to say, *it is what it is.* Nothing else to it.

"I'll have a kid, or more than one, and God willing they'll like each other and lean on each other, and then one of them will take over when I'm gone."

"What about one of these two?" Nate asks.

"They're kids," I say.

I can't explain that it makes me ill to imagine either of them where I am, having to do the things I've done. The things any of us have done. None of our hands are clean but the children's.

"They're just kids." I say again.

It's code for I love them too much to think about their hearts, big as the sky, turning cold and hardened.

"And yours won't be?"

"No, it's just—Angel and Artie are too good. It's something within them, Willa and Sean are so loving, so tender with them. If it's a matter of nature, I can't imagine my kids will be so. . . sweet."

Nate is quiet for a long moment, digesting this I think, or maybe agreeing that my children would be callous little devils.

"I think you'll be a good mom," Nate says. "With Claire and your sisters around, it'd be hard not to be."

We both lean our heads back against the fabric headboard and I let my eyes flutter shut.

"I do have good sisters," I agree.

"Well, one good sister," Nate murmurs. "Mary might scare the baby."

We huff matching laughs through our noses, and I sink a little farther into the bed, into the night, into the quiet warmth of this moment.

"What about you? I bet you want four." I can already imagine his kids—frizzy hair and long limbs, and uncoordinated but curious, and smart; probably just perfect.

"Maybe," he says. "I was an only child and I've always wanted a sibling. I'll teach them things like fractions and card games, and my mom will spoil them rotten."

I crack my eyes open to look at him. His face is close enough that I can count freckles across his cheeks and the high point of his nose. A very good nose.

He will be a good dad. His kids will have green eyes and they will be too-smart, tiny know-it-alls. He's made for a quiet, safe life, with a quiet, safe partner.

"Lucky kids," I blink my eyes closed again and sigh. Nate plucks my mug out of my hands and puts it on the side table and in my drifting state I know he's about to leave.

"Stay," I say, and then, because he looks struck dumb by the request, I add, "They might be sick again."

He doesn't disagree. There's nothing left for them to throw up, surely, and even if there was, I could handle it on my own. I can handle any number of things on my own, but I didn't realize how nice it is, sometimes, to have someone whose job is to handle things with you.

He settles back down beside me, our sides pressed together, and I follow the kids to sleep.

23

VANESSA

James and Ryan Sinclair.

When I said I didn't care which marriage candidates he invited to dinner, Nate invited James Fucking Sinclair and his rat shit little brother Ryan, and of course because they're a family of bottom feeders, Ronaldo had to join, and he had to bring his wife to snoop around and make passive aggressive comments regarding my childless status.

I've been lucky enough to not see Ronaldo for the last two months since I all but banished him from my front room for trying to pawn his nephew on us, and by some cursed luck, Nate chose James and Ryan to interview first and thought that they were the most reasonable candidates to have for a follow-up dinner.

They're getting settled at the patio table outside for some appetizers and I must pretend to be pleased about this. Nate stands with his hands in his pockets none the wiser to what he's just done. It doesn't matter if we've been friendly of late, doesn't matter that he cleaned my nephew's vomit off his clothes this weekend—he's a little goblin man parading as a consigliere in nice clothes with big shoulders and he's been letting this beard grow in a way that looks suspiciously handsome, and *he's invited my least favorite people into my house.*

I look at him until I catch his eye and then incline my head towards the kitchen. Once he meanders in behind me, hands still in those damn pockets, I push him not gently into the pantry, the automatic light clicking on over our heads.

"Get your hands out of your pockets, you look stupid," I say. He does as I say, looking wounded, and I would consider telling him I didn't mean it if I wasn't so angry. "What the hell are they doing here?"

"You said to invite someone for dinner," he says. "Two people. I invited two people."

"What made you choose them?!"

"I didn't have a lot of great options, Vanessa, it was them, the creepy mortician or the man old enough to be your father!" Nate whisper shouts. "How was I supposed to know you hated them more than the others?"

"Maybe by the way I'd drawn violent X's next to their names?"

"The one with the beard seems harmless, just stupid. I thought you were fine with stupid!"

He's right. Ryan Sinclair is stupid, but he's also a Sinclair and I would rather put needles into my toes than have anyone think I'm considering him or his brother as a romantic possibility.

God, Ronaldo must feel so smug about this!

The pantry door swings open revealing my mother, who's got fury in her eyes. It makes me stand up straighter; it doesn't matter how old I am, that expression and *Vanessa Gloriana Morelli* on the tip of her tongue still terrifies me.

"Is there a reason you are hiding from our guests?" she asks.

"I—"

"No," Mom cuts me off. "Yell at each other later. Get out there. Now."

She transforms her face into a syrupy sweet hostess smile

before leaving us with all the dry goods. Her word is law, though, and I follow her out without question.

"Oh, it all makes sense," Nate mutters near my ear. "I thought you must take after your dad, but I get it now. Your *mom* made you scary."

I elbow him in the side, and plaster on my own smile at his grunt before joining everyone outside.

"Forgive me," I say. "Work doesn't break, even for brioche."

"And what a delicious looking brioche it is," Nate says, sliding into the seat next to my mother. "Claire outdid herself with this batch."

"You made this yourself?" Ronaldo's wife (Lisa) says, wary.

Bitch.

To be certain, my mother did not make that bread, but Lisa is a guest in our home and should outwardly believe all self-aggrandizing lies.

"Of course she did," I say.

"Well, then you'll have to share the recipe at our next book club, Claire," Lisa says.

"Alas," I suck my teeth. "It's the kind of recipe that isn't written, more just felt. Muscle memory. Very difficult to recreate."

I dip a slice of said bread into an oil vinegar mix. The bread and oil were most definitely made by Leo (his favorite hobby is baking artisan breads) but he'd let my mom take credit for anything if it was at the expense of Lisa Sinclair.

"Thank you for joining us," I address the table before she can push more about the bread.

"Always a delight to have the Sinclairs for dinner," Mom says. Bless her, she sounds genuine.

"Nathaniel here is a good addition to your team. He's sharp," Ronaldo says, crumbs hanging off his mustache.

Someone who sees sense, he means. A man who sees the worth of his idiot nephews. I turn to look at them instead of justifying that a response. James's floral shirt is unbuttoned almost to his bellybutton, a spare patch of chest hair poking out. I can smell his cologne all the way down the table. Ryan's beard is too solid, I know he uses makeup to fill it in. I have no problem with men wearing makeup, but Ryan has annoyed me since eighth grade, he could be delivering aid to war-torn countries and I would still be annoyed.

"Long time no see, Mary," James says. "You hit a growth spurt yet?"

Brave, considering Mary could kill either of them in more ways than any of us could fathom.

"Are you any less of a disappointment to your mother yet?" Mary shoots back and then, with as sweet of a smile as she's able, she says, "I hear she's quite enjoying her *travels*."

James and Ryan both scowl at this. Their mom and dad left the country to avoid arrest for tax evasion and the talk is that they're enjoying their time and frequently visiting swinger resorts. The real pride of our community.

"Leo, Mary, why don't you help me grab the food?" Mom says. Leo's chair scratches against the floor as he rushes to vacate the table. Mary follows, her chunky high-heeled boots thumping against the concrete. I hope they know that 5' 4" or not, she could (and would) crush their throats in those shoes.

A beat of silence hangs in the air while we wait, one that Willa would fill with ease if she was here. She's with her walking group again, the new generation of Mothers much like our own mom and Lisa's cohort.

"Ryan, how are you liking your new job?" I ask.

"It's great," he says. "NFTs are so much more than we thought at first, really the future of everything. Not just monkey illustrations. Real ground level shit. You'll see. Still waiting for you to come visit me."

As if I have any need for dick head investments. Last thing I need.

"I'll have my accountants look into it," I lie. "Or, you know what, Nate's background is in finance, maybe I'll send him to talk shop."

Nate shoots me a look like he would very much *not* like to talk shop with him. He's saved from this when Mom, Leo, and Mary exit holding platters of greens, seared chicken, and white wine pasta.

A meal this good should never be wasted on bad company.

There's peace and murmurs of delight at the food, and for about six minutes, I think we just might be able to get through dinner without more incident, but then Ronaldo must speak.

"How is the Washington Street building going?" Ronaldo asks.

It's a trick question. He knows how it is: horrible.

"Moving right along," I say after taking a sip of water. No wine tonight, I need all my faculties to deal with them without shooting someone.

"Nice to hear after so many setbacks," Lisa says.

The Washington Street development was hit hard by unforeseen circumstances with the site, first asbestos in the demolition, and then a hundred grand later, the prospectors discovered a water deposit. Amid dealing with this, one of our employees unearthed human remains on the property. The bones were a century old and not our fault, but they became our problem when we had to comply with a three-week investigation. Any one of these issues would be a setback, but all three? Logistical nightmare.

"All in a day's work for construction. It teaches us to be agile," I say. Please let that be the end of it, please let that—

"Agile? Or too precious," Ronaldo says. Mary goes still next to me; I would guess she's thinking of how she might kill him right now just to get it over with.

"How do you mean?" Nate asks.

The rest of us know exactly how he means.

"Well, you know how it is for some. Wanting everything to be perfect," Ronaldo says. He means women. "In this business, not everything needs to be exactly by the book."

"It's all about getting a faster return on investment," Ryan says.

"Exactly." Ronaldo sounds like a proud uncle as at least someone sees some sense. "Doesn't look good for the company when things don't move on a schedule."

"Looks worse if the building crumbles later due to shoddy craftsmanship and cut corners." I manage to say this with a semblance of a smile, my lips upturned at least. He wants a reaction from me, wants me to feel like an emotional woman to make a point to his nephews that he is stronger, smarter, more composed than the person who makes it possible for him to have food on his table.

"What does the project need to be perfect for?" Ronaldo asks, then turns to James at his left. "Women, see, victims to perfectionism."

I fill my lungs with air as not to react. Their whole family gets on my last nerve, but some of the old heads do listen to him.

There are politics at play here, different from the ones my dad had to deal with, but he prepared me for that. Prepared me to hold my tongue when I need to and retaliate in quiet. But, once again, I really, really wish he was here.

I've not once let myself be a victim—to do so would be a victory to the men who'd like me to be weaker than them.

"Better projects beget more, bigger projects. And bigger projects line your pockets, Ronaldo. Those projects let you build your wife your beautiful home and send your nephews to college," I say. I'm pleasant, but there is a warning there. "Reputation is not something I take lightly."

"I'm just saying that perhaps you wouldn't be having loyalty troubles if you moved faster."

Lisa puts down her fork with a loud clack and it's the only sound that fills the balloon of silence since he spoke. Both of his nephews shift in their seats, stupid, but never stupid enough to talk to me the way this man has. I hurt his ego two months ago and he's not one to let that go.

"It would take a fool to willfully ignore the results of her attention to detail," Nate says, surprising us all. Ronaldo's eyes snap to him. "Sure, there's short term returns, but the year-over-year ROI is astounding and has seen exponential growth with Vanessa at the helm. Maybe a little care for detail was needed to push the company to the next level."

I don't know how Nate knows what he does about our financials, maybe he's searched into our public record and tax filing, but he's right. Things have grown, and my sisters and I have made that happen.

"And the family has never been bigger, *Uncle*," Mary says, though the title sounds more like a poison than a display of respect.

"I didn't realize you were questioning your own loyalty," I say and purse my lips.

"I didn't say that—"

My mother cuts him off. "I thought you must be happy! What, with your new cars and helping pay the down payment on little Ryan's house. Such a good boy he is, too. But if you believe you could do better, Vanessa would love to hear it, I'm sure."

The look on his face is priceless. He's been caught now; it would be impossible for him to pretend any respect for me after saying in no unclear terms that I wasn't up for the job. But what did he think was going to happen?

Everyone is quiet waiting for his response. After a moment he lowers his head. His old, bitter face is flushed red, frown lines on full display.

"Ronaldo, I must be clear," I wait until his eyes meet mine to continue, "this is the second time in as many months you have come into my home with derision and disrespect. My father was fond of you, and because of this, we tolerate you. But you know full well that if he was here, watching you disrespect his legacy, in the home he built with his own hands, he would shoot you where you sit. Uncle." I add this last part as a reminder. He is where he is because I allow him to be.

"Of course. Apologies," Ronaldo says. Lisa lets out the breath she was holding and Mom smiles into her drink. Nate and my eyes meet, and he tips his head.

I pick up my fork and knife. "James." I take on my friendly tone once again. "Tell us about your new car."

24

VANESSA

I'M MOISTURIZED, TEETH FLOSSED, IN MY PAJAMAS AND ALMOST ready to drift into the only place where nobody bothers me when my phone shrills. Mary. I sit up in bed to answer it.

"What happened?" I ask.

"Lockdown shit." Mary sighs, code for something we don't usually deal with but now have come to deal with. "Miller warehouse. Get down here."

I dress quickly in black slacks, a turtleneck, and heeled boots. I don't have time to put on makeup, but I swipe red lipstick on before going downstairs where Leo is already in the garage waiting for me.

"What do we know?" I ask as he drives us out of the estate and towards the warehouse on Miller.

"Mary and I got the alert that cameras went down, and she rushed over. By the time she got there, a bunch of shit was stolen. Five bodies. Slit throats."

"Garza?" I ask. That fucking cartel has been salty with us since we gained the mayor's favor last fall, but our relationship has been cordial enough. A room of slit throats is their calling card, though.

"Or someone who wants us to think it was the Garzas. What would they need with enough explosives to bring down a shopping mall? They never hurt for weapons." Leo blows through one empty red light and then another.

"Dabbling in domestic terrorism?" I ask, sarcasm hiding the way the thought roils my stomach. "Did you call your guy?"

"Not yet. Wanted to get a good look first." Leo's grip tightens on the steering wheel, and we drive in silence for a few minutes.

Of all my family members, Leo is the chummiest with other crime families. He's easy to get along with and has a lot of friends, Santiago Garza being the closest of these. It doesn't hurt that Santi is the youngest brother of the head of the Garza Cartel. Something has been going on between Leo and Santi for years, but Leo assures me it's nothing serious.

There's a reason Leo doesn't date, and I have a feeling it has less to do with his busy schedule and more to do with that youngest Garza boy.

I've expressed my support if he wants to date a man—though, I'm sure the old heads would *really* have something to say about this—and offered to talk about his dating woes, but he won't budge on the topic. Until he does, it's none of my business.

When we arrive, Mary and Willa's cars are already parked in the lot.

It's more of a sideshow than I expected, and I breathe steadily through my nose, as to not get queasy at the sight. There's blood everywhere, splattered on the walls, pooled on the floor, and marring tipped over shelves of product. We don't usually have to be at big scenes like this, where the vile parts of our work are so blatantly on display in front of us. It's nauseating.

Willa stands with a clipboard scribbling notes as she counts product and Mary has dragged each of the dead bodies into a bloody row in the middle of the warehouse. Five of our men.

They were killed in various ways, bullet wounds, blunt force, but all were given the same slit-throat treatment afterwards.

"It's not the Garza's handiwork," Mary mutters when I crouch down to look closer. "Too jagged."

I look over my shoulder to where Leo is waiting, his fists clenched at his sides, and nod. He was right.

He relaxes barely before retreating to make a call.

"What did they take?" I call to Willa. She's in a matching bright pink sweatsuit, JUICY across her ass, and her hair is pushed out of her face with a big cloth headband. I'd guess she was doing her skincare routine when she got the call.

"The rest of the little bombs. A couple of the big. Cameras, too, and some sensors." Willa consults her clipboard. "Any guesses why they would need so much security equipment?"

"Probably to resell it," a male voice responds from the back-door. We all turn to see Cillian who is already rolling up his sleeves as he approaches. "Garzas aren't smart enough to know how to use them."

He hadn't heard Mary's verdict. I wonder if he'll see right away what Mary has, the shoddy craftsmanship of the copycats.

"You sound racist again," Mary calls out.

Cillian holds his middle finger up in Mary's direction. "This has nothing to do with race. The Garzas could be Irish and I'd still think they were stupid."

He stops at my side and tsks as he looks down at the bodies. It's four from the Morellis and one of his. The Donovanns don't usually work warehouse shifts, it's unfortunate that there had to be deaths from both of our families tonight.

"Fucking Garzas." He spits the name. "Nothing but trash on the city's streets."

I meet Mary's eyes, both of us noting his lack of notice. Cillian needs little prompting to go off about the Garzas—he hates them as much as his father did and is a total prick when it comes to them.

The Garzas have a say in most drug movement in this city and they expand to other states too. It's a big fish operation, and Cillian hates to think there are fish bigger than him.

"What are you wearing?" Cillian asks Mary, who glares at him. I hadn't noticed her black mini skirt and cropped tank. And her hair is down instead of pinned or braided out of her face like it typically is. She looks hot. Is this how she goes out when she sneaks out at night? "You have a date or something?"

"None of your business, asshole." Mary flips Cillian off before stomping off to follow Willa around the warehouse as she counts materials.

"What I love most about Mary is her charm," Cillian says. He crouches down next to one of his men and does the sign of the cross. The corpse is a young guy, probably in his early twenties. I can't remember his name.

"When do we attack, then?" Cillian asks.

"We don't," I say. He stands too quickly to his feet, a whole head taller than me, and I already know he's about to fight me. "Listen, we have no proof, and now is not the time to start a turf war."

"What more proof do you need?" Cillian waves an arm at the bodies.

"It wasn't them," Leo says, reentering from the office. Cillian puffs up his chest and fumes, ready to tell my cousin just how wrong he is.

I place a hand on Cillian's forearm. "Look at the cuts."

Cillian closes his mouth and does as I say, walking in a circle around the men. His eyes turn to slits as he glares down at them.

"A hack job," Cillian agrees.

At his side, I see his thumb playing with one of his rings, circling the metal around his finger, one of his thinking ticks. Ever the calm man, Cillian paces away from me and flips a table, the contents on top clattering and rolling with the loud bang of the metal table hitting the concrete floor.

I sigh and wait for his tantrum to be over.

"We can't do nothing," Cillian says. He kicks a water bottle that rolls towards him after his display.

"I know that, but whoever did this wants us to retaliate. They want us to start burning the city down, making enemies in the process," I say. Cillian jerks his head towards me and studies me with those icy eyes, there's such ire there that I think they just might ignite. "We need to be deliberate about this."

"You look like a coward."

I don't flinch at his words, but I feel a muscle in my jaw jump. "Going up against the Garzas when it's clear they didn't do this will make us look like trigger happy fools. Which would you prefer?"

Cillian props his hands on his hips. "What do you suggest then?"

"The Mayor's Gala—" Cillian dramatically throws his head back with a groan before I can finish. "You have to be there, Cillian. Everyone does."

"I hate that fucking party," he spits.

One might think that Cillian would take any chance to show off his expensive clothes, shiny shoes, and diamond watches, but if it means rubbing elbows with the city's more. . . conventionally rich and powerful, he wants nothing to do with it. Unfortunately, though, that's not how this business works.

"You're going. Stop acting like a baby," I say. "You know we don't get to have the life we do without some level of cooperation. We're all going to show up, make small talk, and try to sniff out whatever rat has been getting into places it doesn't belong."

Cillian knows he has to go, he just hates the reminder. We get away with literal murder in this city because those people he terribly resents want the same things we do: power, security, stability, and protection. We provide all of that for them for what I consider to be a small cost (idealist Nate might call that cost their souls, I call it their attention). They look the other way, open doors that we don't have keys to, and in return, we keep them on a list.

Practically part of the family.

The Mayor's Gala is the one night of the year when everyone plays nice. It doesn't matter which family you're a part of nor which business you're in, you show up, you pretend your empire is above board, you drink fancy wine and dance to the live band. It is what it is.

"Someone will talk if we ask the right questions," I say, more confident than I feel.

He stares hard at my face for a moment, a battle of wills, but I haven't once backed down to Cillian Donovann since my father died, and I don't plan on starting now. It's what keeps us on common ground.

He jerks a nod and then paces away from me, probably looking for another table to flip over.

"Quite the temper on that one," Leo murmurs next to me.

I reset my shoulders and look decidedly away from Cillian's retreating back. "What'd your guy say?" I ask.

"He'll ask around, but they aren't interested in disrupting the peace we have going. Garza knows how valuable our ties with the mayor and the port inspector are. They didn't do this."

"I know they didn't." I watch my sisters counting and conferring quietly together, dread coursing through my body at the undeniable truth that my control is slipping through my fingers, and when it's gone, I won't be able to protect anybody.

"Let's get this shit cleaned up," Leo says.

25

NATE

I AM DOZING OFF SOMEWHERE IN THE FOURTH SEASON OF *THE Vampire Diaries* when Ranger jumps down from the bed and starts running in tiny circles at the bedroom door, a sure sign he has to pee. When we get downstairs, though, I see that he doesn't have to pee at this 3 AM juncture, he just heard Vanessa come home and wanted to hang out with her.

He wiggles his whole body at her feet until she bends down to scratch his neck. She still doesn't look pleased about having a dog in the house, but her disdain has been softened in the last couple of weeks. I thought she would shoot him at first, so her petting his head is real progress.

"Working late," I say. She's wearing sleek pants and a turtle-neck, very Steve Jobs if Steve Jobs was a hot Italian woman.

"Yeah. Unfortunately."

"Can I have some?" I nod at the electric tea kettle bubbling in front of her.

"Want chamomile?"

"Sounds great."

She reaches up into the cabinet for the box of tea, and her shirt rides up in the process. I remember the feel of her bare back against my palms, the silky skin, warm in the spring night air.

"Here." She slides me the green mug I've taken a liking to. It's the only one of its kind in the mug cabinet and fits well in my palm. Has she noticed it's the one I like? Or was it by chance she gave it to me now?

I clear my throat.

"Thanks," I say, but my voice is like a truck driving over gravel.

I focus my energy on spooning honey into the mug and pouring the scalding water over it.

"Milk?" I nod and try not to touch her skin as she puts the carton in front of me.

She looks tired, like she always does by the end of the day, her shoulders low and under eyes dark. I know I am part of a privileged few being able to see her like this, in her home, no makeup, hair pulled back into a messy ponytail.

She is not a mafia boss like this, she is just Vanessa, tired from working too hard, stress evident on her skin and in the strain behind her eyes.

"Something happened," I say, and she doesn't deny it. Why else would she be coming home past 3 AM looking like sipping tea is a grueling task?

"Yeah," she whispers and sets her mug down before letting her face fall in her hands. I watch her while she breathes, and she rubs her hands down her face and neck until they rest on her shoulders, crossed over her chest. Ranger huddles closer to her leg.

"I don't know," she says. "I'm good at my job."

"Of course," I say. I don't know if she means the construction or the crime, but I figure this is true of both. "That's obvious."

"I am good, the best even. I make it a point to be this way, to never let anything slip past my notice, but—" A muscle in her jaw ticks. "I'm missing something."

She takes another sip from her mug. It must burn her tongue because she winces. I want to ask what happened, but she's not one to share all the gory details. At least not with me, anyway.

I've given her no reason to believe I'd be a generous ear to such things.

"Have you seen anything like this before?" I ask. "When your dad was alive?"

"When I was young, once. Otherwise, people feared him too much to stir the pot. They fear me too, or at least they did."

"They still do," I reassure, and I try not to let myself think about how strange it is that I am comforting Vanessa by telling her how much people still fear her mighty rule. But it's true. "Not only that, but they respect you."

She scoffs at this.

"I mean it," I say. "These men I've interviewed are absolute tools, but they're scared shitless of you. Or, like, the character of you. You as a concept. They know you can hit them where it hurts at any given time and that's why they want to align with you."

"I guess," she says. "I wish my dad was here."

"What do you think he would tell you if he was?"

Vanessa chews on her bottom lip as she considers this. She does this when she's thinking, unconsciously pulling the inside of her lip between her teeth. I watch the motion too closely and avert my eyes before she can notice me staring.

"He'd tell me that I have every ability to figure it out. No problem too big to be solved," she says. "He was always saying that, and even as a little kid I was worried he was wrong about me."

I've never seen her like this, so down on herself and outwardly defeated. It's depressing. I want to tuck her under a blanket and make her popcorn or pancakes with way too much syrup and protect her from phone calls for a minimum of fifteen hours.

Vanessa takes another sip of tea, her throat moving on the swallow. "He would know what to do. Decisions weren't hard for him like they are for me."

"If it's any consolation, decisions don't seem hard for you," I say. "You're very confident. Ask anyone."

She smiles, a small victory.

"Fake it 'til you make it," she says. "I'm just not sure when I'll feel like I'm no longer faking it."

"I don't know that you ever will."

Her brows lower, wary of my assessment.

"I've been teaching for seven years and I'm better at it now, but every week I am still encountering things that leave me guessing. I bet your dad was the same way."

She doesn't look so sure, but she considers it. She's nice like that, always thinking before speaking one way or another. It's more of a strength than she knows.

"We're all just making things up here," I say. "And you're lucky. You have your family to make it up with you. And a very talented math teacher. For now."

I take a chance that she won't murder me and place a hand over hers and squeeze twice. A quiet note that she's not alone in this, even if reasonably the *this* at hand is deplorable and should probably result in jail time. She doesn't attack, just softens her shoulders and heaves a breath.

"You're right. We'll figure it out," she says. "We always do."

* * *

WHEN I WAKE on Saturday morning, there's a tux hanging on my bathroom door, which tells me that someone was in here while I slept, and I get the heebie jeebies thinking it might have been Mary. I lock the door every night because even though I interact with her daily in training, I am only 60% sure Mary won't try to kill me in my sleep. Good to know that my sense of security with a doorknob lock was false.

Ranger is asleep in his kennel, and I take him downstairs where I find Vanessa, Mary, and Willa all dressed in their usual training clothes, picking at a fruit platter that Claire is making on the counter in front of them.

"It's Saturday," I groan by way of greeting. My shoulders are still sore from the three hours of target practice yesterday. "Why do you all look ready to run a half marathon?"

"Good morning, Nate," Claire says. Ranger is hopping excitedly at her feet, and she throws him a bit of apple. "Did you see the suit? The tie will match your eyes."

"Yes, thank you." I let Ranger out the sliding glass door, then reach for the green mug for my coffee, but Vanessa bats my hands away.

"You're not dressed," Vanessa says.

"You said no training on event days," I argue. Tonight is the illustrious Mayor's Gala which they spent the majority of yesterday primping for by getting facials, manicures, and pedicures. Anette even came to trim all of our hair.

Vanessa shakes her head. "I never said that."

"She would never say that," Mary agrees.

"Probably what she said is no *double* training on event days," Willa says while chewing on a mouthful of grapes. "Hurry up."

"Can I have some coffee first?" I ask.

"No," all three sisters say. I feel a twitch in my right eye, but I am so far outnumbered I don't even think about fighting it.

By the merit of only doing one training for the day, I swear Vanessa sets out to make it as difficult as possible. It's ninety minutes of sparring (*but careful of the faces, or you're so dead*), running, hitting bags, and then more running, which leaves me drenched in sweat, limping, and exhausted. Just how I'd normally want to feel when attending a party. Sure.

I lie flat on my back on the mat, my heart rate probably 250 beats per minute, and Vanessa nudges my side with her shoe.

"You're getting stronger," she says.

The high-pitched sound that comes out of me is half a laugh, half a whimper. I do not feel stronger, though it is true that my body looks different in the mirror. I can keep up much better than I could a month ago. "Thanks."

"Now go shave," she says.

"What?" I touch my chin, which is still mostly smooth from yesterday's shave.

"And let Leo do your hair." She nudges my side again, harder this time, and I roll over to start painfully pushing myself to my feet.

"You don't like how I do my hair?"

"You do your hair?" she asks, and I offer my best glower. She starts pushing me towards the door. "I'm kidding, of course spritzing your bedhead with water counts. Now go."

"Okay, alright, I'm going," I say, and I can't help but smile as I make my way back up the stairs.

Mary, like a ghost, is standing at the landing and I jump when I see her. Her eyes narrow, drawing unknown conclusions about me, and the smile is wiped clean from my face. I inch towards my room without comment.

* * *

IN THE CAR on the way to the Gala, Vanessa uses a little compact mirror to freshen up her makeup. Watching her do mundane things always feels like I'm being let in on a secret, like when we sit on the couch after everyone's gone to bed and she falls asleep with her feet on my lap or tucked under my leg.

I turn to look out the window at the passing cars. Save for Artie and Angel, who are with a babysitter, the whole family is dressed to the nines in floor length gowns and tuxedos ready for tonight. We had to take three cars, but we arrive as a posse because Vanessa says it's important that the Donovanns and Morellis walk in together.

As soon as we step out at valet, Vanessa has turned on every switch in her social arsenal and now exudes power and charisma. I both fear her and do not want to stop looking at her with her posture so strong and solid, every detail down to her fingernail color claiming power and strength that I couldn't imagine containing.

I have the impulse to stare at her until my eyes fall out, but again I turn away to look at anything but her.

"What first?" I ask.

"You and I greet the mayor, I'll introduce you, then we find our seats, we'll eat, there will be an auction, and then there is dancing."

"When do the politics begin?"

Vanessa gives me a small smile, one that feels like a break from her mask. "Those have already begun."

I didn't see why it was necessary that I come to this event, but the whole family was adamant that I needed to be there to uphold the image of the new, ever-mysterious consigliere. Cillian doesn't seem so pleased that Vanessa is by my side and not his, but no less than three glamorous women in low cut gowns flanked him when we came through the doors, so I am certain he is otherwise occupied.

I expected there to be a line to meet the mayor, but instead, he stands in a small group, one hand around a woman I assume to be his wife, and the other holding a fluted glass. His wife looks familiar, though I cannot place why.

With everyone standing and socializing, it feels like a happy hour, but everyone is in the finest clothing I've ever seen. The mayor, Gregory Anderson, is shorter than I thought he would be from all his signs and billboards in the last election cycle. The group around him parts for Vanessa in her blood red gown and the mayor lights up to greet her. One man remains, though, an older guy with a glass of amber liquid beside the mayor.

"Miss Morelli," Mayor Anderson says, and then kisses the back of her hand. People still kiss hands in greeting? In Massachusetts? "Always a pleasure to see you."

"Same to you, Greg." Vanessa leans forward and kisses next to his wife's cheek. "And Donna, you're radiant, as usual."

The woman blushes under Vanessa's compliments, and God she looks familiar. I know I've met her before. "Thank you, that dress is excellent. When are you going to set me up with your stylist?"

"She's not taking on any more clients, or I would," Vanessa lies. Her stylist is just Willa buying new clothing for her every other week. After the first initial closet overhaul, she's done the same for me, coming over for family dinner with new button-ups over her arm. I know they're rich, but she might have a shopping problem.

"Mr. McGowan, it's nice to see you here as well." Vanessa holds out her hand and after a brief hesitation, the old man shakes it. He doesn't look thrilled by the prospect. "Mr. McGowan works with Cillian, longtime friend of the Donovann family," she explains to me. Another criminal, then. This one of the Irish variety.

"Nice to meet you," I say, and shake his hand too.

"And who's your date?" Donna asks. Her head is tilted and, Christ, there's a spark of recognition in her eyes, too.

Wait, *date*?

"This is Nathaniel Gilbert. He's recently joined our team as a financial planner. Very talented."

"Gilbert!" Donna snaps her finger. "I thought I knew you; do you teach at Isles Prep?"

I freeze, not sure how to traverse this territory when Vanessa just introduced me as a financial advisor.

Her son.

I taught her youngest son my first year at the school, before Greg was mayor.

"He does," Vanessa says and squeezes my bicep. Vanessa is touching my arm, telling them that I am a lowly middle school teacher, and not correcting them that I'm her date? "So generous of him, right? Quite the time commitment for someone who already works so hard on his own endeavors."

"It's a pleasure to do it," I say when her nails dig into the soft part of my arm. "I remember your son, sharp kid."

I do not remember much of her son; I can sort of picture his face, but I cannot recall his name for the life of me. I'm not one of those teachers who memorizes every face and keeps them in their heart for the rest of their days.

"What's a teacher doing consulting on company finances?" McGowan asks.

I sense that he is the kind of sour man who is never pleased. And he has something against Vanessa, he looks at her as if staring down his nose, though she is three inches taller than him.

"The finances come first," I explain. "I just love to teach."

"That is quite the service," Mayor Greg says. He holds his glass up almost as if to toast me. "This city needs great teachers."

I'm sure he's said this to every teacher he's met since becoming a politician, but yeah, it works. I'd vote for him in the next election after that.

"Needs quality buildings, too," he adds for Vanessa's benefit. "Thank you again for all the beautiful work you do in this city, Ms. Morelli."

"Of course. And maybe one day Mr. McGowan will let us build one for him." She says this with a cheeky smile on her face. "We'll let you get back to your socializing. Do come for dinner soon. We would love to have you."

Greg's eyes show a flash of apprehension at this, but he and his wife both agree. If Donna knows about Vanessa's true position, she doesn't show it.

Vanessa guides us towards the table Mary and Leo are already seated at. I'd guess they're not ones to socialize much at functions like this, though they both clean up perfectly well. Leo did my hair and it does in fact look way nicer than anything I could have managed.

"You really do look beautiful," I tell her.

The crimson dress has a high neck but a low back, so low that if I touched her back at all I'd be smoothing my fingers across her skin. Her hair is straight down her back, shiny and sleek like it's never been frizzy, not even on the most humid day.

"Beautiful for a monster?" she says, and I gulp.

I don't know how to tell her she's the most beautiful woman, monster or not, that I've ever seen, and with every day that passes in her presence, I'm increasingly certain that there's hardly a bad or cruel or monstrous thing about her.

We've arrived at the table before I can say anything too excruciating, and Leo starts reporting on who is here and who is yet to arrive. Some of the last names I recognize from the interviews, others I've never heard of.

"And these are all crime families?" I ask. How much organized crime can one city have and still stand?

"You could call them that," Mary mutters.

"Garza wants to speak with you," Leo says. "Alone."

Vanessa's mask is immovable, but I see her chest rise and fall with a sigh. "Let's get this over with, then. Mary, I need you to talk with Orlov."

"What? Why?" Mary says in a rare display of unease.

Venessa's brows furrow slightly. "Because Willa and Sean are busy with the Cordonis."

"Fine." Mary downs the remainder of her drink, some bright orange juice cocktail and leaves the table with Vanessa, the pair of them walking together before branching in different directions in the crowd.

"Vanessa's a different person in public," I say to Leo, who's closely observing Vanessa speaking to a pair of Hispanic men across the ballroom. "I didn't realize she was so different at home."

"You should see her in the office," Leo mutters.

I can picture it, Vanessa in her heels and a sharp suit, striding through the halls of the corporate office, instilling fear and awe in the employees. She's a force, impossible to look away from. She demands respect just by entering a room.

At the nearest open bar, I spot Cillian leaning next to a woman in conversation, looking casually cooler than I will ever manage in this lifetime.

"Why hasn't Cillian offered to marry her?" I ask. "They'd make a... handsome pair."

Leo laughs. "He has," he says. "A few times now."

"Is he in love with her?"

Leo releases a long breath as he watches Cillian. "I don't think so. Cillian loves himself, and power. Of course he wants to marry her."

"Would he take care of her?" I don't know why I'm asking, only that I can't stop now that I know he's asked her to marry him before. "Would he be good to her?"

"I don't know. I guess. Guy loves women, though."

Cillian traces his fingers over a piece of the woman's hair, and I can just hear her giggling from here. He's cool and suave and already with power of his own. She should probably accept his proposal if he asks again.

For some reason, my stomach turns.

"Are you seeing anyone?" I ask.

Leo's eyes glance briefly towards the side of the room where Vanessa speaks.

"It's complicated," Leo says. "Though I guess love usually is. Unless you're Willa and Sean."

"Does this person love you back?" I hedge.

"Maybe," Leo says, then shrugs. "I wouldn't say a lack of love is the problem. Maybe more of a lack of opportunity."

"How *Romeo and Juliet* of you."

Leo laughs, then shakes his head like it might be closer to the truth than I know. Leo is much softer than I ever gave him credit for, more forthcoming with his friendship and feelings than others in the family. I admire this about him.

"Well, for what it's worth, I hope it works out," I say.

"Thank you," Leo smiles, but sadly. "Me too."

26

VANESSA

THE NIGHT IS NOT OVER AFTER THE AUCTION, OR AFTER THE FOUR-course meal we were served. Instead, there is desert, dancing, and more talking. Always more talking. By the time either I or one of my siblings has spoken to everyone we needed to, my throat is sore from the ceaseless chatter; my cheeks ache from all of the strategic smiling I've done. My spine feels heavy, but I remain as composed and tall as I have since arriving.

Nate and Leo have been buzzing around together, talking to people, eavesdropping on conversations, or visiting the grazing table. By my count, they've both eaten half a dozen macarons.

"What are they up to?" I ask Mary as I take the glass of water she brought me. She squints up at the two men chatting over their desserts.

"I don't know, probably gossiping. They're obsessed with each other," Mary says.

"Oh my god," I start. "Are you jealous of Nate?"

Leo and Mary have always been two peas in a pod. I had no idea that Leo spending so much time with Nate could possibly feel like an attack on their friendship. I am trying very diligently not to laugh at this idea.

"No," Mary says. "I'm offended you would even think that—"

"Excuse me," a deep voice says from behind us. Mary's face hardens at the newcomer, and I'm surprised to see an Orlov when I turn around. *The* Orlov.

"Maxim Orlov. A pleasure," I say, and hold out a hand to shake his. It's not a lie, either. Maxim is the head of the Orlov crime family, and though his father was a piece of shit, I've only had good interactions with his only son. "You've met my sister, I know."

"I have," Maxim nods politely at my sister.

Mary, on the other hand, looks like she might want to burn his house down. Their conversation earlier tonight seemed cordial enough from her brusque report afterward, but I am certainly missing something.

"I hear congratulations are in order on an engagement?" I ask. His face goes grim.

"No, that didn't pan out, unfortunately." He sounds truly regretful at this. I don't know if he was marrying for love, but I might guess it was to rectify his own lack of an heir.

Opportunity scratches at the back of my brain; he wouldn't make a bad alliance. Maybe not even a bad husband.

I file this information away for later when he speaks again.

"We will be keeping an ear to the ground regarding your pest issue," Maxim says. "I don't mean to overstep, but I recommend you look inward. Sometimes adversary wears the mask of a friend."

"I appreciate that," I say. I do not believe that Maxim is the one sabotaging me, though he has family I am less familiar with. As for his comment about looking internally for the rat, it strikes closer to my insecurities than I think he intended.

"I wonder, Mary, if you'd like to dance?" Maxim asks.

I think she'll say no, maybe even spit at him the way her eyes are blazing, but instead, she straightens her shoulders and hands me her glass before she walks past him to the dance floor full of guests moving together to the music. He gives me one last closed mouth smile before following her there.

How strange.

I haven't spoken to Cillian since he was throwing shit around the warehouse acting like an ass, and I can tell by the smug grin on his face that he's tipsy if not fully drunk from the open bar as he approaches me.

"Nessie, Nessie," Cillian says when he stops by my side, too close. Whatever thousand-dollar cologne he has on fills my nostrils immediately in a way that makes me want to sneeze.

He's been family for thirteen years, and most days I quite like him, but sometimes I loathe him. Usually at parties.

"Have I told you I love this dress?"

"You haven't," I say, unamused.

"Shall we dance? If we get lucky, we might see Mary stab the Russian."

"Sounds like just what this night needs, an *incident*," I say. Cillian plucks the glasses from my hands and deposits them on the tray of a waiter passing by. I can't even say no before his hand is on my back leading me forward. "You should go home, Cillian."

"And miss the fun? I could never." Cillian tugs me towards him, our chests almost touching as the song turns to a slower, swaying tune. He ducks his head near my ear, that whiskey breath hot on my cheek. "You look beautiful."

"So I've heard," I say. Cillian drags a hand down my bare arm and then, gripping my fingers, spins me once before pulling me closer. *Ever one for theatrics.* "You're drunk."

"And you, Vanessa, are the belle of the ball," he says.

"Have you learned anything useful while sneaking into corners to ravish the wives of local politicians?" Cillian's palm is dry, the skin coarse from years of weight training and fighting. I know scars crisscross the knuckles he is scraping lightly across my back.

"I think we should go home together tonight," Cillian says, either evading my question, or ignoring it altogether.

"What the hell, Cillian?" I whisper.

"What? I think it's time you send your yappy little dog back where he came from and call off the search."

I glance over at said yappy dog, who stands at the edge of the room watching us with his hands in his pants pockets. Always with his hands in those pockets.

My eyes meet Nate's for a second only before turning my gaze back up to Cillian's.

"It's not safe for him yet," I say.

"Who cares? So he dies, you owe him no loyalty. You shouldn't have brought him into your home in the first place."

I swallow the lump that's formed in my throat at the thought.

"We look good together," Cillian says. "Hot."

"Perfect reason to spend the rest of our lives married to each other."

"Is it him?" Cillian asks, all levity gone. I don't play dumb. "He's a loser, Vanessa. What could he possibly have that you want?"

I shut my mouth and look away from those hurt icicle eyes. Cillian is a hardened man, one who knows better than anyone the kind of things I'm up against daily. He knows me, is loved by my family, and could accept me for all my flaws and misdoings. He wouldn't offer a strategic advantage, but by all other accounts, of course I should accept his offer.

I look up at him again, his lips, his wide jaw, the scar beneath his left eye, and let myself imagine it. The white dress and black tux, him dipping me back for a kiss, rough hands roaming all over me. It would be a life of relative safety and probably one where I'd be happy enough.

It wouldn't be so bad, would it? And it would solve so many problems; no mothers on my back, no risk of the betrayal that could come from marrying a stranger, and finally an heir. I haven't had a relationship in years, just flings to let off steam every now and then. It could be nice to have someone.

"Ness," Cillian whispers. His face is so close to mine, just waiting for me to close the gap between us.

A throat clears just beside us, breaking the bizarre moment. Nate stands, hands out of his pockets. "May I cut in?"

I look to Nate, holding my breath, and nod, already detaching myself from Cillian. Nate doesn't take his eyes off me while a muscle in Cillian's neck ticks. If there weren't more than a hundred of the city's most refined individuals around us, I would fear for Nate's safety.

"Thank you for the dance," I tell Cillian. "I'll think about what you said."

Cillian doesn't speak, just cooks Nate beneath a hard stare before stalking away.

"Thank you," I say. Nate slides one hand around my waist and lightly grips my fingers with the other. "It's not that I needed saving, I just—"

"It's alright," he says, and we dance lightly in a swaying circle. "It looked like he was talking business after that's all you've done all night. You're just tired."

"Do I look tired?"

"No," he smiles. "I just see it."

I don't ask what he means because he seems to see everything. He observes the workings of things and slips seamlessly into them. It's why my mother loves gardening with him, why the kids adore playing with him. He sees people and meets them where they are.

"You see a lot of things," I murmur. "I feel like I can barely see myself these days."

He pulls me closer and shushes me. My chest is up against his like it was Cillian's, but he's so much warmer, like a blanket wrapping over me. I let myself melt into it.

"You're holding your breath," he says. "Tell me a story."

I breathe out and he doesn't mention that it is a bit shaky.

"Have you been to the chapel on Eighth?" I start. I can't think about marriage, weddings, baptisms, anything, without thinking about that church.

"The tall one? Has a bell tower and stained glass?"

I crack a smile. "You're describing every Catholic church in the city. But yes, it has those things."

"What about it?" Nate prompts.

"Everything has been there. Willa's wedding, Artie and Angel's blessings, my father's funeral."

"I'm sure it's beautiful," he says.

I think of the ornate windows, pointed towards heaven, and full of stained glass that I used to stare at for hours of my child-hood, tracing the iron lines over colored glass in my mind during weddings, mass, funerals, any time I could.

"There's a big window of the Virgin Mary in the front of the church. It's behind where the priest stands, so you can't miss it. It's just her. I used to love going to church so I could look at her for a while. When I was nineteen and engaged, I was so excited to get married there beneath her blessing. I didn't love the man, but I thought I could eventually."

"You were a baby."

"Yeah," I say on a breath. "But we knew by then that I was going to take over for my dad. We thought we had decades, but still, it was only a matter of time. I needed a husband."

"I'm sorry," he says. "That's a lot of pressure for a kid."

"I guess." I nod. "I remember thinking that even if he never loved me, even if I was doomed to sixty or seventy years of a loveless marriage, Mother Mary would be there for all the big events, the baptisms and funerals, and she'd make sure I was still okay. That glass version of her would look out for me."

"What happened? With the guy. You said he was intimidated by you, right?"

I laugh a bitter sound and feel Nate's hand on my waist

squeeze the slightest bit. I recall telling Nate veiled truths about my failed engagement the night of his cousin's wedding.

That feels like a year ago, but it's only been a few months.

"It was our wedding day, and I was in this big white dress—I looked amazing. It was Willa's dress, she has the best taste—and I had these little white and pink butterfly clips in my hair that my dad gave me." I recall how bright they looked against my dark hair and the way my mother and sisters painstakingly added them to my braided updo. "I looked like a princess.

"We went through the ceremony, kissed at the altar. He thought he'd won, and he pulled me into a room afterward to laugh at how I looked and tell me exactly what was going to happen now that he had me. How I needed to act and be, and he informed me that *he* would be the one to really take over after my father died. And he said I would never be able to do a thing about it, because I was his wife. And if I tried, he'd hurt everyone I loved."

"Jesus," Nate whispers. I shrug.

"I believed he would kill them, or take advantage of Mary, who was only sixteen then, or hurt the babies—Willa and Sean were living with us, Artie and Angel were just toddlers."

"How did you get out of it?" he asks. The song we were dancing to ended and bled into the next. A cover of some romantic Ed Sheeran song that Willa loves. She and Sean dance too, all wrapped up in each other.

I inch closer to Nate, my mouth near his ear so I can speak quieter. Images of that day flash through my mind, images I've forced myself to remember, that I won't allow myself to forget. First, I remember the back of his hand slapping across my cheek hard enough to smear my lipstick, then seeing my shocked reflection in the mirror.

Blood spilled over my lower lip, painting it crimson. *You're mine now. You don't threaten me*, he'd said, and I was so afraid.

Afraid of what he would do to me, but more afraid of what he would do to them.

Clean yourself up, he said. *We've got a reception to get to.*

"I killed him," I say. Nate tenses, but he's still breathing, releasing a puff of air on my neck. It sends hot chills down my spine.

I remember what it felt like to stab the man through the heart, the smell that made my stomach lurch as he bled all over my white dress, cursing my name as he died.

"He was my first kill. I was protecting my family, and every time since has been to those same ends," I say. I'm talking so low that I'm barely sure if Nate can hear me over the music and surrounding chatter. "And now he'll never threaten me or my family again."

The song comes to an end and the singer speaks into a microphone about picking things up a little bit for the last songs of the night. Nate breaks away from me like I might have burned him.

This is it, I realize; the moment Nate really sees me for who I am. My mouth creeps up into a sardonic smile as he backs away. Of course, he backs away.

He's not meant for this world, no matter how comfortable he is around my family, or how well he's pretended to be one of us. He doesn't belong here, he could never belong here, and I see that in his rigid posture, his tight smile as we politely clap for the live band. The way he can't meet my eye.

It's clear to me, and now he's gotten his reminder, too. This world isn't meant for him.

It never has been.

27

NATE

It's not until I'm back in my room and under the hot spray of my shower that I finally start to calm down. My heart is still pounding in my ears at Vanessa's admission. I knew she killed people; I literally watched her kill two men behind my apartment building.

But they'd been attacking us, *that* was heat of the moment self-defense!

As I violently scrub soap across my body, I reason that killing a man threatening your family like a cartoonishly evil villain is also self-defense.

It's not the story that's made me freak out. No.

It's how I felt listening to it.

I felt vindicated and relieved that he was dead, a strange sense of celebration when she told me what she did to him. I know who she is, and what she's done, but never have I felt like I *understood*.

It became clear to me. I thought of Artie and Angel clinging to her like a life raft as they slept when they were sick, and about Willa and Sean kissing when he passes her in the kitchen. Even

Mary, and her little snort of a laugh that surprises no one more than it does her. Vanessa lives to protect them.

Everything is to that end.

I might have killed him too, I think. If I was in her shoes that day, I might've done it.

That's what scares me the most.

It's fucked up, all of this, they've gotten into my head after two months of sharing spaces and making them human, seeing them cook and laugh together and tear up watching an action movie in the middle of the night.

I scrub my face so hard that it's bright red when I get out of the shower and I don't want to go downstairs, but Ranger is running in little circles, probably because he wants to see Vanessa, who I've just now decided I am going to stalwartly avoid for the next month.

"Outside," I say when we get to the sliding door. Reluctantly, he complies, bounding towards the grass, his collar jingling as he does. It's dark downstairs, everyone has gone to bed by now. All the lights are off, but bright moonlight floods the kitchen through the big rectangular windows. I stare out the sliding glass door into the full moon, which is heavy in the clearest sky.

There's a scuffing noise behind me and I turn in time to see Vanessa drop a glass, which bounces once before completely shattering.

"Dammit," Vanessa says, and leans down to start picking up pieces. I rush to help, crouching in front of her to get the biggest chunks before retreating to the pantry to get the broom.

"It's okay," she says. "You don't have to help."

"No, it's fine." I make quick work of the little shards, sweeping them into a pile while she transfers the bigger pieces into the trash can. Vanessa whips her hand back from her task and I see one of the pieces has sliced a cut in her fingertip, the incision already welling blood.

I drop the dustpan, making a further mess of the glass, and

grab her arms to pull her up and towards the sink. Glass crunches under our slippers, the only sound before I hold her bleeding hand under cold sink water. It cascades over her palm and splashes red over the sink's surface.

She hisses at first, but I hold her hand tight with her forearm cradled. In the drawer next to me, I retrieve a little towel and hold it against her finger. Maybe I'm squeezing too hard, but when I look up at her, Vanessa's eyes are on mine, closer than when we danced at the gala. Her hair is still damp, dripping water onto her cream silk button-up pajama top.

"Does it hurt?" I whisper. It's so quiet in this moment I think the whole house might hear.

Vanessa shakes her head.

"Let me get you a band aid." I step away, the rest of the kitchen substantially cooler than the space where our bodies were pressed together. I have goosebumps all over my arms.

There's a first aid kit in the pantry and I rifle through it, my hands shaking as I do.

Instead of taking the band aid I offer, Vanessa holds out her finger. It reminds me of when one of my students gets a paper cut and they don't want to mess up putting it on. I return to my place much too close to her and wrangle my breath to a normal (albeit slow) rhythm while wrapping the fabric around her finger.

"It does hurt a little," she says. I've seen her suffer worse blows in training without so much as a complaint, but I do what I think she wants me to do and pull her hand towards my mouth, pressing two slow kisses against her wrapped fingertip. "A bit better."

I should step away now, step back and pick up the dustpan and broom and work on the glass and then go directly upstairs to bed. I should do a lot of things, but I might die if I don't do the one thing I want to do, so I tilt my head closer to hers. She lifts her chin in response. I feel the breath from her nose ghosting across my lips before I kiss her.

It's the briefest touch of our lips, but her lips feel molten—the kind of burn that would blister. I pull away, like maybe I can stop this if I leave right this second, but her free hand grasps the side of my T-shirt asking me to stay. I lean in again, but she pulls her head away, just enough to see my whole face.

Her eyes show something I've never seen, something frantic and vulnerable.

"I'm a criminal," she murmurs in a rush. "I've killed people."

"I know."

"We can't be . . . together. Not for real."

"I know," I echo. She's made it clear that she could never marry someone like me, and I've made it clear I couldn't be with her either, though my reasons feel flimsier each day. "We can pretend. Just tonight."

After a pause, she nods. "Just tonight."

No other words are needed before I pull her mouth to mine again.

She's feverish this time, her lips moving over mine, her tongue pressing into my mouth, and I'm right there with her, meeting her at every stride, pushing against her and pulling her to me. She takes her hand from mine before wrapping her arms around my neck. I duck so she can hug her legs around my waist and then slide her on the granite counter. She gasps at the cold stone on her bare thighs but doesn't stop kissing me.

My hands roam around her back beneath her shirt. It's dizzying to feel the expanse of soft skin I'd thought of all night with her in that damn dress.

"Fuck, Vanessa." I slide my palm down her spine. I think I may be able to fuel enough sexual fantasies for a year from just the memory of feeling her bare back while she sits in her tiny pajama shorts on the counter in front of me.

"More," she whines, and it sends me feral. I'm engulfing her, trying to pull her as close to me as possible, trying to swallow her whole. She bites my lip, and it issues a moaning sound I've certainly never made before.

I want her closer, so I start unbuttoning her shirt until it's all the way open and I have to stop for a moment to just take in what I see beneath. Her stomach is tight, defined with muscles I've seen many times in the gym, but her tits—holy fuck—they're somehow better than my mind had painted them because now they're real, the size of ripe grapefruits, pink nipples that are hard and pointy and so, so tempting that I don't even fight the urge to bring one into my mouth.

She arches her back, pressing her chest against my face with these little labored breaths sounding from her. I suck my way up to her throat and then her jaw, sloppily lapping at her skin until she tugs my hair up so we can make out some more. She's grinding against my front where I am unbearably hard through my sweatpants, and I squeeze my eyes shut not to come right this very second.

"You're the most beautiful person I have ever seen," I say. "It's barely human how much I want you."

"Have me," she says. "Please, right now."

I pick her up off the counter and she gives a little yelp before wrapping her legs again tightly around my middle.

We kiss, little fast kisses on the mouth as I walk over to the door to let in Ranger who's been pawing at it. He circles at my feet, and we break long enough for Vanessa to laugh.

"Put me down, I can walk," she says. I do as she says, and am about to guide her straight upstairs, when I see the dustpan still spilling glass on the tile.

"Lock Ranger upstairs and I'll meet you there."

Vanessa pulls my mouth down to hers for one more searing kiss before leaving me to do what I said. My boner is ridiculous as I gather up the glass as quickly as possible and deposit the shards into the trash. I'll do another pass in the morning.

I've only been in Vanessa's room once; the time Artie and

Angel were sick and I sat next to her while she fell asleep. Now, as I stalk inside, it's just her here, and she's pulling closed her curtains. Only lamps are clicked on, and the space is cozy and inviting.

Once I gently shut the door behind me, she turns around and we watch each other, miles of plush carpet between us. Her shirt is buttoned only a couple of times, the buttons in the wrong holes, and her face is flushed pink.

"Tomorrow, we forget about this," she says, and I nod. Then shake my head.

"I will probably never, ever forget." I stare at the spot between her breasts where her shirt hangs open. "But I will pretend."

"Like it never happened," she says.

I am like a malfunctioning machine, unable to think of anything other than *Vanessa, Vanessa, Vanessa*, but I jerk my head into a nod.

This settles it.

We both move across the room towards each other like magnets, meeting in the middle where she leaps on me. The taste of her is ludicrous, it's making me dizzy and ravenous, I am sliding my tongue into her mouth in the least graceful kiss I've ever had, as eager as I was in high school, and she's meeting me and matching me at each turn.

My hands, too, are gliding all over her body, trying to memorize her curves like if I don't touch every part of her now, I never will again.

"The bed," she says between kisses, and I bring her there without having to be asked twice. She falls back onto the comforter with a huff, but keeps kissing me, reaching up to meet my mouth as I crawl over her.

She pulls my shirt up over my head and I shakily undo the last two buttons on her top before throwing it across the room.

I think I whimper, the sound that comes from me is involuntary and needy as I take in her tits again.

"Have them," she says. "Whatever you want."

I'm distracted cycling through a rolodex of "whatever I want" scenarios, but we only have tonight, I remind myself.

Only tonight, and that will be the end of it.

We will both be satisfied, and we can go on knowing what just once felt like.

I know that this never works in movies, the *just one time to get it out of their systems*, but I am convincing myself as I press messy kisses on her chest that by some miracle, this will be enough.

There is no slow seduction here, nothing smooth about me in this moment. For all the time I secretly fantasized about what this would be like, I am a needy mess now.

Her hands snaking up my torso and around my neck, into my hair, make me feel out of control. I am buzzing, breathing her name into her skin as I kiss and touch her.

I've never had less finesse in my life, but she's reacting in kind.

"Please," she whispers, and I guess I'm not the only needy one here. "Please touch me, Nate. Now."

I am taken aback and also a bit sick with power at her asking so nicely for me to touch her pussy.

"You're perfect," I breathe, which only makes her squirm more. I give in to her pleas, because she did ask so nicely, and I think if I don't sink a finger into her heat in the next minute, my heart will stop.

Her lips are wet and slick, and I slide my fingers through them, circling around her clit for a moment before pressing my middle finger inside of her.

My vision goes white.

"Holy shit, Vanessa," I say, and she just moans. I press another finger inside and I have to close my eyes before I come at the sight of her face scrunched up in pleasure. I really might. I am 19 again, touching a girl for the first time, but this time it's a mafia goddess instead of someone I met at a party.

"Nate," she moans, her voice so high like a whine.

It's another piece of her, another hidden gem given to so few.

"Tell me what you like," I say, and add a third finger to her wet center. She groans. "Tell me."

"This," she says. "And more, please. More."

I drop my face right next to her ear. "Can I taste you? Please say yes."

Her breath catches in her throat, and I push my fingers in more forcefully. "Yes," she groans. "Yes, anything."

I kiss my way down her body and shimmy these flimsy shorts off her hips before looking at the pussy my fingers had just been pumping into. Through my sweats, I grab the base of my cock to keep myself in check.

I again squeeze my eyes shut for a moment as to not really embarrass myself.

It's perfect and dark pink, and so, so wet. She's not waxed or shaved bare, which thrills me. She's neatly trimmed and spread wide open for me. It's another secret, this level of grooming that's just for herself and, again, I feel like the smuggest, luckiest man on the planet that I get to see it, get to taste it. I've won some sort of karmic lottery to be in bed with Vanessa Morelli.

As is everything with her, I dive in with zero finesse.

My tongue is probing into her instead of teasing, it's like I've never done this before, but she groans and writhes anyway, and I keep up my ministrations.

I suck her clit into my mouth, and it makes her legs shake around my shoulders.

I'm at my task for minutes, my cock is as hard as it has ever been at the moans she's making and just savoring the taste of her when I can tell she's close. So close, I can sense it in her body's movements, in the way her breaths are tight and fast, shallow in her throat.

But as she gets closer still, something breaks and she's not quite there. This happens a few times, and I can tell she's retreating, just a bit, embarrassed or frustrated or both.

"I'm sorry," she says. "It's—you don't have to—"

"No, baby," I cut her off. "Tell me what you need."

Her throat moves as she swallows looking down at me, and I keep my face between her legs.

"Your fingers," she says. "And your tongue on my clit. I need both," she admits, and I grin before diving back in. Her cunt squeezes around my fingers as I fuck them into her while rubbing my tongue against her clit.

"That," she gasps, and her hips start shaking, fucking herself on my fingers and my tongue.

"Holy shit," I say, and she only groans louder. Her hands are gripping the comforter on either side of her, though I can tell she wants to hold my hair. I grab one of her hands and put it on my head, where she immediately holds on tight.

The tingles of pain in my scalp are like a drug.

I've never *done* drugs, but I think this is what it might feel like.

I suck her clit into my mouth and increase my speed, thrusting my fingers into her perfect pussy. This time as her breathing picks up speed, she doesn't stop until she's gone over the edge, moaning loud into her room, probably waking the whole house in the process, but I keep fucking her with my hand and my tongue all the way through it, until she's quivering around me, her ragged breath slowing.

I lighten up, languidly licking and fingering her until she's come down.

I crawl my way back up her body and take her limp hands in mine. I massage her palms and kiss every knuckle while her breathing slows.

"Why are you so good at that?" she asks, and she's still flushed. "How much practice have you had?"

"Some," I say. "Never like that though."

"You're so hot when you're horny," she says, and I let out a long laughing groan into her neck. She giggles, actually giggles, but then takes a sharp inhale when I wrap a hand around her and grip her ass.

"Condoms are in the drawer," she says, then like she has to explain herself, "Willa bought them for me when you moved in. I didn't answer her calls for a day."

I laugh, silently thanking her older sister for the foresight, and reach for the unopened box, ignoring the part of my brain begging me to stop and go through every single thing in and on top of her nightstand. I see a little journal and I want to read it so bad. I want to crawl around in her brain and study her messiest handwriting and read her words out loud to myself to see how her thoughts feel coming from my mouth.

When I've retrieved a condom and crawled back on her massive bed, she's maneuvered to her hands and knees in front of me, and I am so shocked by this image that I have to take this opportunity to trace the lines of her silhouette. Her daily training shows in her limbs, the definition of her shoulders and toned thighs. Her back is arched as she peers over her shoulder at me and her hair is mussed. I want to see the red flush to her cheeks always, want to know that I'm the one that put it there.

I draw my finger down her spine, and she shivers.

"I want to have you," I say when my fingers reach her pussy, still wet from my mouth and her own juices. "Here."

Vanessa moans in response, her hips anxious to buck back onto my fingers.

Wanton thing.

I slide the condom on over my shaft and she watches over her shoulder every move. When she finds my eyes on hers, she chews on her lower lip.

"Make it good," she says, and I blink at the meaning, the reminder that I ought to make it good since we just have the once. *Just tonight.*

God, thirty minutes with her and I'd forgotten this isn't something we can do every moment of the day for the rest of forever.

"How many times have you come in one night?" I sound composed enough for a man who's about to die here on the spot as soon as I get my cock in her. I tease her entrance, small circles on her labia. When she tries to push back onto me, I pull back further.

"I don't know, three?"

Three.

We can do better than that.

"Great. We don't stop until, say, five, then?"

"Nate," she groans.

"Six?"

She laughs again, the sound igniting every pleasure receptor in my brain. I lean over her back, a trail of kisses up her shoulder until I'm close enough to speak into her ear. My dick is hard between us. "Come on. Vanessa Morelli isn't a quitter."

Vanessa swallows and I do not imagine her swallowing around my dick, not at all, not for a second.

"Fine," she whispers with a smile. "Five."

"Six," I correct. She groans, but nods.

"Just do it, already," she says. "Please, Nate."

"What, this?" I sink two digits into her heat again and she moans. I might be ruined for any other erotic sound again, like I will be thinking about this any time I have a boner for the rest of my mortal life, and thereafter.

"More," she says. "Please, Nate, I want—"

I kiss her hard on the mouth, swallowing her gasps before kneeling behind her and, without preamble, I give her what we both very much want.

I can tend towards the dramatics, I recognize this. But when I say that Vanessa's pussy wrapped around my cock is the best feeling I've ever experienced, well I'm being modest.

We both groan once I'm fully sunk inside her and I'm trying

to be cool, but there is really nothing cool about me in this moment.

"You're unreal," I say, or more so wheeze. "How are you real?"

She starts wiggling her ass side to side and back and forth and I grip her hips to get her to stop, my thumbs pressing into her soft ass.

She does stop but her little whimpers tell me she's not happy about it.

I pull out and thrust into her as an experiment, thankfully disproving the hypothesis that any movement will make me blow my load on the spot. I move a bit faster, then slower, then faster, all the while keeping her hips in place. She arches her back and we both moan at the new angle it provides.

"This is unnatural," I say as I push further into her and then harder, making her breath hitch with every thrust.

"I'm going to come, Nate. Stop holding back," she says, and I do. I can't help but listen, rutting into her without grace, grunting with her moans, coursing my hands over her sides and down her back. I lose any semblance of rhythm with the building of my release, and when I finally come, it's with heavy pumps into her while she keens beneath me and squeezes around me.

I collapse next to her, and she follows, lying down next to me with her head resting on my chest.

"I'm catching my breath, and then we have four more orgasms on the agenda," I say. Her head lifts from my chest, eyebrows knitted together in the middle.

I push up to an elbow to meet her at eye level.

"Just tonight," I say again. "But like, all night."

That dimple makes an appearance on her cheek, and because it's just tonight, I lean forward and kiss it before going to her bathroom to clean myself up.

We've got a full evening ahead of us.

NATE

THE DAY AFTER MY ONE AND ONLY NIGHT WITH VANESSA, I AM reasonably exhausted, but because I am in the employ of the Morelli family, there is no rest.

Vanessa got ready after probably three hours of sleep and was out of the house on family business with Mary before 9 AM. I pulled myself together enough to interview three men from different crime families and was admittedly too smug writing down clever notes about each of them to laugh about with Vanessa later.

Then we met Mary for another shooting lesson and, unfortunately, I don't think I'm getting any better at guns. I know how I'm supposed to hold my body now; the way my legs should stand in different shooting stances, how high my arms should be, and where my eyes should be looking, but something in me always seizes when I pull the trigger. If I really focus, I can get the bullet near to where I want it on the paper, but there's always a wince or recoil that puts me just slightly off target.

Leo is always nice about it, giving practical advice about aim and form and otherwise cheering me on. Mary is not so gentle of a teacher, but she's got a damn good shot, so I am inclined to listen to her.

"Stop holding your breath," she says and thumps her fist on my shoulder. "Again."

I steady myself, shoot the large handgun again, my wrist sore from all the rounds I've already gone through. This shot hits worse than the last.

Mary releases a belabored sigh. "Put the gun down."

I do as she says without question. The less I have to hold the gun, the better. It's like a live wire in my hand.

"Look at me."

I turn my whole body to look at Mary. She's the smallest of the Morelli sisters, but she doesn't hold herself like she's aware of that. She could be ten feet tall the way her eyes blaze.

"Could you shoot a person? If worse came to worse, could you hold that up to someone and pull the trigger?"

My mouth is dry at the very idea, it makes my stomach roll over to imagine. "I don't know."

"You have to know," Mary says. "You have to decide what you can live with to protect the people you care about."

This is the most words I've heard her speak at once since moving in with the Morellis. She speaks well, deliberate and with utmost gravity to her words. This is life or death she's talking about.

"So? Could you shoot a person?"

I think about my parents and Jenna, who I know would bail me out of any situation, but would they kill for me? Would I kill for them?

"If I had to do it, if there was no other way to protect them, I think I could do it," I say, then correct myself, "I could do it. I would."

Mary nods. Her full attention on me, I can spot all the ways she and Vanessa are alike and different, their brown eyes aren't the same shade but they sit beneath their brows in similar shapes.

Their noses slope alike, but have different ends. Mary has more freckles, she looks younger, though harder. She is unfazed by questions like these.

"Pick up the gun."

I do as I'm told, first reloading it and then turning to the target which she brings closer using the button next to the stall.

"Close your eyes."

This I am opposed to because I am still afraid of what Mary could do to me if I'm off my guard (hell, even if I am *on* my guard, she'd fuck me up), but I'm too tired to be contrarian.

"Someone has broken into your home," she starts, not unlike when I'm interviewing men. I crack one eye open and she glares at me. "A man five times your size. He is about to plunge the largest knife you've ever seen into your father's chest. Tell me what you do, and then do it."

My dad, who's going on an Alaskan cruise this fall that he can't wait for.

"I shoot the man's hand. The one holding the knife," I say before opening my eyes, focusing on the upper left target and shooting. It's not in the center, but it's closer than the other shots.

"The man is hurt, but now he's pissed, too. He storms towards you."

I swallow what saliva I can. "I shoot him again, this time in the chest." I move the gun, shoot again, this time in the center target.

"Nice shot, you hit a lung."

This is the first praise I've heard from Mary and it's a surprising delight. She hits the button to move the target another five yards away.

"Move faster. There's someone about to shoot your mother in the upper right."

I take only a moment to focus before shooting; it doesn't meet the target, so I lineup one immediately after and shoot again, then one more time for good measure. Two of them hit.

She moves the target farther again, I squint at it, my mind

already creating gruesome visages of my loved ones and what could happen to them. It's the stuff my nightmares are made of, the kind of thing I avoid thinking about at all costs.

"Three men stand between you and my sister, she's—"

I don't even hear the rest of the scenario, already aiming and shooting the upper two targets then the middle one, pulling the trigger with precision three times before emptying the rest of the magazine into the middle target. I'm panting when it clicks open, no ammo left to shoot.

Hot bullet shells scatter around my feet.

When I look to Mary, my chest is still racing through breaths, up and down. There is something knowing on her face, and something like respect there. I know she will not ask about this, nor bring it up.

"Again, this time with the .45," Mary says, already moving the target.

* * *

I'M PACING around my bedroom, my cock indecently hard even though I just jacked off about ninety minutes ago, when there's a tiny knock on my door. I move my cock under the band of my sweatpants so I'm not tenting whoever's on the other side.

I hope it's Leo here to tell me that despite the late hour, we need to run five miles. Boss' order. But no, it's the boss herself, the reason I've had to relieve myself twice since waking up in her bed this morning. She's wearing wool socks even though it's the middle of June, and a hunter green silky night dress with little loose sleeves and I want to take it from her and hide it where she will never find it so I can keep it until I die. I'll be buried with it.

Green is my new favorite color.

"Hi," she whispers even though my only neighbor in the hall is Mary who is still in the basement probably sharpening knives or whatever scary shit she does down there for another hour.

"Hi," I say. She teeters on the balls of her feet at the doorway and her eyes are a bit wild, her face is cleaned of any makeup, like she was about to go to bed but came to knock on my door instead.

"Last night—"

"We don't have to talk about it," I rush to say. "It's okay, really. Water under the bridge. Consider it over and done."

"No, stop it. I mean, it's night again."

I nod, but I don't follow. "It is."

If she's not here to tell me we should forget all about the otherworldly sex we had last night, then am I forgetting something? Some appointment we made?

"Do you. . . want to watch a movie, or?"

"It's night again," she says, emphatic. "It's *tonight* again."

The flush on her neck is traveling towards her face and my eyes fixate on where her teeth bite her lower lip.

I do not dare let myself think she means what I hope she does. "It . . . is tonight again."

"Just tonight," she reminds. I nod because holy fuck she is saying what I thought she was saying.

"Just tonight," I agree, and catch her legs around my waist before her mouth crashes into mine. I kick the door shut behind us and deposit Vanessa onto my bed where I plan to, once again, get way too few hours of sleep.

29

VANESSA

Nate is already downstairs when I finally make it out of the shower and pull myself together enough to call myself "ready for work." Although "ready" is generous.

No amount of concealer can hide my under-eye bags, which isn't to say I didn't try. He looks tired too, but he also has the shadow of a smile across his face as he reads something on my iPad. I hate that he knows the passcode, but I have an absurd satisfaction that someone knows it and feels comfortable enough to use it. These pesky domestic butterflies in my gut have been bothering me for two weeks now.

Two weeks of waking up snuggled up to Nate in one of our beds, me vowing to myself that I will not sleep with him again only to do just that.

For once, I have no discipline. Unacceptable.

"Good morning," I say, and he and Mom both look up in unison.

"Are you sick, baby?" Mom asks, already standing to come fuss over me.

"No." I dodge her hands from feeling all over my face (they'd come back with a layer of makeup if she did). "I just didn't sleep well, is all."

"Stress?" Mom asks.

It's been quiet since the gala, almost *too* quiet. Just because nobody has attacked in a few weeks, doesn't mean that they *won't* if we don't keep our guards up.

"Nightmares, if I had to guess," Mary says, brushing past us into the kitchen. "I heard. . . heavy breathing."

I glare at her, but she stares fastidiously down at the chopped fruit she spoons into her oatmeal. Most nights, Mary is out prowling the town doing only God knows what, but last night she decided to stay home?

Rich, rich.

"Oh, sweetheart." Mom pulls me in for a hug, which I return like a board. Mary waggles her eyebrows at me and I flip her off behind Mom's head.

They've been dancing around this for weeks and I've been letting the silence drag on as long as possible.

"His face hides nothing," Mom whispers in my ear, and I let out a sigh much too large for seven in the morning. "And really, you do need to sleep sometime."

I do sleep. Some nights I get seven whole hours. Just not often these days.

"Nate, will you go check on the garden?" My mom asks.

He stops with his coffee cup at his mouth and I give him a look that I hope he reads as *save yourself from the grueling conversation that is about to ensue*.

"If we're sending Nate on errands, go remind Leo that he owes me forty dollars," Mary pats his shoulder. The two of them haven't been chummy per se, but they exchange a dozen words sometimes now, which is big progress.

Nate flips the black iPad case back over the screen and offers a salute before slipping out of the back door, promptly putting his hands in his pockets as he strolls away from the house.

"Sweetie," Mom starts.

"What?" I snap, a little too harsh. I slump my shoulders, immediately contrite.

"How long is this going to go on?" She's so gentle with me, not judgmental, just worried.

"I don't know, probably until he pulls a husband out of a hat?" I take a sip from my green mug on the counter only to wince at how absurdly sugary it is. Nate couldn't drink black coffee to save his life. "It's not safe for him to leave yet. Plus, there are still a few more men to interview."

I don't miss the looks Mary and Mom share across the island.

"What?"

Mom looks uncomfortable, like she's trying to find a way to phrase this nicely. Mary has no such reservations.

"Why not Nate?" She asks, point blank.

"What?"

"Well, why not him? You're fucking him—"

"Mary," Mom chides.

"I'm not fucking him," I defend. "We're just. . ."

Mary raises her eyebrows.

"Okay, yeah, I've been fucking him," I say. Mom throws up her hands, any attempts to police our cursing futile. "But it's not like that, we aren't together."

"And what's so wrong with him?" Mary asks.

I never expected to greet a morning where Mary would be defending a guy, much less Nate, who she has on many occasions called a 'weak, strange little man.'

"What happened to you hating him?" I ask the traitor.

"That was before," Mary says. She puts a big bite of oatmeal in her mouth before speaking again. "He's okay now."

"Before what?"

"Before," Mary shrugs. "Before he got good at shooting. Before he got a haircut."

I thought sending her to teach him how to shoot was a bad

idea for his safety. I could not have cooked up the possibility of them becoming friendly from this. What alternate world am I living in right now?

"There's nothing wrong with him, he just. . . isn't meant for this life. He's said so himself plenty of times."

"He could learn," Mom says.

"He's *been* learning," Mary points out.

"I just worry that you aren't being careful, baby," Mom brushes a hand over my hair in soothing strokes.

"Of course we're careful," I say. Nate has faithfully worn condoms because while I *do* need an heir, a baby out of wedlock might be just the thing that makes the Mothers attack me themselves.

"Gross, Ness," Mary says. "She's talking about feelings."

I blink at my sister then turn to look up at my mother, who has that sympathetic, all-knowing thing about her. What do they think? I'm going to find a husband and be brokenhearted when Nate inevitably leaves? All because of some sex?

"I'll be fine," I say. Why would I not be fine with this? Do they not know me at all? I'm always fine.

"Nate is a good person, Vanessa," Mom says. "And he was already half in love with you when you brought him here."

"No, he," I break off and look away, searching my brain for any truth in what she says.

When he moved in, he made it very clear that he loathed me, my occupation, and his predicament. By my estimate, he barely started tolerating me a month ago. He's just horny. We just have chemistry. It's just convenient. He just—

"He'll leave as soon as all this husband business is wrapped up. When we know who's been sabotaging us," I say.

"Does he know that's still the plan?" Mom asks.

"If he's not an option, you need to tell him that before he starts getting ideas," Mary says. Her spoon scrapes on the inside of her porcelain bowl.

I open the fridge and grab the first thing I can find, an apple and a container of baby carrots. This conversation is giving me hives on my neck. Nothing in my life has felt normal and Nate is the one thing that makes me feel like a normal, warm-blooded woman in a normal, uncomplicated situationship.

I can't be thinking about this anymore today, not when I have an unbearably full agenda and projects with increasingly tenuous deadlines.

"Nate is an adult and he can make his own decisions," I say. "He will be just fine."

"Vanessa, don't be a bitch about this," Mary starts, but I am already on my bitch path and am too exhausted to stop it.

"I'm not!" I say, retreating from the kitchen without glancing back at them.

* * *

I AVOID NATE, my mother, and my younger sister for the whole day, opting to eat out for dinner with Leo instead of going home to their judgmental stares and knowing glances. Nate finds me around midnight, when I'm so tired reviewing contracts that I can hardly read the words. He toes the office door shut and walks over to me with a glass of water in hand. When I take it, he drops a couple of ibuprofen in my palm.

"How's it going in here?"

"Never better," I muse, though the slump in my spine tells a different story.

He snakes his hands around my shoulders and digs his thumbs into the tight muscles in a way that is so soothing it should be illegal. This easy intimacy that has bloomed from the last two weeks brings to mind my mom's concerns.

"You need to sleep," he says.

"You're not the boss of me," I say, but I take the medicine and down the water before I lean back in my chair, my head falling back against his stomach as he stands behind me. My eyes are burning, so I rest them closed for a few moments. "Thank you."

"What are we looking at?"

We.

I press my thumb and middle finger to either side of my temple.

"Willa sent me a contract with some sections flagged for final review but I'm so tired that I think it might be written in Latin. We've been in legal limbo for weeks and the buyer is a sexist shithead who's impossible to work with. You met him once; old guy, last name McGowan."

"The grumpy dude, right? From the gala?"

I nod at his spot-on assessment.

"It sounds like he doesn't deserve your business," Nate says.

Business is so simple to him. Right or wrong, black or white.

I crack a smile and flip a few pages before pointing at the bottom line. The whopping 437 million dollars being discussed.

Nate whistles and leans in to get a closer look. I smell on his neck a lingering hint of cologne that Willa bought for him before he started doing interviews. It's expensive and heady and one I'll never be able to smell again without thinking about smooth hot hands and a stubbly jaw scraping against my skin.

I clear my throat and shift in my seat. "I can't blame McGowan for wanting to be careful, but he's willfully difficult when I'm involved."

"Well, then I hope you're just as difficult for him," Nate says.

"I'm not making it easy, at least."

This deal could have been done a month ago if I had far undercut our worth and agreed to his outrageous demands. But I'm stubborn.

McGowan never would have tried this shit on my dad. I'm not sure if that's because my dad was a man, or if it's because he was better at business.

The niggling imposter syndrome worms around my gut

again, too familiar these past weeks. Without Cillian this deal wouldn't even exist. I have no problem getting other builds around town, and good ones, but not usually "$400 million" good.

"I just hate being taken advantage of. Makes me feel small."

"You're a giant," Nate whispers, and kisses me on my head because, in private, I guess this is what we do now. When shrouded by the night and the promise that none of this is permanent, it's easy to let him hold and touch and kiss me as if he's my person. We can pretend whatever we like when no one is here to see it.

"You'll do better work if you sleep past seven, eat some of the quiche Leo has prepped in the fridge, and look at the contract with fresh eyes in the morning."

Sleeping in sounds like a dream to me, a luxury, one I don't think I can afford right now. Maybe not ever again.

He kisses me on my cheek, then my jaw, then my neck. His lips press against my skin for longer moments as he travels down my neck. I feel quite awake now that I have his mouth on me.

"I'll help you get ready for bed."

"Nate," I start as if to stop him, but I'm already readjusting so he has easier access to my chest.

"Shh." He starts unbuttoning the tiny buttons on the front of my dress. "Just tonight," he mutters, and I can't help the smile that takes over my face. "I love this dress."

"This old thing?" I say, but I know he loves it. Last time I wore the flowy, floral dress, his eyes traced my body every time I entered a room with him the whole day.

He reaches in the dress and pulls down the cups of my bra until my nipples are on display for him and he immediately takes one in his mouth. He groans as he does, and my breathing is already labored. He's so good at touching me, like he's been learning my body for years instead of just weeks. Fourteen tonights.

I slip my fingers through his hair, which is so soft and slightly curling at the ends. He needs another haircut soon, but I love the length, love the noises he makes when I pull on it or tug his head closer to me.

One of his hands slides down my body and up the hem of my skirt until he's at the peak of my thighs, teasing the silky fabric that covers me.

"You're so good," I breathe, surprising myself. It's true, though, he *is* really very good.

"I have to be," he says, moving to pay equal attention to my other breast. "I see the competition every day and they are very handsome."

I giggle, then hiccup as he presses circles on my clit.

"You're hotter than them," I say. It's not a lie; I can't imagine a single person on that list I would want kneeling between my legs more than Nate. "And nicer."

He gives me a wry glare, like he doesn't believe me, but pulls my underwear aside and presses two fingers into me anyway. My back arches pressing my hips to the very edge of the chair.

"You just want me for my orgasms," he says.

Panting, I grin. "I do like the orgasms."

Perhaps sensing that we are toeing too close to something real —something like the feelings bubbling around in my stomach— Nate stands and pulls me up to sit on my desk in front of him. He kisses me deep, his tongue clashing with mine before pulling my lower lip between his teeth.

I work open his leather belt, then his slacks, pulling his already hard cock out between us. His body tenses every time my hand touches him, and I revel in the power. From his back pocket he pulls out a condom and makes quick work of sheathing himself with it.

"Ms. Morelli," he murmurs, and kisses a line up the side of my neck.

"Yes, Mr. Gilbert?"

"I'm going to fuck you now," he says. I grin, putting up no fight as he pushes my panties aside and slides into me. We both gasp. I think I'm growing too reliant on the feeling of him inside of me at the end of each day.

"How do you keep getting better?" Nate asks. His shallow breaths and moans are right at my ear, and they make me delirious.

It's been two weeks of this—sneaking to each other's rooms, his sweet words in my ears, the feeling of his skin against mine, waking with his arm around my stomach, holding me to him. If I let myself think critically, we are growing too close for comfort, but then I remind myself that his time here is limited. He'll be gone before the fall, and I'll be engaged to someone he finds for me.

I arch my back and let him take me deeper, faster, his words becoming gibberish in my ear while we both climb towards our peak. I reach mine first, and bite on my lower lip as to not cry out too loud as I pulse around him, my legs shaking around his hips.

"That's right, you did so good," he grunts. "You let me take care of you."

I can only try to catch my breath and revel in the intense feel of him inside of me while his pace becomes erratic and comes with a long groan and a bite on my shoulder.

We both breathe for a moment, wrapped around each other.

"You're wicked," I whisper. "I thought you were helping me get ready for bed."

He pulls his head away from the curve of my neck and I fail not to be charmed by that smirk of his. "You're not relaxed?"

I shrug and slide my palms down his biceps. I am relaxed, way more than I was twenty minutes ago.

"My bad, then." Nate pulls out of me and slides my panties back in place before tying off the condom and dropping it in the trash. "Come on." Nate clicks off my desk lamp and holds out a hand for me to take. I could fight him, could scold him for waltzing in here and comforting me and fucking me and telling me what to do. I should, I think. But I'm too tired to pretend I don't like having someone to fuss after me and take care of me while I give my best attempt to take care of everything else.

So I let him take me upstairs and draw me a bath and, when I've fallen asleep against his chest in the tub's warm water, I let him carry me to bed, tuck me beneath the covers, and scratch my back as I fall asleep.

30

NATE

I'VE DONE SO MANY OF THESE INTERVIEWS THAT I'VE FORGOTTEN what it feels like to have faith in a man.

I am beginning to wonder if my standards for Vanessa are impossible to meet. It's not like every one of them have failed, but even the ones that do mostly well have one flaw that I cannot look over. And Leo agrees. He's been in the room for almost every one of these interviews and with each one, he gives a shake of his head with varying levels of intensity or, on rare occasion, a weak shrug.

Today will be my thirty-ninth interview since starting on this mad chase for Vanessa, and after that, I might just have to sign her up for *Love is Blind* or begin searching outside of the mafia. Maybe to the pool of state politicians. We've gone out of the immediate circle. I've now interviewed gangsters from California, the nephews of bosses in Chicago (twins, both dicks), and half a dozen guys from Italy who barely spoke English, but did understand the words sex, money, and dinner.

Today Leo and I sit at the old iron table in the backyard waiting for our latest interview. Leo tells me about the baseball team he likes, and I pick tiny green grapes off a vine and burst

KATH RICHARDS

them on my tongue. It reminds me of another taste on my tongue just last night, and then I have to readjust my pants.

He's seventeen minutes late. Maxim Orlov. A new addition Claire recommended after the gala, some Russian man I didn't have the pleasure of running into that night.

Just when I am sure that the man is never going to show up and I will have a few minutes to dissociate thinking about what I will do tonight in peace, Claire leads a huge man through the sliding back door, laughing at something he's just said to her. Ranger hops up from his spot in the shade and runs at the man's feet in an instant. He stops to scratch my dog behind the ears, earning Ranger's forever love and devotion.

I stand to greet him, offering my hand which he gives a firm and respectable shake. No funny business about it. His shoulders are impossibly broad and large, more like a refrigerator than a man, but he makes it look cool. A rather suave refrigerator.

I think all his suits must be custom made, and his hair cut is no less than three hundred dollars, probably every Tuesday.

He is no neighbor's-uncle's-nephew, this man is a boss from the fucking Russian mob and he looks every bit the part. He's got two bodyguards just as big as him trailing behind him and likewise attend to Ranger with the same kindness and ease that earns them a forever companion who would abandon me immediately if they had a meat stick.

"Nathaniel," I say. We tell everyone that's my name, but it feels especially important now because saying my name is Nate in front of him might be like giving a nickname to the queen.

"Maxim Orlov," he says. "Good to meet you."

Leo and I share a glance and I'm glad I'm not the only one noticing after only fifteen seconds how this man is different from the others we've interviewed this summer.

"Sit." I motion for the chair that Leo just vacated, and Maxim makes it look tiny and special at the same time. Like the chair doesn't fit him, but in a much more real sense, it was made for him.

"Thank you for coming here," I say. He nods to one of his guards who brings forth from nowhere a bottle of wine.

"That's kind of you," I say, "I'll make sure Vanessa gets this—"

"No," Maxim says. "It's for you."

I think he's joking, but when a quiet minute passes and his face remains earnest, I mutter my thanks and take the expensive vintage and set it next to my notebook.

"Let's begin."

"Please." Maxim clasps together his hands on the table in front of him. The way this man holds himself, his direct focus on me, ready to listen and answer—he's so unlike the others. They all looked at this conversation as a formality, one they would easily blow past to get in front of Vanessa. Like it was a given. Maxim looks serious.

"You were recently engaged," I say, referring to my notes. "What happened there?"

"Didn't work out. She's now married to someone else and they're expecting their first child."

Vague, but at least she's not dead.

"Why are you here?" I ask, forgoing the usual first questions. Maxim is wearing a black tie over a black dress shirt. There are tattoos poking from beneath his cuffs and snaking across his hands, belying a different man beneath his exterior sheen of luxury fabrics and leather shoes.

"I'll admit I was surprised to hear that Vanessa Morelli was looking for a husband and using such means to do so," Maxim says. "But then again, I am unmarried and yet without a successor. If I'd had the idea, maybe I'd be hosting interviews of my own."

Maxim looks at the grape vines and I do not speak, certain he's not done.

"I need a wife," he says. "I have always respected Vanessa, she's intelligent, independent, and I believe she would do anything to keep her child safe. So, I am here. Because I would be a fool not to be."

Over his shoulder, Leo's eyebrows are high on his head, as impressed with Maxim's assessment and candor as I feel.

"So, you need a child," I start, and Maxim nods. "What if there could only be one and that one was a girl?"

"My community is a difficult one. Traditional. I won't lie, leading would not be easy for her, but then again it isn't easy for any of us. I would support her, Vanessa would show her how, and I would kill anyone who deemed her unworthy."

I set my pen down next to my notebook, not a clever quip to jot down or a pros and cons column to be made.

"Your business is mostly clubs and casinos, right?" Maxim inclines his head side to side as if to say for the most part. "You both work grueling schedules, her all day and you all night. Would you sleep with other women?"

"No," Maxim says definitively, his expression hardening. "And I would expect the same courtesy."

"Even if there is no love between you? There is no one who would tempt you?"

Maxim hesitates. I imagine he's flipping through a mental rolodex of women, considering the scenarios. "No," he says, softer this time. "No."

I'm not even glancing down at my questions; it would feel asinine to give Maxim one of the outlandish scenarios I usually do, what with his security detail and earnest answers about devotion?

I lower my voice and lean on the table.

"How do I know you won't try to take over her business? That this isn't just to secure her power?"

"Of course I want her power," Maxim says. "We'll need it if we're going to raise a child with blood ties to this city's most powerful entities. And as for taking her business, I have no interest in construction, nor the moving of large weapons. It will do us no good if I try to take over her position, spreading me so thin would only make us weaker."

Maxim leans back in his chair and his hands go to the metal arm rests. One side of his mouth quirks, the first almost-smile I've seen from him. "Not to mention that enforcer of hers would kill me for considering it."

Mary. He's right about this, Mary would have no issue murdering him, even if he was married to her sister.

"You must care for Vanessa," Maxim says, and I stiffen. Can this dude fucking read minds too? "These questions are thorough and show a lot of thought. I would want nothing less for one of my own friends."

I swallow the saliva to wet my dry throat and nearly choke on it. "Well, a woman in her position has to be selective."

"She is lucky then to have you in her corner." His flattery doesn't feel false, and that makes this uneasiness in my stomach heavier. I pick up my paper and rove my eyes over remaining questions.

"I have a few more, let's keep going."

VANESSA

AFTER DINNER, WHEN IT'S TIME TO REVIEW THE WEEK'S candidates, Nate is more tense than he usually is. He's been shifting on his feet, and I've caught him staring off at things like they might've betrayed him or confounded him. He's deep in his head.

"You're being weird," I said as he helped load the dishwasher.

"You're weird," he said back, like we are in the third grade.

Now, all of us splayed across different couches in the living room, Nate clicks on the TV to a photo of the only man he interviewed in the last few days.

"Maxim Orlov?" Willa asks. "I thought he was engaged."

"They broke up," Mary says. "How did I hear that gossip before you?"

The picture is one of the many tabloid shots of him, wearing a long winter coat looking more like a clothing model than a boss. At my side, Mary looks bored down at her fingernails, chipping off little pieces of black paint onto the carpet.

I had the idea to add his name to the list, but I never got around to actually doing it. Someone else must've.

"When you danced with him at the gala, did you tell him about this?" I ask.

"He'd already heard," Mary says.

Mom puts a hand on her chest. "He is—"

"Big," Willa finishes. "Handsome."

Sean nods in agreement.

"Maxim Orlov. Thirty-seven and the head of the Orlov family and, in turn, all Russian mobsters in this city," Nate says by way of introduction.

"The whole state, really," Leo says. "Everyone knows the Orlovs."

The Orlov family is not one we've had much trouble with, especially since Maxim took his father's place. My dad always looked at that man with distaste, though his son, he said, wasn't half so awful. He was engaged until very recently to another Russian woman whose name I cannot remember.

Nate is quiet, practically holding up the wall the way he is leaning on it.

"Well?" Mary prompts.

"Give us the bad news," Mom says on a sigh, and we all wait. After another moment, Nate stands up straight.

"He passed. He did great."

There's a pregnant pause in the room as we all wait for the imminent *but*.

Nate just shrugs.

I'm still coming to terms with the fact that Maxim sat for an interview in the first place, now to hear he's. . . passed?

"You're kidding," I say. I look to Leo for back up, but his face is drawn solemn.

"He was good," Nate says. "Reasonable responses to my questions, no immediate signs of anger. Plus, he's got three sisters."

"Is he strong?" Willa asks. We've all seen the man, he's enormous. I can't imagine him not being completely cut beneath his suits.

"I've seen him fight," Leo chimes in. "He's a beast."

"Me too," Mary says, and that's as glowing a review as she could give.

"How many people has he killed?" Mom asks.

"Eight by his own hand," Nate says, referring to his notes. "Notably, three who messed up his littlest sister."

I'm leaning forward now, we all are.

"How did he talk about his ex?" Willa asks.

"Said she was a wonderful woman and hoped she was happy with the man she left him for. Said he would kill him if he laid a hand on her."

"Holy shit," Willa breathes, and I have to agree.

"Is he still in love with her?" I ask. A pining husband wouldn't be the worst thing until he decides to leave me for his old fling. Mortifying.

"I don't think so," Nate says. "Said he wouldn't dare cheat, not after what it did to his own mother."

"No fucking way," Mary says while Willa says, "Is he lying?"

"He seemed legit," Leo says, and Nate agrees, though it looks like it pains him to do so.

I stare at Nate's face, the five o'clock shadow and swatches of gray under his eyes showing his own tiredness, maybe just from today, maybe from all of this—the interviews, the crime, the weeks of *just tonight*. When I catch my mom's eye, she is looking intently at me, communicating in her wordless way so much love and patience, but hard truths too. I need to stop doing this to him before he breaks. Before I do.

I stand from the couch.

"Invite him to dinner," I say. "Tomorrow."

* * *

EVERYONE IS tense while we wait for the Russian. Or at least, I think everyone is tense, but it's more likely that they all can sense how tense I am and it's making them antsy. I've snipped at Willa three times in the last hour, twice while she was just trying to make my hair look nice (nothing I did would make it lay right, nothing, and I was admittedly getting intensely angry about it) and then once just now when she told everyone to pretend to be normal.

I don't want her kids to have to pretend not to be their fun selves, I don't want any of us to have to be dressed in our nice dinner outfits getting to know a mob boss who wants to enter into the economic agreement that is marriage. I want to take off these fucking heels and have spaghetti and watch that asinine Mario movie that Angel and Artie want to watch for the ninetieth time and be as weird as we all want.

It's not Willa's fault, and she knows that. I shoot her a look that I hope tells how sorry I feel about all of it, and she squeezes my hand. We're eating outside again tonight, the patio warm and wonderful looking over at the pool and the lush garden. Nate is running around in the grass with the kids and Ranger, who is barking and bouncing around with the weight of our combined frantic energy. There's a growing ache in my chest at the sound of the kids' laughs mingling with Nate's.

Leo hears something from his earpiece and nods at me across the table before retreating into the house to lead our visitor out to meet us. Everyone gets quiet, the kids even milling towards their seats in preparation for Maxim Orlov. Objectively, it looks like we are waiting for a funeral.

I smooth my palms down my dress, adjust the clasp of my necklace, then fix my posture. Nate's wearing a pea green button up that makes his eyes look like bright emeralds, especially in the sun. I try to look anywhere else.

"Everyone laugh," Willa says and after a moment of confusion, we all fall into an unnatural round of laughter, Angel laughing the loudest, until we are all laughing for real at the absurdity of it. It's just a moment of levity, but it does the trick as Leo exits the house, a tall man behind him carrying a bouquet of tiny roses and greenery.

"Morelli family," Leo begins, "Maxim Orlov."

Maxim makes his way around the circle, shaking hands with first my mother, then Sean, Willa, and the kids before finally stopping at me. He takes a longer moment to shake my hand, his warm and engulfing my own palm.

We've all met before, but now the circumstances are different.

He hands me the roses, which I accept with a smile before handing them off to Willa like they're my bridal bouquet and I'm at the end of the aisle.

"Welcome to our home," I say.

Mary clears her throat to my left, waiting for her own handshake of respect. Maxim startles, his eyes falling on Mary with an intensity that was absent for me. It's so brief; there, then gone in an instant. He shakes her hand and then moves on to Nate, who he greets like an old friend.

He's got two guards, big guys who dress sharp. Maxim introduces them by name, but they stay back, just observing.

"Let's eat," I say and gesture at the spread on the table. Sean grilled steaks and chicken; Leo made two salads. I did nothing to prepare the meal because, again, my hair was all wrong.

The small talk that ensues puts me on edge. Mom is every bit the social butterfly, a skill honed from being by my dad's side for so many years. Willa, too, is a pro at this, but I've never been so good at pleasantries in these settings. If I'm too pleasant, I may be seen as weak, and if I'm not pleasant enough, I'm a shrew bitch. A bulldog.

I suppose I'd rather be a bitch than a floor mat.

I tune in as Maxim tells what must be a charming story based on the mooning expressions of half of the table. He's got Willa and Sean wrapped around his finger, and my mother too looks well pleased. The table chuckles at the end of his story and I clear my throat instead of joining in.

"The man had many enemies," Maxim says, I guess about his father. "It's been a trial mending those relationships."

"How many years has it been?" I ask. "Since he died."

Since you came into power would be too intense for a family dinner.

"Seven years," he says. "I was thirty."

I remember this happening. I was in my undergrad; I came home for the weekend and we all celebrated the senior Orlov's demise. He had been a brutal force in the city, a constant source of terror for any gangster. He'd been killed. I never found out who did it.

"Good riddance," Mary murmurs and I kick her beneath the table as quietly as I can. She doesn't wince, just gives a tight-lipped smile.

Mom is quick to step in. "She means—"

"No, that's alright," Maxim says. "He was a difficult man."

Difficult is a mild assessment, but with my heel pressing against the tender part of her shin, Mary does not say so.

"Cleaning up his messes has been my greatest challenge. Trust is something earned over generations in our business."

I am surprised to find that I agree with what he is saying.

I was lucky my father was as upstanding as he was (well, as upstanding as he could be, he was a criminal like the rest of us). He was fair, at least, and never needed extreme violence to be respected. The senior Orlov was the opposite, notorious for his retaliation and torture methods.

"And aligning yourself with us would help or hinder this effort?" I ask.

Maxim thinks before answering, an admirable trait. Many do not, usually men, but also Mary, who never thinks before saying anything. It's her chaotic alignment, Willa says.

"I believe that there is a place for tradition, but when the tradition no longer serves you, it ought to be excised. Aligning with the Morelli family would be another step in this direction, one that I would like to make one way or another, circumstances not limited to these."

These circumstances being a potential business arrangement with a fancy cake and white gown.

"We would like that, too," I agree, and Maxim gives me a warm smile before I nod to his plate and we all get to eating in earnest.

Maxim tells more stories and is genuine and benevolent in answering everyone's questions. We're going around the table discussing our favorite desserts when I again see something in Maxim's eyes that speaks of some spark just beneath the surface.

"And you, Marianna?"

Mary's head snaps towards him, her eyes no longer absently tracing the evening clouds.

"It's just Mary," she says. Nobody's called her Marianna since Dad died, not even Mom.

"Mary," he corrects. "Your favorite dessert then?" She's the only one who hasn't shared, her mind wandering elsewhere as it so often does during a long family dinner.

"Half-frozen cream puffs," she says. "Or chocolate croissants, but the chocolate inside can't be melted."

Mary resumes her staring at only God knows what in the distance, and we move on to the next topics until dinner is finished and Maxim asks if he can show the children a lawn game that requires only three people, a bucket, and a ball.

"He's perfect," Willa says when he, Sean, and the kids have moved to the lawn.

"He's Russian," Mary points out, and Mom snickers.

"What did you think of him, Princess?" Mom asks.

I am making a strong effort not to look at Nate, who I feel looking directly at the side of my face, his eyes boring holes into my skin.

I drop my shoulders. "Seems genuine at least. But you can never really know someone's intentions."

"You can't," Mom agrees. "Trust is difficult to build, even harder to maintain. Especially in our world."

"For what it's worth, he *might* be perfect," Leo adds. The worst thing is that for as wary as I am, I can't bring myself to disagree.

I watch Maxim in his suit, coat shed and discarded on the back of his chair, coaching the kids on how they might school their dad at this game. The sky bleeds from the purple of sunset to the pale blue of the evening over their heads and I desperately try not to imagine someone else in his place.

32

NATE

I HAVE DECIDED COUNTLESS TIMES THAT I WILL NOT GO SEEK OUT
Vanessa tonight. Not after she and the whole Morelli family were
charmed half to death by Maxim Orlov—whose name literally
translates into Greatest Eagle (I googled it) which makes me even
angrier somehow.

He was comically decent, handsome, and broad like a line-
backer, with all these noble ambitions to make the Russian mafia
a better place. What the fuck is that? If Jenna wasn't still touring
Greece on her Eat-Pray-What-the-hell-ever adventure, I would
call her and she would agree that the whole thing is surreal.

He was as good, if not better, than he was in his interview,
and if Vanessa didn't think that she should have Maxim's beautiful, broad-shouldered babies before, she does now. Or she
should.

Me interviewing and delivering him to her feet like a
recruiter doesn't make the thought of them together sting any
less. In fact, it pisses me off more—the fact that I have no right to
be mad and yet I'm pacing around my room, which is just her
guest room, fuming.

We've been wrapped up in this secret fantasy since the gala, her body and mine, sweet kisses, talking until one of us falls asleep, too tired to keep our eyes open. Some nights she's out doing mafia shit with Leo and Mary when I go to sleep, but in the middle of the night, she'll crawl into my bed with damp hair to cuddle and pretend a little longer that this is something sustainable. I live for these nights.

I don't know how to stop. Worse, I can't imagine wanting to stop. Nearly a month of her hands, her mouth, her moans in my ear like an incantation to her thrall. But we can't have that anymore. I cannot have that anymore.

We shouldn't, not when she's soon to be engaged to the one noble mob boss in the universe.

What we've had is enough. It has to be enough.

I decide that I will seek her out tonight, not for sex but to tell her this, that there will be no more *just tonight* in our future and that the sooner she marries that man, the sooner they can figure out who's been targeting them, the sooner I can get out of her house and her life forevermore, amen and amen.

It's only *tomorrow* from now on, *just tonight* is canceled.

I would love to stomp across the hall to her room, but I don't want to disturb Mary, so I settle for shuffling along the plush carpet, and when I get to Vanessa's door, it swings open before I can knock, putting Vanessa directly in front of me.

"Oh," she says, and that tell-tale red flush is already climbing up her neck.

"Vanessa—" It's on my tongue to tell her all that I've been thinking, the monologue I planned, but when I start to speak, what comes out of my mouth is: "I don't want you to marry that guy."

She appears as shocked to hear this as I am having said it.

"Come in," she says, and closes the door behind me.

I take three long breaths to think through what I'm going to say next, but I'm operating on a previously unknown part of my brain now, the section in my mental command center that plants me right in front of Vanessa and picks her hands up in mine.

"Don't marry him," I say.

"You said he was perfect," she says.

"He is," I agree. "You could have a healthy, protected life with him. Even if you don't love each other, I believe he won't cheat on you or try to undermine your authority."

Vanessa's face is screwed up in some anguished confusion. "What are you saying then?"

"I can't fucking lose you, I don't want to," I say. "I like you so bad. Too much."

"You do?"

"God, yes." I breathe out a heavy exhale and the weight I've felt since before dinner lessens. "Obviously I do."

"But you said—"

"I know what I said."

Vanessa pulls her hands from mine and perches on the side of her bed. I follow and drop down next to her with a few inches between us to give her some semblance of space that I really don't want to offer after that bombshell.

"You know what I am," Vanessa says.

"I do. I think you're the greatest thing that's ever happened to me."

Vanessa puts her face in her hands. Muffled, she speaks again: "How can you say things like that when we both know you think everything about me is abominable?"

I wanted to keep my hands off her, but it's a short and futile battle as I grip her biceps and make her turn towards me.

"That's just it. I don't think that at all. I did at first, but you keep being wonderful, the best woman I've ever met, and every time I thought you were evil or deranged, you've proved to be just the opposite."

"And my life? I'm not going to just get another job, Nate. This isn't a temporary thing you can save me from, this is forever for me. For my kids."

"I wouldn't ask you to," I say, and I realize for the first time that I mean it. These thoughts have been living in my mind where I tried to pretend they weren't real, nestled in beside my very real feelings for Vanessa. She pulls away from my grip and stalks to the other side of the room, once again putting distance between us that makes me feel like I'm floating alone on a raft in the middle of the ocean.

Vanessa worries her hands together and chews on the inside of her cheek. She halts her pacing and meets my desperate gaze.

"I need you to be very clear about what you're saying," Vanessa says, and her voice isn't confident, but nearly shaking. Timid.

I just want to keep touching her, I want to hold her against me —showing my feelings would be easier than speaking them, but I know that wouldn't be enough, so I take a big breath and try.

"Maxim is a better choice. He's perfect for you," I start. "But I want you to choose me instead."

Vanessa's lips part, her brown eyes betraying her shock at the admission.

"I know I'm not strong, I barely know how to fight, and I throw up when I see blood, but I can learn. I'm *learning*. Mary's lessons—she'll teach me how to defend myself better, I can keep working at the school, or I can do accounting for you, I can learn whatever you need, I'd learn for you."

"And the bad stuff? What about when I have to bring a criminal into our home? Someone unsavory in the basement, where I will have to do horrible, unsavory things? What about when I come home with blood on my hands?"

I swallow down the dry lump in my throat, really wishing I'd thought to bring a water bottle. "I'll help you clean them," I say, my mind straying to the night of the gala, her own blood dripping into the kitchen sink. "You have your reasons, and they're always good. You aren't some monster killing for sport, I know that now."

"This isn't—" Vanessa takes a clarifying breath. "I can't date you, Nate. It's all or nothing with me. It's marriage and a fleet of little babies who will have to see and hear and do very difficult things when they grow up. I can't just date someone until they get tired of the bad business and shitty coworkers."

"I know that," I say, though she's right to think that I haven't thought as far down the road as our children having blood on their *own* hands. I only know what our private nights look like. I don't know what being together for real, in the light of day, would look like in practice—in the reality of a marriage, a life together. It terrifies me. "And I still want you."

"You'll change your mind," she says, and her eyes are welling with tears that I want to wipe away with my thumbs. "You can't want this."

I do step closer now, anxious to touch her and hold her and kiss all over her face, put hickeys on her neck so everyone knows she's mine.

"I don't understand it either," I admit. "But I want you all the time. Forever. And I can't keep pretending that interviewing these men doesn't make my blood boil imagining any one of them touching you, standing by you, putting a baby in you. There's not a man on this planet good enough for you, not me, not even the Russian, but I want to try."

I don't reach out to her, but we are close enough now that she has to look up at me beneath her big black lashes.

"Let me try," I whisper.

"You would hate it here." Her quiet voice breaks and a tear spills over. "This place is a graveyard."

I cringe remembering how cruel I was when she brought me here, how she opened her home to protect me, and I spent the better part of a week telling her how wrong she was for it.

"I thought I would hate it. I really tried to, but there's nothing rotten about this place, or your family, or you."

She groans, more emphatic now. "But the night of the gala, *you said—*"

"I lied, Vanessa!" I press on even with the cracking of my voice. "I lied. You scared the shit out of me, and I was falling in love with you, and I thought you could never be with me, and I lied."

Vanessa says nothing, her face searching mine like a cross-word, tears still tracing lines to her chin.

I step closer still and she doesn't flinch when I swipe my thumbs across her cheeks.

"I do, I do. I love you. *Please,*" I whisper, but I don't even know what I'm begging for. "Please."

She must get the message though, because she grips the collar of my sweatshirt and pulls my mouth down to hers.

That does it.

We are mouths and hands and limbs—a cacophony of sensation. I press Vanessa against the wall, pouring a moan into her mouth while she grinds against me until she pulls back and mutters "bed" into my ear.

I press her down onto the mattress and help her wiggle off her shorts before I pull her top up and latch onto her tits as soon as they're in view. She groans, tugging at my hair until I feel pricks of pain in my scalp that light me aflame.

I bite her tits, up her chest, on her neck where I do leave hickeys beneath her collarbone and a light one on the base of her throat, and she lets out the prettiest little moans grinding against my thigh while I do.

"Fuck me," she breathes into my ear. "Now, no condom."

The sound that comes out of me is inhuman, a man possessed. But I do as she says, making quick work of my clothes.

"Turn over," I demand, and she listens. Her ass in the air, hands fisting her comforter, I am dumbstruck. I am paralyzed watching her wiggle beneath me until she lets out a moan, and I am spurred into action. She wants to be fucked, but I must lick her first, I am a starved man, parched, and I lap at her relentlessly as she squirms.

"Nate," she moans, then more stern, "Now."

I would toy with her longer if I had any control, but if she'll have me, I'll have forever to torment her, bring her to the edge and make her beg; today is not that day.

I kneel behind her on the bed, sheathing myself inside of her in two thrusts, making us both groan.

I want to cry, or come immediately, fill her up with it and watch as it drips out after. It's caveman speak and probably not very feminist of me, but I want to fill her up and keep it there, I want to come across her chest, her back, her ass, and then I want her to ask for more. I'm dizzy thinking about it.

My hands grip her hips as I press into her again and again, the feeling of her hot cunt addicting around me and her moans making me delirious. I press harder, faster, until she's moaning into her sheets, her face against the mattress while I hold up her hips and slam into her again and again.

She's going to come, I think, and I see her hand snaking down to rub her clit to take her there.

"Yes, baby," I say. "Make yourself come for me."

She just moans louder, her pussy squeezing around me as I move faster. I keep muttering things, not holding back from showering her with praise and all the filthy thoughts that have been swimming through my head. I tell her she's perfect, that she's mine, that I don't want her to even think about another man, not ever, that I want to hear her come and then I want to hear her come again.

And then she comes, moaning so loud I can only pray that Mary is still in the basement punishing a punching bag. The way Vanessa tightens around me sends me over the edge, all of me spilling into her as my thrusts get more erratic and entirely unco-ordinated.

I try to catch my breath while she comes down, while I come down. We are both sweating, panting messes, and she's poten-tially got bruises on her hips from where I was grabbing her.

I flip her on her back and enter her again, slower languid movements as my dick is growing flaccid. She watches me while I do, and I'm afraid to speak the words aloud but I want her to see them, in my eyes, in my touch. I lean to her ear and whisper them.

"I want to be the one. I love you," I say, and then I say it ten more times, a chant against her ear. "Let me be the one. Please, please."

When I pull away, she looks serious, assessing how serious I am, and whatever she finds makes her nod.

"Okay," she whispers. "Yes."

33

VANESSA

Willa loves affirmations, absolutely loves them. I regard them as optimistic attempts to gaslight yourself into getting through another day without confronting the horrors of this life, but she remains steadfast.

Her favorite is: "Everything always works out for me," and she has me repeat it to her sometimes half a dozen times when I'm having a bad day.

As I drifted to sleep tonight, heavy limbs wrapped in Nate's arms, his soft breath on my forehead, I was inclined to believe her. Things are often, in fact, working out for me.

But it was premature. We aren't asleep for two hours before the cold, harsh hand of reality returns, and it clutches its hand around my neck. Because of course, why wouldn't it?

Mary crashes into the room with Leo hot on her heels, flicking on the overhead light behind them. At first, I think they're here to tell me I shouldn't be sleeping with Nate and I almost tell them, "no it's okay, we're allowed to do that now," but neither of them look fazed as I sit up in the bed. Nate tries to stuff a pillow over his face to block the light.

"We've got more bodies. It's the Washington Street project,"

Mary says. She's already digging in my dresser and tossing black items of clothes at me, a long sleeve shirt, a pair of leggings. "Get up."

She tosses sneakers on the comforter.

"What happened?" I ask, already moving, pulling my hair up, wrestling a bra over my head. "How many?"

"Seven that we know of. Leo sent Rafael to check after the first group of guys went down, and he said it was a bloodbath. Bodies, but no sign of who left them."

"Damnit," I hiss.

"We leave in three," Leo says before he and Mary stalk out of the room to leave me to finish getting dressed.

I pull on the rest of the clothes quickly and to my surprise, Nate is up doing the same. He trips while trying to get his legs into the sweats he was wearing, his hoodie halfway over his head.

"You can't come," I say. "It's not safe."

It very well may be safe, especially if the attackers have left, but he would be most safe *here*. Sleeping in the bed with Ranger snoring at his feet.

Nate gives me a look like I'm being obtuse. "I'm going."

"Hurry!" Mary yells from downstairs.

I stay locked in a battle of stares with Nate for a moment longer before he speaks again. "I'm in this."

"Okay." I stop only to grab my chest holster hanging in the closet and two handguns and an earpiece from the top drawer before heading out, Nate's sneakers squeaking on the stairs behind me.

"What do we know?" I ask Mary once we climb into the car.

"One of the night patrols made a call about something suspicious at the site, he was dead before backup could get there, and then *the backup* stopped responding shortly after. Next was Rafael, but by the time he got there, he said cars were peeling away."

"What kind of cars?" I ask.

"He saw two vans, black, didn't get a look at the plates because one of them shot at him."

Well, that narrows it down to absolutely fucking nothing.

Leo's phone buzzes from where he tossed it onto the dashboard and Mary curses when she reads the screen.

"Distress text from Rafael," she says. "Four of them."

"Shit," I murmur and load the magazine into my dad's old gun.

"Don't you have lackeys to take care of this?" Nate asks, alarm apparent in his voice. "Should we wait for manpower before walking into what might be a massacre?"

He's right, but if we've already lost seven men—possibly eight if Raf isn't alright—then we need to get there and figure this shit out. If one of the attackers is still there, we might be able to get more information from them. It might be the best lead we have.

"Lockdown," Mary reminds, and I bob my head in agreement. We need to take care of this ourselves.

"I've already called Cillian, he's sending guys, but they're twenty minutes out," Leo says. He deftly moves us through the streets, by far my best driver.

As much as I want to make Nate stay in the car where he might be safer, he was the one just a few hours ago claiming to be here for whatever, for the long haul, so I fight the urge. I turn to Nate and put a gun in his hand. He no longer holds it like it's a live fish in his hand, so that's an improvement.

"If someone points a gun at you, shoot them first," I say.

Mary adds her own coaching, "If they even look like they're going to attack you, shoot them. Aim for the chest," she says. Telling him to aim for the head would be too ambitious. "You know how."

"What if the person I shoot is one of your guys?"

I shake my head. "None of our guys would attack you."

"What if it's too dark to tell?"

"If someone is approaching you, or holding a gun in your direction, you shoot," Mary says. "Stay near one of us."

Nate's lips press into a line, but he nods in agreement. When we pull up to the property, the gates are open. Leo parks on the street by the back gate entrance, and we make our way out of the car.

The property is a huge five story office building. Structurally, it's complete, but the exterior is still in progress. The wall length windows are slated to be installed next week. Rafael's car is empty just inside the open gates, an old Toyota. There's a summer chill in the air, but that's not what's making the hairs on my neck stand on end.

The first of the bodies is face-down in the dirt, a puddle like oil spread out beneath him.

"Split up," I say. "You two take the basement and the first two floors, we'll search the perimeter and floors three to five."

Leo and Mary nod before taking off quietly behind the building.

I give Nate one more long look. He is trying not to look at the body we just passed, already looking queasy. This is monumentally fucked, but he's the one who said he could do this, and I would like to believe him.

I incline my head to the gate. We traipse around the building until reaching the front entrance. We step through one of the empty windows and I try not to shush Nate for walking so loudly, but I do give a pointed look at his feet and he tries to move a little quieter.

"Basement is clear," Leo says through my earpiece.

"Two of ours dead on one," Mary reports.

We make our way up the stairwell, which is markedly darker than the rest of the building for the lack of windows. It's only the sound of our sneakers on the concrete steps for two full flights, when we hear a stairwell door above us slam shut.

Nate curses under his breath.

I hold down the little button on the earpiece to make sure it's on. "Someone's on one of the upper floors," I murmur.

Lurking around a building at night with guns and tech is the most spy-like part of the job, but it feels more like walking through a haunted house than anything else. Like the worst part of a horror movie, where you just want the main character to turn back and go home, but they don't, and we can't either. Nate was right that I try to avoid this at all costs—lackeys are great for this kind of thing. Eager to do it, too.

We keep climbing the stairs until we reach the fourth landing. It's better to catch them unawares than to be caught unawares, so I shoulder the door open quickly and aim my gun ahead of me. I don't see anyone, just piles of construction supplies on the floor and a layer of dust visible in the moonlight.

At least it's not a cloudy night.

"No bodies on four, heading to five," I mutter just loud enough that the earpiece will pick it up.

We do a lap of the floor and take the other stairwell to the next. Nate is still behind me, holding his gun with two hands and trying not to be obvious about how much he's shaking. I would speak comforting words to him if I thought it would help or if I was sure that no one would hear me.

The fifth floor immediately shows more life than the fourth, not least of all the drips of red on the concrete floor and the sounds of struggle around the corner.

I use my watch to text "five" to Leo and Mary before creeping towards the sounds following the path of blood.

It smells acrid up here, something sharp that I can't put my finger on. It fills my nose and makes it itch, and it gets stronger as we approach.

Nate stays behind me and now I really am wishing I told him to stay in the car, but it's much too late for that now.

I take a long breath through my nose as quietly as possible before quickly turning the corner and pointing my gun at the sound.

It's Rafael taped up, nearly hanging out of the gaping hole that should be a window. A long strip of black duct tape covers his mouth and around the back of his head, and he makes frantic noises trying to wiggle away from the window.

He's alone.

I do a further sweep of the area, which yields no one before Nate and I grab Raf and pull him away from the window. As we do, it becomes apparent that the rope tying his middle is attached to something dangling outside the building, something heavy. When I peer over the edge, it looks like a gas canister.

Nate pulls the tape down from his mouth as I get to work cutting the rope attached to his middle.

"What happened?" I ask. Raf is bleeding from a wound in his leg, a gunshot if I had to guess, and he's peed himself.

"I thought I was alone," he explains, nearly hyperventilating. "No less than three cars drove off in a hurry, so I was sure that was it, but then—"

He's cut off by the sound of a loud bang on the floor above us, one that rings so loud in my earpiece I have to take it out for fear it's going to destroy my hearing forever.

I turn to Nate and give him the knife I'd been using to cut the rope.

"Get him downstairs," I say.

"What about you?" Nate grabs my wrist. "You can't go alone."

"Load him into the back of the car," I say. "What do you do if you see someone?"

Nate's mouth flounders open and closed.

"Nate."

"I shoot," he says.

"You shoot," I agree. I lean in for one hard kiss against his lips.

"These guys are tough," Raf says. "And they're pouring shit all over the building. Gas."

I nod at Rafael then give Nate as long a look as I can spare before taking off for the stairwell.

34

NATE

I SAW THROUGH THE ROPES BINDING HIS HANDS AND FEET QUICKLY enough, but he groans when I accidentally brush his injured ankle.

"Fuckers shot me," he says, and I am really glad it's not lighter out, because as it is already, I can almost convince myself that the pool and smear of blood is in fact just dirty motor oil. Doesn't do much to abate my queasiness though. The smell makes it worse. He smells like urine, yes, but the gasoline smell in the air is going straight to my brain and making me woozy.

The rope tied to his middle is the hardest to cut, but I saw at it until it breaks and whatever was pulling it down tugs the remaining rope swiftly over the ledge towards the ground.

There are two tense and quiet seconds before it hits the ground with the loudest metal clang and we both wince.

I can be grateful now for the heavy training I've had to do in the last couple of months, because it would have been a huge task to get Rafael off the ground without my added strength. Once he's up and steady on his one good foot and using me as a crutch, we start limping towards the stairs.

We are most of the way there when what sounds like a bomb

goes off outside. It's disorienting, and shakes the building beneath our feet, but I keep moving. The sooner we get out of here the better. Car alarms are going off, and it's only a matter of time before sirens join their call.

One arm around Rafael and the other still holding the loaded gun, we start making our way down the flights of stairs towards the entrance.

It's dark and quiet in the stairwells, but I don't have another hand to hold a flashlight, so we keep on, mostly blind into the pit of darkness below, until finally, we near the first floor.

"You Nate?" Rafael asks as I help him down the last set of stairs.

"Yes," I say.

"My brother was Tony," Rafael says, and my heart lurches. I haven't thought about Tony in weeks, the man who died trying to protect me. "He said he liked you."

"I liked him, too," I say, not a lie.

When I push open the door on the first floor, we are met with dense smoke and smoldering flames. Rafael is spouting out all forms of profanities, muttering about how monumentally screwed we are; I don't disagree, but still, I push us forward toward an exterior wall. None of the windows are in place, so I figure that if we hold to the wall long enough, it will spit us out outside.

Breathing is increasingly difficult, but I was right, and we do find a large hole in the wall where a floor to ceiling window will one day be placed. Or would have been placed. I can't say with certainty that this will ever happen now.

Breathing is easier once we're outside, but not by much until we reach the far gate. It's hard work lugging Rafael, he hops along on with me. He's at least five inches shorter than me, and my muscles are burning on the left side of my back from leaning over as I am.

When we're far enough away that I can see through some of

the smoke, I notice flames licking out of the first three floors of the building, climbing their way up to the fourth and fifth. I don't know where Vanessa is, and I want to find her, or scream for her, but that would mean leaving Rafael to fend for himself, which would mean he would probably die of smoke inhalation.

"Take me to my car," he says. "I have the keys."

We limp along, a bit faster now toward the front of the building where we see that the start of the inferno was the Corolla parked there, now a blistering shell.

I do my best to block out his cries at the sight of his car, his "baby" in flames as we keep to the gate and limp towards the exit.

"I'm gonna kill him," Rafael says.

"Sure buddy, okay watch for the curb, yep big jump, okay."

It's the workout of the year moving him along and we are almost there when I hear my name shouted from somewhere to the left of us.

It's Mary, on the far side of the building, with Leo, pointing ahead of me at something I can't quite make out. I hold up my gun just in case.

A gust of wind picks up some of the smoke and pushes it in the other direction so now I can see that the thing in front of me is not a thing at all, but a person, a tall man in all black holding a gun in my direction.

This is the moment they've been preparing me for, I know this, but as I'm staring at the gun, much closer than I thought it would be, my finger is paralyzed on the trigger.

The split second of thinking is a second too long, and his gun goes off, a bullet whipping past my left side, a horrifying stinging sensation to follow.

It scares the shit out of me, and I almost follow suit in wetting myself, but I just manage to keep it together. I don't think I was actually shot, just grazed, but it still stings horribly.

I look back up at the man and do what I should have done

first: I pull the trigger at the moving target, hitting his arm, then another, this time in his shoulder.

I surprise myself by wishing it had struck his chest instead.

I line up for another and shoot, this one missing. Instead of aiming back at me, the man uses his good arm to shoot towards Leo and Mary, the sound of his gun firing followed immediately by a shout. I shoot three more times as he runs, none landing and then he's gone, running outside the gates and into a car waiting for him that rips down the street.

There's another explosion from inside the building, spurring me to regain my hold on Rafael and keep moving, checking only once to make sure Leo and Mary are making their way, too. They are, but Leo holds Mary in a bridal carry as they approach. She looks alive at least, a scowling grimace on her face, and it's no time at all before they've caught up to us.

"Where is she?" I shout, and Leo nods ahead where sure enough Vanessa is backing up the SUV down the street, screaming at us to hurry up and get in.

Rafael's face is ashen, and Mary is bleeding fucking everywhere from a wound in her shoulder, but we make it into the car and Vanessa whips down the street before the fire department can get there.

"Mary, I'm so—"

"Forget it, you did good," she cuts me off, her voice strained. "Don't hesitate next time."

Vanessa and I make eye contact in the rear view, but she turns her focus back on the road.

"Catalog," Vanessa says.

"Mary was shot in the shoulder, Nate was shot at, did it hit?" Leo asks.

"Grazed my arm. I'm fine. Rafael was shot in the leg and has a broken ankle."

"Any other injuries?" Vanessa demands, her voice uneven.

"Yeah, they blew up my car," Rafael whines from where he sits in the trunk. I pull off my hoodie and look at the damage on my arm. It's bleeding, but not nearly as much as the other two injuries in this car.

"We'll get you a new Corolla," Vanessa says. "Hospital first."

It's a tense ride there. Leo instructs me on how to apply pressure to Mary's shoulder as she gets less lucid from blood loss, and I try not to make a shit situation worse by fainting.

Vanessa makes a few calls on the way to the hospital, one to someone telling them we're going to a hospital and to have beds ready, another to Sean and Willa telling them to go to the site to meet with the cops, a third to her mom telling her everything is okay but she needs to come to the hospital and bring everyone some clean clothes.

When we get to the hospital, Vanessa backs the car into a back entrance where a team with two gurneys wait.

We load Mary and then Rafael up onto them and trail behind as the staff in green scrubs wheel them down empty fluorescent hallways and into examination rooms that we aren't allowed to follow into. We all follow anyway, and they don't press.

The staff is obviously familiar with Vanessa, talking to her like they know her and multi-tasking while they listen to her explain both Mary and Rafael's conditions. One doctor scrawls notes onto her clipboard as Vanessa recites all of her sister's medications, others swiftly and deftly fuss over Mary and Rafael.

When the team has enough information and a plan, they unlock the wheels and push the beds through another door in the room. I stay back, certain that the growing spot of blood coming from Mary will make me pass out if I keep looking at it.

After a few minutes, Vanessa joins me. Her face is covered in soot and there's a trail of dried blood from her left ear and a smeared one from a gash on her lip. She's alive. I'm alive. Everyone is alive. Tonight was a shitshow, but we are alive, and the sun is going to come up in an hour and we will still be okay.

She calls for a nurse to take care of my arm, and I'm ushered into an exam room across the hall where a very kind woman cleans my wound, shoots it with numbing shots, and gives me seven stitches total. She does all of this while chatting amicably, as if we didn't just come in here with two people in horrible condition.

All the while, Vanessa stands and watches, her every muscle tensed and eyes wide and unfocussed. I can't read what she's thinking, but I know it's nothing good.

Forty-five minutes later, I'm patched up and the nurse brings us water bottles before showing us to a quiet, empty waiting room.

Now, all that's left for us to do is wait.

A tense and silent moment passes before she lets me fold her in my arms, her face pressing against my chest. I'm not sure if she knows that what happened to her sister is my fault, that the only reason Mary was shot is because I couldn't get my shit together to pull the trigger when I had a clear shot, that I was as useless as she thought I'd be, too weak to take someone out even though they were right in front of me, gun pointed at me.

"I'm sorry," I murmur into her hair repeatedly, holding the back of her neck to me.

"You could've died," she says, and I feel her back hitch like she's crying, holding in a sob.

I squeeze her tighter and smell her hair, which smells predominantly like smoke, but also like the coconut conditioner in her bathroom. I memorize the scent, certain that she'll never let me hold her again when she knows what I did—what I didn't do, and how unfit I am to be by her side.

"I'm okay," I say, and then I say it again, and rub my palm along her back until she stops crying.

3 5

VANESSA

THE SURGERY ON MARY'S SHOULDER TOOK THREE HOURS, AND
Nate sat with me to wait. We watched the sun rise through the
window of the private waiting room, drank cups of tea and burnt
coffee brought to us by hospital staff, and shared a dense bagel.

Rafael needed surgery too, but his was quick, and he was
already recovering in a room on the sixth floor, two men
stationed at his door just in case. I do not know who attacked us
last night, and the worst thing is that, after months of shit like
this, I don't have even an *idea* who it could be.

I am completely out of depth and have no idea where to go
from here.

The lockdown didn't work. It got Mary and Nate shot. The
ever-growing list of reasons I am not cut out for this is miles long
at this point.

Leo is out doing his own investigation, but I don't imagine
he'll find any evidence that points us in the direction of who it
was. That would be too easy, and nothing about this has been
easy since that first shipment went missing in April.

Nate has been good, a steady presence next to me through the
night, but I know he's spooked. Who wouldn't be? He got shot,

and that wasn't even the first time he was almost killed because of me.

If he stays, it most certainly won't be the last.

Mom arrives around six with Willa on her heels. Sean is at home with the kids, who are anxious to see their aunt Mary better.

"Any news?" Willa asks, though the news is the same as the last time Nate texted her forty minutes ago. Mary is stable, set to make a full recovery. We'll be able to see her in an hour or so.

"You smell like an ashtray," Willa says after another minute. "Go home. Mary will be discharged before the end of the day, and if she's not, you can come back tonight."

It takes another thirty minutes of her and my mother convincing me that they can handle things here before Nate and I walk out of the hospital the way we came, and despite my protests, he drives us home.

It's a quiet ride. I can tell something it is eating at him and I'm too afraid to ask him what it is. I don't want to hear him say that he was wrong, that he takes back what he said and could never be with me. Not when this is my life, and he will have to be afraid for the rest of forever that his life or mine will end with a bullet in one of our skulls.

I get it, I really do. I wouldn't want this either if I were him. He deserves someone nice, a sweet thing who is good at gardening, has lots of recreational hobbies, someone who will be a good mother to the horde of children he wants to have. I can provide him none of this.

I cry silently, he grips my hand with the one not steering. I'm overdue for my semi-monthly stress cry, and now it all bubbles out of me in hot streams down my cheeks and neck.

All I have to offer him is pain, bloodshed, violence, a life of crime always maintaining our power on the top and sniffing out rats when threatened. I won't be a good mother, not one who will do anything to protect their baby from the horrors of the world, I will have to show them these horrors firsthand and teach them how to fight the demons that crawl in the shadows. It's not something I can escape.

He doesn't leave my side when we get home, both of us stripping out of our dirty clothes before stepping into the shower together. I let myself cry a little more with the hot water streaming down my face, and he washes my hair with gentle fingers massaging my scalp before rinsing it and repeating the process with conditioner. He does the same with the soap, lathering up his hands and sweeping them over my body, not missing any place from behind my ears to my feet.

I help him and don't pull away when his lips fall on mine, soft and sweet kisses on my lips before they travel down my neck. They feel like a plea or an apology, and I wonder if he knows the same truth that's settling over me like a heavy curse:

This is the last I will have him.

I'd already decided as soon as I'd heard that gunshot when Mary called his name. I knew then I couldn't do this to him, I couldn't ask him to live this life. It's not him who can't do this, it's me—I won't let this man live in danger like this for me, it's not fair.

I will not be the death of Nate Gilbert. I refuse to be the reason he doesn't breathe on this Earth. It's selfish, and I know he is an adult, old enough to make his own decisions, but he has no idea what it will be like.

He knows three months in my house, summer nights watching movies and swimming with us in a warm pool. He knows being with my family around the dinner table and practicing fighting in a basement. He doesn't know what it will be like really, how it will feel to be married to someone who must be cold and ruthless every day of the year. He can't imagine what it will feel like to know who I've killed, and to have to know his kids will kill too.

If he doesn't get hurt or killed, he will get resentful, and I can't take that, I won't.

So, yes, I am selfish. I let him kiss up and down my body and carry me, still dripping from the shower to the bed, and there I let him make love to me until I cry, and then I let him hold me, because it's the last time. Just tonight. I will sleep, and pretend the world hasn't stopped spinning, and when the sun sets tonight, I will be engaged to someone else.

I'll lose my nerve if I wait—he will wear me down with sweet kisses and proclamations of love repeated like a prayer in my ear.

It has to be tonight.

* * *

MARY IS FINE, stitched up and ready to go home, but the doctors want her to stay for another day, so despite her protestations and the number of texts demanding that I "just tell them to let me go," she will come home tomorrow morning.

We didn't have long to sleep this morning before I had to be on the site talking with city commissioners with Willa, who'd come straight from the hospital.

The day was a mess of paperwork, phone calls, and trying to figure out who the hell shot my sister and destroyed a project costing several million dollars and months of work.

We have no leads.

I would've kept working into the evening, but Nate and my mother ganged up on me and forced me out of the library.

They made me wash my face, and mom even put an eye mask on me before tucking me into bed, all before nine.

I pretended to sleep, slowed my breathing enough to make it look like I was relaxed, but my mind was still circling the drain, spiraling downwards and around one truth: I am not powerful enough to protect everyone I love.

It's the rudest of awakenings, one I haven't let myself fully believe all summer. Even with the shipments missing, and the attacks, I thought I could handle it.

I cannot.

Dad, you picked the wrong daughter.

I can't imagine what he would do in this situation, but a large part of me believes that he wouldn't be in this situation in the first place.

He was beloved, revered, and feared. I am liked well enough by some and loathed by others. It's not just because I'm a woman either. I'm too business focused, always trying to expand our company dealings and power in the city, not fostering my community enough.

Dad was notoriously a father, not just of us three, but of everyone in the Family. I am not as loving, or paternal. I am an unmarried 28-year-old who killed her first fiancé and has been interviewing marriage candidates like a twisted reality TV show.

I need to pivot.

Once I'm certain Nate is asleep beside me, I lay a kiss on his cheek, a light one to not wake him, and then I crawl out of the bed. I don't want him to hear me rifling through my closet, so I borrow some of Mary's clothes, a pair of black jeans that look more like capris on me and a tight T-shirt. It'll have to do.

We haven't talked about yesterday, but I know it's been eating him up. He's been quiet all day, helping where he can, but he's shaken. He's trying to find a good time to tell me that he can't do this, can't be with me, not when it costs so much. I can see in his eyes, he's tortured.

When I get to Maxim's club, it's well-past midnight but the music is still thudding outside.

The bouncer lets me in without asking my name and it's a nice touch, a point for Maxim in this asinine game I've been playing, rating him against someone nothing like him, someone who I like infinitely more.

The club is spacious and electric, a lowered dance floor with standing tables and lounging booths on the raised areas against every wall. There's a long bar elevated on a platform to one side and a stage across the room where a live DJ plays. The club is packed, dancing bodies pressing against each other in the thrall of neon drinks and punching music. I'm underdressed—or overdressed if we're talking about the sheer amount of fabric on my body.

I go unnoticed by patrons, all of them too distracted with the joy of their evenings, who they will meet, what they will do. A woman in a sharp suit finds me before I can venture into the club farther and leads me with a light smile to a glass staircase.

She leads me wordlessly to a table in the VIP area with a full view of the main floor where I find Maxim sitting alone with a glass of scotch. He's less buttoned up than yesterday, a tailored black shirt with the top three buttons undone and sleeves rolled over his forearms. His hair is mussed too like he's ran his hands through it too many times tonight. This is the look I expected from him, dark and powerful. Lethal. He's a broader version of Cillian with darker features.

He watches me respectfully, like he's pleased to see me but not surprised that I'm here.

"Nice club," I say, but I don't sit down. He leans forward, resting his elbows on his knees.

"My first project with Morelli Construction," he says, which I already knew. It was an olive branch after his father passed, when Maxim made it clear that the blood between us didn't need to be spoiled. "Something to drink?"

"Is there somewhere quieter we can go?" I say instead.

Maxim stands; Willa was right, he really is a huge man. He's bigger than Leo, which is a genetic feat. He leads me through the second floor towards an elevator that brings us up and out to the roof. We can still hear the music, but barely.

"I heard about your project," Maxim says after we look quietly over the city for a few moments.

"Was it you?" I ask.

Maxim sighs, shakes his head. I believe him. I knew it wasn't, there was something personal about last night's attack. Hitting us where we were down, then going for Nate and Mary.

"I will be clear, and I expect the same from you," I start, and when he inclines his head, I go on. "I will not guarantee love. I cannot."

He leans on the rail and turns towards me. In this position he is almost the same height as me.

"Nathaniel," he says.

I give him the same honesty I expect from him. "Yes." My voice doesn't wobble nor crack. "But I will be loyal to you, and I would expect the same in exactness."

"You do not choose him?"

"I choose for him to live."

Maxim does not question this, and I am grateful. He runs a hand across his jaw, the shadow of a beard beneath his palm.

"I agree to those terms," he says. "Are you very cruel?"

I give the question the thought it deserves. Beneath us, a couple emerges from the dive bar across the street, giggling and hanging all over one another.

"Some would say I am," I say. "Though I would prefer fair."

He looks to understand the sentiment.

"Are you? Cruel?"

He considers this as his eyes travel over the skyline, a sea of lights twinkling beyond.

"My father taught me to be very cruel. Exacting." He examines his hands, the backs of which are marred with smooth scars on his flesh. "But my mother was different. She was forced into a marriage with a horrible man who tortured her relentlessly, lacked control in every area of her life, but she held her own rebellions. Tiny ones, in our rooms at night where she taught us to be kind.

"So yes, I have been all manner of cruel in this life, enough for ten lifetimes. But I do prefer to be kind."

Good enough. Better than most, even. "What do you seek to gain?"

"Same as you. An heir and more bodies to protect them, and if not love, then companionship. Someone smarter than me who will tell me when I'm being an asshole."

Two months ago, this would have been music to my ears. He is everything I wanted in a match. But now the words only serve to remind me what the arrangement will not be and who it will not be with.

Same as you.

If Nate can live a peaceful life, I will have gained much more from the arrangement.

"Someone has been after me," I say. If he knows who it is, his lack of reaction is compelling acting.

"The rat Mary mentioned. At the gala."

"Yes," I say. "I've been trying to handle it, but last night went too far. They hurt my family."

This catches Maxim's attention, a part of the story he didn't hear. We pay out the ass for discreet hospital staff, and it's good to know that's paid off.

"Mary," I say, "My little sister. She was shot."

"Is she—" Maxim's eyes are wild at the news, just a flash, but enough to confirm my suspicions.

"She's fine," I give him a wry look. "Maxim, I will never ask again but tell me now if you're in love with her."

Maxim says nothing for a time, which I take to be answer enough. Mary does not make herself easy to care for. This news would be refreshing if the situation wasn't what it is.

"She's come into my club before," he explains, and this surprises me. Mary is the last person I would ever expect to come to a club alone, but she is a creature of many secrets, always skulking off into the night. To go clubbing, apparently. "She fascinates me, is all. It will pass."

I don't believe it will, but if he marries me, the object of his fascination will torment him forever. Mine will move to Connecticut. Not sure which of us is worse off.

"You can never have her if you're with me." I am sorry to say it.

"Of course," he agrees. "It's not something to worry about."

I can sense his finality in this. Even if the discussion at hand wasn't about our potential marriage, I wonder if he would see Mary as a viable option. She's the blade of the family, honed to a fine point and sharp edge; she doesn't go out of her way to be liked. In another life I might've enjoyed seeing this man, a decade older than her and double her size, try to win her. But we aren't afforded a life where people like Maxim Orlov and me get to marry who we'd like.

"I'm doing what I can to keep business moving while searching for the people who want to see me fail. But until I do, this is my baggage," I say.

"I will help you find them," Maxim says, a new determined lilt to his voice. When I raise an eyebrow, he goes on, "It serves both of our best interests if we take them down quickly."

Searching means more interrogations, more blood, more bodies. But he is right.

It never gets easier being the one with final say, the one who makes decisions, shakes hands, reports it to others. It's a constant second guessing, imposter syndrome bubbling in my stomach that I must pretend doesn't exist.

I wish again that my father was here to make this decision for me.

"You have until we announce the engagement to wrap up any romantic entanglements you may have," I say.

He dips his chin in agreement. Steadying myself, I hold out a hand to Maxim.

"Maxim Orlov, will you marry me?"

A smile tugs on his lips. "I will," he says, and shakes my hand.

36

VANESSA

Nate is awake when I get home, sitting at the island in the kitchen with a glass of water half empty on the counter in front of him. I can't see Ranger but I hear his tiny snores coming from the dog bed in the living room.

A day ago he was telling me he loves me. Tonight I am engaged to someone else.

I want to retreat to avoid the conversation entirely. If I can sleep right now, it can stay a secret. If nobody knows for another six hours maybe it won't be real until then, and maybe he won't hate me more than he already does.

Or maybe Nate will feel relieved that he doesn't have to go back on the promises he made last night before he knew.

I don't know which is worse.

He looks over his shoulder at me standing in the doorway.

"Hey," he says. It's dark in here, dimmed cupboard lights and the moon on the countertops. It reminds me of the night of the Mayor's Gala, the first time.

"Hi." I make my way to the other side of the counter opposite him where we stay in silence until the sprinklers in the backyard click on.

We both start to speak at the same time and cut off. He waves at me to go first.

"I have to marry Maxim," I say.

The look on his face is so much worse than I'd prepared for. He's never been good at hiding how he feels—I've seen him angry, then nervous, then disgusted. I loved most to see him lustful, in love. He held a warm softness to his green eyes that saw his own feelings reflected in my own. Now, I see him gutted, and it turns my insides over to know I am the cause.

"Is that where you were?"

"Yes," I say and my voice is so small.

"Hm."

I want to explain everything, spew word-vomit about how I will never be good enough to be with him. I've put him in enough danger and I refuse to do it any more even though I desperately want to. Even though it makes me sick to think about living without him next to me telling me when I'm being rude, or unfair. I want to tell him I already miss him, like there's a vital organ in my abdomen that he's carrying around with him, and that I'll even miss that stupid dog, I'll miss everything about Nate. I want to tell him this and more, but instead I just let my head bob on my neck as I try to swallow back the stinging in my eyes.

A tear spills over, and then another, and I wipe them both away.

"It's not personal." I try to contain the shaking in my voice, but it cracks. "It's not you. If this was different, if *I* was different. . . it's not you."

He doesn't cry, much more held together than me, but he does stare hard at me like he can still see straight through me.

"Don't do this," he says. "You don't want to do this, Vanessa, *so don't*."

He reaches across the counter to grip my hand, but I pull it away from him. Hurt flashes again in his eyes before they harden to something else.

"I can't convince you," he says. Not a question, but I shake my head anyway.

Perhaps it would be easier for him if I lied. If I said I *wanted* to marry Maxim over him. But that lie would hurt too much to speak, and just like the rest of me, he'd see the truth behind my carefully curated walls.

Nate smacks a hand on the counter. "You're so fucking *stubborn*, Ness. Why?"

Tears keep falling from my eyes, there is no stopping them.

I want to ask him if he'll hold me, if we can have one more tonight, just one more, but it's not fair to him and if I touch him again, I might be liable to never let him go.

"I have to do this."

Nate stands up to leave and pauses like he might say something, and I selfishly pray that he will say anything at all about how he wants it to be him, how Maxim will never get me like he does, how his life will feel as empty as mine already does in this moment.

He doesn't, just retreats from the kitchen, up the stairs, and into his room.

I'm left alone in the cold kitchen; Ranger's snoring, the sprinklers stuttering on, and my own soft crying are the only sounds that remain.

* * *

A WEEK HAS PASSED since I told Maxim Orlov I would marry him, and it has been filled with wedding planning and tracking down who shot Mary.

My family took the news fine when I told them I would be marrying Maxim. They all shared looks with each other, and Willa tried to give me one of her sisterly talks, but I told them that I wouldn't be hearing any of it and now was the time for them to remember to respect my decisions. They all agreed after that, but nobody congratulated me. It would've been an empty gesture; one I didn't need nor want.

Nate has kept to himself, largely avoiding me or acting like I didn't rip out his heart and mine and put them into a blender. Conversations with him are stilted and brief. No more sitting on the couch watching movies until one of us falls asleep, no more glances over meals, stolen touches in hallways, no more just tonights.

Mary's not allowed to train while her shoulder heals—her personal hell—so she's been terrorizing Nate with lessons of self-defense and shooting. He won't be here forever, so it's a relief to know that when he's on his own he will be able to defend himself.

Willa has been in her own kind of hell dealing with the insurance, buyers, and investors for the Washington Street project. I do not envy her, but I don't envy myself either; Leo and I have been working with Sean investigating, it's some of the worst work we have to do.

There's lots of interrogating and threatening and watching lifelessly as Leo beats the shit out of someone until there's nothing left to do but speak. We tracked down one of the vans, only to find that it was one of *our* vans stolen out of a parking garage last week and more video evidence was tampered with. After a particularly difficult conversation with the security guard on duty in the lot that night, he confessed that someone had paid him off to give them the key and threatened his wife and daughter to keep it secret. Classic move.

When pressed further, it became evident that the man didn't know who the thief was. They'd been in thick black masks, not even their eyes were visible, and they had some sort of tech to modulate their voices.

This news drove Sean nuts because that tech is familiar, something he and Cillian had brought in and sold late last year.

He was certain it had to be a match and had been checking books for every buyer.

We've been chasing threads, desperate to get to the bottom of them before they're cut short. There have been three attempts on the system this week alone, so on top of searching through last sales, Sean had his hands full making sure our cyber security was safeguarding us from further damage.

It's been a shitshow, to say the very, very least.

While all of us have been doing our part to not make it look like we aren't chickens with our heads cut off, Mother planned an engagement party and has already started planning the wedding that will happen next month.

We are on an expedited schedule, though trying to be discreet.

The announcement will come tomorrow at the engagement party when any number of Russian and Italian mobsters will be annoyed to hear that the town's two most eligible criminals will be getting married to each other.

Mom brought a seamstress over to do some alterations to a gown made just for the party. None of the ones I had made enough of a statement. Which I think was code for: *Your closet of blood-red slut dresses will not cut it for your engagement party, and this is hopefully your last one, so you'll let me do what I want.*

We stand in her room in front of her tall mirror while the seamstress fixes the hem on the green silk gown, the exact color of the emerald eyes that will haunt me forever.

"Green signifies new beginnings," she says. "I wore green to my own engagement party."

"You did?" I've never seen pictures of that night, only the wedding where she looked like a goddess with huge, curled hair all over her shoulders.

"I was so nervous," she says, her eyes dreamy into a near distance. "I grew up watching your father at weddings and parties, he was ten years older than me, practically a prince to me and my friends."

A smile flits across her lips, and I'm reminded how young she is, fifty-three. She married my dad when she was twenty-two and had Willa right after. Once their parents decided they would be married, Dad wanted to marry her immediately, but she made him wait until she was out of college. Said it was important to be educated, even if she'd never want for anything for the rest of her life.

She didn't know she would be left wanting for her own husband.

"Any advice?" I ask, because I'll cry if I keep thinking about how much she misses my father. How much I miss him.

The seamstress pulls tight at the skirt, and then lets it fall, repeats this a few times and adjusts a pin.

"Oh, sweetie." Mom meets my eyes in the mirror. "You are so much smarter than I was. You have a brilliant head on your shoulders."

There's a 'but' there, I can feel it.

"Spin," the man working on my dress says, and I follow his instructions. "Perfect."

He helps me out of the dress carefully before Mom can continue, and it's another seven minutes before he's gone, leaving me and her in the quiet of her room. I used to hide in here when I was a girl, when I was too tired to consider doing another training session with Dad. I would come hide behind their curtains, waiting for mom to find me. I wish I could do that now.

"All I want for my babies is happiness," she says. "My biggest advice is to find a champion for you and hold on as tight as you can until the end of the line."

She's talking about Nate, but we both also know that he's not an option anymore.

"Maxim will be good to me," I say. "He will love our children and fight to protect them. I think this is as much as I can ask for."

Her eyes swim with sadness at this.

"Are you sure about this?" she asks.

I turn to face her; I'm wearing her old slip, the one she wore beneath her wedding dress, that Willa wore beneath hers.

"I'm not sure," I admit, just a whisper, and it's a weight off my chest to finally say it aloud to someone. "I'm not."

Mom pulls me to her chest where I don't cry, but I do stay, holding her and being held, remembering the thousands of times she's comforted me this way in my life. Like I haven't let her in years.

"I didn't realize how lonely I've been," I confess in a whisper. She keeps stroking a hand through my hair and down my back until there's an imprint on my cheek from where it was pressed against her shirt.

It's time to keep moving.

"I'm going to marry Maxim." I sit up to face her again. There are unshed tears pooled beneath her brown eyes that look like mine. "And somewhere along the way, there will be happiness."

Mom gives my arm one more long squeeze before crossing the room to her armoire and pulling it open to look at her jewelry. After a moment she closes it, retreating with a black felt box I recognize instantly as the object of 40% of my adolescent longings. She pulled out the box for every big event—sometimes letting my sisters and I try it on in front of her bathroom mirror.

Now, she inclines her head to the mirror like she did then, and I gulp before following her there.

Mom pulls out the necklace, and I hold up my hair so she can fasten it on my neck, the thin gold chain holding up a ruby pendant that lies in the middle of my chest.

"Your grandmother gave this to me when I needed it. You need it now, and when there comes a time one of your sisters needs it, you'll give it to them."

I touch the stone, bright red and a weight against my skin. A comfort.

"Thank you," I say, and set my shoulders, lifting my chin.

37

VANESSA

WILLA DEMANDS TO DO MY MAKEUP FOR THE ENGAGEMENT PARTY, and she chatters on about any and everything as she does. This was her plan, I'm sure. To distract me from the night ahead with anecdotes about Taylor Swift and all the theories around her next album, or by describing in depth the plot of the show she's been watching with Angel and Artie. Anything to not think about work, or Nate, if I had to guess, and for the most part, it works. Mary lounges in a chair chiming in too, a real team effort to keep my mind from wandering.

I'm grateful for all of it.

The three of us laughing in my bathroom, Willa chiding me for moving too much or sneezing, it feels like high school. For any number of school dances, parties, or weddings, the same rituals have been completed; sisters putting on makeup, doing each other's hair, curling or straightening or crimping if we are talking about Willa's first homecoming.

There is a comfort in the practice of it. I would do anything to protect this from breaking, and the thought straightens my spine reminding me why I am doing this.

Willa uses a big brush to apply powder to my whole face,

especially my forehead which she says is genetically predisposed to get greasy, and then she squeals.

"Mary, tell your sister she looks beautiful."

Mary looks up from her phone and squints assessing me.

"You do look beautiful," she says, and then stands to look at all three of us in the mirror. "We all do."

We do. Undoubtedly sisters, there are a dozen micro-similarities in our faces, though uniquely our own. Mary's hair is in the same curly, dark A-line it's been in since high school and Willa's honey hair lies in big curls down her back. Mine is straight, held behind my ears by pins with little red gems on them, and parted down the middle.

"But me the most, right?" I ask, and they both snort a laugh.

They help me into the heels and green gown next. For a moment, I can almost forget my troubles, until someone clears their throat from the door. Our three sets of eyes swivel to the door and it's Nate looking nervous and tired in a crisp suit, a new one. Willa's doing, I have no doubt.

"Can I have a minute?" Nate asks.

Willa and Mary turn to me, ready to shoo him from the room if that's what I need. Without looking back at either of them I give as much of a nod as I'm able when my heart is beating in my throat.

"We'll be downstairs," Willa says and grabs her makeup bag before she and Mary retreat from the room, closing the door behind them, leaving me and Nate alone.

Nate's face breaks from the collected mask he had in place. "Don't do this."

I release all of the breath I was holding in one huff, and he comes closer.

"Vanessa, don't do this. You're rushing into something very permanent with someone you don't know."

"I have to, Nate. I—"

"You *don't*," he cuts in. "You really don't have to do this. You are the strongest, scariest woman I know, you don't need to marry *anyone*."

"I need to keep my family safe," I say. "I need to keep *you* safe, Nate. You're not safe with me, you've been attacked three times since that parent teacher conference."

"You've been protecting me just fine."

"Not enough!" We are both quiet in the aftermath of the sound. I work to steady my breathing again or to lower my heart rate, anything to keep me from exploding. "It hasn't been enough."

Nate runs his hands through his hair, which is a mess. He steps closer, then thinks better of it and paces to the window.

"You've wanted to go home since the moment I brought you here," I say. "This will help make that happen."

"For Christ's sake," he mutters, and now it's my turn to approach him, to beg him to understand.

"You'll be okay, Nate. You can move home and no one will ever bother you again. You won't have to think about the mafia, or organized crime, or anything else for as long as you live, and you and your family, you'll all be safe again—"

"God damnit Vanessa." Nate thuds the side of his fist against the wall and closes the distance between us before he grips my face between his two hands. His fingers on my neck thread through my hair, and I can look at nothing but him.

"I don't give a shit about living some boring ass life teaching math in Connecticut, so if you're doing this for me, then you need to stop right now." He puts his forehead against mine. "Please, just say you won't marry him."

"Nate—"

He cuts me off with a kiss, one so heady and intense that I want to fall into it. I want to forget every bad thing happening and forget how helpless I feel, but I force myself to memorize it. I need to remember his thumbs and his palms, his lips that are so unbelievably giving, his eyes that tell me all his secrets. I make myself commit everything about this kiss to memory and then, knowing I will never be satisfied, I pull away.

He looks like I've just broken him, and maybe I have. I've broken myself.

"I'm marrying him," I say. Nate squeezes his eyes shut as he grips the back of my neck.

After another excruciating moment of my heart being stomped to a pulp, he pulls back and regains control of himself.

He straightens my necklace, his fingers ghosting over my collarbones and neck once more.

"I know," he says.

A knock falls on my door and Leo pokes his head into my room.

"He's here," Leo says.

I straighten my shoulders again, my spine tired from all the standing tall I've been forcing it to do over the last week.

"Thank you, I'll be right down."

Leo retreats, leaving the door cracked, and I take a moment to pat my face to make sure my makeup is still good. I swipe a fresh layer of red lipstick on and run a comb through my hair before risking one last glance at Nate and leaving my room.

My future husband awaits.

NATE

THREE MONTHS AGO, BEING AT A PARTY WITH A SEA OF MAFIOSOS, each strapped with guns or knives, or guns and knives, would've been the recipe for an anxious stomachache. Probably hives, too. I feel sickly now, but not because I'm afraid for my life and the life of my dog (though considering I interviewed half of them, and this party will be proof that I found them wanting, I suppose I should be more afraid one of them is looking to kill me this evening.)

Leo manifests by my side without sound, as is his way, holding two glasses of bubbly. "I'd get you something stronger, but I'm afraid a lot of men here will need it after this," Leo says. We both laugh, but it's a mirthless sound.

The way he's looked at me the last week was nothing short of heartbroken for both me and Vanessa. He wears it all on his sleeve when he's not being bodyguard supreme.

"Where is she?" I ask.

"Planning a speech with the Russian." Nice of him not to call Maxim by name when I know he thinks the guy is awesome. Very loyal.

I'll miss Leo when I'm shipped off to my parents' house. Will I ever see him or speak to him again?

I notice an older gentleman in a brown suit standing alone, looking less than pleased to be here. It's the prick with the drawn out project. Mr. McGowan? Last I heard, they were still hammering out his godforsaken contract, but the family probably invited him only because he's about to line the Morelli's pockets with a shit ton of money.

"Did the deal close?" I incline my head towards the man. Leo rolls his eyes.

"Wednesday it did. $430 mil. No time to celebrate."

"Hm."

We stand together as guests chatter around us. The backyard has been set up beautifully by decorators that swarmed the house this afternoon. Standing lamps and tables on the grass along with fresh flower arrangements. It's a gorgeous party, with delicious food and drinks, but it makes my stomach turn remembering *why* we're here.

Mary walks up to us, slow enough not to draw attention, though still rushing. "Leo," she says in greeting. "Come inside for a second. Please."

My instinct is to tag along, which is an urge I need to fight because I'm no longer a member of this team. This is family business, and Vanessa has made it clear that I am not going to be a part of that. The rejection doesn't sting so much as it aches. Brutally, so.

Leo and Mary head back for the house and I meander over to the old man whose net worth must be absurd.

"Mr. McGowan," I greet. There's no recognition behind his eyes, no way he remembers me.

"Thank you, son," he says, and takes my half-drunk champagne from my hand, having a sip. I pretend this was its intended destination.

"Nathaniel," I remind him. "We met at the Mayor's gala."

"The teacher?" he says, and I nod. In this world, that is all I will ever be. Nothing more than a blip in their memories. The realization hurts more than it should.

"I hear my congratulations are in order regarding your building. A hotel?" I say.

"Mm." McGowan raises his overgrown white eyebrows. "Yes, I'm looking forward to having a bit more space to . . . grow."

I offer my most knowing look, the Boy's Club one I practiced in all those interviews.

"I'm certain it will be the best quality, as they always are. Everything the Morellis touch turns to gold, after all."

"I would hope so." McGowan drains the rest of the glass and hands it back to me. "For $600 million, it better turn to diamonds."

I stare at the man, about to correct him when he catches the eye of someone he knows and excuses himself. Surely he misspoke. No way would that man pay over $430 million after the fight he put up—but *600*?

I looked over the contract early last week and we all gawked at the big number together, it most certainly wasn't *that* big of a number.

There's a tapping against glass, ringing out like a bell drawing everyone's attention to Claire standing on the deck.

"Thank you all for being here," she says with a wide smile on her face. "I am sure you're all anxious to hear what's brought us all together this evening."

Everyone murmurs, some laughing and nodding.

"But first, food. Please, serve yourself, and enjoy." She motions to the large buffet set up on the lawn and light applause comes from the family. Everyone is buzzing, out of their minds about why Vanessa Morelli would host a multicultural celebration in her home on a random Friday evening.

"I hear wedding bells," someone says as they walk past me, and the barely formed scab on my heart is scratched anew. I don't know that this one will ever heal over. When she announces their engagement will they kiss?

God.

I grab another glass from a table and take a long sip, wincing at the carbonation. This may just be the longest night of my life.

39

VANESSA

I ALLOW MYSELF ONE LAST QUIET MOMENT ALONE, FINGERS AND palms stretched at my sides as I force myself to meet my own gaze in the mirror. My eyes aren't bright, though Willa worked magic beneath them to make the dark circles practically invisible. She also put sparkles on my eyelids because she said it would look cute. Cute it is, though the blood-red lip and the dress are anything but.

I remind myself of why I'm doing this, saying every one of their names in my head three times before exhaling one final breath and leaving the bathroom. It's almost time for our announcement, and I should be seen mingling before the time comes.

I'm making my way down the hall when a palm snakes out of my office door, pulling me in. I'm ready to fight off whoever dragged me into the dark room, but it's just Cillian, a devilish little smirk on his face.

"You're looking mighty nice," he says, and I flip him off. He laughs, ever amused. "What's the occasion for all this?"

The question surprises me. I suppose all conversations with

KATH RICHARDS

him for the last week were about the McGowan deal or the mad goose chase. "Sean didn't tell you?"

His smile appears suspended as he squints. "What."

"Isn't it obvious?" I hold up my left hand, back side facing him. There's no ring yet on my finger, but I waggle it anyway.

"The teacher?" he asks.

"Maxim Orlov."

His face crosses from confused to concerned in seconds. "The Russian?"

"He's a good match," I say with a shrug.

"Good match for who? He's Russian."

"He's got power," I say simply. "People. Bodies. They're in markets we haven't even thought to touch." I'm unsure why I have to defend myself to him. He may be a friend, but he's related by marriage, not blood and though we are allies, he cannot pretend to have control over my dealings.

He smiles like I'm playing a joke on him, but when I remain silent his face falls again. He goes preternaturally still. "You're not serious."

"What part of my situation is unserious to you, Cillian?"

Cillian blinks, then pushes shut the library door so it's quieter. I still hear faint noise of the festivities beyond.

"This is a horrible idea," he says, and I cross my arms over my chest.

I wonder how many more people will be chomping at the bit to tell me the same thing before the night is over, before I marry Maxim in a month's time.

"You know nothing about the man," Cillian says.

"I know enough."

"He's an Orlov, darling. He's a loose cannon. How can you be sure he won't take everything from you?"

"There are safeguards in place," I say. "It's in both of our best interests if he doesn't. I trust that."

"Don't be stupid, Vanessa. Why him? Why now?"

"You know I've been searching for a husband; this isn't news to you."

"So that the neighborhood mammies stop bothering you? Please, you have more power than a gaggle of sixty-year-old women."

"It's not just that—"

"Is this about Washington Street? Because that's just a minor setback, just a team of thugs trying to make you sweat, how do you know that wasn't Orlov's guys trying to make you feel desperate? He could take everything—"

"If I don't marry him, there will be nothing to take!"

We fall silent following my outburst, and I try to maintain my composure. I shouldn't have to defend myself to him, not when he knows as well as me what we've been going through all summer.

"Marry me instead."

"We've talked about this."

"No, I mean it," Cillian stands taller. "I will treat you well, I respect you, I care about you already, you can trust me more than a stranger."

"And what of all your women?"

"What about them?"

"You cannot be married to me while keeping up the revolving door of beautiful strangers coming into your home." He opens his mouth to rebut, but I go on. "And I've told you that as your friend I would never ask you to commit yourself to a loveless partnership."

"You have no such reservations for the Russian."

"He knows what he's getting into. It's as worthwhile for him as it will be for me." My heart is too tender now to imagine that I'll ever be in love again, but maybe there will one day be tenderness for Maxim. Over time, maybe. "Now, if you'll excuse—"

"And what if there could be love?"

I halt my exit and turn back to him. With just the low yellow lamp light illuminating his bright blue eyes he looks like a man possessed. A section of his blond hair has escaped the gel and hangs over his forehead.

"I have always admired you and that respect has turned to friendship. Why couldn't it also turn to love?"

I'm speechless for once, imagining it again. First a wedding, companionship instead of just partnership, eventually intimacy when a child is needed. But love? The thought slashes through my abdomen, a reminder of who I really want this with, who would be my pick over all of them if I could only be right for him.

"We could be so good together," Cillian insists. "I've been trying to tell you. To show you."

He lifts my hand in his, scarred and callused from years of the kind of work Nate could never do, the kind that would corrupt him.

"We could rule this city, more than we already do, can't you imagine it?"

There's something wriggling in my brain as I picture it, a worm of alarm that I can't quite put my finger on.

I want to tell him no, but before I can, his lips are on mine, warm and insistent, but his kiss is a strange thing. It's inviting, gentler than I expected, but as if he's trying to convince me. Trying to show me, I suppose, this life that could be.

And as his hands wrap around my waist, pulling me closer to him, I can almost picture it. He's not a stranger, he's practically family, the brother of my brother-in-law, marrying him wouldn't be messy, it wouldn't cause some uproar amongst families, it would be just fine. Expected.

His hand snakes into my hair as his tongue tries to press into my mouth, and I let him kiss me, let him remind me how no kiss has lit me up like Nate's will and probably none ever will again.

But this one should, by all counts. He is sexy, he is powerful, he is a friend. I should feel something from this kiss, from the way his body presses against mine, but I feel nothing. Just the sliding of limbs, the wetness of his tongue in my mouth. No heat roiling in my stomach and busting through my fingertips, not the electric current I've grown accustomed to, the way my ears ring and every piece of skin feels like a live wire.

There's none of that here.

As gently as I can, I push him away.

He searches my face like he's looking for the yes in my eyes, but I can't give it to him.

"I can't, Cillian," I say. "I won't. Everything's set, I'm marrying Maxim."

Cillian doesn't speak, barely acknowledges that he's heard me, I straighten out my dress and turn the knob. I need to touch up my lipstick before I'm ready to stand tall before all our guests and pretend to be elated about my forthcoming nuptials.

I'm about to step out of the room when Cillian moves suddenly, a blur of motion to my right before there's a sickening slam at the back of my head.

Everything goes completely black.

40

VANESSA

I wake with a gasp, like in a dream where you step off a ledge and feel like you're falling, but upon landing, I'm not in my bed at all.

There's a morning light that feels like it's piercing into my eyes when I open them, it's two minutes of rapidly blinking before I can look at my surroundings fully.

I'm in a metal chair, both of my arms and legs are tied down hard enough that I can barely wiggle them. My skull is pounding and there's a sharp ache in my spine, which I equate to being knocked out in this chair for hours. I'm not wearing what I was at the engagement party, the green floor-length dress now replaced by a white linen one with intricate embroidery along the skirt and sleeves.

"What the fuck," I mutter and turn my eyes to my surroundings. I'm in an office building that hasn't been built out yet, all exposed ceilings and concrete floors.

I can't see well out the windows from where I am, but we must be high in the city. It's not one of our builds, an older one that's been gutted if I had to guess by the condition of the exposed brick and cracked concrete. There's a gutter around the perimeter of the floor where sheetrock used to be installed in front of the brick.

The floor is empty save for me and my chair, and if my eyesight isn't betraying me, my dress and heels are in a dark green pile by the door. My skin crawls at the knowledge that someone changed my clothes while I was unconscious.

I've never been in trouble like this.

How did I get here? There was the engagement announcement—wait, no, I never got to see the announcement, did I? Did they give it without me?

Steps sound from down the hall and I wiggle in my bindings to no avail. Whoever tied me up knew what they were doing.

Cillian steps around the doorway wearing a clean suit, smart and fitted to him perfectly. I remember at once the kiss, the way he pleaded for me to marry him instead, the party—*the party*. What did they do without me there? Are they looking for me?

"You're up," he says, and I snarl at him, renewed strength in trying to break my bonds. They don't budge, and my skin aches like a bruise beneath the rope. "Good morning."

"What the fuck is wrong with you?" I spit, followed by a slew of unbecoming curse words that he pretends he pays no mind to.

Cillian pulls up a chair from behind me and sets it down in front of mine. He sits on it backward, so his chest is against the bars of the seat back. He clicks his tongue.

"Darling, don't fuss, you'll bruise," he says.

"Oh, and that would be an issue for you?"

Cillian tilts his head at a 45 degree angle, and leans closer. I smell his cologne and aftershave, heady and wrong. My nose burns. His hand reaches slowly for my face, and I want to bite it. He pushes strands of hair that had fallen into my eyes behind my ear and then slides an index finger down my jaw, then down my neck to where he touches the ruby necklace that still hangs above my breasts.

I spit on him, right in the face, and he doesn't move, just

smiles at me before removing a hankie from his chest pocket and wiping his face clean. I regret that I didn't get more in his eye.

"Nessie," he chides, and I almost spit again.

"Don't call me that." Any version of Ness is reserved for family and dear friends, not fucking maniacs who force themselves on me and then knock me out for not agreeing to marry them.

"I'll call you whatever I like, bride."

I still, looking down with new eyes at the white gown I'm wearing.

"I won't."

"But you will," Cillian says.

"They'll come for me. You think Mary will let you live after hearing what you did to me?"

Cillian laughs. "She won't hear. You're not going to tell her."

It's my turn for my eyes to search his face, trying to determine just what he's getting at. "We're going to elope," he says. "Beautiful ceremony, an intimate one, just the two of us, the priest, and God. When we come back, they'll be surprised, but so happy for us."

"I wouldn't marry you."

"You wouldn't marry your friend? The one everyone trusts, the brother of your sister's husband, who's been asking for months? Please. You'll be able to sell it."

"I refuse."

"Do you think you are better than me, Vanessa? You were about to marry a stranger to get what you want from him. You were about to tie an innocent man to a woman who could never love him."

I do think I am better than him, and I will not let him make me feel bad for asking an adult man to enter a consensual contract that would be mutually beneficial to both of us. He can't make me feel guilty for sacrificing this.

"There's nothing scrappy or self-made about you. You're a selfish brat, and a bitch," Cillian spits.

"I am better than you," I say. "I can beat you in a fight and your business would be in shambles if Sean hadn't married Willa. Without us, you're just a fucking gangster."

A muscle ticks in Cillian's neck.

"There is one way you're weak, dove."

The pet name falls on my ears like acid.

"You care too deeply," he says, like it's simple math. "You love too much. You keep too many people close to you and it makes you weak."

"Family is what this is built on," I say, I'd yell if my throat didn't burn so bad. "It's what everything is built on."

"No. You know better than most that loyalty must be paired with fear to last. *Fear* is what this is all built on. And you open yourself up to more fear than anyone should. It's why you are not fit to lead, why you were never *meant* to."

A carousel of faces flash through my mind; my sisters, my mother, Angel and Artie, Leo, *Nate, Nate, Nate*. How could I care for any of them less? My father was the strongest man I've known and he loved dearly, with everything. His love was his reason.

"This is what's going to happen." Cillian stands behind me and pulls my hair behind my shoulders, lightly running his fingers through the tangles. "You and I are going to get married. Lovely little ceremony, you'll be sorry you couldn't invite your family, but you were just feeling so trapped, and I offered, and you couldn't say no. You'll say that you've secretly been wanting me for years, you just didn't want to tell anyone because you thought it might be weird, brother-in-law and all. You'll say whatever you need to say to convince them."

"They'll never believe me."

Cillian fists the hair he was playing with and tugs, pulling my head back until I'm looking up at him. I try to suppress a whimper from the pain in my already sore neck.

"Don't pretend you don't know how to act. You were prepared to convince a house full of guests that your engagement was a good thing. To a *Russian* whose family has only ever caused yours pain. I've known you for years, practically family, business partners. It'll be an easier sell."

He lets go of my hair and walks away from me, now typing something into his phone. I hope it's his final will and testament because I am going to kill his ass with excruciating slowness.

"I will kill you," I say. "I will never, ever stop fighting you. You can force me to marry you, but you will never *have me*."

He glances up from his screen looking bored, then rolls his eyes.

"Look," Cillian says after a few more moments tapping at his screen. He holds it out for me now to see and begrudgingly I do look.

It's open to some app with two rows, one of names and the adjacent toggles that read "armed."

My mind races over the names so fast it takes me three times to realize what I'm seeing.

Mary Bedroom, Guest House, Artie Room, Angel Room, Willa SUV, Sean Motorbike, Nate, Garden, Green House, Kitchen, Basement, Garage, the rows read, each a location where I am certain a bomb is planted, one of those damn little ones from the May shipment. The ones that went missing.

"You wouldn't," I breathe, and Cillian has the gall to laugh. A loud and brutal sound bursting from his chest.

"You have no fucking clue, do you?" Cillian asks and squats in front of me like he's talking to a child. "Your family is a scourge, Vanessa. I never thought Sean should marry your bitch sister, but I wasn't in charge then. They didn't listen to me."

I've never been one to bite my tongue, though sometimes I wish I could. "We gave you power."

"You *made us look weak*." Bits of spit lands on my face, but I refuse to wince. "We didn't need to have an alliance; we were in better business without you. You act like you are so high and mighty, so many fucking morals for criminals—no skin trade, no organs, none of the shit that actually makes money.

"And we listened. My father was a fool, trusting like you, removed us from circles to get into your father's good graces. Weapons are more lucrative than girls, he said, your dad's words, and he believed them. Just went along with whatever he said. It made my father look like a feeble little man."

"But he was right," I say. "You've gotten into less trouble and doubled your profits over the last decade, how is that not gain?"

"Because now I'm your little bitch, Vanessa. I've been in the shadow of your 'genius' but you're not a genius. You're a novelty."

I swallow down his words, the sting of them acid on my already dry and stinging throat. He's lying, or he's wrong and deranged, but part of me has always wondered when the party trick that is the woman mafia boss would lose its shine.

"And soon, you'll be a wife. A mother. You think their patience will still be there when you have a kid at home being raised by your mother? You forget your roots, your tradition. You're too American."

There is nothing in my stomach but I'm moments away from heaving. From the shame and the embarrassment, from the hatred and sick loathing, and most of all, the fear that he might be right.

"We can be happy together, Vanessa." Cillian puts his hand on my face again, tilting until my eyes are forced on his. The worst part is that he looks sincere. He really believes I could be happy with him? "I have wanted this for so long. You just have to see."

I shut my eyes tight and turn my head until his fingers brush softly over my lips. It's supplicating, intimate.

"You see the vision, don't you?" Cillian asks, and I nod again before opening my mouth and biting down on the meaty part of his thumb, hard, until I taste blood.

Cillian's other hand punches me in the head, my skull reverberating with the blow so much I let him go, a trail of saliva and blood trailing from the marks on his hand.

After a moment, Cillian makes a sound that's almost a laugh. He's too crazed for it to sound amused, though. He looks violent.

"I will have you. You will see that we are right for each other," he says. "And if you don't, you'll get to choose who goes first."

He holds the phone up again, reminding me of the screen, the dozen bombs dormant beneath my loved ones, cobras ready to strike and blow my whole world to pieces.

"Who will you choose? Angel? The teacher? Or maybe my brother first. Easiest to kill, not a blood relation."

I'm going to be sick, but I force myself not to gag. I can't show him more just how much he's getting under my skin.

"I'll let you think about it," Cillian buttons on his suit coat, smoothing it out. "Wedding's at eight." I bite my cheek so hard it bleeds while I watch him walk away, leaving me alone in the building.

41

NATE

I DIDN'T SLEEP. I DID TRY ONCE EVERYONE WENT HOME, disappointed to not hear a wedding announcement. Vanessa vanished, leaving only a typed note on her computer. A two line note on a word document.

I can't do this.

-V

Mary was concerned, seeking out Vanessa all over the house before discreetly calling a family huddle in the kitchen. They all got to looking through rooms, and when they found the note, Mary brought me into the room, too, which made me feel important and part of the family for a little longer.

"What is this?" Willa asked, studying the laptop screen.

"It's bullshit is what it is," Mary said. "I just checked her room and Vanessa didn't bring her phone, her gun, not even a knife except for the one she was wearing."

We all chewed on this information.

"Why would she run without him?" Sean asked, nodding to me. Again, I was touched, but obviously they didn't know that Vanessa had brutally rejected me, twice, in the last seven days. The last time just an hour prior.

"She didn't want me."

"Bullshit," Mary said again.

"Say we humor the note. She left. She didn't take a car. Where would she go on foot, with no weapons?" Willa asks, bringing us back to the problem at hand.

The Russian chose that moment to make his appearance, asking for himself where his fiancé-to-be was hiding.

"Good question," Claire said. "The masses are getting restless."

Willa relayed the information to Maxim, who looked increasingly worried with every interjection from Mary until she had him convinced that Vanessa was buried somewhere. And now that he was convinced, I was growing sure of this too. My mind raced over possible fates, horror after horror, Vanessa's bones broken, face bloodied, dirt piling up on top of her bare skin, alone and afraid and—

"Don't be dramatic," Willa said, but she sounded nervous too. Willa stared at the message a moment longer then stood tall, taking charge in her sister's absence. "Mom, make the announcement that the Orlov and Morelli families have set aside any sour blood and are looking forward to a long and fulfilling partnership. Ask them to welcome the Orlovs with open arms. Apologize for Vanessa who's suffering a bout of food poisoning but sends her very best."

Claire nodded and quickly left the room.

"I want to help look for her," Maxim said, as if he wasn't already chivalrous enough. "My resources are at your disposal."

Willa pressed her lips together and nodded.

"We appreciate that. Help my mother with the announcement. We search as soon as toasts are made."

Sean put a reassuring arm around his wife's waist, though his face showed the same concern as the rest of us. Well, I wasn't sure what my face showed exactly, probably the green pallor of someone who was about to vomit all the hors d'oeuvres he'd slammed in the last 45 minutes.

I could do nothing to help them. I slipped around the house, searching behind every door for her, but I knew she was not there. I chewed on my thumb nail until it started to bleed, I paced until I was so full of restless energy that I wanted to scream.

The party went as well as Willa hoped it would. People clapped cordially at Claire's announcement, though they obviously wanted something more salacious to go home and gossip about.

As soon as the Morelli children's presences were made known, the search began.

It was three hours before Sean received a call from his brother letting him know that he had Vanessa, she was safe and sleeping. Apparently, she'd caught him before coming into the party, begged him to take her somewhere, anywhere else, because she couldn't go through with marrying a stranger.

Sean put him on speaker and Mary asked about two dozen questions and demanded he put her sister on the phone.

"She was pretty torn up," Cillian said. "She's sleeping now. I'll have her call you in the morning."

The call ended shortly after, as did the search, everyone somewhere between relieved and disconcerted.

Mary was pissed, visibly fuming as she stormed out of the house.

"She was scared," Willa explained. "Mary hates being scared."

I nodded, but something didn't sit right with me.

This was the least Vanessa-thing she could have done, running away from her obligations without so much as a word to her sisters.

The staff had cleaned up and gone by this point, so I paced outside a while, Ranger huffing by the door wanting to go inside for once. I walked around the pool, watched the water lap lightly against the blue tiles, and thought through every conversation I'd had with her over the last week.

She was so sure. I saw the sorrow and heartbreak in her eyes

—I'm not so self-deprecating to say I don't know where the pain came from. She wanted me but needed *him*. She needed an advantageous match, someone with power to help protect her family.

She wouldn't willfully give up protection.

As the minutes passed, I thought about every person I spoke to at the party. The family, yes, but I touched in with others, too. The Sinclairs were there, and some of the other marriage candidates who considered me their buddies. I think most of them secretly hoped she was announcing that she wanted to marry one of *them*. Like she might offer her final rose in front of everyone.

Could one of them have found out? Hurt her?

No, none of them are smart enough, nor skilled enough, to pull that off.

I kept returning to my chat with Mr. McGowan, the number inconsistency.

I called Willa, who answered on the third ring even though it was the middle of the night.

"How much was the McGowan contract for?" I asked.

"$430 million," she said.

"You're sure?"

"I wrote the contract, Nate. Yes, I'm sure." Her annoyance was valid, but I couldn't drop what the old man said.

"I need the passwords to Vanessa's computer," I said. "Oh, and access to the contracts. Something is wrong."

After a moment of silence through the phone line, she acquiesced, too tired to fight me, and maybe even knowing that I was right. Something was wrong with all of this. From the moment they found the note, nothing was making sense.

I spent the rest of the night auditing old contracts with payments received. I'd compiled a list of twenty projects that were suspect, and as soon as the clock struck 8 AM, I called each of them in turn, pretending to be from the Morelli legal office, questioning if they'd be willing to remind us of some key details regarding their builds. I told them we had a new system in place and needed to make sure everything was transferred properly. Everyone was all too willing to comply.

Mary came in after I'd called three of them. She hadn't come home in the night, and still wore her clothes from last night.

"Something is wrong," I said.

"I know," she said, and brought me another cup of coffee.

Ranger had been loyal, sleeping at my feet the entire night, no doubt having checked Vanessa's bed and found it cold.

"What can I do?" Mary asked.

I explained the process to her and gave her a copy of the names and phone numbers to call. She took half. It became apparent that her style was much more abrupt than mine, stating her name and asking they share the numbers, no explanation given.

It took zero back and forth for them to comply.

With her help, we worked through the list and sure enough, twelve of the twenty calls indicated discrepancies between their contract and the contract Morelli Construction had on file.

We didn't tell any of them any of this, but made eye contact every time the number was wrong, sometimes by tens of millions of dollars, hundreds in the case of McGowan.

"What the fuck is going on with these numbers?" Mary asked after we'd gone through the whole list and another ten contracts for good measure. Willa and Sean were on their way with bagels by this point, so Mary and I took a break to shower (I needed it, horribly), and now have the anxious attention of Willa and Sean back in Vanessa's office.

I'm nervous to voice my hypothesis, especially with Sean in the room, but I go on anyway, telling them about the conversation with McGowan, the contracts, the calls, all of it.

"If these numbers are correct, there's a discrepancy of half a billion dollars from the last four years," I explain.

Willa leans closer and Sean whistles.

"Like what, an accounting error?" Willa asks.

"Some accounting error," Mary mutters.

"No, it's contractual. Just one might be an error, but this is a pattern." I turn Vanessa's computer screen to face them. Almost all the clients were willing to send over their contracts for reference, each of these displaying the obvious price difference when laid side by side, though identical signatures.

"These clients signed for millions more than what was reported in your system and vending through a third party bank before depositing into company accounts."

"Where did the extra money go?"

"I'm not sure," I admit, then scroll to the top of the document. "There is one common denominator though."

I pull up a separate document and let them sit side by side.

"I don't see the issue," Willa admits.

"Tell them," Mary says.

"It's Cillian," I say. "He's the closer on every one of the duplicated contracts."

The room is silent for what feels like three minutes, and I am half-certain they're going to kick me out for even offering such an idea, but then Willa grabs the laptop and Sean kneels beside her while she clicks and types and scrolls for ten minutes.

"You're right," Sean breathes.

He already has his phone out.

"Wait," Mary puts her hand over his. "Don't call him yet."

"Did you know about this?" I ask him, considering Cillian is his brother.

Sean looks like I've kicked Ranger right in front of him, like even asking is the biggest betrayal I could have managed.

"I wouldn't." Sean could be lying, but he'd have to be an exceptional actor for that to be the case.

"He wouldn't," Willa agrees. "This is all Cillian."

"It's got his rat ass name written all over it," Mary says.

"He's been stealing that kind of money right from under our

noses, who knows what else he'd been taking," Willa says and slams the laptop shut.

"The shipments?" I ask and all three of them look up at me in unison. The implications aren't lost on them: if he oversaw stealing those shipments, he was also probably the one in charge of the building fire. Of Mary getting shot.

"And now he has Vanessa," Sean says before I have to.

42

VANESSA

I don't know how many hours pass before I see Cillian again. My wrists are scraped raw from trying to free myself from the bonds and my arms ache both from my futile efforts and from being held so tightly in place for so long.

My stomach feels like a gnawing pit, tearing at itself in hunger, and the burning in my throat has only gotten worse. There's an acute ache behind my left eye that has been throbbing as the sun has traveled across the sky. It hasn't set yet but it's low enough that I know it's evening already.

I've realized that torture might be most effective in an empty floor full of windows. You can't pretend more or less time has passed when you can see just how much sun is lighting up the sky. It might be more grueling than a basement.

He strolls in with a tray of food with him that makes my stomach growl instantly. His hand is also bandaged, and it fills me with a spark of glee to see that I left a mark. If he lives through this, I hope it scars.

"How was your time to think?" he asks, ever chipper.

"Comfortable."

"Good." He pulls up his chair again and sits down in front of me. If I had access to my hands, I would claw his face. "I brought you dinner."

I am exceptionally wary of anything this man wants to offer me. Certainly, it's drugged. When I press my lips shut at his offered spoonful of soup he sighs and takes a bite himself.

"See? Harmless."

Nothing from this man could ever be harmless, but when I'm hungry, I get faint and if I lose consciousness, my opportunity for escape drops to near zero.

He offers another spoonful, and this time I do take it. It's soothing on my throat and I am ravenous for more, which he dutifully feeds me.

"Is this what married life will be like?" I ask after he gives me a sip of water through a straw. "Me tied up in the attic and you feeding me three meals a day by hand?"

Cillian laughs through his nose.

"I won't need to keep you tied up," he says. "You'll learn."

I want to scream at him until I lose my voice, tell him I will never love him, tell him I have no intention of marrying him or learning to keep quiet, that I am smarter than him and always will be, but I take another bite of chicken and rice soup and try to hide the scorching blaze of hatred from my eyes.

Cillian moves onto the bread, biting off a piece for himself before feeding me the rest. I already feel better, marginally more energy now that I have some food in my system. It won't be enough to get out, though, not when I'm this weak and he's got bombs on every one of my loved ones.

"What are you thinking, dove?"

"Why do you call me that?" I ask instead of answering.

He takes a bite of the last thing on the tray, bread pudding, and when he shows me his tongue to prove he swallowed it, I let him feed me that, too. It's intimate having his hand so close to my face to feed me and wipe a napkin under my lips. I detest the closeness with him.

"Everyone loves a dove," he says. "They're romantic birds, some even mate for life." I chew and swallow the last bite of pudding before he speaks again. "But at the heart of it, doves aren't so far removed from pigeons, are they? And everyone hates a pigeon."

Cillian sets the tray down on the chair and walks behind me.

"Jensen," he yells, and the man I recognize as one of Cillian's goons steps into the room. Was he just standing silently in the hall awaiting beckoning?

Jensen is a big man, but one of his arms is in a sling, which makes him look a lot less scary than I know he can be.

He looks at me with mild disgust written across his face.

It dawns on me, then. He was shot. By *Nate*.

"You tried to kill my sister," I say, my whole body tense. That day on the site. Of course Cillian was behind that too, sabotaging everything. And then Jensen *shot* her. She can't fight because of him.

"Nothing the bitch doesn't deserve," Jensen says. "But it's not personal. I just wanted to get the teacher."

A chill runs down my spine at this admission.

Cillian starts to untie the series of ropes that have me locked in place and I'm already formulating a plan to incapacitate them both when his breath skates over my ear.

"Mary will go first if you even think about it, Vanessa. Feel free to test me, I've been waiting for an excuse to kill her for years."

I still, letting this news sink in before giving one jerky nod.

That's enough for him, I guess, because soon as the rope is undone he's helping me stand. My legs are completely asleep, and as soon as I try to step, I fall right into his arms, my face pressed against his chest. That cologne is so strong I could almost throw up the whole meal I just ate.

"I hate you," I whisper.

"That's okay," he says and kisses the top of my head.

As soon as I'm able, I stand away from him and try to shake some life into my limbs.

"You look nice in this dress," he says. "It suits you."

I look down at the thing. Now that I'm standing, I can see it clearly, a low square cut on my chest and puffy sleeves. A sort of princess look. The kind of dress I would have killed for as a little girl.

"Shall we? There's a wedding we don't want to be late to."

I give one long look that he meets with a hard one in kind. One that says he wasn't lying about what he was going to do to my family. I duck my head. I need to think.

"Good girl."

Cillian slides palms down both of my arms until landing on my wrists which he squeezes lightly before cuffing them again in front of me, this time with zip ties that will cut into my skin if I struggle.

"You're so beautiful when you behave."

MY HEART DROPS FURTHER into the ever-growing pit of my stomach when I realize where we're going. My church, the Saint Mary, not ten miles from my home, the backdrop of so many memories, and now to be sullied with this. It's fitting, I suppose. I always wanted to be married here.

When we arrive, the sun is almost set, half of the sky is now a purple twilight. Cillian ushers me into an empty old building, save for a man I don't recognize at the altar. Outside there were about a dozen armed guards, maybe more, which gives me hope that he's worried someone might know where he is. Someone that might be dangerous to his plan.

He let me use the restroom before we left, but watched the

KATH RICHARDS

whole time. No funny business, he said, can't take any chances I'd try something.

He even held the dress up for me, a smug smirk all the while. Quite the gentleman.

The last light of the day filters through the stained-glass face of the Virgin Mary as she looks down on us. It doesn't provide comfort today, just a sad foreboding. If I was her, I would know what to do, I think. Maybe I'd have some divine intervention.

I'm good at thinking on my feet, but as soon as I realized Cillian had weapons pointed at everyone I love, my mind went blank.

I wasn't meant to be the choice maker; I wasn't meant to be a boss. My dad would never have ended up here, not ever. He was smart and discerning. He knew who he could trust, and when he couldn't, he dispensed of them with regret but readiness.

I wonder about the signs I missed as Cillian slowly marches me up the aisle. What didn't I see in the last three months, in the last thirteen years, that led us here?

"Did you get the license?" the man asks.

"Of course," Cillian says, and pulls an envelope from inside his suit's chest pocket. Cillian always has made light work of expediting official documents.

"A beautiful occasion," the man at the altar says, and I can see now that he is a priest, though not one I recognize.

I could almost laugh. A supposed man of God stands at the head of this beautiful place about to marry a wicked man to a woman whose hands are zip tied in front of her. My mind wonders over what Cillian must've threatened him with. Or bribed, I suppose.

"Indeed," Cillian says. "I thought you'd want to be married in your church. Such a beautiful wedding your sister had. Yours could've been as grand a celebration as hers, but," Cillian shrugs at the priest, "it is what it is."

"Indeed," the priest echoes. "Shall we get right to it, then?"

Cillian nods and takes my bound hands in his, his thumb tracing small circles over my knuckles. His touch is gentle, like he's trying to soothe me, but his eyes speak something different. They promise pain, violence, and all manner of cruelty if I mess this up.

I lift my chin and meet his eyes as the priest begins reading off the marriage ceremony from his old leather book. There are candles lit on the altar and in sconces around the old church, a yellow-glow hue illuminating the scene as the sky darkens to night.

The priest starts with prayer, and Cillian winks up at me from his head bowed in mock reverence. This isn't a normal wedding, none of the repeated prayers and songs, just a homily. The priest speaks briefly about the bonds of marriage, the sacred nature of it, and how we will be one for the rest of our long lives here on earth. He shares some scriptures, but I don't hear them; I'm too deep in the pit of my mind willing every ill-intention I've ever had into my eyes.

Cillian just smirks. Amused.

"Do you have the rings?" The priest asked Cillian.

"Yes." Cillian lets go of my hands only to pull two gold bands from his breast pocket. The one for me is dainty, with an intricate vine design carved on the outside. He slides it on my left ring finger, though it's tight with all the blood that's rushed to my hands since being tied up. He puts his own ring on instead of making me try in my state.

"Cillian, do you promise to be a companion to Vanessa in all of her successes and failures, her happiness and sadness, to always give to her your unwavering support and above all else, the freedom to be herself?"

"I do," he says. The hollow promise guts me, and without meaning to, a drop falls from my eye and rolls down my cheek. Cillian wipes it with the pad of his thumb then licks it off.

"And Vanessa—"

A phone starts buzzing in Cillian's suit, halting the priest. Cillian pulls it from his breast pocket, reading over the screen briefly before nodding. "Continue."

"Vanessa, do you promise to be a companion to Cillian in all of his successes and failures, his happiness and sadness, to always give to him your unwavering support and above all else, the freedom to be himself?

My mouth is dry, like I've swallowed cotton balls. If I say yes to this, what am I promising?

How long will I have to endure pretending before I catch him unawares? Weeks, or months? Years? Will I need to have a child with him? Suffer through sleeping with him and then bear his children?

I don't care what he believes, I will never, ever love him.

I think to say as much, just as a reminder. When Cillian raises a brow, daring me to test him. Jensen stands guard at the entrance. It would take just a nod from Cillian to make his threats reality.

"I do," I whisper.

"Hm?" Cillian prompts.

I clear my throat. "I do."

I will have to pretend, but it won't be forever. I will beat him somehow, it's the only option—

His phone buzzes again, and after a glance at Jensen, he nods and ignores it. The priest says a few more words that I don't hear, only thinking about the smug grin spreading over Cillian's face, the indeterminate years of torture I've just promised myself to.

"You may now kiss the bride," the priest says, and Cillian wastes no time pulling me to him, dipping me back until I'm suspended almost parallel with the ground and pressing his mouth against mine.

His lips are lukewarm and probing, but I won't yield this, not again, not when I let him kiss me thoroughly last night when I thought he was just my confused friend.

There's that phone again, vibrating loud, and this time, I feel it against my chest, pressed up against him as I am.

He lets up for just a breath.

And then it feels like the whole place explodes.

43

VANESSA

I'm dropped to the ground as soon as it happens, my side hitting the hardwood floor before I roll down the two steps in a way that makes white pain sing through my shoulder. It's unbelievable, the noise, so loud and raucous that my ears quickly turn to ringing, the exploding of the windows barely audible.

Glass shards fly inward slicing through the air and raining down on us like ice. Cillian follows me to the ground, covering my body with his. With a moment to process, my ears ring with a high-pitched squeal and I think my shoulder might be dislocated, the pain is so acute.

Cillian's face drips blood onto my gown, flowing from a slice on his cheek where a shard of purple glass sticks from his skin. The Mother Mary window, I realize. It's been shattered with the rest. Explosives, of some kind.

He plucks it from his cheek without much regard and tosses it to the wood floor.

My ears are still ringing when he yanks me up by my bad arm and leads me to the wooden stairs to the second level. I trip on the steps, but he just tugs me behind him, his punishing grip on my bicep. The pain in my shoulder is excruciating, so I follow as close as I'm able. He's pulling on it with abandon and I think I'm screaming, but I still can't hear anything. By the time we get to the second story overlooking the chapel, a team of people have flooded into the building.

I see Willa with blood spattered on her face and her honey-streaked hair pulled into a ponytail, and Sean behind her. They both hold guns. The priest is on the floor, a bullet through his chest, and the ringing in my ear is beginning to subside just in time for Cillian to pull my back flush against his chest. The cold barrel of a gun presses against my temple.

"I will do it," he shouts over the banister. "I swear that I will."

A dozen guns are trained on us from below, and Cillian's hands shake around me.

I see my sister Mary, fury written on her face, one hand gripping her pistol and the other arm still in its sling. Maxim stands just behind her.

And Nate—*God*, it's Nate standing there in all black holding a gun like he knows how to use it, and as soon as I see him, I can't look away. I don't want him to see this, to see what will happen to me next. Cillian is not a man, but a fury of madness, one desperate to possess me.

"I will kill your precious princess, and you will all have to watch." His voice is a bellowing in my ear, one I feel reverberating through his chest against my back. He's going to do it, I'm sure. And if I'm dead then I can't protect them.

"Stand down," I say, then louder, through my gasps, "Stand down—*please*."

None of them lower their guns, not a single one of them willing to lose this fight.

"Damnit." Cillian cocks the gun and shoots above my head, destroying any hearing I had in my left ear after the explosions. Plaster from the ceiling rains down somewhere to the right of us. I look between the people I love, all there ready to kill for me, I make eye contact briefly with Willa, pleading with her to convince them.

She shakes her head, just barely.

"You're surrounded, *dearthái*r," Sean says. I hear anguish there. His own brother.

Cillian pulls me so that my whole body shields his own. To kill him, they would have to shoot through me first.

"She will die, then." Cillian pulls the hammer of his revolver back and I wince but don't close my eyes. I won't let the last thing I see be blackness when my family is here.

"Okay! Okay." Mary lowers her gun first, and one by one, the rest of the family follows suit, Nate last. Cillian begins to inch down the aisle, the gun still against my head and my back against his chest moving us towards a door. He shoulders it open and shoves me inside.

44

NATE

As soon as we hear a door slam shut behind them, Mary curses and springs into action. Everyone does, either stalking to a different corner of the church or, in the case of Willa and Maxim, taking out their phones and making calls for backup.

"Nate," Mary barks, and I follow behind her. Willa wouldn't let Mary take her arm out of the sling that secures her elbow to her torso, but Mary is a pretty good shot even with just one hand. She looks like a ball of wrath, so I hurry.

"We split up. You take that staircase, I'll go outside," she says. "Whoever finds the bastard first gets to shoot him."

I nod in agreement and slink away. There was a small battalion of men outside when we got here, but Maxim and Mary are fucking beasts and took out ten of them on their own. Willa and Sean, too. Between the four of them, there was only the man inside the church left by the time we set up the explosives, and he got taken out by Maxim as soon as the bombs went off.

My heart has been jackhammering in my chest, but my options are do nothing and let him take Vanessa, or do *something* and hope it's enough.

I creep up the stairs and hold my breath once I reach the door they disappeared into. I can't hear anything on the other side, but that doesn't mean Cillian isn't waiting with his gun still to Vanessa's head. I hold up my gun, and before I can count all the way to three, push the door open in a rush.

It's quiet, no movement, nor sign of life other than a heavy wooden door left ajar on the other side of the room.

With the windows shattered and a slight evening breeze slipping through, the room feels haunted. I gulp and take another slow step forward into the room.

Still nothing. Their dad's pistol is heavy in my hand and the handle is hot from my grip, but I keep it ready to shoot.

There are a few pews here, and an ornate wooden confessional booth. I step past all of them and peer through the door. This one leads down a narrow hallway with old creaking stairs down and out of the church.

I am alone in the outdoor corridor, only one of Cillian's men lying face down in a patch of darkened grass. I look around me and my arms shudder involuntarily.

From here I see only a small building that must be the priest's apartment, and what looks like the entrance to. . . a cellar?

I storm for that door, pulling it open not at all gracefully before stomping down the few stairs until I reach a stone hallway. Not quite a cellar, unless cellars are old stone corridors beneath old stone churches. Tunnels.

When I force myself to still for a moment, I hear something—a scuffle, a voice—quiet, but here, underground.

I curse and follow it, moving as quickly as I can without stomping like a horse. I have to use my phone's flashlight as I get farther away from the light of the entrance. There are lights on the walls but they're all off, and when I come to an intersection of crossing paths, I hold my breath, listening for anything at all other than my jackhammering heart.

There. Something like footsteps, down the hall to my left. I turn course and follow, speeding up slightly. The hall turns once more and—how long have I been walking? We've most certainly extended beyond the church grounds. Geography has never been my strong suit, so unless I close my eyes and retrace my steps mentally, I'm not even sure which direction I'm headed.

With one last turn, I stifle a gasp and halt my steps. At the end of this corridor, a yellow light emits from behind a cracked door. I can hear footsteps and the low murmuring of a voice I am almost certain belongs to Cillian.

I turn off my flashlight and silence my phone before creeping as quietly as I can forward towards the room. My shoe hits something like a pebble that skitters across the floor and I freeze, but the sound in the room goes uninterrupted.

Stepping carefully, I venture closer. And if I hold myself against the stone wall, I can just barely see inside the room—a chamber? Nothing down here looks like it was built in the last century, save for the addition of electricity.

"I'll call them off," Vanessa says. "I'll explain it to them."

"You won't need to explain anything to them because they'll each have a bullet in their skull—"

"Can you blame them for being worried? You didn't let me call them, or even try to convince them." Vanessa's frantic voice breaks. "I'll fix it, I promise they'll listen to me. Just, please don't hurt them."

Cillian is quiet, and I worry I'm breathing too loud, or that he can just intuit that I'm in the hallway. But after a moment, he steps just into view, prowling towards where I imagine Vanessa stands. He doesn't look murderous, he looks calculating.

"If you kill them and you take over the business, you'll lose everyone's trust. It might take years to get that back, if you ever do," Vanessa says. "I will help you spin the narrative."

"I can make it look like an accident," Cillian says.

"And if you do, then you might as well kill me too," Vanessa says. "They live, you get my cooperation. They die, you will get my corpse."

Cillian blinks at this, then throws his head back in a laugh. I am close enough that I might be able to shoot him, but I would need to fling the door open first. Cillian still holds his own pistol, ready to fire at any second.

"You're such a bitch, you know that?" Cillian says. "I think we're soulmates."

Vanessa says nothing, and Cillian's phone beeps. He pulls it out of his jacket and glances at it.

"Ride's here," he says. "Come."

He walks out of my sightline, and I slide the last steps away from the door until I'm right in front of it.

"I can't climb like this," Vanessa says. Her hands must still be bound in front of her. "I need them free to get up the ladder."

Cillian thinks on this before his voice gets so low I almost don't hear it. "If you try something, I *will* kill him first."

"I won't," she says. She sounds so dejected that even I believe her.

I need to barge in there. I need to act, I can't just wait for an opening, but my limbs are frozen. If I go in too soon and he shoots Vanessa, it will be my fault; I need to be fast, and certain. If he's climbing a ladder. . . maybe I can get him then. He will be distracted—

An obvious scuffle sounds from the room, Vanessa grunting as what sounds like fists hit flesh. An instant later, she shrieks, and that's all it takes for me to bolt into action. I shoulder open the door and raise my gun. None too soon because that prick is on top of her, his lip now bloody, but pinning her down with fury in his eyes. He's choking her, tattooed hands around her throat.

I don't think about it.

I line up my shot and shoot, then shoot again, both shots directly into his skull.

He's the first person I've ever killed.

His blood coats the stone wall behind him, his body thuds onto Vanessa, who gasps for breath beneath him. I rush to her and push Cillian's corpse off her, speaking incoherent comforting nonsense as I draw her close to me. There's hot red staining the bodice of her white dress.

"You killed him," she says. She grips my face with one of her hands, the other arm limp at her side. Her touch is a miracle to me. Everything about her alive in front of me is nothing short of a revelation.

"You're safe," I breathe, then say it five more times until I believe it.

She's safe, whole in front of me, and Cillian is dead.

He's dead because I killed him.

I killed him.

My eyes are stinging with relief as I bring her to me in a tight embrace, placing kisses on her shoulder and neck.

I killed Cillian.

I would do it again.

There is a time to do bad things. When the people you love are in danger, lines become blurred between good and bad—and I would do a great number of things to keep Vanessa safe.

A loud creak sounds above our heads, and a pit opens in my stomach.

Cillian had said their ride was here—they were about to climb the ladder to meet them—

Vanessa grabs the gun I dropped at her side and points it to the hatch door that is heaving open above us. She cocks the gun but lowers her arm back to her side with a strangled sob of relief when the person who pokes their head in the room is Mary.

"Whose blood is that?" Mary demands. Her voice is frantic and loud. "Are you hurt?"

"I'm okay," Vanessa says.

Mary's gaze falls to Cillian and her eyes narrow into slits. I didn't know a scowl could look so satisfied.

"Good fucking riddance," Mary says, her voice wobbling. She

swipes a tear from beneath her eyes and starts down the short ladder, a feat with only one arm.

"Vanessa?" Another voice calls, high pitched and panicked. "Is she down there?"

Willa's face comes into view; she follows Mary down the ladder before she drops to her knees beside her sisters and me.

A steady pool of crimson seeps beneath us, soaking the hem of Vanessa's white gown, but Willa and Mary just fuss over their sister, dropping kisses on her hair and wiping blood spatter from her cheeks.

Vanessa doesn't let us take her from the room until she's very certain Cillian is dead. She watches his body with wide eyes like he'll rise again and shoot one of us, even with two bullets through his brain.

When Leo confirms that there's no heartbeat and has us cover our ears while he shoots Cillian in the chest for good measure, she finally lets us lead her out through the tunnels, still holding tight to my hand, her nails digging crescent moons into my skin. Her other arm hangs limp and I tell the EMT's to be careful with it.

They snip the puffy sleeves from around her arm and sure enough, her shoulder is dislocated. Her eyes are vacant as they assess her for other injuries and lie her back onto a gurney.

Her makeup from last night is smeared with blood around her face. Mascara surrounds her eyes and runs in black lines with Cillian's dried blood down her cheeks and jaw. She's alive, and she is beautiful.

They let me ride in the ambulance with her and she grips my hand the entire way.

I brush her hair off her forehead murmuring into her ear about how it's alright now, she's alright, everyone is alright.

Eventually, she closes her eyes. The paramedics sedated her; her heart rate was through the roof, and her muscles tensed.

She drifts into unconsciousness before we even get to the hospital.

45

VANESSA

As soon as I wake up, I know I'm in a hospital room because the lighting is godawful and there's a hazy heaviness over all of my limbs. I force my eyes open, though they want to sink back closed, and within a moment of this internal wrestling to stay awake, my sisters are there.

Willa, Mary, and my mother all crowd around me, showering me in kisses and hugs and brushing their hands over my hair, my cheeks, my arms. My mom weeps and mutters in Italian. It helps wake me up.

The relief I feel is so sudden and intense that I can't help but cry with them. I thought they were going to die—that Cillian was going to kill them. I thought he was going to kill me, too, his hands wrapped around my neck and ire in his eyes. Part of him knew he would never possess me, and I think the knowledge might have made him snap and kill me himself if not for Nate.

Nate.

I can't see him as my family fawns over me—a nurse comes in and scolds them for startling me after just waking up, but I see him. He leans against the wall near the door, watching with steady eyes. Not an ounce of the anxiety I know so well from him, just a still confidence in eyes that hold mine.

The nurse takes a few minutes checking my vitals, then checking for hearing in my left ear, which Willa reports was bleeding when we got here. The second time in as many weeks that my ear bled from the trauma of a loud shot—I'm lucky I can hear out of it at all. It's muted, like I'm listening through water, but there's something at least.

The nurse assures that they'll do more tests later. She then props my pillows, checks the swelling of my shoulder, and administers more pain medicine through the IV in my arm, leaving an unpleasant taste in my mouth.

My eyes trail back to Nate, and don't leave him, not when the nurse shuffles out of the room with promises to return in thirty minutes, not when my sisters and mother file out in a line, and not when he approaches my side.

He's a beautiful man. Grass green eyes watching mine, a strong unshaven jaw, curly hair that's mussed and unruly like he's been raking his hands through it.

I want to keep him.

"How do you feel?" he asks.

"Horrible," I say, and we both let out a semblance of laughs. It feels good, smiling with him. "Nate—"

"Please, can I go first?" He sits on the side of the hospital bed and wraps both warm hands around the one of mine that isn't held to my chest with a sling matching Mary's. "Please."

I shut my mouth and nod for him to continue. I want to keep him, but maybe this is it. I won't force him to be with me.

"I love you," he says, pauses, then rushes on, "I am criminally, fatally in love with you, and you can try to marry someone else, but I'm not going to leave. I like your house too much and I like you too much to ever be away from you."

For once, I do not interrupt because I can tell he has more to say, and I want to hear every one of his reasons.

"I know that Maxim is better for you, I get that on paper he is the perfect fit, but he isn't. It's me, Vanessa. It's you and me, I can't explain how I know it, but I do. It's us. We're meant to be, and I will not let some Russian mob boss come between that. If he tries, I guess I'll just have to kill him," he says.

There's no holding back my tearful laugh.

"I never wanted you to have to kill someone," I croak. It's a heavy price to pay to be with me, one I never would have asked of him.

"I didn't either," he admits. "I never wanted to be a part of this world. But here I am and it's my choice to make, and you can try to kick me out, but I'm not going anywhere."

His words break something in me—a piece of me that I thought was unlovable dissolves, and all that's left is love and relief. I've deluded myself into believing that the only people who could want me were the ones who had me by blood or the ones who were worse than me. I didn't let myself hope that he could want me, or that I could let myself have him back. Not permanently, at least.

I weep openly for the third time today, and Nate lets me while he takes his turn kissing all over my face, slow kisses in a line across my forehead, on each of my eyelids, and finally against my lips.

"I love you," I whisper. "I love you so bad, Nate. You challenge me and push me to be better, you make me laugh, you're the brightest man I've ever met."

He smiles against my mouth and kisses me deeper, it's a tender and gentle kiss, but long. I've got snot running beneath my nose and Nate's cheeks are wet with my tears and some of his own. We are a sappy, snotty mess. A perfect mess.

"I'm pitiful," I say.

"You're perfect," he says. "And you're stuck with me. When your arm isn't swollen from being yanked out of its socket, I'm going to put a ring on your finger and marry you in front of every criminal in this city, and if anyone has a problem with that, they'll have you to deal with, and clearly, you are no one to mess with."

"Nate," I whisper, and we kiss for a long time, until Angel and Artie barge into the room, Sean and Leo on their heels for another round of family fussing. Nate grins, and I do too, because I know that here with this family of loud, loving criminals, is exactly where we're supposed to be.

EPILOGUE

NATE

Six Months Later

THE MORELLIS ARE A FAMILY OF A GREAT MANY TRADITIONS, AND they have begun to include my dear parents in all of the wholesome ones.

Claire and Vanessa both thought it would be a good idea to have my parents here for the holidays, and to that end, they've been staying in my old room since the week before Christmas. Keeping the criminal parts of everyone's daily life hidden has been easier than I thought; at dinner, nobody talks about debt-collection, threats, or illegal shipments, and instead, they discuss hobbies, interests, work, and other completely personable things. It's all been very friendly and normal, even if it may have seemed to them strange and out of character for Willa to get her siblings and husband new handguns as Christmas presents.

The feat of convincing my parents that nothing is amiss with my new in-laws has proved to be more difficult at the Morelli Family New Year's Eve Party. No less than two hundred criminals (Irish, Italian, *and* Russian) gather in a hotel ballroom, dancing, drinking, and sharing hors d'oeuvres over conversations about business.

I've spent most of the evening following my parents around, directing any conversation steadfastly *away* from crime when they decide to chat up someone new—which is often because they really are exceptionally chatty. Now, they're sitting at a table with Jenna and her girlfriend, and I can only hope they stay there for the rest of the evening. I've barely seen Vanessa, who has been making the expected rounds at the party, charming every guest she speaks to.

She can't help it.

Business has been good since Cillian died. This cordial, even friendly, mix of criminals is a sign of the times—fewer enemies, and more shared power thanks to Vanessa, Maxim, and now Sean. The three youngest bosses in the city. Shipments stopped disappearing; those who were at Cillian's beck and call were found and dealt with. And with Vanessa wearing her mom's engagement ring, even The Mothers fell into an appeased peace.

I catch Vanessa's eye across the ballroom, and she excuses herself to make her way to me. She's beautiful, radiant in a deep purple satin dress with sparkling silver clips pinning her hair out of her face. Her mother's red necklace sits around her neck.

I want to escape to an alcove of some sort and take the clothes off her immediately, but I am a man of class and decorum, so I settle for wrapping an arm around her waist and pressing a kiss to her temple.

"Husband," she muses.

"Wife," I say. "I've missed you."

"I've been right here," she says, but smirks. "I've missed you too, so do not even think about leaving my side for the rest of the night."

"Yes, Captain."

Artie and Angel breeze past with some other kids their age and younger, the boys with their button-up shirts untucked and short ties long forgotten. Angel wears the blue dress she wore at our wedding, and a warmth sits in my chest remembering the softness of that day.

Late summer, on the day Vanessa planned on marrying Maxim, I married her instead. My parents cried happy tears, as did we all. The Morellis, it turns out, are a sappy bunch. Ranger jumped and barked around our feet as we kissed, and our guests cheered. The whole day was like something out of a movie.

The single best choice I've ever made.

"Ness," Willa singsongs as she approaches. Her hugely pregnant stomach bumps against Vanessa as she leans towards us both. "It's time."

"Already?" I ask, but when I look at my watch, sure enough, there's only about thirty minutes until midnight.

"Give me five," Vanessa says. A nervous energy buzzes off her as Willa walks away, and Vanessa's eyes snake around the room. I pull her tighter to me, and she grips the side of my shirt.

"She's still here," I nod in the direction of her younger sister. "At the bar."

Vanessa turns her eyes to Mary and sighs.

"Do you think this is the right thing?" she asks.

I think about my answer, though it's the same one I've given the last ten times she's asked. "Mary is an adult, and a fearsome one. She'll be just fine."

Vanessa chews on the inside of her cheek. I duck my head close to her ear. "Have you ever known her to do something she doesn't want to do?"

Vanessa takes a big breath and sets her shoulders. Any concern that just showed on her face has been replaced with a cool confidence.

"Let's do this," she says.

I squeeze her hand and give her one last kiss before walking beside her to the front of the room. Waiters are already passing out glasses of champagne, and I snag one for me and one for Vanessa, too, though she won't drink it.

Her pregnancy was a wanted surprise just before Christmas. Our heir. She's too early to be showing at all, but the whole family is tickled about the fact that Willa's baby will have a cousin less than a year younger than her. The family continues to grow, and with this announcement, it will even more.

The music quiets to a stop and the guests' attention turns to their gracious host. I give a slight nod to my wife, and she smiles wide at everyone.

"It's been an eventful year," she starts. Some chuckles sound from the crowd at the understatement. "I'm grateful for every one of you. The support, the care, and the love that you show my family and each other. We would not exist without family."

Vanessa gulps. "And to the Orlovs, many of whom this is your first New Year's Eve party with us, thank you for being here. Your partnership has been so valuable these last months."

She pauses for some polite applause, and her smile softens. She doesn't look at me but at her little sister. Mary stands in a black dress, alone at the side of the room.

"As we close this year, I pray that next year will be even more fruitful and healthy for us all. I hope we will see more growth and feel united in our aims for a better future. In that vein, I would like to offer a toast to all of us, but especially to two people I love dearly." Vanessa's throat bobs with a swallow, and she raises her glass. "To my sister Mary, and to Maxim Orlov, who I'm thrilled to announce will be wed this February."

The crowd buzzes at this news, turning to look for the new guests of honor. Maxim joins Mary's side and holds his own glass up in a mirror of Vanessa's.

"Cheers to them, and to all of us," Vanessa says. In the shocked murmuring that has settled over the room, the crowd raises their glasses in cheers. "And now that the cheers are out of the way, please dance, drink, and enjoy the last twenty or so minutes we have of this year!"

The music starts back up and Vanessa hands off the microphone before returning to my side. I put both of our glasses onto the tray of a passing waiter and pull her to me for a kiss.

"The hard part is over," I say.

"Don't jinx it, the wedding hasn't even happened yet."

"They'll be fine," I say. We both glance over to where Mary and Maxim receive congratulations from a host of guests. Mary looks stiff, but more approachable than she usually does. She's smiling, at least. "She's good with this."

"I know, I just. . . I wanted her to get married for love. Dad would have wanted that for all of us."

"Your dad didn't marry for love, right? At least not at first? And look how that turned out."

"She's good with it," Vanessa echoes, reminding herself that she's not some over-lording sister *forcing* Mary to wed a man twelve years older than her for an alliance. "Two of the most dangerous people in Boston, what could possibly go wrong?"

Vanessa squeezes my arm and kisses me on the lips. It still thrills me that I'm the man she kisses in front of everyone—the one she calls her husband, the one who will be the father of her children. I am the single most lucky man in the state of Massachusetts, and beyond.

"I think we should take this party to a closet somewhere," Vanessa says with a grin in her voice. "Just tonight."

"Lead the way, love," I say.

I will never not be thrilled to follow where she goes.

THE END

ACKNOWLEDGMENTS

So much of writing means sitting alone in front of my computer, but at every step in the process I have found rich collaboration and community. There's no way I could list every person who's cheered me on as this book has come to be. If you did, *thank you*; your encouragement made a meaningful impact on days when I was tired, overwhelmed, and unsure how to proceed. Here is a laundry list of specific thank-yous I want to include:

To my sister, Jackie. Thank you for being the first to read any novel I write, no matter how messy of a draft, and for *always* telling me it's great.

To Rebecca for the hours (so many hours) of brainstorming, cheerleading, reading, and offering thoughtful feedback as I drafted and revised this novel. At this point, walking on a track with you is a creative act.

To my writing besties. Lizzie, Rachel, and Shayla—ILYSM. I am the most fortunate gal to have a squad as tight as mine.

To my writing group (AKA The Plot Heads). Micah, Hattie, Lauren, and Dylan, ILYSM. You help me be a much better writer.

To my editor, Ellie. You are so thorough, thoughtful, and patient with my mind-boggling number of run-on sentences.

To my agent Bethany for encouraging me to publish this novel, cheering me on, and answering dozens of clueless questions from me. I am lucky to work with you.

To Sophie and Cass. You are a dream team for beautiful book covers, and I could not be more thrilled with how the book looks.

To my family: my parents, by blood and by marriage, who I love and credit for teaching me to believe in myself and all my wildest dreams. And to my siblings, Jackie (again), Randy, and Shelby, for the lifetime of shenanigans and love. I hit the family jackpot.

To anyone involved in the making of *The Fast and Furious* movies at any point in time.

To Brayden for never making my dreams feel unimportant. I love you so bad.

And to you. If you picked up this novel, thank you, thank you, thank you.

COMING 2025

A Love Most Brutal

See more of the Morelli Crime Family and what happens when Mary Morelli and Maxim Orlov are married to seal the alliance between their families. Mary is many, many things, but is she fit to be a wife?

Pre-Order *A Love Most Brutal* now.

To keep up to date on Kath Richards and all things Morelli Crime Family, subscribe to her newsletter or follow her online. Find all information at kathrichards.com

ABOUT THE AUTHOR

Kath Richards is a romance writer living and writing in Utah. She graduated with a bachelor's in technology engineering and an MFA in creative writing, both from BYU. She writes poetry, short stories, and romance novels, and has a fascination with relationships, connection, and love stories of all kinds. You can find her short work in many journals and magazines, but *A Love Most Fatal* is her debut novel.

She is represented by Bethany Weaver at Weaver Literary.

Printed in Great Britain
by Amazon

48064024R00199